BLUNT
FORCE

BLUNT
FORCE

Lynda La Plante was born in Liverpool. She trained for the stage at RADA and worked with the National Theatre and RDC before becoming a television actress. She then turned to writing and made her breakthrough with the phenomenally successful TV series *Widows*. She has written over thirty international novels, all of which have been bestsellers, and is the creator of the Anna Travis, Lorraine Page and the *Trial and Retribution* series. Her original script for the much-acclaimed *Prime Suspect* won awards from BAFTA, Emmy, British Broadcasting and Royal Television Society, as well as the 1993 Edgar Allan Poe Award.

Lynda is one of only three screenwriters to have been made an honorary fellow of the British Film Institute and was awarded the BAFTA Dennis Potter Best Writer Award in 2000. In 2008, she was awarded a CBE in the Queen's Birthday Honours List for services to Literature, Drama and Charity.

✉Join the Lynda La Plante Readers' Club at
www.bit.ly/LyndaLaPlanteClub
www.lyndalaplante.com
⬛Facebook @LyndaLaPlanteCBE
🐦Twitter @LaPlanteLynda

Lynda La Plante

BLUNT FORCE

ZAFFRE

Copyright © La Plante Global Limited, 2020

Typeset by IDSUK (Data Connection) Ltd, UK

First published in the United States of America in 2020 by Zaffre
Zaffre is an imprint of Bonnier Books UK
80–81 Wimpole Street, London W1G 9RE

ISBN: 978–1–49986–247–8

Also available as an ebook

For information, contact
251 Park Avenue South, Floor 12, New York, New York 10010
www .bonnierbooks .co .uk

To all my readers who follow me on Twitter and Facebook, and visit my website, your support and messages mean so much to me. Thank you.

CHAPTER ONE

Wearing a worn tracksuit over her tights and leotard, Jane Tennison was hurrying out of Holmes Place Health Club on Fulham Road after a strenuous aerobics class, worried that the time on her parking meter would have expired.

She ran the last few yards to her car as she spotted a traffic warden checking the meter.

'I'm here!' she yelled.

The warden gave her a cursory glance before moving off to check the next meter. Jane was throwing her kit bag and towel into the car when she heard someone call out her name. She turned, not recognizing the voice for a moment.

'Hi, it's Dave Morgan.'

She was still flustered, but then remembered exactly who he was.

'Dabs!' she cried out fondly.

Dabs was the diminutive SOCO she had worked with on the first day she had been with the Flying Squad. He gave her a hug and she quickly pulled away.

'Oh God, Dabs, I must stink! I've just been doing a workout at my club and didn't have time for a shower as my meter was about to expire.'

Dabs nodded in the direction of Holmes Place. 'That's a posh place, isn't it? What are you doing there? Self-defense?'

Jane laughed. 'No, I had enough of that when I was training. I'm doing aerobics.'

'Oh, the Green Goddess? I've seen her on breakfast TV. Fine for most people, but working alongside those macho blokes in the Sweeney, I'd probably take up boxing.'

Jane gave a pensive smile, not wanting to discuss her time with the 'blokes' Dabs had so aptly described.

'So, what have you been up to?' she asked, changing the subject.

He leaned forward. 'Been on a big case . . . Still on it. Checking out a bad situation, a triple murder with a lot of weapons. Seeing the damage some crazy idiot could do with a rifle, I decided I needed some hands-on experience, so I'm doing this course at a gun club. I'll give you my phone number if you're interested . . . I might be able to fast-track you at the club.'

Jane sat sideways on the driving seat of her car as Dabs jotted down his home number and passed it to her. She thanked him, swung her legs in and shut the car door. As she took out her car keys she felt the emotion welling up inside her. She was sure Dabs knew about her situation at the Sweeney, and that was why he had given her the card. The more she thought about it, the more she wondered if this opportunity was just what she needed.

She called him later that day to take up his offer and they arranged to meet near Norbiton train station, in Kingston. Dabs told her to park her car there and he would pick her up and drive her to the shooting club.

'Can't you just give me the address and I'll meet you there?'

'I could, but it's like a rabbit warren of small roads off a big council estate and it's quite hard to find. Plus, there's a secure entrance gate, which you have to have a code for, so it's just easier if I take you there.'

* * *

At 6:30 p.m. the following Thursday Jane followed Dabs's instructions, parked near the station and then stood outside a fish and chip shop waiting to be collected. He turned up a few minutes later driving a rather beat-up green Mini Clubman.

'Sorry for all the junk in the back,' he said, opening the passenger door for her. 'I've been working more or less twenty-four/seven.'

'Well, thank you for giving me your time, Dabs, I really appreciate it.'

He went quiet for a moment as he concentrated on driving through the narrow back streets with large council estates on either side.

'Are you married?' Jane asked.

'I am. Fifteen years. She's a professional carer. We lost our only boy when he was seven. He had myeloid leukemia, and for Joan caring for others has helped her get over it. Same for me, really.'

'I'm so sorry about your son,' Jane said. It was strange how little you really knew the people you worked with. All she had remembered about Dabs was his sheer professionalism and knowledge of ballistics. Now she realized he was also a very decent man.

Dabs put on the headlights as they continued along a narrow, dimly lit road.

'I've been here so many times but I still drive past it. Here it is!'

Jane frowned. 'You sure?'

They were in a narrow dead-end road.

Dabs laughed. 'Well, it's a pretty exclusive place, this. Not many people know about it, unless you're into shooting, even though it's been here for over fifty years. It used to be part of a leisure club attached to the post office in Surbiton back in 1966.'

They stopped by two large wooden gates with a sign on the wall saying 'Surbiton Postal Rifle Club'. Dabs got out of the car and used a set of keys to unlock one side of the gates, sliding it open, then returned to the car. They entered a large car park and Dabs parked, returned to slide the main gate closed, and relocked it. Jane climbed out as Dabs opened the rear double doors of the Mini and took out a black leather duffle bag. He placed it down on the ground beside him as he locked the car.

'I've still got a lot of my equipment in here, but I know this is very secure. Right, follow me.'

They walked to the rear of the car park where there was an iron door with a keypad. Dabs entered a code and waited, then pushed the heavy door open. Jane heard it click behind them as she followed him down a stone corridor lit by an overhead strip light.

She was taken aback when they entered a large room. One corner near the entrance had a coffee bar and a vending machine. There was also a small cooker and kitchen sink. Standing at the sink washing up mugs was an attractive middle-aged woman who Dabs introduced as Vera.

As she and Dabs chatted, Jane was able to have a good look around the large common room filled with sofas and easy chairs, and a long table with sixteen chairs placed around it. Dominating the walls were rows of awards and cups, but it appeared that the three of them were the only people there that evening.

Dabs asked Jane for her ID and took some documents over to the large table for her to complete the membership application. Jane studied the application form, which requested details of her work, medical profile and previous experience with firearms, plus the name of three references.

Dabs tapped the paper. 'Put in here that you had experience with the Flying Squad, you had training at the academy, but you feel this would be useful further experience as there are not that many opportunities.' He gave a chuckle. 'For women and particularly female police officers.'

Jane finished filling in the forms as Dabs joined Vera for a cup of coffee. A tall, broad-shouldered man joined them at the coffee bar.

Dabs shook the man's hand, then turned to Jane. 'This is your instructor, Elliott Norman. He is also the secretary, so he can go through your documents now, while I show you the rest of the club.'

'You're a policewoman,' Elliott said, turning towards her.

'Yes, a detective sergeant.'

He raised an eyebrow and gave a slight smile. His age was uncertain because he was completely bald, but had a youthful face. He was also an impressive size, at least six foot three, and dwarfed the diminutive Dabs.

Jane was led along the length of the common room to a bolted door at the back, which went into a large locker room area. Dabs pointed out that all the members have a locker, and their own keys, as it was imperative it was a secure area. From the moment they had entered the room they had not seen one window. He took out his own keys and opened a locker, showing Jane his rifle. She was impressed and watched as he carefully put it back into the locker and repocketed his keys.

'My wife bought it for our wedding anniversary,' he told her. 'OK, follow me. We're going to go into the long-range shooting area. This is where you learn the military technique of firing when lying down.'

Yet again Jane was stunned at the size of the area, which must have once been a massive underground car park.

They returned to the coffee-bar area, where Elliott was waiting.

'Dabs has told me you want to have some instruction in small-arms shooting. A .22, is that right?'

Jane nodded.

'The .22 is one of the oldest firearm calibers in existence. It survived the jump from black powder to smokeless. As a handgun round, it's pretty much worthless except for training or target shooting. Although you may hear of people carrying these guns for self-defense, this is a horrible idea. Not only is the caliber insufficient, the guns normally designed for this cartridge are not up to standard. On the other hand, the nine millimeter is the most prolific handgun caliber in the world. More cartridges of a nine-millimeter ammunition are produced, sold and fired than almost every other caliber in existence. They are extremely popular because of how cheap the cartridges are and it's normally considered to be the bare minimum for self-defense. It is carried by most militaries and law enforcement agencies in the United States.'

Jane gave a light cough. 'I need to practice with a .22, and at some time in the future, go on to a nine millimeter and then maybe a rifle. But right now, I think I need training that would just basically give me confidence in handling a gun.'

'I'm surprised that the Met don't give weapons training to their recruits.'

Jane flushed. 'I doubt that will ever happen. Some specialist squads and police stations have a small number of officers who are trained as "authorized shots", but even then, firearms can only be issued by a sergeant with good reason. I don't know of any women officers who are authorized. Personally, I'd just like to learn more about guns and handling them. Then if ever I get the opportunity to apply for a firearms course, I can say that I have previous experience.'

Elliott nodded and pushed his chair back. 'I should process your application first, but as you're a police officer I'll take you through to the range where you can get the feel of a handgun. We'll do a few basic exercises and see how it goes.'

Jane looked around for Dabs. Vera gave her a warm smile.

'He's gone to the long range,' she said.

Elliott took off his overcoat and checked the roster. 'Right, Vera, I'm only going to be ten minutes. We've got all stalls available.' He turned to Jane. 'Club starts filling up at around eight p.m. with people coming in after work.'

Jane followed him through a door opposite the coffee bar and down a narrow corridor to another door with a light above it.

'When the light is on red,' Elliott explained, 'you don't enter as there's a practice or often a competition going on. So you have to wait for clearance.'

Elliott gestured for Jane to go ahead of him and closed the door behind them. She wondered when she was going to get hold of a gun and actually start shooting. He walked her right to the end of the twenty-five-yard range where there were six targets with bullseyes in the center.

'Right, Jane, we never have the handgun and the rifle sessions at the same time. Right now, the range is set up for rifle shooting. Take a look at the marksman's astonishing shots from stall two.' He pointed at the bullseye where she could see six small bullet holes.

'The club and all members are very security-conscious. You fire a cartridge, you pick it up, and you never leave a gun loaded in the stall. Now, I want you to stand on the cross in the center of the range.'

Jane went and took up the position as instructed. Elliott stood beside her.

'Now, what I want you to do is put your feet slightly apart so your balance is good. OK?'

'Yes, I feel balanced.'

'Good. Now, you are actually facing target three.'

Jane nodded.

'Are you left- or right-handed?'

'Right.'

'OK. Lift your right hand, stretch out your arm and point to the bullseye on target three.'

Jane did as instructed. Feet apart, pointing directly at the bullseye. Elliott stared at her as she still held out her arm, her finger pointing.

'Good. Now, that is exactly how you fire towards your target. Follow your arm, your hand, then finger pointing to it, then fire. So what we have just learned is balance, eye, target. Now, what I am going to do is show you how you hold your gun.'

Elliott opened his vest and removed a Smith & Wesson .38 revolver from his holster. He released the cylinder catch, opened the cylinder and showed Jane the gun was empty.

'We only load up when standing in the range-firing cubicle. It's the same first principle as for shotgun users. So listen carefully to me.' He looked her in the eye as he spoke.

'I will, I mean, I am,' she replied nervously.

'Never, never let your gun be pointed at anyone. That it may be unloaded matters not the least to me,' he continued, looking serious.

'I'll remember that,' Jane replied, reciting it in her mind.

'Now, you'll be holding the gun in your right hand, but this doesn't mean the support hand is not important. Quite the contrary. The support hand stabilizes the handgun and makes the shooter two to three times more accurate than if the shooter used just one hand. Why? The shooter must perform two tasks with the shooting hand when firing a gun: hold the gun and press the trigger. I deliberately use the word "press" not "pull" because just like pressing a doorbell button, you press the button until the bell rings, and then stop. You don't continue pressing until the button breaks. To me, the word "pulling" is the whole hand and arm, and "squeezing" is something performed by all the fingers.'

He loaded the revolver, handed it to Jane, and told her to aim at the target. He stood behind her and, using his hands on her shoulders, got her to stand in a semi-crouched position, then put his arms on hers to help hold her steady.

'OK, slowly press the trigger and fire one shot only.'

Jane could feel his hot breath on her ear as he spoke. Making sure her fingers and thumb were in the correct position, she aimed at the target and pressed the trigger. The loud bang made her jump and the recoil made her hands jerk upwards, but Elliott held them steady.

'Not bad. You at least hit the target.'

'Only thanks to you helping me.'

'OK, on your own now.' He stepped away from her.

She got into position, took a deep breath, then fired, but missed the target.

'Do you know what you did wrong?' Elliott asked.

'Was I not holding it correctly?'

'No, you were, but you flinched just before you pressed the trigger. It's known as recoil anticipation, and one of the most common reasons shooters miss the target. That said, it's not difficult to fix with some "dry fire" practice.'

'What's dry fire?' she asked.

'Practicing with an empty gun. When dry firing, there's no recoil to worry about, so the anticipation and flinching goes away quickly. The key is to dry fire like it is live fire by maintaining a firm grip, so when there is recoil, the firm grip is there to reduce it. Not up, not down, not sideways, just firm and steady.'

'Practice makes perfect.' She smiled.

He didn't smile back. 'Practice does not make perfect. Perfect practice makes perfect,' he said firmly.

* * *

Dabs had come off the long range and was quite eager to get home, so he came to see how Jane was doing. Jane was now in one of the stalls, wearing ear protection, and a new human silhouette target had been brought to ten yards from the firing line. She fired her three shots in quick succession and removed the ear protection as Elliott pressed clearance on the door and Dabs came in.

'How's it going?'

'Fantastic,' she said with a frown.

Elliott told her to open the gun barrel and make sure the revolver was empty, put the gun on the table and to come and have a look at the target.

'Bit of a calamity, Jane. You only got one shot in the inner ring,' Elliott said.

Jane glanced at Dabs and felt herself flush. 'I'm not sure what I'm doing wrong,' she said nervously.

'Your stance is fine, as is your grip,' Elliott reassured her. 'But you're still anticipating the recoil and flinching before you fire. Like I said, it happens with first-time shooters, so don't let it get you down. You just need to do more dry practice, and there's some other drills I can teach you that will help.'

'On that note, Jane, I really need to get myself home,' Dabs said, looking at his watch.

By the time Jane got back to her car she felt totally drained. For some reason, she had thought that by the end of the evening her old confidence would have returned, but quite the opposite had happened.

* * *

After a long, tedious day at work, Jane felt the evening on the range hadn't been such a bad experience after all, despite her disappointing performance, and while things didn't improve dramatically on the next session, by the fourth lesson she knew she had made great strides forward and her membership was accepted. One of the most important problems she had overcome was the panicked feeling whenever she pressed the trigger.

Elliott had given her one of his lengthy monologues about controlling her breathing to keep her mind calm, and it seemed to have worked. She no longer felt he talked down to her quite so much, and couldn't help respecting his expertise.

After seeing how much she'd improved, Elliott invited her to visit an 'impressive' gun club with him.

'You'll find it similar to a lot of the training in America where they use moving targets representing police officers, innocent bystanders, an armed bank robber and a guy holding a knife. Hopefully Calamity Jane won't let me down like my previous trainee, who not only shot the unarmed pedestrian, but also the police dog,' he joked.

Jane was flattered he had that much confidence in her, but wanted to keep her gun training quiet for the time being.

'Thanks for the offer,' she said with a smile, 'but I think I'd better wait until I'm a bit more proficient.'

CHAPTER TWO

Jane was having dinner with her parents at a small Italian restaurant to celebrate her birthday. It was just the three of them as Pam, her sister, had cancelled due to one of her sons having mumps. Jane was trying to be relaxed but really didn't feel it. She was unhappy about being thirty years old, as well as the fact that she was now working out of Gerald Road police station. She made no mention that her position with the Flying Squad had been short-lived or that she was disappointed to have been sidelined. She was having a problem winding her spaghetti into the spoon as she had a nasty bruise on her thumb from a session at the shooting range, but like everything else in her life, she kept it to herself.

'I don't know where that station is,' her father said, as he expertly wound his spaghetti around his fork.

'It's in the heart of Belgravia. It's a really nice location.'

'Oh yes, close to all those posh shops,' her mother said, not attempting to spin the spaghetti but slicing it up with her knife and fork. Jane's parents were both relieved about her transfer. They'd been concerned for her safety when she had worked with the notorious Sweeney.

As a birthday gift to herself, Jane had traded in her VW and had bought a second-hand Mini Cooper, and she had at last been able to repay her father the money he had loaned her for the deposit on her flat. She was now keen to sell and was looking for something larger – not that she had anyone to share it with, she thought wistfully.

She tried to be as good-humored as she could throughout dinner – even when her mother insisted on asking if she was seeing anybody. She just changed the subject and told them that she had been reunited with an old colleague, Spencer Gibbs, from her early days at Hackney Station and then at Bow Street.

'He feels he's being sidelined as well,' she said.

'What do you mean?' her dad asked.

'I don't want to talk about it, it's just he did something he shouldn't have done and . . . '

'But you said he was sidelined "as well". So have you done something that you shouldn't have done?'

'For goodness' sake, Dad. It's not a question of something I did.'

'But why did you say you were being sidelined as well as Spencer Gibbs if you haven't done something wrong?' her mother said nervously.

'For Christ's sake, it's not something I have done wrong or Spencer has done wrong, just leave it alone.'

'It's only because we are concerned about you,' her father said, obviously shocked by her tone of voice.

Jane tried to control herself. 'There is absolutely nothing to be concerned about. As I told you, I am working at a station in Belgravia that mostly investigates petty crimes. That's all there is to it.' She got up. 'Please excuse me, I need to go to the ladies.'

As soon as Jane was out of sight, Mrs. Tennison lowered her voice. 'Well, something has to be wrong. I have never seen her like this. And she's lost weight.'

Mr. Tennison kept his eyes on the ladies and leaned closer to his wife, almost whispering: 'If something's bothering her, she'll tell us when she's ready.'

'She never has in the past,' Mrs. Tennison replied, not bothering to keep her voice down. 'Oh dear God, what do you think she's keeping from us now? I knew something had happened. Has she been demoted as well, just like her friend Spencer?'

Mr. Tennison quickly signaled for his wife to be quiet as Jane returned to the table. At the same time a waiter appeared with a cupcake on a plate decorated with icing sugar. To make it even worse, stuck into the cupcake was a candle with a silver 30 on it. Jane squirmed in embarrassment as her parents began to sing 'Happy Birthday' and some of the other diners and a couple of waiters joined in. Jane blew out the offending candle and forced herself to keep smiling as the cupcake was sliced into tiny pieces.

When her father took her hand and squeezed it, looking as if he wanted some kind of assurance that she was all right, she nodded.

'Female officers still aren't totally accepted in the force. I suppose I might have rattled a few cages.'

'But you are dealing with it?' he said quietly.

'Yes, Dad, I am dealing with it,' she said with more confidence than she felt.

* * *

The following morning Jane parked her Mini in the street behind the station. She went into the yard and saw Spencer Gibbs' motorbike chained up in the bike shelter.

He's in earlier than usual, she thought.

After a quick breakfast in the canteen, she went to the CID office. A cleaner was just finishing emptying Chinese food cartons from the bin beside his desk, but there was no sign of Spencer.

Jane nodded to the other members of the team already at their desks.

'Is Gibbs in?' she asked a young DC, Gary Dors.

'No, he was at some gig with his band last night over in Camden Town.'

Dors was pale-faced, with a short haircut that made his ears seem to stick out.

Jane hung up her coat and sat down at her desk to look over the night's reports. Two burglaries, a hit and run, a stolen E-Type Jaguar, and a drunk and disorderly charge against a man who was still being held in the police cells. She checked the CID crime reports, which were recorded in a large notebook by the late turn and night duty officers and then had to be allocated to a detective by the early turn DS, which was herself.

'Harrods really need to sharpen up their security,' Dors said.

He flicked over two pages of the report that described how goods were being stolen. The company believed goods for delivery were being reboxed and sent off to a different address by some storeroom workers, and the losses had so far been estimated at over £2,000.

'It's beyond belief. This is the second report this month.'

Tony Johnson, another DC with the desk next to hers, who was equally wet behind the ears, looked over at Jane. The other three desks on the opposite side were empty as the DCs were having breakfast in the canteen.

'Did you see that report on the seventy-five-year-old shoplifter? Eight previous convictions. Wears a mink coat lined with pockets. She was picked up yesterday morning.'

Jane continued reading her reports, only half listening.

'Rich pickings at Harrods,' Dors said, beginning to type.

Johnson nodded. 'Yeah, then there's Burberry and House of Fraser, and you're right by Beauchamp Place with all the posh shops along there, not to mention the high-end jewelry stores next door.'

Jane didn't say anything. Being inundated with shoplifters meant a lot of tedious paperwork, even though the uniforms actually dealt with them. Sometimes Jane had to teach the young probationers how to make these arrests, taking them through the interviews and showing them how to process the prisoner.

There was another report on her desk from the previous week from Harrods' security. They had discovered that boxes of items delivered to their soft furnishings department had been removed using forged Harrods delivery forms redirecting them to a warehouse address. When the legitimate Harrods delivery vans arrived there, the goods were then put on board another van previously stolen by thieves, which was dumped later that day.

The monotonous sound of Dors's heavy-handed, two-finger typing made everything seem even more mundane. Jane had been used to experiencing real excitement in her previous roles.

The incident room door banged open as DCI Leonard 'Lenny' Tyler marched in, carrying a large box of groceries.

'Morning, everybody.'

The team murmured their replies as he maneuvered between the desks towards his private office.

'It's Hannah's tenth birthday party this weekend and I've had to get balloons, party hats and games. The bloody magician won't be pulling any rabbits out of his top hat as he fell off a bus in Edgware Road. That means we're going to have fifteen kids and no entertainment, unless . . .'

He looked towards Dors. 'Unless Big Ears over there can find me a substitute.'

He stood in the doorway to his office and looked around.

'Is Spencer in yet? I've had a complaint from the uniformed chief superintendent that he's taking up two spaces with his motorbike and stopping the chief from getting into his bay. He's got more chains wrapped around that bloody bike than Houdini.'

'He might be in the canteen,' Jane suggested.

Tyler glanced towards one of the empty desks in a coveted corner position by a window, which had a chair with a back-press cushion pushed underneath it.

She couldn't tell whether he'd heard what she'd said as he closed his office door. He was a very easy-going man to work for, but at times it was clear that his own life wasn't always easy. He often left the station in the early afternoon in order to do the school run while his wife was busy studying for a mature student university degree in economics.

But during the short time that Jane had been stationed at Belgravia, she had never heard Tyler raise his voice. He had piercing blue eyes that sometimes appeared to look straight through you. At over six feet tall, he was one of the major players in the Mets rugby team and was clearly very fit. At the rate things were going, however, Jane doubted if she would ever get the opportunity to see if Tyler did have more to him than met the eye.

'How much does he want to pay for this magician?' Dors asked. 'Some of them I've looked into are quite expensive. Does he want someone from the magic circle?'

Jane sighed. 'Just look up children's entertainers, not magicians.'

'I'm only doing what he told me to do, Sarge!' Dors snapped.

'Go and knock on his door and ask how much he wants to pay for the children's entertainer.' Jane returned to work, while the office CID clerk and a typist arrived and took up their desks, carrying in their personalized mugs from the canteen.

Johnson had departed to take a statement from a woman whose handbag had been stolen on the Brompton Road. It had contained a staggering £2,000.

Tyler remained in his office and it was after eleven when a very disheveled Spencer Gibbs walked in, carrying a mug of black coffee. He muttered 'good morning' to everyone as he walked over to his desk. There was already a pile of detectives' reports regarding cases awaiting trial at the Crown Court for him to check over. Jane noticed that he needed a shave and, although she had been working with him for over five weeks now, this was the first time he had looked as if he had slept in his clothes all night.

Back in the days when they had worked together at Hackney, Spencer had often been the butt of jokes regarding his rock and roll attire. Then, when they were together in Peckham, he had changed his style. Spencer had discovered a second-hand gentleman's outfitters and had turned up in an elegant tweed suit, waistcoat and trousers that had the telltale signs of being let down to accommodate his lanky six-foot frame. He took the jokes about him wearing a dead man's outfit in his stride, and boasted that at least the winkle-pickers had been his own – until he found an elegant pair of two-tone brogues that he felt better suited his outfit. When he played with his band, however, he would wear flamboyant frilly shirts and cowboy boots.

'I hear you had a gig last night,' Jane said, turning her swivel chair towards him.

'Yeah, but it was a pain in the ass. I'm getting too old for this. There were two punk bands on that were smashing the place up and I wasn't going to let the buggers damage my speakers. I didn't get out till after twelve, and we only got fifty quid each. Bloody disgusting.'

Spencer lit a cigarette. Jane hated the smell of smoke, which always hung in a cloud above his head. He still had thick curly hair that often stood up on end from his habit of running his fingers through it when he was concentrating. It appeared even more unruly now, as for some reason he had decided to cut the sides short. Spencer was still an attractive man, but his sense of humor seemed to have soured and he was often moody and impatient with probationers.

'Well, this is all very exciting, isn't it?' he muttered. 'This old lady in the fur coat has been arrested how many times? And we have to spend how many hours doing paperwork, taking her to fucking court just so some equally ancient judge will release her because of her age? Someone should tell our guys not to bother arresting her anymore.'

'Have you seen the report about the woman who had her handbag nicked on the Old Brompton Road?' Dors asked. 'She had two thousand quid on her.'

Spencer shrugged his shoulders. 'Really? Isn't that fantastic. Held up at gunpoint, was she?'

'No, a kid on a bicycle nicked it.'

'I was being sarcastic, Gary.'

Jane shared Spencer's frustration. She felt that the dealing with the petty crime that took up all their time was a waste of their experience. Like Spencer, she had years of training behind her. As if reading her mind, he crossed over and sat on the edge of her desk.

'Not sure how much more of this I can take, Jane. I know I've blotted my copybook a few times in the past, but this is really testing my patience. I've applied for a promotion and I've had a couple of interviews but they've led to nothing. No one has had the balls to tell me the reason I've been sidelined. I know you didn't get on with the lads in the Flying Squad, but they're a bunch of wankers anyway. And they turned me down.'

Jane nodded. She knew it was unwise to join in with Spencer's disgruntled rant, and she'd learned to keep her mouth shut. Spencer remained perched on the edge of her desk, kicking the side with the heel of his scruffy shoe.

'I mean, it's bordering on bloody ridiculous. I haven't had a single criminal worth wasting my time on, and the paperwork just gets more and more every day.'

He nodded over to the empty desk that belonged to Detective Inspector Timothy Arnold, lowering his voice. 'I see he's still not back yet. He should have a visitor's book instead of a duty status if you ask me. It's unbelievable. He's a bloody hypochondriac. He doesn't get a simple headache, it has to be a full-blown migraine. He can't just get a cold, it has to be flu. And if he gets flu it's bloody pneumonia!'

Jane felt uncomfortable about the banter, because it showed a complete lack of respect. At the same time, since she had been there, DI Arnold had taken frequent sick days and he had now been absent for almost a week.

Spencer leaned closer. 'You tell me, what kind of man has an effing battery-operated Mickey Mouse pencil sharpener? And he doesn't even have any kids. Mind you, if you saw his wife Bronwyn, it's no wonder.'

Jane turned away, not wanting to listen to any more. Spencer wasn't finished, though he did have the forethought to keep his voice low.

'You know what he's got in his drawer? Antaci̇d tablets, Epsom salts and hemorrhoid cream. And he keeps a St Valentine's Day mug in the canteen.'

'That's enough, Spence,' Jane snapped. 'Apparently he's down with gastroenteritis.' Her desk phone rang. Jane held up her hand as she answered. 'Yes, sir, I'll ask him now.'

She replaced the receiver and looked over at Dors. 'The guv wants to know if you've found a kids' entertainer for the party on Saturday.'

Spencer slid off her desk and raised his arms. 'You see what I mean! What's he bloody going on about a kids' entertainer for? I'm fed up to the back bloody teeth with this. I'm seriously about to throw in the towel.'

Dors pushed back his chair. 'I've got a bloke who can blow up balloons and make them into animals, you know, poodles and things like that.'

Spencer looked at him as if he had two heads. 'What in Christ's name does this have to do with anything? Blowing up ruddy balloons for a profession?'

'He charges fifteen quid an hour, plus transport.'

Spencer shook his head in frustration. 'Maybe I should think about blowing up fucking balloons. Certainly pays better than working here. I'm going for breakfast.'

Jane felt sorry for Spence. He rarely, if ever, discussed his private life, but she knew he had married a young, aristocratic girl called Serena. It was clear that it wasn't a good match. All he'd ever said about it was that after Serena had told Spence she was pregnant, her father had threatened him and he was persuaded to marry her. Serena's parents had bought them a flat in Shepherd's Bush. There had been a miscarriage, and Spencer had inferred that he had been unashamedly relieved.

* * *

The remainder of the week was as mundane as usual. She and Spencer each spent a day in court, but apart from that there had only been a domestic assault inquiry and the search for a missing pupil from the prestigious Hill House. Thanks to the school's odd-looking uniform of burgundy knickerbockers, a beige V-neck sweater and beige socks, the search was soon called off after the pupil was spotted playing with the puppies in Harrods' pet department.

Jane was having lunch in the canteen when Spencer, his tray loaded with shepherd's pie and green fruit jello, came and stood at her table.

'OK if I sit with you?'

Before she could reply he pulled out a chair with his foot and sat opposite her.

'There's been a development. Apparently DI Arnold is now in hospital with a suspected kidney stone. I was thinking of applying for a transfer but if Fatty Arbuckle isn't returning any time soon, then maybe I could get promoted.' He shrugged. 'If not, then I'll just have to sit it out until my bloody pension.'

Jane smiled. 'You'll have a long wait for your pension. You're only thirty-eight. Besides which, if DI Arnold has been diagnosed correctly, he'll be back at work in a few weeks.'

Spencer banged the last of an HP Sauce bottle onto his shepherd's pie. 'How old are you, then?'

Jane hesitated, finding it a rather uncomfortable question, but then replied, 'I'm thirty, Spence.'

Spencer shoveled the food into his mouth, mashing the potatoes into the gravy and the HP Sauce with his fork.

'Did I detect a hint of reservation there, about me being eligible for promotion?'

'I didn't mean it to sound like that, but you shouldn't go on about DI Arnold. He's a very good detective.'

'Do me a fucking favor! I hadn't seen you since we were transferred to this piddlin' station, so I think you might have got the wrong information regarding my being demoted.'

Jane pushed her half-eaten ham salad to one side. 'There's always gossip, Spence; you just have to ignore it.'

He waved his knife in the air. 'Let me give you the real facts. I admit I was well over the limit, but how many times have you or I been on an investigation when never mind the DI but the DCI has been fed peppermints because their breath stank of booze? So, I admit I had a few jars, but I had done a good gig with the guys in a well-known pub in Islington. I was in Serena's dinky little pale blue sports car that her dad had given to her for her twenty-first and, as a big guy, I'm crunched up in the driving seat. Maybe I did jump the lights, but I get this traffic prick pulling me over. So I stop the car and he beckons me with his finger, telling me to get out of the car. Like I said, I'm a big guy and getting out took a while, and the next minute I've got this second bastard on me, who turns out to be a Black Rat,' he added, referring to the common slang used by detectives for traffic police, because rats are known to eat their young.

Spencer threw his hands wide as he swung his legs around the canteen chair.

'I was accused of taking a swing, and of avoiding arrest. The reality is they didn't really give a shit about me being over the limit. It was all down to my abusive tone of voice and the fact that I had thrown a punch.'

Spencer straightened his chair and gesticulated again with both hands.

'That's the truth . . . and I get demoted for it.'

He began to eat his awful-looking green jello as Jane stirred her coffee. There was not a lot she could say. From the gossip she had heard it was not just one accidental swing, he had actually thrown a couple of punches.

'What are you looking at me like that for?'

'I'm not looking at you in any way, Spence. I just think the whole incident was unfortunate and you've paid a high price.' Jane glanced at her wristwatch. 'I should be getting back to work.'

She picked up her plate and took it over to the trolley left out for dirty crockery.

Five minutes later, as Jane was coming out of the ladies' toilets, Spencer was heading down the stairs.

'I suppose you know the gossip about you being transferred here from the Sweeney?'

'I'm really not that interested in any gossip about me,' she replied firmly.

'Well, you should be. I wouldn't like anyone saying I screwed up and as a result of that another officer was wounded.'

Jane stopped dead in her tracks. 'What did you just say?'

Spencer grinned. 'Just repeating the gossip I heard, about the Big Boys being on some armed robbery of a security van, and that it started to look like the gunfight at the O.K. Corral. Word has it that you were unarmed and came face-to-face with one of the raiders, who took a shot at you with a revolver.'

Spencer was enjoying himself, despite the fact that Jane was seething.

'I heard you froze, and another officer had to push you out of the way and he got shot in the shoulder.'

Jane had to take a deep breath and lean against the wall. She felt like bursting into tears, but instead she gritted her teeth and snapped at him, 'Yes, I did freeze, and I admit I was unable to defend myself or anyone near me. But I was *not* to blame for what happened, even if DCI Murphy said that I was a contributory factor to one of his expert officers being shot.' She felt herself sagging. 'He gave me a warning and said that I would be disciplined and might even be demoted.'

Spencer suddenly looked guilty. He tapped a cigarette out from his soft pack and lit it. Even though Jane loathed the smell of tobacco she occasionally smoked when stressed. Her hand was shaking when she took the cigarette and inhaled deeply.

'Murphy wanted to get rid of me from the very first day I joined the Sweeney. Well, he got what he wanted. I'll never forget his sarcasm when he said that after my near-death experience, he felt the Flying Squad was not for me. He told me that if I agreed to a transfer, then his report wouldn't be so harsh.'

Jane dragged on the cigarette again. She was feeling a little bit calmer but was still very emotional.

'I had asked to have weapons training, not once but three times. Murphy ignored me. So then when I did come face-to-face . . .' Jane dropped the cigarette butt on the ground and stubbed it out with her shoe. 'Well, there you have it. I did freeze, because I was terrified.'

Jane was taken aback when Spencer drew her into his arms and held her tightly, but it felt comforting.

'Listen, Jane, don't blame yourself. If I hear one more prat spreading any gossip about you, they'll regret it.' Spencer stepped back and gave her one of his trademark smiles. 'You'd better pick up that butt and put it in the ashtray on the wall, or I'll report you.'

Jane did as she was instructed while Spence headed into the office. She had never told anyone before and she was surprised to find how relieved she felt to have let it all out.

CHAPTER THREE

Spencer gave Jane a fresh croissant when he came into the office. It had been a week since their confrontation, and they had both made no further mention of what had occurred, but this seemed like some sort of peace offering. Spencer stood next to his desk and looked over to the still-empty one belonging to DI Arnold. Arnold had been released from hospital and they were expecting him to return shortly. Spence gave one of his long sighs as he shrugged his shoulders and sauntered over to Jane's desk where she was finishing her croissant.

'I just want something I can get my teeth into, a decent violent crime. When I think of some of the cases I've worked on in the past, and the adrenaline buzz they gave me, it just feels like I've now got a bloody tedious nine to five job.'

'Be careful what you wish for, Spence.'

'You can't tell me you enjoy working day in and day out on these petty crimes.'

The reality was that Jane had also contemplated requesting a transfer. In the last week she had only been involved in one case, when she had been on nights, involving a club in Cromwell Road.

The club had been reported numerous times for breaching their alcohol licensing regulations by staying open long past their closing time and well into the early hours of the morning. They maintained that they were entitled to do this due to the fact that they were a private members-only club. The complaints had been made by a young woman who rented the flat above the club. When Jane had interviewed her in her flat, the smell of stale alcohol and cigarette smoke was overwhelming. The young woman said she could deal with the smell, but it was the deafening thud of the loud music from the live bands that she couldn't cope with. Jane had taken a statement and promised that she would contact the council. It turned out that the complainant had been offered alternative accommodation by the club, and Jane suspected that she might be sitting tight in the hope of being offered financial compensation. The case had been transferred to the station's licensing officer.

The switchboard put a call through to Spencer. He went back to his desk to take the call, introducing himself as Detective Sergeant Spencer Gibbs.

'Could I just take your name?' Spencer asked abruptly.

It was a Mrs. Nora Compton, whose address was in the exclusive Onslow Square.

'If you could just explain the reason for your call.' He listened as the anxious Mrs. Compton told him about her neighbor downstairs, in the basement flat.

'Has something happened to your neighbor?' Spencer asked curtly.

He rolled his eyes as he continued to listen.

'I see . . . it's your neighbor's dog that you're calling about? And it's a long-haired dachshund?'

Mrs. Compton continued, saying that she had become worried because the dog had been barking all night and was still whining this morning. She said that she had gone down to the basement and knocked on the door, but her neighbor, Mr. Charles Foxley, had not answered. The dog had repeatedly scratched at the front door, clearly distressed.

Spencer rolled his eyes again at the tediousness of the call. He suggested to Mrs. Compton that perhaps Mr. Foxley had gone out the previous night and had just not returned home.

Mrs. Compton became very agitated as she explained that Mr. Foxley would always contact her if he intended to leave the dog all night. She said that he had two other dogs that were not at home, but they often slept in his car. He had a very strict regime and always walked them all at about eleven every night, then again at seven every morning.

'Do you have a key to Mr. Foxley's flat?' Spencer asked.

Mrs. Compton replied that she did not, but he had always given her contact details if he was going to be away from home. Spencer thanked her for the call and said that he would arrange for someone to check on Mr. Foxley's flat.

Replacing the receiver, he held his hands up in the air. 'Bloody hell! A long-haired dachshund hasn't been taken for his morning walk. What the fuck has that got to do with us? I'm telling you, the switchboard need a bollocking! Uniforms should be dealing with that.'

Only having heard Spencer's side of the conversation, Jane suggested that, as it seemed out of the ordinary and the pet owner had a strict routine, perhaps they should at least send a uniform to check things out.

Spencer shrugged. 'OK, I'll go down to the duty sergeant and see if there are any uniforms in the area.' He paused by the door. 'Perhaps the dachshund is just pissed off the other two dogs have gone off in the car with the owner.'

As Spencer walked out, Jane went back to checking through the reports. DC Gary Dors, the two-fingered typist, made so many spelling errors in his reports that she was going to have to ask him to redo them. He was on night duty for another week and the other DC, Tony Johnson, was in court.

DCI Tyler had been closeted in his office since nine a.m. He was trying to contact the head of security at Harrods to organize a visit from a crime prevention officer as it was not his department. It felt ironic that petty crime seemed to be the priority at his station, even though this was the area where one of the most notorious crimes in England had taken place: the murder of Lord

Lucan's nanny and his Lordship's subsequent disappearance. Lucan remained on the run, and there had been no sighting of him since the murder had been committed over ten years ago, well before Tyler had taken over the station.

Next, he put in a call to DI Arnold's home and spoke to his wife, Bronwyn, asking for an update on her husband's health. She thanked him profusely for his inquiry and his get-well card in her strong Welsh accent, and told him that Timothy had come through his kidney-stone surgery exceptionally well but was still in some discomfort. He was hoping to be able to return to work within a few days. Tyler asked her to pass on his best wishes, and was halfway to putting the phone down when Bronwyn asked if he could ensure that someone watered the plants in the window boxes at the station's entrance.

'Yes, of course, it's all in hand,' Tyler assured her, having no idea whose job it was to look after the plants. He would ask one of the typists to water them. He checked his watch, deciding it was too early to take a lunch break.

* * *

PC John Lee, the uniformed officer who'd been sent to investigate Mr. Foxley's flat, had walked along Exhibition Road from the Natural History Museum, where there had been complaints about a rowdy school party waiting to go in. He turned left into Old Brompton Road, and fifteen minutes later arrived at Onslow Square.

The properties were all exclusive, a few remaining as single-family homes but the majority of them having been converted into elegant flats. As PC Lee descended the steps to the basement flat, the front door above him opened. A lady in her mid-fifties, wearing a tweed skirt and twin set and pearls, came out. She had a ruddy complexion and short, greying hair.

'I'm Nora Compton. I called the police over an hour ago. Something is very wrong and even the dog has stopped barking now. The curtains are still closed. I'm certain something's happened.'

PC Lee nodded and continued down to the basement. The front door was painted racing green with a brass lion's head knocker and a brass letterplate. There was a small framed notice above it: *No flyers or junk mail.* Beside the front door was a large terracotta planter containing an array of well-tended plants and the patio was immaculately paved with York stone.

Lee rang the doorbell. Mrs. Compton leaned over the railings above him.

'I've been down there ringing the doorbell since early this morning. I can assure you no one is there.'

Lee waited and rang the bell again. He could hear a scuffling sound and a whine, then a hoarse, pitiful bark.

'That's his dog,' Mrs. Compton said. 'He does have two others, but they're not always in his flat. One's a Jack Russell cross and the other is some kind of whippet. It's quite vicious.'

Lee lifted the lion's head knocker and banged it repeatedly. Inside the dog attempted to bark feebly.

Lee bent down, lifted the brass letterplate and peered in. He could see a rolled-up newspaper lying on the doormat, which had probably been delivered that morning. A little dog was staring at him and whining pitifully, and he noticed that the newspaper had been shredded at one end. More disturbingly the dog and the newspaper both seemed to be splattered with what looked like blood.

Lee stood and looked up at Mrs. Compton.

'Do you have access to this flat?'

'No, I do not – I made that clear to the detective I spoke to on the phone earlier.'

Lee climbed the stairs back to street level.

'Is there a back entrance, or a garden area?'

'Yes, Mr. Foxley has his own garden, but no other tenant can gain access to it.'

'So, there's no back door from the main property?'

'I thought I just made that quite clear to you. Mr. Foxley is the only person who has access to the back garden, through his French doors.'

'Have you noticed anything suspicious recently?'

'No, I have not. The only reason I've been concerned is that the dog has been barking all night and morning, and Mr. Foxley is nowhere to be seen.'

Lee thanked her and walked down the road, hoping that Mrs. Compton would go back inside. He called in to the station and the switchboard transferred him to Jane.

* * *

Jane listened to his update and made notes, instructing Lee to remain at the property. She then went up to the canteen to find Spencer, who was sitting eating a sandwich.

'You may just have got what you wished for, Spence. I just took a call from the PC who went over to the long-haired dachshund's property.'

'Don't tell me – he was viciously attacked by the dog?' Spencer said through a mouthful of sandwich.

'No, he couldn't get into the flat, but when he looked through the letterbox the dog appeared to be covered in blood.'

Spencer's jaw dropped. 'You're fucking kidding me.'

She shook her head. 'I think you need to get over there, Spence.'

He stood up and walked briskly out of the canteen. Ten minutes later he was on his way to the flat in one of CID's unmarked red Hillman Hunters, accompanied by DC Gary Dors.

Jane returned to her desk and continued checking through reports and statements until she got a call-out from a uniformed officer about a disturbance at the exclusive Mulberry handbag shop off the Brompton Road. A customer had attempted to run from the shop with a handbag and had inadvertently caused a taxi to swerve into an on-coming vehicle. Although no one was hurt, the taxi driver was furious, and the other vehicle had severe damage down the passenger side.

By the time Jane arrived at the scene, traffic police were already taking particulars and two members of staff had taken the woman back into the shop. She was extremely abusive and had tried to punch and kick her way out of the shop again. Jane tried to calm her down enough to take a statement. In the end she was more shocked by the price of the handbag than the fact that this middle-aged woman had risked getting herself seriously injured by running in front of the taxi. She took all the necessary particulars but the woman was not taken into custody because she agreed to pay for the handbag.

Well, at least I got a break from sitting at my desk looking through tedious reports, Jane reflected.

*   *   *

Gary Dors hurried up to her as she walked into the station.

'Holy shit! You've missed the panic going on here. Just before you left, Spence walked into the most horrific murder scene over at Onslow Square.'

'What? You're joking.'

'I'm bloody not. He called in for forensics, pathologists and a doctor.'

'Is he still over there?' Jane asked.

'No, he's up in the incident room, and more uniforms have been ordered to cordon off the murder site.'

Jane went into the incident room. Spencer was on the phone, his hair looking even untidier than usual.

'Detective Chief Inspector Tyler is at the scene, but he wants a pathologist present as soon as possible. The two we've tried to contact are not available. Yes, it is a fucking emergency! Sorry . . . sorry for swearing, but it's just been a nightmare. Thank you very much.'

Spencer slammed down the phone and turned to Jane. 'You will not fucking believe it. We've had to cordon off half the street. There's blood everywhere and the forensic team, AKA Paul Lawrence, is trying to keep everyone from tramping all over it.'

'Is it a murder?' Jane asked, taking her coat off.

'Murder? I've never seen anything like it. He's been disem-boweled, his head is almost severed, there's pools of blood in the hall, the bedroom and the bathroom. I've never seen so much blood. The poor dog was covered in it. Lawrence had a hard time cutting off some of the dog fur for the laboratory as the little bastard has got teeth like a piranha. He's had a go at everybody. The neighbor said she'd look after it and give it a bath, but she can't keep it for long as she's got two cats.'

'Should I get over there?' Jane asked.

'Right now Tyler's not letting anyone in until a pathologist has had a look at the victim. And you won't believe what happened to me. I was told to get back here, get more uniforms, get the bloody pathologist there, and this woman gets out of a Mercedes 280SL, leaves it parked in the middle of the road, and starts screaming at me that she wants to know what's going on. I mean, right now, Jane, I don't *know* what the hell's going on. It looks like the killer used a cricket bat, left a razor in the bathroom, victim's got blunt-force trauma to the back, front and side of his head, so we can't identify him. The woman upstairs wouldn't come down and take a look at him. She said he's an agent.'

'What, an estate agent?'

'No, no, like a theatrical agent. There are photos of these people all over the flat, and this Mercedes woman starts screaming at me that she wants to know what's happened. I told her that there had been a terrible incident in the flat. She starts pushing and shoving me, demanding that she goes down the steps. The guv comes out because she's screaming the place down, and then she says, "Has something happened to Charles?" She almost pushes me off my feet and starts to go down to the basement, screaming that she was his wife. The guv tries to stop her, meanwhile, we've got blokes putting the corrugated cardboard down to avoid contamination and footprints in all the blood, and she keeps yelling that she is Justine Harris, Charles Foxley's wife, and she has every right to know what is going on. That's when I am told to fuck off and do what I'm told to do.'

The phone rang to interrupt him. Spencer grabbed the receiver and listened before snapping angrily, 'Everybody's waiting. I'll get there as quick as I can.'

He slammed the receiver down again.

'Pathologist is on his way. It's that bad-tempered guy who works over at Hammersmith – nasty little sod.'

Spencer's radio bleeped. 'I'm at the station, guv . . . What?'

Jane could hear Tyler saying that it looked possible that the body was Charles Foxley and that Justine Harris had been removed from the premises by uniformed officers as her car was holding up the traffic. They would, however, still need to get a formal identification, as the woman was so hysterical, he couldn't let her near the body.

'Listen, if I hadn't dragged her out, it looked as if she wanted to give him a kicking.'

'Tennison is here, guv. Do you want her over there?'

'Not yet. As soon as we are able to move the body, I want you both here. There's enough traffic here at the moment. In the meantime, you and Jane see what you can find out about the victim. I want uniform assistance to start house-to-house inquiries ASAP.'

Spencer switched off his radio.

'Did you hear that? Charles Foxley, theatrical agent. Let's get started.'

It was another two hours before the pathologist gave permission for the body bags to be brought in and the SOCOs could start assisting Paul Lawrence. He had a specialist in blood pattern analysis and two back-up scientists to focus on the bathroom, the hallway and the bedroom where the body had been found. It appeared that the victim had been attacked first in the hallway. The weapon, a cricket bat, was already bagged and tagged to go to the laboratory. Judging from the blood spattering on both sides of the hallway, it was possible the victim had then been dragged into the bathroom. There were blood-soaked clothes, torn into shreds, and an open cut-throat razor left in the bath, with deep blood pooling around it.

The trail of bloodstains suggested that the body had then been taken into the bedroom, where a silk bedspread, carpet and pillows were also soaked in blood. The victim was wearing only pants and socks, and attached to his right wrist was a closed handcuff, the other cuff lying loose.

* * *

Jane and Spencer, alongside the rest of the team, began to gather as many details as possible, bringing in civilian staff and a couple of probationary officers to assist them. They were now working on the assumption that the victim was the successful theatrical agent Charles Foxley, even though no formal identification had been done yet, since the body had been found in his residence.

Justine Harris, it turned out, was his ex-wife. DS Lawrence had asked the team to check with BT urgently to discover what last numbers Foxley had called from his home phone.

Tyler came out of his office to enquire how much progress they had made. Jane glanced at Spencer as he turned over page after page of his notebook.

'Well, sir, we were informed that he had offices in Wardour Street and a substantial list of television actors. The company name is Foxley & Myers.'

He glanced towards Jane and she tapped her notebook. 'When we discovered how well-known Mr. Foxley was, we contacted the press office and we got a lot more background information.'

Spencer nodded. 'Guv, Foxley was forty-two years old and divorced from Justine Harris. They have one daughter, aged ten, called Clara.'

Jane lifted her hand. 'She's apparently at boarding school, guv. We got a fax detailing a lot of press releases saying his ex-wife was living in the marital home in Barnes, valued at 1.5 million pounds.'

Tyler whistled.

Spencer added that the Driver and Vehicle Licensing Agency had confirmed that Foxley owned a Jaguar XK120 sports car and an eight-year-old Volvo estate. Usually the cars were kept in the garage in Barnes. He had a parking permit for Onslow Square.

Jane interrupted. 'According to Companies House, guv, Foxley & Myers had a turnover of 2.3 million pounds last year.'

Tyler puffed out his cheeks. 'Oh shit, this is getting nastier by the minute. It's going to be a right handful to deal with.'

'We also know that Foxley & Myers employed four subsidiary agents, two receptionists and three secretaries,' Jane added.

All three turned as DC Dors called out that he had something of interest. They watched the fax machine slowly coughing out numerous black and white photographs of Justine Harris.

Dors carried the pictures over. 'She's a famous actress,' he said. 'She was in *Upstairs, Downstairs.*'

Tyler just stood there, looking wrecked. He turned to Jane, loosening his tie.

'Right, Justine Harris needs to be contacted ASAP to give us a formal fucking identification.'

Jane raised her hand. 'Sir, I have been calling her home and the number for her in Barnes, but I'm getting no reply.'

'Well, keep trying. And in the meantime I could do with a coffee and a sandwich from the canteen.'

Tyler went into his office and gestured for Spencer to join him and closed the door.

'I'm not pissing around when I say we need a press blanket on this. If the victim is who we think he is and knows all these famous people, the journalists will be crawling all over us like bed bugs.'

'Didn't his wife ID him for you, guv?'

'For Christ's sake, I told you the woman was hysterical. Anyway, she couldn't see his face properly. There was so much blood you couldn't even tell what color his hair was. I don't know if you also took on board that he had a handcuff on his right wrist. It's gone with him to the mortuary. Poor old Lawrence reckons it is going to take a couple more hours at the very least. If we can't get hold of Justine Harris we need to find someone else to ID him. Or we'll have to get his fucking dentist to do it.'

'I'd say the best bet would be to get in touch with his business partner, James Myers. They own the company together.'

'OK, so quietly does it. I want you and Jane to go over to . . . where are the offices?'

'Paramount House, Wardour Street. It's full of film companies and agents.'

Tyler nodded. 'OK, but no warning phone call. I want you both over there. Have a quiet chat with this so-called business partner Marsh—'

'It's Myers, guv.'

'Myers, then. Take him to the mortuary. I'll tell them to clean up Foxley's face as best they can. As soon as he identifies him, I'll see you back at the crime scene.'

There was a knock on his door as Jane entered with a ham sandwich and a cup of coffee. Tyler smiled.

'Thanks, Jane. I hope you don't mind me asking you to get this for me. You and Spencer have done a great job so far but we have to keep a lid on this horror show as best we can. I want you and Spencer to go and see this . . . ' He rubbed his head. 'What's his business partner's name again?'

Spencer sighed. 'James Jarvis Myers, sir.'

'OK, off you go.' Tyler bit into his sandwich as Spencer closed the door behind them. He nudged Jane to look at DI Arnold's empty chair.

'This could be just the opportunity I'm looking for.'

* * *

Jane and Spencer drove to Wardour Street. It was a busy one-way street and difficult to find a parking space directly outside the building, so Spencer left the police car log book on the dashboard so that any traffic wardens would recognize it as a police car and not give them a ticket.

Jane had combed her hair and put some fresh lipstick on but she wished she was wearing something smarter. She lent Spencer her comb as his hair was still standing on end.

They went through the glass doors to the reception where there was a small desk pushed to one side. On a plaque on the wall there was a list of the various companies who occupied the building and it appeared that Foxley & Myers Theatrical Agents had the entire first floor. There was an 'out of order' notice taped to the lift so they walked up the wide staircase to the first floor.

On the landing there were two doors with 'Foxley & Myers Agents' printed on one, and 'Foxley & Myers Reception' printed on the other. They headed towards the reception.

Spencer looked at Jane. 'Doesn't look very theatrical to me.'

They pushed open the door and Jane smiled at what it revealed. Ahead of them was a corridor with a name plaque on each door. The walls were covered in framed film posters and actors' awards. On the right was a half-moon desk with four leather and chrome chairs beside it. Two girls sat behind the desk, one weighing and stamping large envelopes and one typing. Behind them were rows of files and volumes of *Spotlight*, the bible for all theatrical and film contacts.

The two receptionists were perched on high stools. One had bleached blonde hair with heavy make-up, glossy lips and false eyelashes. The other girl had bright red dyed hair, with matching lipstick. Both appeared to be in their mid-twenties and, rather incongruously, Jane couldn't help noticing behind them a large wall poster for *Night of the Living Dead*.

The blonde girl was talking into one of the handsets of the four phones on the desk in front of them.

'I have the details and I will pass them on to Mr. Foxley as soon as he comes in. I do know he has a very full diary for the next few days, but I am sure he will call you back when he gets this message.' She replaced the receiver, muttering, 'What an arsehole.'

The redhead appeared to be reading a contract. Both girls totally ignored the fact Spencer and Jane were standing in front of them. Eventually Spencer tapped the desk.

'I'm Detective Sergeant Spencer Gibbs, and this is Detective Sergeant Jane Tennison. We have an urgent matter to discuss with Mr. Myers.'

'Do you have an appointment?' the blonde girl asked.

'No, but as I just said, it is an urgent police matter.'

'If it's about the parking, we've already had someone here from Scotland Yard.'

Spencer glared at her. 'Show me to his office, will you? Do you think you'd have two detective sergeants here in person to discuss a parking problem?'

'No need to be rude,' said the redhead huffily.

Perhaps detecting something in Spencer's manner, the blonde girl got off her stool, leaned over the desk and pointed to the end of the corridor. 'That's his office at the end. Do you mind if I just call and tell him you're coming to see him?'

Spencer waved his hand and gestured for Jane to follow him. As they walked away they could hear a high-pitched voice saying, 'There are two high-ranking police people coming to see you. They didn't explain what it was about.'

Before they had a chance to knock on the rather impressive door to the office at the end of the corridor, it swung open.

'Yes?'

'Are you Mr. James Myers?' Spencer asked quietly.

'I am.'

Spencer introduced himself and Jane as he walked into the office, forcing Myers to take a step back.

'I'd like to discuss our reason for being here in private, so would you mind shutting the door?' Spencer asked.

Myers closed the door and gestured for them both to sit on an expensive-looking, thickly cushioned sofa in front of his desk.

As with the outside corridor, his office was lined wall to wall with photographs of clients, or posters of the films they'd been in.

At first sight, Jane found Myers a difficult man to read. He was very slight, about five foot nine, wearing exceedingly tight fawn trousers and brown leather boots with Cuban heels. He had a pale blue corduroy shirt tucked in tightly at his waist.

You couldn't really describe him as handsome or good-looking, she thought, but he had very neat features with expressive eyes.

'This all looks very serious,' Myers said with a smile.

Spencer took the lead. 'I'm afraid it is, sir. We are here on a very unfortunate matter. I understand that you and Charles Foxley are partners. Is that true?'

'Well, only in a business sense,' Myers said, flippantly waving his hand.

'Well, this is a very personal matter.'

Myers leaned back. 'Oh God, what's he done now?'

'It's not what he's done, sir, it's what's been done to him. His body was found early this morning. I am afraid we will need you to formally identify him as we've been unable to contact his wife.'

Myers sat up in his chair. 'I don't quite understand . . . Are you telling me he's dead?'

'I'm afraid that is why we are here, sir.'

'Jesus Christ!' Myers muttered, clutching the arms of his chair. 'What happened? Was it a heart attack?'

'No, I'm afraid he was brutally murdered.'

Myers gasped. 'Where?'

'He was found in his flat this morning. I'm afraid I can't go into any more detail, Mr. Myers, but we would appreciate you accompanying us to identify Mr. Foxley, unless you know of any relatives.'

Myers shook his head. 'Both his parents are deceased, and I have no idea about anyone else.'

Five minutes later Myers had put on a grey cashmere coat and picked up his soft leather satchel. He had been asked not to make the reason for his departure public, so simply waved his hand towards the reception desk. Then he paused.

'Rita, will you make sure my dogs are collected from the groomers?' He turned to Spencer. 'How long is this going to take?'

'Not long, sir, and we'll return you to your office when we've finished.'

'So about half an hour? An hour?'

'I'd say around forty-five minutes.'

As they headed down the stairs, Jane studied Myers. She was finding it difficult to understand his lack of reaction on being told that his business partner had been found dead.

Myers didn't speak during the journey to the mortuary at Lambeth, and as soon as they arrived, asked if he could check whether his dogs had been taken to his office.

Spencer raised his eyebrows. 'I'm sure there's a phone that you can use, sir.'

Jane and Spencer watched Myers make the call from a pay-phone in the reception area.

'Can you believe this guy?' Spencer said.

'No, I can't,' Jane said, shaking her head. 'He seems more worried about his dogs than his dead business partner.'

They were given permission to go into the mortuary area, where the body would usually have been laid out in the small chapel of rest for identification purposes. But their victim was still waiting for an autopsy, so his body was on the slab covered by a green sheet, with only his head visible. They had cleaned his face up as best as they could, but a number of teeth had been smashed, his nose broken, and one eye had been driven into his skull. They had managed to wash most of the blood from his hair, which was now its original strawberry blond color.

'Are you ready, Mr. Myers?' Jane asked quietly.

He nodded, and a mortician led them to the table.

Spencer looked directly ahead with Myers standing to his right and Jane just a little behind, in case Myers felt faint and keeled over backwards.

'Could you please look at the man on the table and tell me if you recognize him?'

Myers remained completely still, slowly lowering his head to look closer. He frowned, took a deep breath and sighed.

'Yes, this is him. This is Charles Foxley.' He turned towards Jane. 'Can you get me out of here, please?'

* * *

'Maybe this is not the time, sir, but I will need to talk to you, and we will obviously have numerous questions to ask,' Spencer told him on their way out of the mortuary. 'Can I request that you do not make any contact with the press regarding Mr. Foxley's death? It is imperative we are able to investigate the crime without being hampered by overzealous reporters and journalists. I would also be grateful if you would accompany us to the station where we could take a formal statement from you.'

'What? Do you mean right now? No, no, it's impossible. I have an incredibly important meeting with a client; in fact, I have back-to-back meetings all day – and, of course, I need time to recover from this appalling news.'

'Would it be convenient to speak to you at nine tomorrow morning?' Spencer asked.

Myers pursed his lips. 'I'll have to move a couple of appointments, but yes, I suppose I could be available.' He paused. 'Charles did have an awful lot of enemies.'

Jane glanced at Spencer as they walked behind Myers, who was now intent on hailing a taxi.

'One moment please, sir,' Jane said sharply. 'You just said Mr. Foxley had a lot of enemies. Is there anyone in particular you were referring to?'

'Dear God! I was being flippant. It's the shock. I'm in a state of shock.'

A taxi pulled up, and before they could stop him, Myers had hurriedly climbed in, slamming the door shut behind him.

Jane and Spencer watched the taxi drive off.

'Incredible. He didn't appear to give a shit that his partner had been murdered,' Jane muttered.

Spencer shrugged. 'Yeah, well, we'll see him again tomorrow. Come on, we should go and catch up with the boss at the crime scene.'

* * *

At Paramount House Myers ran up the stairs two at a time, bursting into the reception area. 'How are my babies?' he demanded.

'Oh, they're back and all lovely – nails cut and coats shampooed. They smell divine,' said the blonde girl.

Myers hurried down the corridor and opened his office door. Two Pekingese dogs raised their heads in unison from their hand-woven Harrods dog basket. He closed the door quietly behind him, took off his coat and sat behind his desk. Plucking a handful of tissues from the box, he twisted them in his hands, then burst into tears.

'You stupid bastard, you stupid bastard . . .' he repeated over and over again as he tried to stifle his sobs.

CHAPTER FOUR

Two uniformed officers remained at the entrance to Foxley's flat, which had been cordoned off with yellow tape. Spencer showed his ID and Jane followed him down the steps to the open front door. There was cardboard across the entrance and placed like stepping stones along the hallway. DS Lawrence was at the end of the corridor and turned towards them, removing his latex gloves. He gave a small nod of recognition to Jane.

'It's been a very long day. I'll come back first thing in the morning, but I need to get to the lab to work on all the evidence we have removed so far. I'm asking everyone to keep to the cardboard to avoid contamination. By morning I should be able to give a clear account of what I believe happened.'

Spencer looked at him quizzically. 'It's pretty obvious, isn't it, Paul? Killer used the cricket bat, hammered him at the front door.'

Lawrence put up his hand. 'Don't make assumptions, Spence. So far we don't know which blunt-force trauma occurred first. By that I mean whether he was hit first from behind, suggesting that his assailant was already inside the flat. As yet we have had no indication of forced entry.'

Duly chastised, Spencer muttered his apologies. Jane smiled at Lawrence.

'Is DCI Tyler here?' she asked.

Lawrence nodded and gestured towards the kitchen. 'In there.'

As he finished packing up, Jane had the opportunity to take in the flat's luxurious furnishings. There were antique oil paintings along one side of the hallway, and a small Georgian side table opposite. The elaborate gold-framed mirror was spattered with blood. The hall carpet was a pale blue, the weave so thick that the corrugated cardboard sank into it. The ceiling cornices had gilt decorated scrolls and Jane looked up at the ornate chandelier, made from numerous pieces of beautifully colored glass.

'Murano glass,' Lawrence said. 'Probably 1920s.'

Spencer glanced up at the chandelier. 'Looks quite cheap to me.'

'No, it's very, very expensive,' Lawrence replied.

Suddenly they heard Tyler's voice from the kitchen. 'If you antique aficionados are finished assessing the value of the furnishings, could you come over here?'

Jane followed Spencer into the kitchen, and couldn't help gasping in surprise. It was in a totally different style to the ornate hall and Jane had never seen such modern equipment. There was a state-of-the-art stove, and all the cupboards and worktops were black granite and silver. The white tile floor had been partly covered with corrugated cardboard to protect it and there was a kitchen bar with chrome and black leather stools. Every available wall space was occupied by kitchen cabinets. Tyler had a large notebook open on the counter and a takeaway coffee. He gestured for them to sit down, then jerked his thumb towards one of the cabinets.

'That's a dishwasher in there, next to it is a deep-freeze and next to that is a fridge. You've got a coffee percolator that looks like a power-station and I would say they must've lowered the ceiling for these spotlights.'

Spencer nodded. 'Yeah, we found out he's worth a bob or two. His partner has formally identified him. He didn't show any emotion at all. Not a thing.'

'Well, somebody certainly got very emotional towards Foxley,' Tyler said. 'I've never seen anything like it. Until we've had the postmortem and we meet with Paul Lawrence again, our priority is to identify a suspect. It's very difficult to ascertain if robbery was involved, but I'll walk you through the bedroom and the drawing room, so you can get a feel of the place. Apart from the blood bath, nothing looks disturbed. So that means we have to consider that this horror may have been staged, the killer making it look as if he acted in a fit of uncontrolled rage, and then the dismemberment done to make us think we're looking for a psychopath.'

They spent another twenty minutes discussing the neighbor who had alerted them, agreeing that she needed to be spoken to again to verify the timeline Spencer had made a note of when she called the station.

They also urgently needed to talk to Foxley's ex-wife.

Tyler led them from the kitchen into the large drawing room. One set of barred windows looked out to the stone steps at the entrance. On the opposite wall were large French windows with elegantly draped curtains, which opened onto a York-stoned patio with steps leading up to a small walled garden with mature trees and flower beds.

Spencer examined the French windows, which showed no signs of a forced entry. There were also no bloodstains in this room, which had polished pine floors and an elaborate Persian rug, two white sofas and a large tapestry depicting Tudor couples performing some kind of dance. On the opposite side of the room were beautifully carved floor to ceiling bookcases. In the center of the room was a glass-topped coffee table displaying an array of architectural books.

'As you can see, nothing looks out of place here,' Tyler said.

'Is that him?' Jane asked. Along one shelf of the bookcases were silver-framed photographs. In one of them the victim was smiling broadly, wearing an evening suit, his arm around Roger Moore.

'That's James Bond,' Spencer said.

All three stood together looking from one photograph to the other. Charles Foxley was photographed at various premieres, always smiling, always immaculately dressed. The photographs were signed 'With thanks' or 'With love'. One of the large framed photographs had a crack across the glass. The photograph was of Foxley standing beside a white pony with a pretty little girl. Jane looked closer.

'This could be his daughter, Clara. Interesting: if you look closely, the photograph has been folded.'

Tyler nodded at Jane, and with her protective gloves, aware the glass was cracked, she carefully laid the frame face-down to remove the clips from the back and ease off the cardboard backing.

'I'm right! Look.' The folded-under part of the photograph showed Foxley's ex-wife, Justine, with a black felt-tip cross over her face.

'I want that bagged,' Tyler said.

The same pale blue carpet ran through into the bedroom. The simplicity of the room was enhanced by the almost match-ing pale blue silk-covered walls and the white fitted wardrobes. The vast king-sized bed had an array of blue silk throw pillows and a quilted silk bedspread. There were pieces of cardboard running along the carpet to the bed, where the pooling blood had taken on a hideous body shape. There was a gold ormolu clock on the bedside table and a selection of leather-bound books on the opposite matching table. Tyler stepped carefully across the cardboard to ease open a wardrobe door. Behind it was a safe and a number of slender drawers. He crooked his finger to pull out a drawer.

'Nice array of watches, wouldn't you say? We haven't yet had access to the safe, but we should get that open tomorrow morn-ing.' Tyler then pointed upwards to the ceiling, where there was an enormous mirror. 'What do you think of that? When Lawrence was here, he took a lot of pictures of the blood spatter.'

Just by the open door was a large, dirty velvet dog bed with an empty water bowl beside it. The only indication that they were in a basement came from the dank smell that pervaded the air. Jane was beginning to feel nauseous.

'OK, last but not least.' The smell became stronger as Tyler pushed open the connecting door. The elegant bathroom had obviously been designed by the same architect as the kitchen. But instead of black marble, everything was porcelain white.

'The pathologist reckoned this was where his throat was cut. The weapon, a cut-throat razor, has been taken in to be tested for fingerprints. It was found in the bathtub. The suggestion is that the body was dragged from the bathroom and disemboweled in the bedroom.'

Tyler looked at his watch. It was coming up to seven p.m. and already getting dark.

'Right, I'm going to head back to the station and start on the reports. I think it's imperative we don't waste any time. I need to have a statement from the ex-wife and the neighbor by tonight. You can work on it between you or do one each. There'll be two uniformed officers on duty here around the clock as the premises need to remain secure.'

As Tyler left, Spencer looked at Jane. 'Do you want to do it together?'

'I don't mind. I mean, the neighbor is only upstairs so we could do that now, and then head over to Barnes,' Jane said.

'I'll have to call the wife,' Spencer said. 'It's been a long day.'

'I don't mind going to Barnes by myself, Spence. And we have to meet Mr. Myers tomorrow morning.'

'OK, let's do it that way,' Spence said as they headed out. They paused at the front door as they heard one of the uniformed officers saying loudly, 'I'm very sorry, sir, but you are not allowed to enter the premises.'

There was a good deal of barking going on.

'I have every fucking right to be down there and I want to know what the fuck is going on.'

'There is no need to swear at me, sir,' they heard the uniform insisting. 'I am just doing my job. You cannot enter these premises.'

'Listen, mate, I've had his dogs all fucking day and I have a job to do.'

Spencer came out just as a small, wizened man wearing a trilby and a stained wax jacket looked as if he was about to throw a punch at the officer. As he was restraining two dogs on leads at the time, he was slightly off-balance and looked as though he was about to fall over. Spencer walked quickly up the stairs.

'Can I help you?'

'Yes, I've got to leave his dogs – I've had them all night and day and I've got things to do.'

The neighbor was caring for Foxley's dachshund, so Spencer assumed these were the Jack Russell and whippet cross, who were now being returned.

'I'm afraid I cannot allow you into the premises. There has been an incident.'

'I just want to leave the fucking dogs. I've already had them longer than he pays me for – I'm a dog walker not a dog babysitter.'

Spencer lifted his hand. 'Just a minute, sir.'

Jane pulled the front door closed behind her and checked the yellow tape was secure. She looked up as the irate dog walker handed the leads for the two dogs to Spencer.

'What's your name please, sir?'

'Mind your own fucking business.'

'I really need to know your name, sir. I am Detective Sergeant Gibbs.' He showed his ID.

Jane walked up the steps.

'Oh, fucking hell. Has the place been burgled?'

'No, I'm afraid it's far more serious than that. I really do require you name,' Gibbs said firmly.

'Eric Newman.'

'Do you have any identification?'

'I don't believe this! What's so serious you need ID? Will my unemployment benefit card do?'

Mr. Newman took out an old crumpled document.

'Are you employed by Mr. Foxley?' Jane asked, as Gibbs passed her Newman's benefit card.

'I do a few cash-in-hand jobs. I'm not on any payroll. I walk his dogs when he can't. If he has business I look after them. Like I said, it's just cash-in-hand, but he usually gives me good warning. I've had them all night and all day – I've been calling him but there's been no reply.'

'Do you ever house-sit for Mr. Foxley?' Jane asked, passing his document back.

'What do you mean?' Newman looked evasive.

'Exactly what I asked. Do you ever stay in Mr. Foxley's flat when he is not there?'

'No . . . no, never.'

'Do you come to his flat to pick up the dogs?'

'No. He calls me if he needs me to walk the dogs. What he does is he takes the dogs to his office and I pick them up from there. Sometimes he asks if I can keep them for the afternoon. Then what I do is I bring them back here. Or if he's away, he pays me extra and I have them with me. But he's not told me to keep 'em.'

'What about the dachshund?' Spencer asked.

'I never have her. Mr. Foxley's ex looks after her as she can be vicious – goes for the ankles.' Mr. Newman seemed to be getting more nervous by the second.

'Do you have a key to Mr. Foxley's premises?'

'Shit, no! No, I don't have a key. He's been burgled, hasn't he? That's what it is.'

'Mr. Newman, I am going to ask you if you could please keep the dogs and you will be contacted first thing in the morning,' Jane said calmly.

'I can't take them. I have a job to do. That's why I've come round now.'

Spencer could hardly believe it. Newman turned as if to walk off but Spencer grabbed him by the arm. 'Just a minute, sir.'

Spencer quickly withdrew his arm as the ferret-faced Newman whipped around.

'Don't you lay your hands on me. I've done nothing wrong. You got my name, you got my address. I'm not taking charge of them dogs no more. He owes me fifteen quid.'

Spencer caught the smirk between the uniformed officers and gave them a sharp look. 'This isn't funny.'

'Well, at least they're well-behaved,' Jane said. She looked at Newman. 'It would be exceedingly helpful to us if you took the dogs this evening. We are scheduled to be at Mr. Foxley's office at nine a.m. tomorrow. If you, or someone else, can meet us there, we will have the dogs taken care of. In the meantime, my colleague will give you twenty quid to take them tonight.'

Spencer, known by his colleagues for being tight, was forced to open his wallet, and grudgingly handed over a well-worn twenty-pound note. Newman then moved off quickly with both dogs.

One of the uniformed officers smiled to Spence. 'That was the easiest twenty quid I've ever seen earned.'

Spencer angrily instructed the uniforms to remain on duty until they were relieved and walked off with Jane, who was trying not to laugh herself.

'As you handled the dog situation so well, Spence, I'll leave the next-door neighbor to you. I'm going back to the station to grab a bite to eat before seeing the ex-wife in Barnes.'

Spencer was eager to get home so he headed up the steps to the neighbor's flat and rang the bell. He could hear the sound of the dog yapping and a loud voice saying, 'No, get down, no!' He had to wait for a few minutes before the door was opened, still with the security chain in place.

Spencer held out his ID. 'Mrs. Compton, it's Detective Sergeant Spencer Gibbs.'

She frowned at him. 'Nobody told me I would have to look after this dog for the entire afternoon. I've had to wash it, dry it and feed it, and keep my cat in his cat basket in a different room.'

'Mrs. Compton, I do apologize for any inconvenience. You have my sincere thanks for taking care of Mr. Foxley's dog.'

'I really didn't have any option, did I?' she snapped.

'We are very grateful, but do you think I could possibly come in, as I need to take a formal statement from you?'

Mrs. Compton unhooked the door chain. 'All right, but I really don't have much time. *Coronation Street* is about to start. Quickly, quickly. I don't want to let it out.' She slammed the door shut.

The entire conversation was overheard by the uniformed officer who had witnessed the earlier interaction with Eric Newman. He turned to his partner. 'He's a glutton for punishment, isn't he?'

* * *

Back at the station, Jane could hear the click-clack of typewriter keys as she passed Tyler's office. She went up to the canteen and was able to get a rather stale sandwich and a cup of tea just before it closed for the evening. She sat at her desk typing up her report, looking over the empty desks of both of the young DCs who she knew would have their work cut out for them in the morning. She typed quickly, attempting to make the interaction with Mr. Newman as humorless as possible. She then contacted the collator at Hammersmith police station, remembering that Newman's address was in that area, and asked if he could look into Newman's history. It didn't take long before she was informed that Mr. Newman had a lengthy record of petty crimes and was well-known on the greyhound circuits. Jane added the new information to her report.

It was 8:30 p.m. by the time she'd finished, so she left the station and collected her Mini to go and see Foxley's ex-wife, narrowly missing a grumpy-looking Spencer heading into the station with a wire-haired dachshund under his arm.

Jane drove through Putney and then Barnes before arriving at a substantial-looking house on Vine Road with a Mercedes 280SL convertible parked in the drive. As she approached the front door, a security light came on and she heard the sound of dogs barking. She rang the front doorbell and waited. The barking grew louder and then a brusque male voice came through the intercom by the side of the door.

'Yes?'

Jane leaned forward and pressed the intercom button. 'I'm Detective Sergeant Jane Tennison from—'

The intercom crackled loudly and dogs could be heard barking frantically.

'Wait a minute.'

Through the two stained-glass windows embedded in the panel door, Jane could see the shadowy figure of a very tall man. He appeared to be shouting to quiet the dogs before unlocking the door. A slim, handsome man wearing a black turtle-neck sweater and jeans with monogrammed slippers stood in the doorway.

'Could I see your identification, please?' He had a low, plummy voice.

Jane had her ID card ready. 'I'm Detective Sergeant Jane Tennison. I'm hoping to speak to Justine Harris.'

'I'm afraid that won't be possible,' he said, handing back her ID.

'It is very important. May I ask who you are?'

'I am not sure it is any of your business, but I'm George Henson.'

Jane didn't know if the name should mean anything to her, but there was something theatrical about his manner and something quite familiar about his face.

'It's about her husband, or ex-husband, isn't it?'

Jane nodded. 'Yes, I don't know how much you've been told.'

'Detective, you will not be able to speak to Justine because she attempted suicide this afternoon and is at St Mary's Hospital.'

Jane gasped. 'I'm so sorry.'

'As soon as I was alerted to Justine's situation,' Henson continued, 'I came over to secure the house. I'm a close family friend. While I was here, her ex-husband's dog walker deposited two of his animals. I have no option but to look after them now.'

Jane was still taken aback, not only about the information regarding Justine Harris, but she also found Mr. Henson's attitude unnerving.

'I will obviously need to contact Ms. Harris again after she's hopefully made a full recovery. Thank you for your time, Mr. Henson.'

He shrugged. 'Think nothing of it.' He hesitated for a moment, then added, 'He was a despicable human being, a detestable man who treated his wife and his only child with a blatant disregard for their feelings. Whoever killed him has done everyone who had to deal with him a great favor.'

Jane was shocked, but this time she was able to meet Henson's piercing gaze.

'Was he your agent?'

Henson laughed, shaking his head. 'Thankfully, he didn't represent me. Goodnight.' He shut the door, sliding the bolt across.

Jane drove to the nearest phone kiosk and called the station, asking for a message to be relayed to DCI Tyler that Justine Harris had been admitted to St Mary's Hospital, after a failed suicide attempt.

She also wanted the unpleasant Mr. Henson to be checked out.

CHAPTER FIVE

When Jane got home she had eight calls on her answering machine. She kicked off her shoes and pressed play. The first one was from DCI Tyler. 'Please contact me ASAP. I'm still at the station.'

There were three previous calls, all from Tyler and equally abrupt. There was also a call from her mother and one from her sister, which Jane fast-forwarded through as she dialed Tyler's direct number.

The phone was snatched up immediately. 'DCI Leonard Tyler.'

'It's Jane Tennison, sir.'

'About bloody time! It's already after ten so I won't ask you to come in, but I'm calling a seven a.m. meeting at the station tomorrow. I have been able to secure ten officers who will be doing the house-to-house inquiries, and there will be a press conference at eight a.m. Justine Harris appears to be making a good recovery after taking a substantial but non-fatal amount of Nembutal. I've spoken to Mr. Henson and, off the record, he said this was not her first suicide attempt. I also had a lengthy conversation with Mr. Myers at Foxley's agency, and asked if he could compile a list of people with grievances against Charles Foxley. He was a bit sarcastic about that, saying it would take considerable time. I also asked him to put together a press release, which I can use in the morning.'

Tyler then listed all the names of the sub-agents at the agency who he wanted Jane and Spencer to interview at 9 a.m. Jane quickly jotted down the names as Tyler angrily added that they were now looking after a long-haired dachshund that Spencer had brought back to the station until Battersea Dogs Home could arrange a collection.

'Maybe the dog could be delivered to Justine Harris's home as Foxley's other two dogs are being looked after by George Henson,' Jane suggested.

No sooner had Jane put the receiver down than the phone rang again. It was Spencer.

'Has the guvnor been in touch?' he asked.

Jane relayed back all the instructions, adding that she had been impressed by Tyler's efficiency. She glanced at her watch.

'I mean, Spence, it's eleven p.m. and he is still at the station. You know how early he usually gets off. I've often wondered how he would react to a big case. I'm astonished he's got so much done in such a short time.'

'You must be bloody joking. He's had me running around like a blue-arsed fly since I got back to the station. Gave me a load of verbal abuse because of this fucking dachshund the neighbor refused to look after. Anyway, one of the secretaries gave the dog a ham sandwich. She's called Toots, by the way. Dunno if that has any connection to cocaine.'

Jane smiled. 'Where are you?'

'I am sitting on a hardback chair at St Mary's Hospital. The guv instructed me to stay here until our ex-Mrs. Foxley has recovered, and I'm waiting for a uniform to take over. I had a quiet word with a rather tasty receptionist who told me on the QT that our ex-Mrs. Foxley was quite a frequent patient. She's had her stomach pumped and is still being monitored. I tell you something else, Jane, my wife is not going to believe what's been going on tonight. I called her but she's not answering the bloody phone.'

'Listen, Spence, I'm going to make myself a hot chocolate and go to bed. I'll see you in the morning.'

'All right for some,' Spence muttered. 'I'll see you tomorrow.'

Jane replaced the receiver. She felt absolutely exhausted. She had a quick shower and didn't even bother with the hot chocolate. She was fast asleep as soon as her head hit the pillow.

* * *

The following morning Jane bought a takeaway coffee and a toasted cheese sandwich on her way into the station. She was at her desk by 6:45 a.m. but was not the first in as DC Gary Dors and DC Tony Johnson were already marking up an evidence board. Two clerical staff were checking through statements from neighbors which had been taken the previous night, and three more uniformed officers were traipsing in and out with more files on the house-to-house inquiries. Spencer arrived shortly after Jane. By his disheveled and unshaven appearance, she doubted he had made it home.

He approached Jane's desk. 'Looks like Justine Harris has made a remarkable recovery and may be released sometime today – I believe she's being put in the care of a right prat called George Henson. He was demanding to see her and got quite abusive when they said he couldn't. He was going on about how Justine's daughter, Clara, should be taken out of school by her grandmother, before the news about her father's murder hit the headlines.'

'Do you know what happened? Do you know if Henson was able to sort it out?'

Spencer nodded. 'I suspect so. The receptionist was all over him like a rash,' he added sourly. 'She called in the duty doctor who'd pumped out Justine's stomach.' He cocked his head to one side. 'You do know who Henson is, don't you?'

'No, but from the way he spoke to me, if he isn't famous, he thinks he should be.'

'Jane, he's one of the top directors in England. Did you ever see *Life on the Speedway*?'

Jane shook her head. 'No.'

'How about *Doomsday Killers*?'

'Nope.'

'*Riot Run*?'

'Definitely not.'

'*Depraved Slave*?'

'Seriously, Spence, do I seem like the type of person who would pay money to go and see films like that?'

'But Jane, they're very sexy, especially *Depraved Slave*.'

Jane laughed as Spencer headed towards his desk. There was the sound of high-pitched barking as Toots, the dachshund, hurtled across the incident room to attack Spencer's trouser leg. At the same time, DCI Tyler opened his door and bellowed, 'Would somebody get that bloody dog out!'

Spencer picked it up by the scruff of its neck and hurriedly left the incident room in search of the woman who was supposed to be looking after it. Still smiling, Jane made her way to the meeting.

By 7:05 a.m., the boardroom was jammed. Eventually people were standing and a couple were leaning on a window ledge. Rather than the usual hubbub of chit-chat, there seemed to be a feeling of apprehension. Tyler entered, accompanied by a middle-aged clerk carrying a stack of notebooks. DC Dors began passing the notebooks out like a pack of cards to the officers sitting at the table. Tyler removed his jacket and rolled up his shirtsleeves, then gave a concise but comprehensive update on the murder of Charles Foxley.

'An incident board is being written up with scene of crime photographs and as many details as possible from the forensic department,' he said finally.

He looked around the room.

'I suggest some of the photographs be covered up as they're very graphic. Right now we're obviously waiting for further details from the postmortem, but it seems unlikely I will have anything until mid-afternoon.'

The room was quiet as Tyler said they had had little result from the house-to-house inquiries but these would be continued, with statements taken from every homeowner and tenant living in proximity to Foxley's basement flat.

The room was becoming stiflingly hot with so many people, but the officers leaning on the windowsill made no attempt to open the windows.

'I want you all to understand this is going to be a sensitive case and we're going to have journalists sniffing around like a pack of dogs. Charles Foxley may not be a well-known name, but he represented some big stars. So tread carefully and be wary of any journalists trying to get information.'

Like everyone else, Jane listened attentively. But as she already knew the facts of the case better than most of the detectives gathered there, her mind wandered as she sized Tyler up.

Jane admired the way he behaved like one of the team but was clearly in command – something that that she had never seen in him before. He also seemed better-looking than she had seen before. Jane was jolted out of her daydreaming when Tyler began to allocate everyone's duties for the day, emphasizing that it was imperative they find a suspect as quickly as possible.

'Right, I've got fifteen minutes for a Q&A,' he said finally, and, with perfect timing, the door was opened by one of the ladies from the canteen pushing a trolley filled with coffee, tea and plates of doughnuts.

Spencer had just bitten into a doughnut when Tyler gestured for him to come to one side. He spoke quietly: 'Listen, Spence, I'm going to have to go to Scotland Yard for this press conference and I want you and Jane to get over to that agency. Start digging but keep on your toes; these are all theatre people who lie through their teeth to make a living.'

* * *

'First off, we talk to James Myers as he's expecting us, then we interview Emma Ransom,' Spencer said.

Jane flipped opened her notebook. 'OK, she's one of the agents. Then we also have Laura Queen and Daniel Bergman. It means they all have separate offices.'

Spencer almost shot a red light. 'Apparently they're taking Foxley's Jag XK120 and his Volvo into the yard. And DS Lawrence is back at the murder site.'

Jane stared out of the window. 'I'd say the forensic department have their work cut out for them. We don't even know if the killer was known to him and was waiting inside the flat, as there were no signs of a break-in, or if Foxley let him in. We'll probably have to wait for the postmortem results to give us some clues regarding his blunt-force injuries.'

They drove along Shaftesbury Avenue, turned left into Wardour Street, and parked outside Paramount House. The lift had the same 'Out of Order' notice taped to it so they walked up to the first floor.

'I think we need to have a chat with the receptionists. Are we going to work the interviews together or solo?' Jane asked.

Spencer headed towards the agency's reception doors. 'I think we work this together. I don't want to put my big foot in it. I'm going to need your intuitive skills. To be perfectly honest with you, I'm completely fucking knackered.'

'Do we know the receptionists' names?'

Spencer held up his notebook. 'Got to hand it to the boss, I think he's even got the name of the cleaner. Rita Wood and Angela Merton.'

He pushed open the double doors with Jane just behind him. They could see that only one of the girls was at the reception desk. She was blowing her nose into a wad of tissues.

'Good morning. I'm Detective Sergeant Spencer Gibbs and this is Detective Sergeant Jane Tennison. We have an appointment with James Myers. You are . . . Rita?'

'No, I'm Angela, but everyone calls me Angie.' She blew her nose again. 'We've all just heard the news. It's terrible . . . I can't believe it. Poor Rita has had to go to the toilets 'cause she can't stop crying. It's shockin' . . . absolutely shockin.'

The phone rang as she spoke. She picked it up and spoke in an entirely different, and much posher, voice.

'Good morning, this is Foxley & Myers Theatrical Agents. Can I help you? No, he's not available. Yes, please call back.' She replaced the phone, eyes brimming with tears.

'We've been told not to say a word to anyone about what's happened.' She blew her nose again. 'Mr. Myers says we have to be very careful if we get any calls from the press and we're not to say nothing. But we don't really know anything.' She sniffed back her tears. 'What's happened to his dogs?'

Jane stepped forward. 'They're being taken care of, Angie. We would appreciate it if you and Rita would give us a few moments later on.'

She nodded. 'I'll just ring through and tell him you're here. He's expecting you.'

As they were heading down the corridor, one of the double entry doors opened and a short man came out, fixing his eyes on Angie.

'I've been expecting four scripts that were apparently delivered yesterday fucking morning. My secretary even fucking warned you that they were important. I need to get them out to my clients yesterday. You two cunts rap and yack all day long. If I now find these scripts, I'm going to have you fucking fired!'

Jane could hardly believe it. The man leaned over the reception desk and began snatching at the large manila envelopes stacked to one side, muttering, 'You fucking cunts, fucking cunts, where's my stuff?'

Even more surprising was the way Angie, instead of being intimidated, began sifting through the envelopes with him.

'If you don't mind me saying so, your secretary is a dozy cow and if I had an urgent delivery to you, you would've bloody got it,' she said. 'Rita's probably over in your office now, giving it to your secretary.'

The man spun on his Cuban heels, his tight jeans showing off his spindly legs underneath a large safari-type jacket. At that moment James Myers came out of his office at the end of the corridor and clocked Jane's shocked expression.

'Ah, I see you've met Daniel Bergman. You'll have to ignore him. He tends to fly off the handle now and again. It's the pressure of work. Fortunately, we're quite used to him here. Can I offer you any tea or coffee?'

'Coffee would be fine,' Spencer said and Jane nodded. Myers then gestured for them to go into his office before turning to Angela.

'Can you get Rita to bring three coffees? Make sure it's Illy and the milk isn't off.' He followed Jane and Spencer into his office, closing the door behind him.

'I called everyone in this morning and explained the terrible situation. I said it's imperative we did not take any calls from the press.'

He moved to sit behind his desk as Jane and Spencer sat side by side on the sofa. He opened a file in front of him.

'I had a lengthy conversation with DCI Tyler and I've compiled a list of . . . ' He waved his hand rather theatrically. 'I don't really want to call them suspects, but these are people who I believe had a grievance against Foxley. I've put them into categories. Category one are employees who were fired by him. The second category are artists that have had battles with Charles, over contracts, misrepresentation and, in two cases, there was a possible sexual relationship.'

At this point Spencer raised his hand. 'Excuse me for interrupting you, Mr. Myers, but I'm finding all this a bit difficult to understand. I thought Mr. Foxley was a very successful agent?'

Myers frowned. 'He was, but you have to understand that Mr. Foxley was an agent for over twenty-five years. You cannot exist in this business without making enemies.' He waved a hand. 'Now, do you want me to continue or should I have not bothered spending time on these lists?'

Jane tapped Spencer's knee for him to shut up. 'Mr. Myers, we are very grateful for all the help you can give us.'

He sniffed. 'Very well, I shall continue. Now, as you will see from this list, there are a few well-known names. As such, I have not given you their private numbers. If you wish to interview them, I suggest we do it via my office. The third category is made up of people who I know had a personal grudge against Charles. There is an architect who had begun designing sets for the National Theatre, the Royal Opera House and other prominent theatre companies. He sold the basement flat to Charles, and he was bankrupt. There are also two producers and two directors who believed that Foxley destroyed their careers. I've done my best to produce a comprehensive list. So can I please ask you to respect not only my position, but that of the artists?'

He closed the file and passed it to Spencer as the door was gently kicked open as Rita, the blonde receptionist, carried in the tray of coffees. She placed the tray on the desk, her eyes red-rimmed from crying, with her mascara smudged.

'Thank you, Rita,' Myers said. 'Can you call home to see if my babies are all right?' He glanced at Jane. 'I didn't think, under the circumstances, I should have them in the office with me as I am sure it is going to be a very busy day.'

He handed Jane and Spencer their coffees.

'Mr. Myers, we really appreciate the time you've taken to put this list together,' Jane said. 'We will need to go through it and might have to ask you for additional information.'

Myers pointedly looked at his watch. 'I want to be as helpful as possible, I really do, but at the same time, this is going to be a very difficult time. As soon as Charles's clients hear the news of his demise, for want of a better word, I'm sure the phones won't stop ringing.'

Jane nodded. 'We know that Mr. Foxley came into work on the Monday morning. Could you tell us if there was anything out of the ordinary about his behavior?'

'Well, I only saw him very briefly as I had an early morning meeting with a client. I had a few words with him, and I think he mentioned something about having Toots spayed as he felt she was coming into season. He knew I have an excellent vet.'

Jane leaned forward. 'That's the dachshund?'

'Yes. Apart from that I had no other conversation with him. I think he left the office in the early afternoon.'

'Can you be more specific about the time?' Jane asked.

'Well, it would have been about half past one or quarter to two. He called out that he was leaving, but I was on the phone.'

'We will need to have a list of his calls from that morning.'

'They should be listed in his diary, or Julia, his secretary, will know.'

Spencer placed his coffee cup back on the tray. 'Is there anyone on the list you feel we should focus on immediately?'

Myers shrugged. 'If I were you, I would talk to his ex-wife. She is clearly a very disturbed woman. Even before the divorce, she was a complete nightmare. She can be violent and abusive.

I think she has accused every single woman who works here of having a relationship with her ex-husband.'

Jane held up her hand. 'When you say violent, can you recall any specific incidents?'

'Oh my God, how many do you want me to tell you about? I think you should ask Laura Queen. She came back into her office one morning to find that some clothes she had left in her closet had been shredded. Miss Queen often does a full day's work, then goes straight out to a production or a premiere in the evening, so she keeps some evening wear in the office.'

'Did Justine Harris have access to the premises at night?' Jane asked.

'Yes, at one time she worked here, so she would have all the security codes. I think she came here quite often.'

'Was there animosity between Miss Queen and Justine Harris?' Jane asked.

'I would call it a lot more than animosity. We are very fortunate that Laura still remains with us. Any other woman, after being spoken to and threatened the way she was, would've joined another agency. We were forced to have a lengthy conversation with Justine, and I believe she did apologize for her behavior. But that was always short-lived as she would then find someone else to accuse of having sexual relationships with Charles.'

Suddenly a cacophony of phone ringing began and the light on Myers' desk started blinking. Jane and Spencer stood up.

'Thank you for your time, Mr. Myers,' Spencer said. 'I think we're going to talk to Emma Ransom next.'

'Ah, Charles's right hand. Her office is just opposite,' Myers said, then added, sotto voce, 'You'll probably find her reading *Vogue*.'

Jane tapped on the door, which was slightly ajar, and a voice called out, 'Yes, come in.'

Emma Ransom was tall and slim, with a pale, not very attractive face almost devoid of make-up but with what Jane could tell was a simple but expensive haircut. Her eyes were very blue, and she looked as if she'd been crying. Her office was very different in style to Myers', with a large glass-topped chrome table, one fawn leather desk chair and two fawn leather bucket chairs. The walls were lined with scripts, books and numerous posters and photographs. Her desk was free of any clutter, with just a large notepad, a stack of fashion magazines and two phones.

As Spencer introduced himself and Jane, Emma picked up one of the phones and pressed an intercom. 'Rita, please hold my calls.'

As they sat down in the bucket chairs, Emma swiveled her desk chair around to face them.

'Could you tell us if on Monday there was anything out of the ordinary about Mr. Foxley's manner?' Spencer asked.

'Monday mornings are always a bit hectic,' Emma replied. 'I had two meetings that morning and it would have been about mid-morning when I saw him in the corridor. He was carrying his dachshund and seemed annoyed. Apparently, his dog walker had refused to take her. That was the only conversation I had with him.'

She frowned and Jane wondered if she was going to start crying again.

Jane leaned forward slightly. 'I'm sure you must find this very difficult and we'll try and make it as brief as possible. You've been described as Mr. Foxley's right hand?'

'I wouldn't exactly call myself that. I began working for him fifteen years ago, for the last five years as an agent in the company. So that means I have my own clients, mostly directors, writers and producers.'

Spencer nodded. 'What about Mr. Foxley's clients? How many of them would you say were unsatisfied by Mr. Foxley's representation?'

She sighed. 'That's normal in this business, I'm afraid. Charles had an astonishing ability to spot raw talent, by that I mean he could go to an amateur production or an end-of-term production at RADA and he would know intuitively which one of these hopefuls had the potential to be a star. But once they become successful, that's when the problems start, and they quickly go from being grateful to wanting more. That's when dissatisfaction and even bitterness can go alongside success, and that's when things can go wrong. Innumerable times, Charles made a star out of a nobody, and the next thing, they're alcoholics and unable to be on a film set, and he has to start doing damage control.'

Her eyes watered as she swiveled around in her desk chair and pulled a tissue from a box.

'I'm sorry. I'm finding this very difficult. I'm still hardly able to believe that Charles has gone, and in such a terrible way.'

Spencer nodded. 'I do understand. If you'd rather, we can return at another time. But it would be really helpful if we could ask just a few more questions.'

She sniffed and blinked her eyes. 'It's fine. Go ahead.'

'Do you know anyone who had a motive for killing Mr. Foxley?'

Jane noticed that Emma's right foot had started twitching.

'I really can't think of anyone who would want to hurt him. I mean, obviously we have to deal with a lot of people being disappointed – you know, an actor losing a big role, a director being fired from a film, a writer's work being discarded. But I can't think anyone like that would want Charles . . . dead.'

'What about his wife?' Spencer asked.

Emma sat bolt upright. 'I'm not prepared to say anything against Justine. Yes, she used to get very emotional because she still loved Charles after the divorce. She was jealous at times, but I think she was also very sad, because he was not an easy man to love.'

'What do you mean by that?' Jane asked.

'Just what I said. He wasn't an easy man. He could be annoying and devious, but at the same time he was also an astute businessman – he had to be.'

Before she could continue, Jane interrupted. 'Was Foxley also a womanizer?'

Emma pursed her lips. 'I suppose you could say that. He was a very attractive man and, in his position, he could be a bit of a magnet.'

'We have to look into the possibility that he was having an affair with a married woman and there could be a jealous husband,' Jane continued. 'So if you know about anybody . . . '

Emma shook her head, looking fiercely at Jane. 'I refuse to speak ill of Charles at this terrible time. You can ask other people about his sexual habits if you like, but I simply worked alongside him. And I admired him. I find this very upsetting. I don't want to say any more.'

'There's just one more thing, Miss Ransom,' Jane said. 'I understand that Mr. Foxley had an appointments diary?'

'Yes, we all do. Most of us leave our diaries on our desks when we leave the office, in case when we are out at an appointment something needs to be checked. Charles also has a secretary who keeps a record of his appointments . . . ' She paused, then corrected herself. 'Julia Summers *was* his secretary. I believe she is visiting a sick relative in Devon at the moment. I'm going to have to tell her the terrible news.'

Emma stood up and opened the office door, leaving Spencer and Jane no option but to leave. She closed the door behind them. As they passed the internal window, Jane glanced through and saw Emma plucking more tissues from the box.

The shrill sounds of phones ringing echoed down the corridor as they now headed towards Laura Queen's office. Laura Queen was an altogether different type of woman from Emma Ransom. She was petite, with glorious, naturally curly auburn hair, perfectly made-up, wearing a flattering black dress and high-heeled Prada wedges. Her office had a large window and along the windowsill were flowering orchids. There was also an orchid in a beautiful glass bowl on her stylish, pale wood desk with drawers either side. On the opposite wall were shelves filled with books and numerous photographs of well-known actors. There was quite a high desk chair and two pale blue velvet easy chairs.

'Please do sit down. Can I offer you a tea or a coffee?' Laura had a sweet, soft voice.

'We've already had some, thanks. And thank you for giving us your time,' Spencer said.

Jane took over. 'We need to ask you a few rather personal questions about Charles Foxley. We've already had a great deal of help from Mr. Myers, and also Miss Ransom.'

When she heard Emma's name, Laura's eyebrows lifted. 'I'm surprised she looked up from her *Vogue* to give you any time at all,' she said sarcastically, then waved her hand with her long pale pink nails. 'I'm sorry, that must sound awful, but Charles was always making a joke of it. Sometimes he would stand in the corridor outside her window and say, "My God, she's already halfway through *Tatler* and it's only ten!" But he was actually very fond of her. I was obviously deeply shocked to hear that he has been murdered – I can't even take the reality of it in yet.'

'Did you see him on the Monday morning?' Jane asked.

'Yes, he came into my office. He asked if I'd had a good week-end and I said that I'd been to an opening night and that on Sunday I had had a game of tennis at the Queen's Club. He was quite sporty, you know, but I hated playing tennis with him because he was such a poor loser.' She bit her lip, near to tears.

'Did he have any enemies?' Spencer asked.

Laura gave a light laugh. 'You know, in this business you can accumulate an awful lot of enemies without really trying, but someone who would want to kill him? I can't imagine that. I'm aware that Charles was a complex individual. He was a man who detested failure. Let me explain what I mean by that: if, for example, he represented a director who got the break of his life with a big American movie, and it bombed, the director would not get any sympathy from Charles. So, yes, he did acquire enemies. However, I have my own clients and in the past few years the two of us have been quite distant, so if there was any recent altercation, I wouldn't know about it.'

'What about his ex-wife?' Spencer asked.

She smiled wryly. 'I was expecting you to ask about her at some point. It's common knowledge that Justine hated me. She believed, incorrectly, that I was having an affair with Charles. I can assure you nothing was further from the truth – it would not only have been unprofessional, but . . . he had a deviant side to him, which I found repellent.'

Spencer leaned forward. 'What exactly do you mean by that?'

Laura hesitated and started to flush, clearly wishing she hadn't mentioned it.

Jane now took over. 'Miss Queen, it is important that you explain what you have just said – it is obviously strictly confidential.'

Laura picked up a pencil and tapped it on the notebook in front of her.

Jane continued. 'Was Mr. Foxley having a relationship with Emma Ransom?'

Laura leaned back, shaking her head with a half smile. 'I'm afraid she is far too plain for him to even notice she was female.'

Yet again Laura appeared to be slightly embarrassed by what she had said.

'I'm sorry, I must sound such a bitch . . . I really don't know why I came out with that about Emma. The truth is, and I'm not the only one to be aware of this, Charles had a predilection for prostitutes – and not particularly glamorous ones; in fact, I believe he preferred obese women.'

Spencer glanced at Jane. 'Was he into S&M?'

Laura shook her head. 'I don't know. Look, it's wrong of me to repeat gossip. I think we should just stop there.'

Jane closed the notebook in which she had been jotting down notes. Spencer took this as meaning the interview was over, but actually it was an old trick Jane had learned. Let them relax and think, just as Spencer had done, that there were no more questions.

'Although you said you did not have a physical relationship with Mr. Foxley, you had a confrontation with his ex-wife, didn't you?' Jane said quickly, catching Laura off-guard.

'Jesus Christ!' Laura pushed back her desk chair. 'Justine is mentally unstable. She had accused me of having an affair with her husband on numerous occasions but she never accepted my denials. Then one time, when he had left his dachshund in my office because she was in heat, she kicked my door open. She had one of the dog leads with a chain on the end and she swung it at me. It very nearly hit me in the face. She was screaming . . . I think she was calling me a whore. I managed to get the dog lead away from her but in the scuffle she fell and hit her head against the side of my desk.'

Jane and Spencer stayed silent as Laura pulled her chair back to her desk and picked up her pencil again.

'She wasn't unconscious, thank goodness. But the entire thing had been overheard by Rita and Angie, and I don't know who else was passing in the corridor. It was humiliating and embarrassing. I wanted to hand in my notice, but Charles persuaded me to stay. I eventually agreed on the condition that he kept his wife, or now ex-wife, under control.'

'When did this incident take place?' Jane asked.

'Two years ago, perhaps more. But I would say if you're looking for someone capable of murder, you should question the ex-Mrs. Foxley.'

Spencer stood up. 'Thank you very much for your time.'

Laura ushered them out of her office. 'I do hope you don't think badly of me. But I'm sure under these awful circumstances you want the truth.'

As the door shut behind them, Spencer let out a deep sigh. 'Bloody hell, this is a snake pit.'

'And we've only just started,' Jane added.

* * *

Charles Foxley's Jaguar and Volvo were taken into the station yard. Three young forensic scientists examined the Volvo, which appeared to have been the main transport for his dogs. There were dirty blankets, dog bowls, packets of dog treats and two worn dog leads, and the interior hadn't been cleaned for some considerable time. Numerous unidentified fingerprints were taken. In total contrast, his Jaguar was in pristine condition. They had found no bloodstains, and no evidence that anyone other than Charles Foxley had driven it. However, in the glove compartment, they found a number of parking tickets and these were taken into the incident room to have the locations checked out.

Meanwhile, DS Lawrence had returned to the murder site to continue collecting evidence. He was accompanied by three more officers who were checking through Foxley's personal effects and had been given the authority to open the safe. They found a considerable amount of money, a few documents regarding his divorce and custody of his daughter, his will, and the mortgage deeds for his house in Barnes and the purchase of his basement flat. So far, there was no evidence that the basement flat had been broken into.

Tyler was sure Foxley had been killed by someone he knew, but so far, none of the forensic evidence had produced a significant lead or pointed them towards a suspect. They would have to wait for the postmortem to see if that told them anything new.

CHAPTER SIX

DCI Tyler had been gowned and booted up for the last hour and a half as the postmortem on Charles Foxley continued. One of the main conclusions that the pathologist had come to, after examining the victim's skull, was that he was hit from behind, and this could have been the first blunt-force trauma the victim had suffered. The blow, he believed, would have knocked the victim forward, possibly to the ground, where he was then struck on the right side of the skull, and finally a lesser blow to the left. Tyler deduced from this that the attacker was already in the flat hallway when the attack began.

'Would the blows have knocked him unconscious?' Tyler asked.

'Altogether, yes, without a doubt,' the pathologist replied.

'And the cricket bat was definitely the weapon?'

'Yes.'

'Would he have been alive when his throat was cut?' Tyler then asked.

'Very likely. But he was almost certainly dead when he was disemboweled.'

'The cut-throat razor that was found in the bath of the victim's home, was it the only other weapon used?' Tyler asked.

The pathologist was less certain about this. 'Some injuries are consistent with a cut-throat razor, but a large, very sharp serrated knife may have been used to disembowel the victim as the cut was deep and had left marks on the rear ribcage and spine.'

Tyler frowned. As yet, no large blood-stained knife had been found at the scene. He had no choice but to go back to the station to see if the house-to-house inquiries had turned anything up – someone seen carrying a cricket bat on the night of the murder, for instance. He also wanted to talk to Eric Newman, the dog walker. He could possibly be the last person to have seen Charles Foxley alive, apart from the killer, and might also know if he had a cricket bat in the flat, but they had been unable to trace him, and he was not at his home.

* * *

At the agency, Jane and Spencer were on their second round of coffees. They were talking to Rita, who remained inconsolable. Unlike everyone else they had spoken to, she felt that Charles Foxley was not only a wonderful boss, but one who paid well and had a great sense of humor – though he did often make the receptionists lie about his whereabouts. She cheered up for a moment as she remembered something.

'There was this actress – I can't tell you her name but she was really famous – and Mr. Foxley had got her to take this part in a play, and then when it got terrible reviews she turned up 'ere all guns blazing.' She started laughing and had to blow her nose. 'He was in the broom cupboard . . . he 'id in there 'cause he knew she was after 'im. He was stuck in the cupboard for half an hour until we convinced her he wasn't in the office – we had such a laugh. But all the other people who work here didn't half have a go at him 'cause his dogs piss and shit all over the carpet. Mr. snooty-up-the-corridor's dogs are too posh to shit, but we know half the carpet stains are from his Pekingese.'

Rita seemed on the point of telling another story when Jane interrupted.

'What was your impression of Justine Harris?'

'Ooh, she was really famous once upon a time, beautiful too. She had a temper all right, but she always apologized after she'd thrown a wobbly.'

When it was her turn to be questioned, Angie also spoke fondly about Charles Foxley and was equally kind about Justine.

Both girls had said he was his usual self on the Monday morning, chatting amiably, expressing his concern that Jack the Jack Russell had been humping Toots and he was worried she was coming into season. He left earlier than usual, but didn't say where he was going.

'Everything will be in his desk diary, though,' Angie told them.

'So, Angie, were you hired originally by Mr. Foxley?' Jane asked.

'Yes, we both were.'

Spencer leaned forward. 'There seem to be a lot of other agents alongside Mr. Foxley.'

Angie nodded. 'Well, yeah . . . It used to be just his company. Then it got to be so successful, he hired other agents. I think they all bought shares in it.'

'So, who exactly owns the company?' Jane asked.

Angie shrugged. 'If you really want to know, we have a legal department across the hall, along with an accountant, John Nathan, who does all the contracts.'

They thanked Angie and started walking towards the other offices but were stopped in their tracks when they heard what sounded like a howl of rage and then the booming voice of Daniel Bergman.

'Pregnant? Are you telling me she is pregnant? The stupid fucking bitch. I'm not having a go at you, but for Christ's sake. She's done this on purpose, or the stupid son of a bitch of her husband has got her pregnant, and he's the fucking director!'

Jane looked at Spencer as Bergman continued his rant.

'We only got the movie financed because his wife was going to star in it. He probably got her up the spout intentionally because he couldn't face working with her. Now the whole deal could go up in smoke.'

At that moment a slim young man scurried out of the office, closing Bergman's door behind him.

'Angie just called and told me you want to meet John. He's in the office at the end of the corridor.'

'And you are?' Jane asked.

'Oh, I'm sorry, I'm Simon Quinn. I've only just started working here. If you want to talk to me, I'm in that annex down there.' He pointed to an office partition. He was wearing a white T-shirt with a large Duran Duran logo on the front, a black waistcoat, pale blue skin-tight jeans and trainers. He appeared to be in his early twenties.

As Jane and Spencer headed down the corridor, there was a muffled scream from Bergman's office.

'Bloody madhouse,' Spencer muttered under his breath, knocking on John Nathan's door. It was opened almost immediately. Compared with everyone else they had met so far at the agency, Mr. Nathan looked out of place. He wore an ill-fitting grey suit, white shirt and tie. He had thin, wispy hair with a receding hairline, and wore gold-rimmed glasses.

'I was expecting you,' he said quietly, and closed the door behind them.

The office had banks of files from floor to ceiling against every wall, and the floor was covered with cardboard boxes containing scripts, files, notebooks and books. In the middle of the chaos was a plain desk with two calculating machines and a telephone.

'Have you had coffee?' Nathan asked, seeming nervous. 'I'm so sorry, I don't have any extra chairs.'

'That's all right,' Jane said. 'And we've had coffee, thank you. We just want to find out who might benefit from Mr. Foxley's death. We're a little confused about who owns the company and the position of the various agents.'

Nathan clicked the top of his retractable pen. 'Well, it is quite complicated, but the primary shareholder of Foxley & Myers is – or was – Charles Foxley. Originally Mr. Foxley and Mr. Myers were not exactly partners. Mr. Myers was the first agent to join the company. I believe shortly after that, they both decided on bringing in more agents.'

Jane opened her notebook. 'So that would be Emma Ransom, Laura Queen and Daniel Bergman?'

'Yes. Recently the agents you mentioned bought shares in the company, which enabled them to handle their own clients in the agency's name. So, you have Emma, who has actors and actresses, Laura, who mostly does writers, producers and directors, and Daniel has a lot of theatre stars.'

Jane looked up from her notebook. 'We just met a Simon Quinn?'

Nathan continued to click his pen and a film of sweat broke out on his thin upper lip. 'Well, it is quite complicated because Simon has only just joined the agency and he is very much part of . . . ' He paused. 'I'm sorry, *was* part of a new venture Charles had been working on for the past six months. They were setting up a modelingagency called KatWalk and contracting some well-known sports stars, mostly for advertising and promotional work, but it's all still in its infancy.'

Spencer shifted his weight. The office felt stifling and his back was starting to ache from having to stand.

'So, Myers is now the majority shareholder?'

Nathan nodded. 'Yes, but he would not be able to make any changes to the present structure until Mr. Foxley's estate and beneficiaries are legally sorted.'

Jane closed her notebook. 'Can you think of anyone with a motive to kill Mr. Foxley?'

She was surprised by his reaction because for the first time there was a glimmer of a smile on Nathan's face. 'Well, I would say there are an awful lot of people with grievances, but I doubt any of them would want him dead.'

'What about his ex-wife?' Jane asked.

Nathan kept clicking his pen. 'I know Justine was devastated by the divorce, and perhaps she is the main beneficiary of his will . . . I really don't know. I hardly ever had anything to do with her.'

He placed his pen down on the cluttered desk and Spencer glanced towards Jane to indicate they should leave. He thanked Nathan for his time and turned towards the door.

'You're welcome. She was a very successful actress, you know. When the company first started, I believe Justine financed it. I don't know if that's any help.'

Spencer didn't reply as he opened the door and ushered Jane out. A tearful secretary scurried past them and they headed further down the corridor. Daniel Bergman threw open his office door.

'Margaret, come back in here this minute!' he shouted. 'Oh . . .' He looked at Jane and Spencer. 'Secretaries.' He shrugged. 'For some reason I seem to go through a large number of them, but Miss Pratt really and truly suited her name. You must be Jane Tennison.' He reached out to shake her hand. He then turned to Spencer. 'And you, I believe, are Detective Sergeant Spencer Gibbs? Do come in and sit down. I think you've already been offered coffee, but would you like a fresh cup? Or I have a variety of teas. Herbal, mint . . .'

Spencer lifted his hand to indicate that they were fine. Mr. Bergman's office was spacious, with a window looking out onto a yard behind the building, with a partly opened white blind. Bookcases were stacked on two walls and glass-fronted cabinets beneath them housed hundreds of scripts. Two comfortable-looking sofas formed a 'V' in front of his desk. Bergman waited until they had both sat down before moving around his desk to sit in a large leather swivel chair. They were now able to get a good look at the man they had earlier heard screaming and cursing. Daniel had dark, curly hair, an unusually long face with a prominent nose, and a small, pinched mouth, but his most striking feature was his dark brown eyes, which were set unusually close together. He spread his hands on the top of his desk and attempted a pleasant smile.

'We are all in a state of shock,' he said softly. 'We haven't really been told any details, but James said that he had identified him and that he was shocked to see the injuries to his face. Obviously I'll do all I can to help you to find who did this to him, but you have to understand that, although we all work together under the same roof, we are very separate and private people and do not mix socially with each other unless it's for premieres or discussing casting between agents. By that I mean, if I have a movie and require an actress that I know is represented by Emma, and so of course we discuss things. But it is always strictly business.' Bergman spoke quietly and softly, as if he was a different person to the one they had heard screaming abuse earlier. Jane found it slightly disturbing.

'Even so, can you think of anyone who would have a motive to kill Charles Foxley?' Spencer asked.

'I am aware there was a very unpleasant situation with regard to Charles's purchase of his flat, which was previously owned by a set designer, but that was quite a long time ago. He didn't talk about it that much, but he was quite upset when it all blew up and the designer, Sebastian Martinez, made a big fuss.'

'Can you explain what the fuss was about?' Jane asked.

'Not really. I think it was connected to something about a set Martinez had built, which went catastrophically wrong. But I was never privy to any of the details. Charles is – or was – a very likeable man, who made friends easily, but beneath that bon viveur there was, I know, a darker side. He hated failure, but the strange thing is that he hated success almost as much. There was something masochistic about it.'

Spencer glanced at the list of people that Myers had given them and saw that Sebastian Martinez, with his address and contact number, was on the list.

'But I would say that Charles hated any sort of direct confrontation,' Bergman added.

Jane looked up from her notebook. The red light on Bergman's phone was blinking furiously. She was trying to make sense of what he had just said, but before she could put anything into words, Spencer asked Bergman about his relationship with Justine Harris. For the first time, Bergman became animated.

'She was an abusive alcoholic and made Charles's life hell. Before the divorce she would come into the office and cause trouble, throwing all sorts of accusations around. One time, I was just leaving when she appeared, and I told her that her presence was unacceptable.' He opened his mouth and tapped a tooth. 'She punched me in the face so hard that she knocked this tooth out. I fell down the staircase.' He shrugged. 'I hope that answers your question.'

Spencer stood up. 'Thank you for your time. I hope we haven't inconvenienced you too much. And if we do need to talk to you again, we will obviously give you prior warning.'

They left Bergman's office as his phone started ringing. By now both Spencer and Jane were feeling exhausted.

'Do you think we should have a talk to the new guy, Simon Quinn, before we go?'

Jane suggested they leave it for another time as they still needed to see Foxley's office. By rights it should have been first on their agenda. As they crossed back towards the reception area, Angie walked past with her arms full of manila envelopes.

'That poor cow,' Rita explained, shaking her head sadly. 'She's only been here a couple of weeks. They never last more than a few months with him. He's a nasty little sod. But this time it was Angie's fault because some scripts had been delivered and she put them in the wrong place.'

Jane looked at her watch. 'We just need to have a look at Mr. Foxley's office.'

'Oh right, it's up the corridor, next to Mr. Myers'.'

It was surprising how different all the agents' offices were to each other. Charles Foxley's office, although the same size as Myers', was more like a study in someone's Victorian manor. There was a giant oak desk with claw feet, cabinets bursting with manuscripts, old bound-leather books and numerous faded photographs covering the walls. There was an exercise bike and on top of the original, worn fitted carpet was an expensive antique Persian rug. Instead of a desk chair there was a wing-back chair covered in worn fabric with three equally worn cushions on the seat. A matching wing-back chair was on one side of the desk and on the other, a leather studded sofa. Two dog baskets and dog bowls were on the other side of the desk and there were dog hairs everywhere. There was also a wooden carved waste-paper basket, still full of screwed-up pages. Foxley's desk displayed an array of slightly tarnished, silver-framed photographs that seemed to be of family and friends. On the desk there was also an old leather blotter, a Rolodex, a portable typewriter, and stashed in one corner a large electric typewriter and a fax machine.

'We better not take anything from here without a warrant,' she said, looking around the room.

Spencer was already flicking through the Rolodex. 'Where's his diary?' He pulled open one of the drawers in the oak desk. 'Bloody hell.'

Jane came over to look. 'What?'

'Vitamins. I've never seen so many vitamins in my life! There's every kind in here. Vitamin B, Vitamin C, D. Oil of primrose. A blood pressure band . . . ' He shut the drawer and opened the one beneath it. It was full of bags and tins of dog food.

Jane continued to look around the office, which somehow felt very decadent. It was so different from the elegant basement flat where Foxley's body had been found. It also did not appear to be very clean. Everything seemed to be covered in dog hair.

'Well, I can't see any diary,' Spencer said.

'I'll go and ask Emma.'

Jane closed the door behind her as Spencer began to sift through a wastepaper basket full of screwed-up papers and some torn typed notes. He started cramming them into his pockets and whipped around as Jane walked back in.

'Caught me!' He grinned. 'But it's only rubbish so we won't need a warrant.'

'We might need one for Mr. Foxley's diary,' Jane said. 'According to Emma Ransom, it was a large red leather-bound thing with Foxley's initials in gold. She also mentioned that all the agents were supposed to leave their diaries on their desks in case someone needed to check them.'

Spencer stuffed the last few papers into his pocket. 'Funny it's not here, then. On our way out I'll ask Angie if she can track it down for us.'

* * *

It was only a short time later that an irate Eric Newman appeared in the agency's reception and let all three dogs loose in the corridor of the offices.

'What have you brought them here for, Eric?' Rita screeched. 'Don't you know what's happened to Mr. Foxley? We can't have the dogs here. Are you stupid?'

Eric jabbed his finger at her. 'Hey, don't you go talking like that to me, darling. I won't have it. I got a phone call from George Henson. You know who he is?'

Rita pursed her lips. 'Of course I do.'

'Right, well, Mr. Henson, who is living in Mr. Foxley's ex-wife's house, he tells me I gotta help out because the police have sent Toots over in an effing taxi and he tells me that he can't look after the effing dachshund, because he's got to go and take the ex-Mrs. Foxley to Ascot.'

'What's the matter with her?' Rita asked.

'I have no fucking idea. But I'm owed money. And Mr. Henson tells me that if I take Toots I'll be paid by someone here at the agency. So I borrowed me friend's van – that I need to pay him for – and pick up Toots and the other two, and I'm here 'cause I'm still owed fifteen quid and if I'm not paid now, I'm ruddy well leaving them here.'

'You can't do that,' Rita said firmly.

The three dogs, Jack, the Jack Russell cross, Stick, the whippet cross and Toots, the dachshund, ran up the corridor, barking madly, tails wagging, scratching at Foxley's door until it opened. They ran widely around the room excitedly until eventually they seemed to realize that Foxley wasn't there. All three jumped onto one of the wing-back chairs and huddled together, whimpering sadly.

CHAPTER SEVEN

Tyler called a briefing with Jane and Spencer as soon as they returned to the station. Spencer now had a thudding headache and Jane only had time to grab a sandwich for them both before returning to the incident room. The crime scene photographs were displayed on the board, along with all the notes that had been compiled in their absence, detailing two statements that the house-to-house inquiries had produced.

Foxley had been seen walking Toots at around three p.m. on the day of the murder, while another neighbor had reported seeing Foxley arguing with a man on the street outside his basement flat very early in the morning of the day before he died. They described the man as being a thin-faced and surly, wearing a cloth cap, and 'Eric Newman?' was written on the board. There were also photographs from the postmortem pinned up, but due to their shocking content they had been covered by sheets of paper.

Tyler was now waiting impatiently for Jane and Spencer to join him in the boardroom. He had made copious notes but avoided showing them the photos of the postmortem as Spencer was still eating his egg sandwich. Neither of them had had time to type up their reports of their morning at Foxley's agency, so Jane gave Tyler a condensed version. Tyler listened intently and asked a few questions.

'We still need to do more investigation to discover a possible motive,' Jane concluded. 'And until we know the beneficiaries of Foxley's will, we don't know who gains anything from his death. But there was no one who had a good word to say about his ex-wife, Justine Harris, who seems to be a violent alcoholic.'

'Do you think this ex-wife could be capable of murder?' Tyler asked.

Spencer shrugged. 'Apparently she gave one of the other agents a right uppercut that knocked his tooth out, but to be honest he's a bit of an arsehole so I don't really blame her.'

'Sir, you know that Justine Harris attempted suicide, which could be due to her emotional distress at seeing the appalling state the body was in,' Jane said.

Tyler leaned back in his chair. 'She was definitely hysterical, but at the same time she seemed angry that he was dead. By rights I shouldn't have allowed her inside the crime scene, but frankly she was unstoppable – plus she might have been able to give us a positive identification. But I swear she was going to kick him. We had to drag her out in the end and—'

There was a knock at the door and DC Dors put his head around. 'Excuse me, guv, there's a Mrs. Florence Harris on the phone who wishes to talk to, as she puts it, "the man in charge".'

Tyler frowned.

'I know you said you didn't want to be interrupted,' Dors said, 'but I think it's Justine Harris's mother.'

'For Christ's sake, just put her through,' Tyler snapped.

Tyler was tight-lipped, waiting for his phone to ring, but he didn't snatch it up; instead, he carefully picked up the receiver. 'Mrs. Harris, this is DCI Tyler. How can I help you?'

Although neither Jane nor Spencer could hear clearly what Mrs. Harris was saying, there was a strident, aristocratic voice on the other end of the phone, and Tyler had to hold it away from his ear while he made a few scrawled notes.

'Thank you for the update, Mrs. Harris. Much appreciated.'

Tyler replaced the receiver and turned to them both. 'Well, Justine Harris was released early this morning from St Mary's and she's been taken to her mother's home in Ascot. Apparently Mrs. Harris is taking her granddaughter out of boarding school and is trying to get Justine to see her previous psychiatrist at the Priory.'

'Is Justine Harris now with her mother?' Jane asked.

'I presume so.'

Spencer brushed the crumbs of his sandwich off his jacket and tossed the plastic container into the bin.

'Foxley's business partner, James Myers, gave us a long list of people he thought had grievances against Foxley. But so far the only other possible motive we've uncovered regards the previous owner of Foxley's flat, Sebastian Martinez. We haven't got all the details yet.'

Spencer put the file on the table and Tyler started flicking through it.

'Bloody hell! Have you seen how many people he has listed?'

'To be honest, guv, I was at the hospital nearly all night, we've been at the agency all morning and then we came straight here. I haven't even had time to look at it.'

'We'll need to sift through this list as soon as we're finished. Right, let's take a look at the postmortem report. The pathologist concluded that the cricket bat was used to inflict the blunt-force injuries to Foxley's head. The blood grouping on the cricket bat was matched to the victim's. No surprises there. The forensic team are expected in at any moment and I hope Detective Sergeant Lawrence will have some more details.'

'Could robbery have been a motive?' Spencer asked.

'Doubtful, as we have no forced entry and no drawers or cupboards were ransacked. The safe contained jewelry, money, Foxley's will and mortgage papers. Again, Paul Lawrence might have more, as they have numerous fingerprints from the scene. We also have clear footprints in the victim's blood from, we believe, quite a common sneaker-type shoe.'

'Do we have anyone who can fill us in about Foxley's private life? And who he might have allowed into his flat?'

Tyler shook his head. 'We had a lengthy interview with his cleaner, Frieda Lunn – when she wasn't crying her eyes out – but she didn't really know much. She did mention that Mr. Foxley occasionally had people sleeping over, mostly on weekends. She worked on Mondays, Wednesday and Fridays, from nine until twelve, and he was not at home on the Monday when she went in. Toots the dachshund was there, and she left just after ten for a dentist's appointment. If Foxley had had guests at the weekend, he would have left the bed linen ready to go to the laundry. And on the Friday he would have left her a shopping list if he was going to be entertaining at the weekend.'

'How long had she worked for him?' Jane asked.

'Two and a half years. She had previously worked as a cleaner in his office, and she had only recently been doing three days a week for him. She said he was generous and likeable, if rather untidy. The three dogs made a lot of work for her shedding their fur all over the place.'

'Did you ask her about the ex-wife?'

'Miss Lunn said she'd been very rude to her on several occasions. Foxley was always apologetic and explained that his ex-wife was in psychiatric care. Frieda had met his daughter a few times but said that when the daughter was on holiday from school she would stay with her mother or grandmother.'

There was a tap on the door and Paul Lawrence walked in carrying a takeaway coffee.

'We've just about wrapped up at the murder site, sir. I'll need to go back to the lab for a couple of hours to double-check on progress.'

He sat down and glanced towards Jane and Spencer as he opened his briefcase.

'I spent a considerable amount of time with the pathologist and together we have put together a timeline of events. The assailant was in the basement flat. There must have been some altercation, which resulted in a frenzied and brutal attack. We know the cricket bat was Foxley's as his name is scrawled on one side. There is blood spattering by the front door, which could have been caused by the bleeding from the nose and mouth. Foxley then fell forward and was dragged down the hallway and into the bathroom, bleeding profusely from his head wounds. The second weapon, an old-fashioned cut-throat razor, was found in the bath. Foxley's body was possibly hauled up by his hair – we found a considerable amount of hair around the bathtub. When he was positioned over the bath his throat was cut. There are blood spurts on the tiles, the bath and the walls. The body was dragged into the master bedroom, Foxley was then positioned spread-eagled on the bed, and he was disemboweled. According to the pathologist, a third weapon was used – a very sharp serrated knife, around ten inches long and two inches wide. As you know, this weapon has not been recovered.'

As Lawrence talked, Tyler brought out the photographs he had held back while Spencer had been eating. Jane slowly moved through one photograph after another.

'Was he stripped of his clothes in the bathroom?'

Lawrence sifted through the photographs and pulled one out that showed a blood-soaked shirt and a pair of corduroy trousers.

'I think the victim was unconscious and his assailant stripped him, as you see on photograph fourteen, down to his white underpants and white socks. We found his shoes in the bathroom, along with his bloody clothes. I would say he was stripped before his throat was cut. There are numerous finger-prints, some in blood, some possibly left from a previous occasion, which would say that this was not the first time our killer had been in that flat.'

Tyler gathered up the photographs and stacked them like a pack of large cards, before sliding them into a large brown manila envelope. Lawrence did likewise with the photos he had brought.

'The killer would have to be physically strong and probably quite muscular to be able to drag Foxley to the bathroom and the bedroom,' Lawrence added.

'So most likely a young man?' Jane asked hesitantly.

'Who knows? He could be middle-aged and fit . . . I can't tell you for certain. All I can say is that this was a rage-driven murder.'

'Is there a possibility there were two killers?' Jane asked.

'It's possible, if one was keeping lookout and didn't get involved in the attack, but I only found one set of bloody shoeprints,' Lawrence replied.

Spencer flicked through his notebook. 'What about the handcuffs?'

'They are police issue. There must be thousands out there. He didn't have any abrasions to either wrist.'

Jane scribbled in her notebook. 'Was there any indication that Foxley was a sadomasochist?'

Lawrence shook his head. 'I didn't find any pornography or S&M magazines. In fact, we didn't find very much. It's unusual not to find any papers, letters or diary, anything that would give us an insight into Foxley's private life.'

'Any drugs?' Spencer asked.

'No, just a lot of vitamins and health drinks. The toxicology report will come back in a couple of weeks. The pathologist did observe that the victim's nasal cavities seemed raw. He took samples so we'll wait for the results. Obviously he examined the body for injuries and bruising, and also checked his anus for any signs that he was raped or in a homosexual relationship.'

Tyler stood up, thanked Lawrence and asked if he could join him in the incident room as some of the other officers would like to ask him questions. He picked up the file from James Myers and held it up in the air.

'We'll need to go through this and decide who interviews who. But first off, let's bring in this bloody dog walker, Eric Newman.'

Tyler and Lawrence walked out.

Jane turned to Spencer and saw he was nodding off to sleep. She poked him in the arm. 'Spence!'

He opened his eyes wearily. 'Jane, I've got to have a kip . . . I can't take it all in. I'm too knackered.'

'Well, have a sleep in here. I'll go and start putting together some reports from this morning.'

She watched as he rolled his jacket up into a cushion and crawled under the boardroom table.

As Jane walked over to her desk and started typing, Tyler came over and was about say something when DC Dors piped up: 'We've got Eric Newman. He's in interview room one.'

'About bloody time.' Tyler tapped Jane on the shoulder. 'Come and interview him with me.'

* * *

Eric Newman's body odor filled the small interview room. He had a rat-like face, with a thin moustache. He was still wearing the same stained jacket and around his neck he had a thick woolen scarf. He was tapping his dirty fingernails on the table.

'I'd like to know what I've been brought in here for. I've done nothing wrong, me rent's been paid up, and I've been straight now for ten years.'

'You're not under arrest, Mr. Newman, but you have been somewhat elusive, so we thought it best to interview you here at the station. We are just interested in your relationship with Charles Foxley,' said Tyler.

'Well, I wouldn't call it a relationship. I walk his effing dogs. He's got three of them.'

'We are aware of that, Mr. Newman. What we need to know is when exactly was the last time you saw Mr. Foxley?'

'That would be around about three p.m. last Monday.'

'And where did you see him?'

'I went to his flat. He wanted me to take his other two dogs, Stick and Jack, because his dachshund was coming into heat. I've told him about this before because even though the Jack Russell has lost his balls, he'll hump anything and goes crazy.'

'So it was unusual for you to collect the two dogs that afternoon?'

Newman scratched his nose. 'Yeah, it was unusual. He asked if I could walk them and keep them overnight, away from the sausage.'

'Would you say you had an argument with Mr. Foxley?'

'I was a bit tetchy, 'cause that fuckin' Toots gets the other dogs going apeshit. I told him I wouldn't take her. I got a poodle and a Dalmatian I walk as well, so I was pretty firm about it. I might have raised me voice a notch when I refused to take her.'

Jane was making notes. 'So, the following day, when you returned with Mr. Foxley's dogs, you were met by the uniformed police officers?'

'Yeah, I was. I rung him and he didn't answer me. I even called his office and no one seemed to know where he was. But he owed me money for keeping the dogs overnight.'

'The day before, when you went to get the two dogs, how did Mr. Foxley seem to you?'

'How do you mean?'

'Was he agitated, nervous . . . ?'

'He didn't seem any different from normal. He gave me the dogs on their leads and the car keys, then I left.'

'What car were the keys for, Mr. Newman?'

'The Volvo. I couldn't carry the dogs back and forth on the bus, could I?'

'Was this the usual arrangement?'

'No, it was a bit different this time. Not our usual arrangement.'

Tyler was becoming impatient. 'Mr. Newman, could you tell me what your usual arrangement was?'

'Right . . . Mr. Foxley would go into his office around seven thirty or eight in the morning. He would call me to pick up all three dogs. Then I would walk them and feed them and take them back to his office late afternoon and give him back his keys.' He looked at Jane. 'Am I going too fast for you, love?'

'No. I'm fine, thank you, Mr. Newman.'

'This arrangement was mostly during the week and he would pay me extra if he was going away on a weekend and wanted me to keep them overnight. But he should have had that bloody sausage dog spayed when I told him to. That's why he had her and I had the other two.'

Jane looked up. 'Did you know Mr. Foxley's ex-wife?'

'Oh, yes. Sometimes I used to take the dogs over to her place. His daughter Clara loved having the dogs. I don't think his missus did, though. But those times I'd drive them over to her house in Barnes and leave her the keys to the Volvo. When I knew about this situation, God rest his soul, I was getting worried that I'd be dumped with the bloody dogs and I'd be right out of pocket – and he owes me anyway.'

'Were you always paid in cash?' Jane asked.

'Always. If the dogs stayed overnight, I'd get ten quid. That's picking them up, taking them for a walk, feeding them and taking them back the next day. So then I get a call from George.'

Tyler raised his hand. 'George who?'

'George Henson. He's a film director, a friend of the ex-Mrs. Foxley. He calls me to ask if I could pick up Toots and still look after the dogs. I told him I was owed money and I needed transport. But I've got a mate who said he'd lend me his van for a tenner. George told me there wasn't going to be anybody in later.'

Tyler raised his hand again. 'So, you took a van with two dogs to Justine Harris's house, where George Henson was, and you collected the third dog?'

'Correct.'

'Did he pay you?'

'He gave me eight quid, which was not the full amount if I was to keep these dogs, and there was the extra money for the van, so I decided I'd had enough and took them to the agency and left them there.'

'Did you ever meet any of Mr. Foxley's associates?'

'I met the two silly cows at the reception desk and a couple of others, but I was basically in and out.'

'What about his friends?'

Newman grinned, shaking his head. 'Do me a favor, do I look like someone who would be mixing in the same social circles as Charles Foxley? Not that I didn't get along with him. He was down-to-earth, no airs and graces, you know? He liked a flutter on the gee-gees, as it happens.'

'Did you put any bets on for him?'

'Yeah, now and then . . . And the dogs. If he won big, he'd always give me a cut, and when he lost, he didn't get too cut up about it. He was a good bloke.'

'So, along with walking his dogs and placing bets for him, was there anything else you did for Mr. Foxley?'

For the first time Newman shifted around in his seat. 'How'd you mean?'

'It's a simple question, Mr. Newman.'

His small eyes glinted as he chewed at the corner of his droopy moustache. 'I've done nothing wrong. I've been straight for ten years. All I do is walk dogs for people who can't walk them themselves and I declare all my earnings, too.'

Tyler slapped the table hard. Jane almost jumped and Newman froze.

'Just tell us what else you did for Mr. Foxley.'

Newman licked his lips. 'You mean putting him in touch with Mandy?'

Tyler nodded as if he knew what Newman was talking about. 'Why would Mr. Foxley want to contact Mandy?'

Newman shrugged his shoulders and looked down at the desk. 'This is nothing to do with me. I've never got into that kinda thing ... but each to their own. I'd been walking her Doberman because the bloke that did security for her had got sciatica and I knew him from the tracks.'

'Get to the point,' Tyler snapped.

'I'm getting there, I'm getting there. Mr. Foxley was asking about the Doberman because I left a studded collar in the Volvo. I swear to God, that's how it happened.'

'What happened?' Tyler asked, leaning forward.

'I told him it belonged to Mandy. Mandy Pilkington. I mean, I didn't really know her, you gotta understand that. Like, I know she's into S&M. I made a joke that maybe the collar was for one of her clients. Mr. Foxley seemed interested, wanted to know more, so I told him. He asked for her address, so I give it to him. It was just in conversation, really. Then my mate, the one with the sciatica, tells me I'm not needed to walk Bruno again, but Mandy said to give me a tenner because I'd sent her some new business. To be honest, I don't even know why she needs security 'cause she's got to be almost three hundred pounds. I swear, that's all I know.'

After Newman had been released, Spencer ran Mandy Pilkington's name through the records. When the results appeared, Spencer did a little dance step, ending with a spinning turn. 'Well, what do you know? Our Mandy Pilkington has quite a record. Arrests for prostitution and soliciting and she's now advertising herself as a dominatrix.' Spence placed Mandy Pilkington's mugshot on Jane's desk. 'And it looks like our Mr. Foxley was a regular client.'

CHAPTER EIGHT

Tyler was just wrapping up the meeting in the boardroom where he'd allocated the names from Myers' list to be questioned. He gestured to Jane. 'Have you made contact with Justine Harris? Virtually everyone at that theatrical agency seems to think she was more than capable of murder.'

Jane tapped a page in her notebook. 'I did speak to her mother, Florence Harris, sir, and she said Justine would not be staying long with her in Ascot. She agreed to see me tomorrow morning.'

'Good. I also want another round of house-to-house inquiries. And those officers who were assigned to them earlier in the day, go back and check over the properties where the occupant was absent.'

There was an audible groan.

'Look,' Tyler said sternly, 'I've got the press on my back and there's already all sorts of rumors going around. We need to get a result – and quick.'

They filed out of the boardroom and got to work. Jane had agreed to do two of the house calls as a favor to one of the officers whose wife was expecting a baby.

Jane spoke to one flat owner who had never met Charles Foxley and didn't even know which flat he lived in. The second occupant did recall seeing him with his dogs and said that his next-door neighbor had had a loud argument with Foxley about his dogs, telling him that he should use poo bags, but he'd never had a conversation with him himself. He was a rather dapper, middle-aged bachelor, with wavy white hair. He was dressed in an immaculate pin-striped suit with a rather flamboyant pink tie, and worked as an investment banker. He even offered Jane a glass of sherry, which she politely refused. She was just about to leave when he said that he *had* met the previous owner, a Mr. Martinez.

'He created a lot of animosity among some of the residents because he renovated the basement and the work went on for a lengthy period. It was all very inconvenient as some of the residents' parking was taken up by the skips. But he was very apologetic, and I believe he gave bottles of champagne to his closest neighbors.'

'Did you actually meet Mr. Martinez?'

'Yes, I did. He was such a charming man. He invited several residents to his house-warming drinks. It was beautifully catered and he served cocktails in the small garden, and so any ill-feeling that anyone had about the building works soon evaporated.'

'Thank you very much. You've been very helpful.' Jane hesitated. 'Do you recall how long ago Mr. Foxley moved into his flat?'

'I don't have the exact date, but it would be at least a year ago. I was rather surprised, to be honest, because Mr. Martinez had spent so much time and money on his renovations.'

'Do you recall the name of the estate agent that handled the sale?'

'No, there was no board put up. I think it was a private sale. Are you sure you wouldn't be tempted by a nice glass of sherry?'

Jane was eager to get home as it was almost ten p.m. 'Thanks, but I need to get going.'

As she was heading towards her car she saw, towards the end of Onslow Square, the uniformed police officer standing outside Charles Foxley's flat. The yellow crime scene ribbons were still attached to the railings and she could see that the bright porch light was on. She walked towards the officer.

'Good evening.' She showed her warrant. 'Is there someone in the flat?'

'Yes, sarge. It's DS Lawrence. He's been in there for a couple of hours.' He shuffled his feet. 'I don't know . . . apparently some people don't have a home to go to. I'm on duty until he leaves, then I have to lock up.'

'So, the around-the-clock has been cancelled?' Jane asked.

'Yes, sarge, but I think they have someone here in the day.'

She headed past him and down the steps. The front door was ajar, and she could see the strips of cardboard were still down. She pushed open the door and stepped inside, calling out Lawrence's name.

After a moment, he walked out from the bedroom.

'I was just finishing some house-to-house inquiries and saw the lights on,' Jane said.

Lawrence gestured towards the kitchen. 'I can make you a cup of tea if you like?'

'I wouldn't mind one.'

Lawrence pulled off his rubber gloves. 'So, I hear you've been seeing Dave "Dabs" Morgan.'

Jane was taken aback, wondering how much Dabs had told Lawrence about her new hobby.

'He was at the lab doing some work with the ballistic experts and we just got talking about this case. He asked who I was working with and I mentioned you.'

'What did you talk about?' Jane asked.

Lawrence gave her a quizzical glance. 'Nothing much, but he did say you'd joined a gun club or something.'

Jane shrugged. 'I did but I haven't really had any time. So how's it been going here?'

'We still haven't found the weapon which was used to dis-embowel him. I checked all the knives but there doesn't appear to be one missing. Our victim also had a very good selection of chef's carving knives, but they're all still in their boxes. As for the razor, Foxley used an electric shaver.'

'Well, according to a neighbor I just spoke to, the previous owner, Sebastian Martinez, designed the place, and Charles Foxley bought it already furnished and kitted out.'

'Ah . . . ' Lawrence said as he filled the kettle and put it on.

'He was set designer or architect . . . I'm not sure.'

Lawrence put teabags into two fine china mugs and poured boiling water over them. He then took a carton of milk from a cooler bag. 'Do you take sugar?'

'No, that's fine,' Jane replied. She could see the ever-professional Lawrence also had a jar of instant coffee and two Tupperware boxes with the remains of his sandwiches.

'Would you like a Kit-Kat?' he asked.

'No thanks. You certainly come prepared.' She smiled.

'Yeah, well, you know me. I should've left hours ago, but something just doesn't feel right.'

She laughed softly. 'Well, I doubt finding a disemboweled body feels right at any time.'

He smiled. 'No, I don't mean that. I've been told that our victim lived here for at least a year, but there doesn't seem to be any imprint of who he was. There are just the few photographs that you saw earlier, there's very little food in any of the cupboards, the fridge is almost empty. But if you come through with me . . . '

He stood up, carrying his mug of tea, and Jane followed him into the bedroom.

She watched as Lawrence carefully maneuvered himself across the cardboard strips protecting the bloodstains and opened a wardrobe door.

'OK, we have good quality shirts, we have two designer suits, a couple of pairs of corduroy trousers . . . ' He looked down to the base of the wardrobe. 'Some cheap trainers – maybe used them for dog walking – but no other shoes.'

'That's odd, isn't it?' Jane agreed. 'Did you know we found a big supply of vitamins in his office?'

Lawrence shut the wardrobe door. 'Interesting. We found a large supply of vitamins in the bathroom cabinet.'

Lawrence then guided Jane to the chest of drawers, easing one open after another. 'Underpants, socks, a few cashmere sweaters, that's it.'

Jane looked around the ornate bedroom. 'His office was rather like going into an old Victorian house. All the furniture is worn and covered in dog hairs. I don't see that much evidence of the dogs here.'

Lawrence nodded. 'Well, there is the dog basket. But, apart from the blood, the place is pristine.'

'So, what's bothering you?'

Lawrence shrugged. 'I can't put my finger on it, but it feels as though the victim was hardly ever here.' He drained his tea. 'Maybe it's just me, but I can't quite work out what kind of man lived here.'

Jane followed Lawrence back into the kitchen.

'Well, Spence and I interviewed all his coworkers today, and to be honest, they all seem to describe him as a boyish charmer. A couple inferred there was a darker side to him. Tonight, we talked to the guy who walked his dogs and he told us that Charles Foxley may possibly have been visiting a dominatrix, but we haven't verified that yet.'

Lawrence took her mug and rinsed both of them under the tap before drying them and putting them back in the cupboard.

'Well, that might explain the handcuffs. But I still find it difficult to build up a picture of his character. He has an ex-wife, a daughter, and yet I can't find any family-orientated notes, books, letters, mementos . . .'

Jane yawned. 'Thanks for the tea, Paul, but I'm going to call it quits.'

'Yeah, I'll be packing up in a minute too,' Lawrence said.

Jane headed down the hall, pausing outside the bedroom. 'Maybe we'll find out more when we get to the bottom of the situation with this designer, Martinez. There was some sort of ill-feeling about the purchase, apparently. Also, one of the agents said something that I can't quite make sense of: that Foxley was a man who fed on success but became masochistic towards failure.'

Lawrence shrugged. 'Well, that's a bit obtuse.'

Jane laughed. 'Anyway, goodnight, Paul, I'm off home. Some of us do have one to go to.'

* * *

Jane made herself a cup of tea and dialed Dabs's number.

'Hello, Dabs, it's Jane. Sorry to call so late.'

'Hello, love. My God, you've got a nasty one. I saw Paul Lawrence over at the lab this morning.'

'Yes, he mentioned he had seen you. I'm calling because I feel quite bad about not going to the rifle club for another session with Elliott.'

'I'm sure he understood, Jane. Work takes priority. But let me give you his number if you want to talk to him. Just remember, he's a very private bloke, so keep it to yourself.'

Jane laughed softly. 'I'm not likely to tell anyone, Dabs. I really don't want anyone on the team knowing I'm joining the club.'

'I understand. I keep my out-of-work hobby to myself.'

'Well, thanks, Dabs, I really appreciate this.' She jotted down the number before hanging up. She finished her cup of tea and called Elliott. It rang once and was picked up.

'Yes?' The voice was low and quiet.

'Is this Elliott?' Jane asked.

'Yes.'

'This is Jane Tennison. I hope you don't mind me calling. I want to firstly apologize for not being able to see you this evening due to work commitments.'

'Yes, Dabs let me know.'

'I really would like to have another training session with you.'

There was a slight pause. 'If you can be at the rifle club by 6:45 a.m. tomorrow I can give you half an hour. Did you get your membership?'

'No, it hasn't come through yet, but I can be there tomorrow morning.'

'Good. I'll see you at the entrance to the car park to let you in.' He hung up and Jane was left holding the receiver, wondering if such an early start was going to become her routine.

* * *

The next morning she put on a tracksuit and sneakers for the session. She had given herself plenty of time to get from Marylebone to Norbiton but had not considered early morning traffic on the A40 or the congestion at Shepherd's Bush roundabout even at that time of day.

She hit traffic once again as she started on the A316 and finally made her way into Norbiton. Then, starting to get nervous, she missed the turning to the rifle club and found herself going round and round the small streets. By the time she found the narrow road leading to the club, it was already almost seven. Elliott was waiting by the open underground door. He was wearing a grey tracksuit and pristine white trainers, standing with his arms folded.

She drove towards the entry door to the club as Elliott slid the door closed to the car park. He moved quickly to stand in front of her as he put the code in to unlock the entry door, then once inside he deactivated the security alarm. She started to apologize for being late, explaining about the traffic and getting lost, but he made no reply until they entered the club. He had obviously been there earlier as there was a mug of coffee on the counter of the small coffee bar.

'You mind if I just say something, Jane?' he said finally. 'I would have hoped, as a detective, you would have been aware of the traffic and planned things a little better. My time is as valuable as yours.'

Jane could hardly believe it. She was unsure how to even reply.

Elliott looked at his watch. 'We'll only have the small-arms range for fifteen minutes now.' He picked up a metal briefcase and Jane followed him into the range, where he switched on the strip lighting.

'Until the secretary gets here, we will have to use one of my personal revolvers. I have a .38 Smith & Wesson, but you're not ready for that so we'll continue using the .22 revolver.'

Jane stood to one side as he clicked open the gun case. She could see there were four small handguns nestling in the black sponge protector.

'Let's see if you can remember everything I told you at the last session.'

Jane had never ever come across anyone like Elliott. He handed her the gun, then immediately snapped: 'Check there are no bullets in it first!' He said it so sternly that she physically jumped.

'Now, go to the area you were in before, with the crosses, and face the target.'

Jane did as requested, standing with her feet apart and arms raised in the correct position.

'Good,' he said, and then took her by surprise by asking if she had ever played Grandmother's Footsteps.

She lowered her arms. 'I don't think so.'

'Kids play it. You stand with your back to them, and they have to practice creeping up on you. Each time you turn and catch anyone moving, they have to start again. I'm going to go right back to the booths and try and sneak up on you, and you have to stand with the gun in position to shoot. That means both arms straight, thumb over thumb. Be ready to fire.'

Jane was completely nonplussed. He'd gone from a cold aloofness to talking to her about a child's game as if she was six.

She waited, and then he said softly, 'The game starts.'

She could hear nothing, and she waited, counting the seconds, and turned. He was standing no more than six feet away from her, absolutely still. She turned back, arms still stretched, and by now she could feel the muscles in her forearm really hurting. Silence ... and then suddenly he had two fingers cocked like a gun pressed into her neck.

'Bang.'

Jane was so shocked she screeched, almost dropped the gun, and her whole body started shaking. He gently took the gun from her.

'Is that what happened to you, Jane?'

'I didn't . . . have a gun,' she managed to say.

'I know you didn't. But you froze when you saw someone facing you with a weapon, and one member of your team was shot. Fortunately, not fatally.'

Anger started to take over from humiliation, and with her teeth clenched Jane moved away from him. 'I didn't come here to play childish games.'

He held his hands out. 'I'm sorry if playing that game has upset you. But that was my intention. You have to learn to control your fear, and the only way you can do that it is by facing it. Now, I want you to go into the stalls and I'll bring the target closer.' He pulled back a cuff and glanced at his watch. 'You only have five minutes left. But before you start practicing, I want to give you some breathing exercises to do every time you have that feeling of panic.'

Jane followed him to the stall as he switched on the no-entry red light. She was slowly calming down as he came to stand close beside her.

'Have you heard of an opera singer called Joan Sutherland?'

Jane shook her head.

'I was just listening to an interview with Pavarotti. You must have heard of him. When he was a young opera singer, he worked with Joan Sutherland and was amazed by the control she had with her diaphragm, which gave her the ability to hold notes perfectly.'

Jane was startled when Elliott placed his hand on her diaphragm.

'Now, take a deep breath.' He pressed firmly against her stomach. 'OK, hold it tight. Then slowly release it. Let me feel my hand move. It's the muscles in your lower stomach that should be controlling your breath.'

Far from feeling calmer, she almost felt like fainting.

'I can't do this,' she said.

He spoke very softly. 'Yes, you can. Now breathe in again.'

After a few moments, Jane began to relax. By the time he allowed her to shoot at the target, she had to admit she felt much steadier.

After she'd finished shooting, Elliott walked her back to her car and leaned on the door as she got in.

'I can do these early morning sessions two mornings a week. Call me if you want to do it.'

He slammed her door shut and walked over to the garage entry gate so she could drive out. He didn't look at her as she drove past.

Jane just had time to go to her health club in Fulham, have a shower and change into her work clothes. She'd begun to feel less angry about her interaction with Elliott, but she was still angry with Dabs for telling him about what had happened with the Sweeney. She used the health club's payphone and called Dabs at his home, preferring not to make the call from the station in case anyone overheard. Her privacy had already been compromised enough.

'Everything all right, Jane?' Dabs asked.

'Not really. I've just finished a session with Elliott, and I have to say that I find him quite difficult to deal with—'

Before she could continue, Dabs laughed.

'Well, he is a bit of an oddball, but you couldn't have a more professional instructor.'

'I'm sure he is very professional, but my beef is that he knows about my situation at the Sweeney, and I just wish you hadn't gossiped. I'm obviously very sensitive about what happened. If I thought that you were going to discuss my problems with a stranger . . . '

'Hey, hang on a second, Jane. All I said is what you told me – that you had a situation when you were with the Sweeney and you wanted to have some gun-handling experience. I've never discussed your personal life with him, and I'm just sorry if it's not working out.'

'OK, Dabs. Sorry if I jumped to conclusions,' Jane said. 'Look, I'm late. I'd better go.'

She put the phone down, feeling more confused than ever.

* * *

DI Arnold had returned to the station that morning and had brought in a large box of jam doughnuts for everyone before catching up on developments with Tyler.

Spencer was now munching one as he sat at his desk, checking the morning's assignments. He was to interview Mandy Pilkington first thing and Jane was to travel to Ascot to talk to Justine Harris. He had still not sifted through all the scraps of papers he had removed from Foxley's office and was about to tip them out of the plastic bag he was keeping them in when DI Arnold, carrying a bulging briefcase, walked out of Tyler's office.

'Morning, guv, glad to have you back. Feeling better?' Spencer asked.

'Yes. It was an experience I wouldn't wish on my worst enemies. They say it's as bad as giving birth, having kidney stones removed. I just hope that's the end of it.'

'I'm sure we all hope so, too,' Spencer said.

Arnold moved closer to Spencer's desk. 'You're interviewing Mandy Pilkington at Clapham? That could be interesting. What have you got there?' Arnold indicated the plastic bag full of crumpled paper.

'I removed it all from Foxley's waste bin yesterday. I've still got to sift through it to see if there's anything of interest.'

'Right, well, we want that missing diary, so that has to be a priority. You need to get the secretary, Julia Summers, interviewed tomorrow as well.'

If Arnold was attempting to prove he was up to speed on the investigation, Spencer wasn't impressed.

Arnold then turned to everyone in the room.

'Thank you all for your good wishes. I'm off to see my doctor. I know I still have a lot of catching up to do but I shall be back later.'

Spencer said nothing. Nobody else appeared to be concerned that DI Arnold was leaving after only a few hours at the station. He shoved the plastic bag into a drawer and then, with a sigh, took it out again.

If I don't do it now, I'm never going to do it, he thought.

A number of the crumpled notes had no time or date on them but referenced horse racing bets. There was also a partly typed memo regarding a contract for a film. It appeared to have been written the week before his death. There were numerous receipts from restaurants, one relating to dog food delivery and a torn bank statement for two cash withdrawals of £2,000 and £3,000. There appeared to be no indication of anything particularly suspicious, but Spencer would investigate the cash withdrawals and find out if there was anything significant about the film contract.

* * *

Jane drove herself to Ascot. On the way there she used her small tape recorder to make a note of things she felt were important. One was to discuss Charles Foxley's diary with his secretary Julia Summers, as it had not been in the office. She also made a mental note to question Justine about the possibility of her ex-husband having another residence.

Jane approached the driveway of a substantial property that overlooked the famous Ascot racecourse. Large rhododendron bushes grew either side of the drive, which curved around to pass lawns with numerous cultivated flower beds and a central large fountain that looked as if it had not been in use for some time. The rusted cherub at the top of the stone was missing one arm. Parked outside the house was a highly polished BMW, the model at least five years old. There were four wide steps leading up to a pillared entrance and the front door was painted in racing green with a prominent brass letterbox and knocker.

Jane pressed the old-fashioned bell, which chimed loudly inside. She waited a few minutes then pressed it again. Eventually she heard the click-clack of shoes on a hard floor and the door was opened by an elegant, white-haired woman wearing a floral blouse and a blue pleated skirt. Her white hair was tied back into a loose bun at the nape of her neck. She had piercing blue eyes and high cheekbones.

'Yes?' she said curtly.

Jane showed her ID. 'I'm Detective Sergeant Jane Tennison. I believe you were contacted by my superior, Detective Chief Inspector Tyler?'

'Yes, yes.' She opened the door wider. 'Do come in.'

Jane stepped into a marble mosaic-floored hallway. There was a large Georgian mirror with a mahogany table placed in front of it with a vase containing a beautiful floral arrangement.

'I'm Florence Harris.' She gestured towards a wide staircase. 'My daughter will be down shortly. I have just taken her breakfast.'

She walked through some double doors, and Jane followed her into a beautifully furnished sitting room. The polished parquet wood floor surrounded a thickly ornate patterned carpet. There were velvet sofas and easy chairs, all in muted greens, with draped silk curtains and Austrian blinds. The bay windows looked out over the front garden.

'Can I offer you some refreshment?' she asked, waving for Jane to sit on one of the sofas.

'I would love a coffee, please.'

'I won't be a moment.'

Florence turned and strode back through the double doors. Jane could hear the receding footsteps on the marble flooring. She had a good chance to look around the room with its numerous paintings, carved marble mantelpiece and a variety of silver-framed photographs. She was just about to get up to have a closer look at the photographs when she saw the young girl at the open door. This had to be Clara, as she not only looked like her mother, but also her grandmother. Her eyes were strangely expressionless, and she had long, rather lank blonde hair with unusually pallid skin. The girl was wearing a worn blue quilted dressing gown over pajamas, with bunny slippers.

Jane smiled. 'Hello, you must be Clara.'

'What do you want?' the girl asked, not moving from the doorway.

'I've come to talk to your mummy.'

'She's upstairs in bed.'

'Yes, I've been told. I'm waiting to see her.'

'I was taken out of school. Do you know why?'

Jane nodded. 'Yes, I do.'

'Nobody gives a shit about him anyway.'

Jane was shocked at the venom in the girl's voice, but before she could react, Florence Harris appeared with a small silver tray.

'Clara, go to your room now.'

'Yes, Grandma, no, Grandma, three-fucking-bags-full, Grandma.'

'That's enough, Clara! Now go up to your room immediately!'

The child turned slowly and walked casually away as Mrs. Harris pushed the door closed with her hip.

'I'm sorry, the poor child has taken this all very badly. But I'm going to take her away for a special girls' shopping trip to Paris.'

Florence passed the tray to Jane then fetched a small side table and placed it beside her.

'Thank you very much,' Jane said, as Mrs. Harris moved halfway across the room to sit in a very large velvet-covered chair.

'Justine's having a shower and will be right down. I don't want to speak out of turn, but my daughter is very fragile. You must be aware that after she found out what happened to Charles, she took an overdose. And you probably know it is not the first time my daughter has attempted suicide.'

Jane nodded. 'Yes, and obviously we are very concerned. It must be a relief that she is now here with you and her daughter.'

'Well, it is a great relief, with her psychiatric history. And her psychiatrist felt it would be beneficial for Justine to come home into my care. I think discovering what happened to Charles must have been very traumatic, but my daughter also has a very determined streak. She probably won't stay here very long, but I have Clara for most of her school holidays and will be taking care of her throughout this ordeal. My husband always was against Justine getting married; she was very young and very foolish and didn't pay any attention to his warnings.'

Jane hesitated, not wanting to put her foot in it. 'Is your husband still alive?'

Mrs. Harris gave a short laugh. 'Yes, dear, he is very much alive and living in Guernsey with a very common woman with false teeth. We have been divorced for a long time.'

To hide her embarrassment, Jane continued, 'You said your ex-husband didn't approve of Charles Foxley?'

'Good God, no. He didn't have a pot to piss in, and no career, really. Whereas Justine had already starred in two costume dramas for the BBC, and obviously her father gave her a substantial allowance. Even when he threatened to cut it off, she still went ahead and married Charles. And now look what's happened.'

'They were married for some time, though?' Jane said.

'Yes, and if Justine hadn't financed his agency, he probably would've gambled everything away. But he could turn on the charm, and even though I was as against her marriage as my ex-husband, Charles could be a really delightful man, or really a boy. I don't think he ever grew up.'

'Why do you say that?'

Florence turned her face to look out of the window.

'I believe his business was very successful?' Jane pressed.

'Yes, so I have been told,' Florence said curtly.

Florence seemed ill at ease, as if she had said too much. Jane finished the small cup of coffee, eager now to have a conversation with Justine. Florence stood up and went over to a silver cigarette box on a beautifully carved round table. She took out a cigarette and lit it with a heavy silver lighter. She remained with her back towards Jane.

'He could also be a monster. When I say he was boyish, he had rages and temper tantrums like a child. He could be vicious. I don't think he was ever physically violent, but he was a man full of self-loathing and low self-esteem. He took it out on my daughter. She gave up her career for him, and it was her money, her contacts ... Without them he would never have had even a modicum of success. Tragically, they couldn't live with each other and they couldn't live without each other. They tormented each other. That's why my daughter has tried to kill herself and that's why I refused to allow Clara to spend any time with him, her so-called father.' The smoke drifted from her cigarette as she inhaled deeply. 'I hated him. I know he has been brutally murdered, but I don't think you will find many people who really care.'

At that moment the double doors opened widely as Justine entered. She looked at her mother.

'Please leave the room, Mother.'

Mrs. Harris stubbed her cigarette out in a large glass bowl and picked up the little silver tray on which she had served Jane her coffee.

'I suppose you were listening at the door.'

Justine watched as her mother exited the room, closing the doors behind her.

'So, now you've met my mother,' Justine said, as she walked slowly across the room and sat in the same chair her mother had used.

She was wearing a beautiful black Chanel dress and black sheer tights with soft ballet shoes. Her blonde hair, although similar to her daughter's, looked freshly washed, healthy and glossy. She wore no make-up and her skin was flawless, her eyes the same brilliant color as her mother's. But unlike Florence's, there was a washed-out sadness in them and from her expression it looked as if a heavy weight was pressing down on her.

'What do you need to know?' she asked softly, as she lit a cigarette from the same silver box.

'When did you last see your ex-husband?'

'I spoke to him early that Monday, but I had not seen him for over a week.'

'What time was that?'

'I called him at the office. It was about nine a.m.'

'How did he sound?'

'He sounded his usual self. I asked whether or not he would be coming to a parent-and-teacher meeting at Clara's school and he said he would let me know nearer the date, which is what he always said. Then he always found an excuse not to go. Charles showed little or no interest in Clara.' She gave a small shrug.

'Do you know of anyone who would have a motive to kill your husband?'

'I think you will probably find a number of people. He could be cruel. He controlled a lot of people's lives and an awful lot of people detested him.' She dragged heavily on the cigarette, taking the smoke deep into her lungs. 'I think you could say I was probably one of those people.' Her voice had a slight quaver to it.

Jane was trying to assess whether Justine was being truthful, or giving a very good performance.

'Your mother said you and Charles had a love-hate relationship and that although you are divorced, you couldn't live with or without each other. Would you say that was true?'

'Not quite. I could live without Charles, but he found it very difficult to live without me. Even though we were divorced, he would never leave me alone. If I formed a relationship with anyone else he would make abusive phone calls and threaten them. No matter how hard I tried, he refused to let me live my life without him. In all honesty, I have wished him dead many times.'

'Do you know anyone else who wanted him dead?'

'I just told you. There are many people. We tried at the beginning to salvage our marriage. He could be a very kind and generous man . . . but he was also a compulsive liar. I found out that he had been unfaithful so many times, but I really tried hard to make things work. At one time I even protected him. That was when the rot really set in.'

'I don't quite understand,' Jane said.

'Charles was a sexual deviant. He frequently used prostitutes, and when I discovered his disgusting and sickening sexual predilections, I couldn't stand it any longer and that is when we divorced.'

'You said you protected him?'

Justine got up and stubbed her cigarette out in the same glass bowl her mother had used. 'Yes, I did. You can probably check it out in police records. There was a prostitute murdered about five years ago. He had been with her and was so afraid it would be made public. So I lied and gave him an alibi and said he had been with me. That became my weapon to force him to divorce me.'

'Do you recall the name of the murdered woman?' Jane asked.

'No. It happened five years ago. Charles came to me, begging for my help and crying like a child. As I said, I protected him.'

'Do you know if your ex-husband ever had any other homes, other than your house in Barnes and his flat in Kensington?' Jane asked.

Justine shrugged her shoulders. 'Quite possibly . . . but I don't know about him living anywhere else. In fact, he often used to sleep in his office and invariably found an excuse to stay at the house in Barnes – which always made it incredibly difficult for me to form a relationship with anybody else.'

'We've been unable to interview your ex-husband's secretary, Julia Summers. Apparently she has a sick relative. Do you know if Miss Summers used to take Charles's diary with her when she wasn't in the office?' Jane asked.

'I have absolutely no idea. In fact, I only met her a few times, usually when she was at her wits' end, as Charles was incredibly difficult. He had no notion of time and was always missing appointments – as well as his daughter's birthdays.'

There was the loud hoot of a car horn and Justine crossed to the window and looked out. 'I need to rest now.'

The double doors opened and Florence Harris led in George Henson.

'Darling, George has come to take you home, dear,' Florence said, looking at Justine.

Jane watched the actress move slowly across the room to rest her head on George's shoulder.

'Have you met Mr. Henson?' Florence asked.

'Yes, we have,' George said, his arm around Justine.

'Have you finished your interview, Detective Tennison?' Florence asked, clearly keen for Jane to go.

The actress in Justine appeared again as she held out her hand and thanked Jane profusely for agreeing to come to Ascot to interview her. 'Do just let me know if you need to speak to me again about anything.'

Before she could reply, Jane found herself ushered out into the marble hallway, through the front door and down the steps towards her car. She got in the car and slammed the door shut, frowning. Spencer had suggested that Charles Foxley's office was a nest of vipers and Jane was beginning to feel that the house she'd just left was too.

*　*　*

The morning's briefing was already underway in the board-room. Jane had hurried to the canteen to grab a sandwich and a coffee before she joined them. Tyler nodded his head towards her as he continued describing the lack of progress. Jane sat next to DI Arnold and whispered to him that she was glad to see he was back. He acknowledged her with a small smile and then concentrated on Tyler, making small notes in an open notebook in front of him. The blackboard had scrawled names crossed out and newspaper articles detailing the murder littered the board-room table.

DC Dors entered the room carrying two large carrier bags containing video cassettes collected from Foxley's office. Tyler looked in the bag and glanced at the titles on the spines. They seemed to be mostly 'CF at Premiere' or 'CF at Theatre Opening'. He turned to Dors.

'Take these up to the tech division and ask them to splice together all the footage of Foxley. I'm not wasting time trawling through all his red-carpet functions.'

Dors gathered up the bags of video cassettes and left the room. The briefing continued as various detectives described the interviews they had had so far with people on Myers' list. They had been able to eliminate them as suspects due to their alibis being confirmed, but they still had about thirty more people they needed to interview.

Tyler turned to Jane and asked if she had gained anything positive from the ex-wife. Jane quickly summarized her time in Ascot, saying that she felt it was imperative she interview Justine Harris again, at her own home. She felt the interview had been dominated by Florence's presence. Jane also told him that Justine had mentioned that, at some point around five years ago, Foxley had visited a prostitute who had been found murdered.

'She admitted that at the time she had lied for her husband and given him an alibi, which is obviously perjury but also, of course, an indication that she is a very able liar. I will double-check with records to see what we have and if anyone was arrested and charged with the murder.'

'Well, it would be bloody useful if we had the tart's name,' Tyler muttered. 'Did you have any joy with the missing diary?'

'We have made contact with Julia Summers. She was staying with a relative and will bring the diary in later today.'

Tyler ran his hands through his hair, looking frustrated. Standing with his hands on his hips, he nodded to the blackboard.

'Well, we were all interested in tracing the previous owner of the victim's flat as he was on the agent's hit list. We know exactly where Sebastian Martinez is – he was cremated two years ago. Coroner's report confirmed suicide – he hanged himself in a hotel room. Interestingly, that was six months after Charles Foxley had purchased Martinez's flat for under half the market value. So we need to do some more digging around into that; local police would have attended the incident and a report must have been made for the coroner's inquest.'

Arnold held up his pencil. 'I'll check into that, guv.'

Spencer barged in with a cup of takeaway coffee, looking rather pleased with himself. He had a thick folder in his other hand, which he tossed onto the table.

'I've just come back from Clapham. Miss Pilkington.'

Tyler loosened his tie. 'I sincerely hope you've got something we can use, Spencer. Right now, we have fuck all!'

Spencer grinned. 'I had to make a few promises to get to the nitty-gritty. Miss Pilkington is a dominatrix. Her entire cellar is equipped like a dungeon: chains, whips, a vaulting horse . . . There's a padded room and another really sick one with a large baby's cot. She deals with heavy-duty fetishes. Like I said, I had to make a few promises that I was not there to investigate how much money she was making, but I would say it's a fair whack. From outside, it looks like any other terraced house, right down to the net curtains. But inside it's full of rubber suits, masks and mirrors above all the beds . . . '

'For fuck's sake, Spence, get to the point! I think we can all work out what a dominatrix's place looks like!' Tyler shouted.

There were a few guffaws around the table, and a couple of the detectives muttered, 'Never having been in one . . .'

'I'm getting to it, I'm getting to it. But you need to get the full picture.'

'Are you suggesting that this dominatrix killed Foxley?'

'Hell, no! She's about three hundred fifty pounds! Besides, Charles Foxley was her cash cow. It was only after I told her the only person I was interested in was him, and I didn't want to know the names of any other clients, that she started to open up. Foxley was not just a regular client, he was obsessive. He would go there three or four times a week. Mandy Pilkington said that he would go at lunchtime, early evening and often very early in the morning, but never at the weekends. He only liked obese women and it was sometimes hard finding the right women at short notice.'

Spencer opened the file. 'These are just a few photographs showing what she has on offer, most of them from magazines. But our victim liked the shit beaten out of him.'

There was an odd silence in the room as they looked at the photographs and took on board this latest bizarre development.

'OK,' Tyler said. 'Let's take a break and reconvene as soon as we get the footage from tech support. This is all very interesting, but it still doesn't give us a suspect. We've all got work to do.'

'I'll organize a TV and a video player, since the station doesn't have one,' Arnold volunteered.

'Good, Tim. And see if you can get a reasonably sized one so we can get a decent picture,' Tyler replied.

Jane and Spencer hung back while everyone left. Spencer turned to Jane.

'He only did half a day yesterday then scurried off home. Now he's so far up Tyler's arse . . . He pisses me off.'

'For goodness' sake, Spence, give him a break. He's lost quite a bit of weight and he looks pale.'

Spencer shook his head. 'Apparently having kidney stones is as painful as giving birth! Give me strength.'

'I am not getting into this with you, Spence.'

'Fine,' Spencer shrugged. 'Did you know the guv was interviewed this morning for BBC News? He kept it very short, just saying that a thorough investigation was underway.'

'Wait until you read my reports about Florence Harris. More poisonous than you would believe,' Jane replied.

Jane had started typing up her report from her visit to Ascot when Arnold stopped at her desk.

'I pulled in a few favors and I might have something on that incident Justine Harris mentioned.'

'What? Was Foxley involved?'

'No no, someone else was convicted of the murder. It's the description of the victim that's the possible connection to Foxley. Arlene Wicks, originally from Liverpool, worked out of a small massage parlor in World's End, Chelsea. It was shut down a few years ago but . . . ' He passed Jane a fax print-out dated seven years previously. Jane looked at the rather blurred and faded black and white mug shot. It had the word 'DECEASED' stamped across it. The description read: *Born in Bootle, Liverpool, aged 22, 5 foot, 1 inch, 215 pounds, arrested for soliciting three times.*'

Jane looked up as Arnold shrugged. 'His ex-wife lied for him. They got the guy that killed the poor girl, but if it's the right incident then it shows that all that time ago Foxley was using the same type of whore.'

Jane passed back the fax sheet to Arnold, noticing that he had some sticking plaster around his very heavy gold wedding band. He caught her looking and gave her a smile.

'Lost weight and I'm scared to death of it dropping off. If I lose it, Bronwyn would never forgive me. And I have to wear a belt on my trousers to hold them up now. Think I've lost about twenty-five pounds. All the years I've been on diets, but it was the hospital food that did it. I couldn't eat the stuff!'

'It suits you.' Jane smiled.

She watched as he added Arlene Wicks's details to the blackboard, then turned to Spencer.

'Those betting slips you found in Foxley's office – might be worth checking out the betting shops he frequented. We are also waiting on the lists of in- and outgoing calls Foxley made from his office and the basement flat.'

'On it, guv,' Spencer said, tight-lipped.

A little over an hour later they reconvened in the boardroom. A large TV screen had been wheeled in with a video recorder attached. They all drew their chairs up to one end of the room and the blinds were drawn. The tech support officer explained that they had worked flat-out to splice the tapes, but only some of the footage had sound, and a lot of the imagery was blurred.

Jane sat beside Spencer. There had been no time yet to discuss his visit to Mandy Pilkington's. 'That must have been a fascinating morning,' she whispered.

'You're telling me!' he replied with a grin. 'There are some sick pervs out there all right. That giant baby's cot and big plastic baby bottles and pacifiers – she said she gets a lot of clients that want to be dressed up in nappies. Or those rubber suits . . . Jesus, I don't know how they get into them.'

Tyler clapped his hands. 'OK, attention, everyone. Thanks to Tim here we've got it up and rolling now. So let's have a look at him.'

Arnold inserted a tape and after a few moments the screen came to life. What they were looking at seemed to be a film premiere as there were banks of photographers milling around, and then the glamorous figure of a well-known film star in a beautiful couture gown appeared and the flashing cameras went crazy.

Tyler pointed at the screen. 'There he is!'

Charles Foxley was walking a few paces behind the film star, wearing an evening suit and black tie. He had wavy blond hair just down to his shirt collar. Jane was surprised how good-looking he was. The next shot was of a similar event, and Jane and Spencer recognized Emma Ransom talking animatedly to Foxley.

They all sat watching the footage of fifteen similar events, and Foxley was always there somewhere on the periphery of the action. One showed a crowded after-show party and Foxley appeared to be working the room, smiling and greeting everyone there, kissing one glamorous woman after another.

Eventually Tyler stood up. 'Anyone who wants to keep watching, go ahead, but I think we've seen enough of the smarmy bastard, and as you're all aware, we still haven't identified a single serious suspect, let alone a motive. I want the rest of the names that Myers gave us checked out, and, more importantly, I want that missing diary.'

Tyler left the room and the rest of the detectives followed, as the video footage continued to play.

Spencer drained his coffee and chucked the empty cup into the bin. 'You get anything from the ex-wife?'

Jane shrugged. 'Not a lot. I think she's having a relationship with George Henson – he was there. Apparently our victim used to spend a lot of time at the old marital home in Barnes.'

She looked at the screen, then reached for the remote control and pressed the pause button. She rewound the tape.

'You know, Spence, it's so strange, watching him at these premieres, rubbing shoulders with all these celebrities and being charming, while we know he had a sick perversion, so perverted that he was going there before he started work, at his lunchtimes . . . How do you slow the video down?'

Spence grabbed the remote control. 'You can't. I can freeze-frame it, though. What are you looking for?'

'His eyes. Look at his eyes, Spence.'

They sat side by side and watched one frame after another. On the surface Foxley appeared to be confident and animated, but Jane went close up to the screen and tapped it with her pencil. 'He has dead eyes. He hates himself.'

CHAPTER NINE

Jane and Spencer arrived at Foxley's offices just before two p.m. Rita was the only girl in reception. She looked forlornly at Jane.

'Julia Summers will be back any moment, but she's in a shockin' state. Everyone's asking when the funeral's gonna be, but we've not been told nothin'.'

Jane nodded sympathetically. 'Is Mr. Bergman in?'

'He's always in,' Rita replied, picking up the phone. 'You've got the detectives here to see you, Mr. Bergman. Shall I show them through?'

She held the phone away from her ear as Bergman replied, then replaced the receiver.

'He's a rude bastard, that one. Just go on through.'

As they crossed the hallway into the other office, Bergman could be heard shouting at his usual volume.

'I'm just telling you she's found out the leading actor is getting paid more than she is. No, just fucking listen to me! She's a much bigger name – you know it, I know it. So you're telling me you had no option because the previous leading actor got appendicitis and you were over a barrel. Fine, you tell her that. Yes, *you*. Then call me back!'

Jane knocked lightly on the door and walked in. Bergman waved his hand at them.

'Rita, hold all my calls – but if Vanessa rings I'm going to have to take it.' He put the receiver down with a sigh. 'Sorry about that, but I've got this fucking actress throwing a wobbly on the set and refusing to continue shooting. The stupid cow has somehow found out that the actor playing opposite her is being paid more money and she's throwing a fit. They've told her that she can keep two very costly designer outfits as compensation but she's not buying it.'

Bergman then looked at them inquiringly as they sat down on the sofa.

'We just need to ask you for some more detail with regard to Sebastian Martinez,' said Jane. 'You said there was some sort of "situation" regarding the purchase of Mr. Martinez's flat?'

Bergman sat back in his chair. 'Well, it was common knowledge that Charles bought it for half the market value. All I do know, as I have told you, is that there was a very unpleasant situation.' Bergman shrugged his narrow shoulders. 'You know how gays can be. He was in here screaming his head off, accusing Charles of destroying his career – but I have no idea what that was all about. You could probably get more information from Emma Ransom. Shortly after Charles did the deed, the poor old queen topped himself.'

The light on Bergman's desk phone started blinking. There was a knock on the door and the flustered face of his secretary, Margaret, appeared.

'Mr. Bergman, Vanessa really needs to talk to you urgently.'

'Shit! Would you excuse me?' He snatched up the phone.

'Vanessa, darling. Update?' He sprang to his feet, gripping the phone, while his face went puce. 'The stupid cunt did what?! I don't fucking believe it! Listen, Vanessa, I'll get into a taxi right now. I promise you I will sort this out.' He slammed the phone down.

'The stupid bitch of an actress. I told you they were giving her two designer dresses – one from Chanel costing an absolute fortune and the other one from Valentino – and now the stupid bitch has gone into the wardrobe department and taken a pair of scissors to all the other costumes.'

Jane and Spencer looked on wide-eyed. Bergman grabbed a suede coat from the back of his chair, muttered a fleeting apology and hurried out of his office. They heard him screaming for Margaret to get him a taxi.

Jane and Spencer looked at each other, shaking their heads. After a few moments, Rita popped her head around the door.

'Julia Summers is in reception for you.'

Julia Summers looked typically posh. Her hair was held back with a neat Alice band and she wore a maroon suit, pale stockings and court shoes, with a strand of expensive-looking pearls around her neck. Her eyes were red-rimmed, and she had obviously been crying.

'I came as soon as I heard the dreadful news,' she said.

Jane turned to Rita. 'Is there somewhere we can talk in private?'

'Well, 'is office is obviously empty now.'

Julia shook her head. 'Could we go to the little coffee annex?'

'That would be fine,' Jane replied.

Julia led them down the corridor and through a side door. There was a small kitchen area with a table and four chairs. Julia sat down between them, with a small overnight bag beside her.

'It must have been a great shock for you, Julia,' Spencer said gently.

Her eyes brimmed with tears. 'I still can't believe it.'

'When was the last time you saw Mr. Foxley?' he asked.

She took a deep breath. 'It would have been the day before I left. My aunt had got severe angina, and her housekeeper had some family matter to attend to, and when I explained this to Charles he said I must go.'

'So that would have been on . . . ?' Spencer started taking notes.

'Monday. And I really only expected to be there overnight, but my aunt's condition worsened, so I called in and spoke to Rita to say that I would stay in Devon.' She fumbled in her pocket and took out a tissue to blow her nose. 'I'm awfully sorry, but I still just can't believe it.'

'How long have you worked for Mr. Foxley?' Jane asked.

'Almost eighteen months.'

'Could I ask how old you are?' Jane said with a smile.

'Yes, I've just turned eighteen. To be honest, I'm really a sort of go-between for Mr. Foxley and Emma. Or rather, I started that way, but more recently I've worked mostly for Charl ... Mr. Foxley.'

'Do you have his diary?' Jane asked quietly.

'Do you mean his desk diary?'

'Yes, do you have his desk diary?'

'I was only expecting to be away for one night, you see. I didn't think my aunt would need me and often I would take the diary home because I had so many arrangements to make with collections and deliveries, and I needed to be sure I got everything right. I didn't do anything that I wasn't supposed to do. As soon as I heard what had happened, I came straight here.'

'So, before you left, how did Mr. Foxley seem to you?' Jane asked.

'He was the same as always. A lot of people found him quite difficult to work with. He was very disorganized. He was always misplacing things – his passport, his car keys, his wallet. It was often very difficult to make sure he made his appointments on time, let alone his flights to the US. He was very trying at times, but I genuinely liked him, and he was incredibly generous. But I did find looking after his dogs difficult. He would forget where they were, and when his dog walker was coming or going.'

The more she talked, all the time playing with the pearls around her neck, the more she seemed to relax.

'Can you think of anyone who would want to harm Mr. Foxley?' Spencer asked.

That made her smile for the first time.

'Oh, lots of people disliked him. He was a very tough negotiator.'

'Were you aware that Mr. Foxley paid considerable amounts of money for prostitutes?'

Her smile vanished, and she put her hand to her mouth with a gasp.

'Did Mr. Foxley ever make any advances towards you?' Spencer asked.

'No, never! Has his ex-wife been saying things about him? She seemed to think any woman who went near Mr. Foxley was having an affair with him – but in reality nothing could have been further from any of our minds . . . ' She suddenly stopped.

Jane and Spencer let the pause hang in the air, as Julia bowed her head.

'Sorry, I'm speaking completely out of turn. I don't think I should answer any more questions.' She bent down and lifted her overnight bag onto her lap. 'You wanted Mr. Foxley's diary.' She took out a large manila envelope and passed it to Spencer. 'In his office, you'll also find the previous three years of diaries.'

Jane pushed her chair back and stood up. 'Thank you very much for your help, Miss Summers.'

Julia zipped her overnight bag closed. 'I'm going to see Mr. Myers, now,' she said, then walked past Spencer, out of the annex, with her eyes down.

Jane looked at Spencer. 'What do you make of her?'

'Well, I hope her shorthand and typing is good. She seems a bit feather-brained to me.'

Jane nodded in agreement. 'I'm just going to the ladies. Do you want to wait for me in reception?'

The ladies bathroom had three cubicles, with three wash basins and a roller towel. Jane was washing her hands when the door opened and Emma Ransom walked in.

'We were just talking to Julia Summers,' Jane said affably, as she pulled down the roller towel.

'Yes, I was told she had hurried back from Devon with Charles's diary. You have no idea how many times I have told her that she should not remove it from the office, but I don't think the lift stops on all floors with Julia. Trying to organize Charles was quite a complicated exercise and one I constantly had to monitor.'

'I would've thought that as he was such a successful agent, Mr. Foxley would have required an experienced secretary or personal assistant,' Jane said.

Emma nodded. 'He most certainly did, which is why I had more work than I should have had. But then there were other reasons for hiring Julia. Her father is what is known as an angel in our business. He's a phenomenally wealthy man who invests in stage productions and, more recently, British movies. Her mother is also from a very aristocratic family, so Julia is very well-connected. For all her ineptness, she did bring in a lot of her aspiring model friends to Charles's new venture, KatWalk. But frankly, now that he's gone, I doubt she will be staying at the company. And Simon Quinn will more than likely be out of a job without Charles as well.'

She pushed open one of the cubicle doors.

'Can I just ask you something?' Jane said. 'I believe you were the agent for Sebastian Martinez?'

'Yes, I was.'

'I've heard various stories about there being some unpleasant interactions with Charles Foxley in connection with the purchase of Mr. Martinez's flat in Kensington.'

Emma pursed her lips. 'I did represent Sebastian. He was an exceedingly talented designer. He had also qualified as an architect and a lot of his sets were extraordinarily complicated structures. He worked not only for major theatres but also opera houses.'

'Could you tell me about the animosity between those two?'

'It was a difference of opinions. At the time, Charles also represented him as a client, and I didn't really know the details.' She turned as if to go into the cubicle.

'But he committed suicide, didn't he?'

Emma turned back, frowning angrily. 'I really don't see what that's got to do with anything.'

'I just want to know if his suicide was connected to the sale of the flat.'

This time Emma snapped. 'If you want further details, I suggest you ask Charles's ex-wife. Right now, I really need to take a piss.' She slammed the cubicle door shut.

Spencer was in reception with Rita, listening to the conversation as Rita took a call from Frieda Lunn. It appeared Mr. Foxley's housekeeper had not been paid for a month. Rita assured her that she would take it up with Mr. Myers, and just as she replaced the phone, Myers called out from the end of the corridor.

'Detective, could I speak with you for a minute?'

Spencer headed down the corridor and Myers ushered him into his office.

'Detective, I don't know if you are aware, but Charles's ex-wife has inherited all of his shares in the company. Quite honestly, if she was even to contemplate working here, I very much doubt that the other agents would stay. I, for one, would find it virtually impossible. My hopes are that she sells the shares, to be divided among us all. Emma Ransom has already had another top agent trying to poach her. Meanwhile, Charles's clients are already moving elsewhere.' He shook his head. 'FFA, as we say in the business. Fickle Fucking Actors.'

'How do you know the contents of Mr. Foxley's will?' Spencer asked.

'I was his partner. He had said numerous times that he would change it after his divorce, but then they had this freaky relationship, so you never knew where you were with the two of them. He was often at their marital home, which she fought like a tigress to be awarded, lock, stock and barrel. And she was always on the phone to him, usually using Clara as an excuse.'

Myers' desk phone rang and he snatched it up. He listened for a moment, scowling.

'Rita, I am a very busy man and I don't give a toss about whether or not Mrs. Lunn has been paid for her cleaning services. Tell her to send an invoice to his ex-wife.' He slammed down the phone.

'Unbelievable. As if, in the middle of this nightmare, I've got time to deal with Charles's cleaner. At least we don't have his bloody dogs running amok. I had to get rid of one of the wing-backed chairs they appropriated – it wasn't just full of dog hairs, but fleas.' He gave an odd chuckle. 'He used to find it amusing, you know, when he had one of his FFAs in. He would sit them in that chair and they'd walk out covered in dog hairs. Now, added to the rest of my problems, bloody Daniel Bergman is insisting that he wants to move into Charles's office. I mean, talk about shoving his feet into a dead man's shoes.'

Spencer said, 'Thank you very much for your time, Mr. Myers. I would also like to take this opportunity to take Mr. Foxley's Rolodex from his desk.'

Myers frowned. 'It has some important contact details I need.'

'I'll make a copy of it for you, but I'll need to keep the original as evidence in the investigation.'

After they had driven back to the station, Spencer went into the canteen and grabbed two rather stale cheese sandwiches and two mugs of tea to take into the boardroom. Jane was having the first look through the coveted diary and by the time he joined her she had already made extensive notes.

'I don't know how this man functioned with a secretary who was so dizzy,' she said, shaking her head. 'There is more whiteout in here than there is paper. Some of the pages are clogged with it when he has appointments, breakfast meetings, coffee meetings, lunches . . . but on the days when he was obviously visiting the dominatrix, it just says "family matter". There's a lot of scrawled writing, which I presume is his. "Toadying with FFA". I wonder who FFA is,' Jane said, turning the pages.

Spencer grinned. 'FFA means Fickle Fucking Actor.'

Jane rolled her eyes. 'Well, he certainly has a lot of meetings with them.'

Together Jane and Spencer went through the diary page by page, noting that Julia had covered over some entries. Perhaps because she'd run out of whiteout, she had glued on little bits of paper and written 'cancelled' or 'do not include'.

There were numerous flights back and forth to LA and New York, and on one page, in Foxley's red scrawl, was 'got him' underlined several times, but nothing else that indicated any confrontations or difficult relationships.

Spencer stood up and dug his hands into his pockets. 'Here is a guy who has a hugely successful business. He represents some of the most famous actors in the UK and in the US. He owns a luxurious flat in Kensington. And he spends an inordinate amount of time in a seedy S&M brothel. It just doesn't seem to add up.'

Jane nodded. 'I know what you mean. Paul Lawrence felt there was a lot about his flat that didn't make any sense either. He had very few clothes there and, for a man who was always going to premieres and opening nights, there were no evening suits or smart shoes, only one pair of rather grubby trainers.'

Spencer began to walk around the boardroom table.

'He owns the rundown Volvo to move his dogs around, plus he has a flash Jaguar. What we don't know is what was he doing at the weekends. Where did he go? Did he play golf? What did he do on those blank weekends?'

Jane closed the diary. 'I think we should get a search warrant for the ex-wife's house.'

'Too bloody right! According to DS Lawrence, whoever committed the murder had to have been covered in blood.'

'Yes, we know that,' Jane agreed. 'But we haven't got the results yet on the footprints which were found in the victim's blood.'

'Maybe they could be female? They haven't clarified the actual size and make yet.'

'We know Justine Harris turned up shortly after the murder was discovered and behaved irrationally. According to the guv it felt as if she was going to kick the body. If you ask me, we should have been considering her as a suspect from day one.'

Spencer raised his eyebrows. 'Do you want to run that by the guv?'

Jane shook her head. 'No, it's just a bit of a gut feeling. If we get a warrant, maybe we'll find something incriminating.' Jane stood up and put the diary back into the envelope.

DC Tony Johnson barged into the room, holding the door open awkwardly as he heaved in four folding chairs.

'Guv wants the diary and asked me to tell you there is going to be a briefing. I dunno what time it's going down, but if not this afternoon then tomorrow morning.' He stacked the chairs and walked out as Dors carried in a heavy portable slide projector, setting it up at the end of the table.

'Commander Dartford and Detective Chief Superintendent Walker are in with the guv. They've been closeted in there for half the afternoon.'

'Did something happen while we were out?' Jane asked.

'I dunno. DI Arnold was in with them, that's all I know. Me and Tony are hacked off as we've been back running the station and working shifts for the usual array of shoplifters while you nobs are all interviewing movie stars.'

Spencer put his jacket on and gave a warning look to Dors. 'Mind your mouth.' He turned to Jane. 'I guess we better get cracking on writing our reports about the diary.'

'I haven't even started yet.'

'Well, we better get a move on. I think something serious is going down.'

'Finding a man disemboweled isn't serious enough for you?'

'No, listen to me, Jane. I've heard that Walker, the Divisional Senior Detective – the bloke who monitors murder investigations – is coming in. So the pair of us need to get more information and make sure we are up to speed.'

'Honestly, Spence,' said Jane. 'I've been doing report after report after report. I don't think Arnold is pulling his weight.'

'You're telling me that? Listen, I've been covering a lot of work in Arnold's absence and I've had no thanks for it. If the big chief is coming in, I want to make a good impression because of previously blotting my effing copy book.'

'And being demoted for it.'

Spencer grinned, unrolling a tie from his jacket pocket. 'I am going to prove, DS Tennison, that I am an exceptionally capable officer.'

Jane laughed. 'Well, if I were you, Spence, I would hold that tie over the spout of the steaming kettle first. It looks as if you slept in it.'

Spencer headed for the electric kettle, muttering to himself, as Jane took out her compact. If Spencer wanted to make an impression, she was damn well going to make one herself.

CHAPTER TEN

Jane had passed the diary over to one of the clerks, who had hurriedly taken it in to Tyler's office. She could hear the low voices from inside his office but did not know for sure who was in there. She went back to working on her report.

Other members of the team were arriving in dribs and drabs, some hurriedly typing up reports, others bringing in teas and coffees. The room felt stiflingly hot and clouds of cigarette smoke hung in the air. Jane printed out her report and went over to Spencer's desk.

'Are you going to suggest a search warrant?' she asked quietly.

'Yeah, yeah . . . ' He leaned towards her. 'What do you think is going on in there?'

She shrugged. 'I don't know, but it's got to be something big. I overheard one of the detectives saying something like Harry Belafonte was coming in.'

Spencer looked up. 'You're fucking joking! The actor? He's not on any list from the agency.'

'I think he was referring to some high-ranking fixer from Scotland Yard, not the movie star.'

She looked around the room as even more officers were arriving. Jane decided to grab a bite to eat in the canteen before the meeting started.

By the time Jane had washed her hands and tidied her hair, it was coming up to four p.m. When she got back to the boardroom, it was packed full. Detectives were seated around the table, apart from five empty chairs at the top. The folding chairs were mostly occupied as well, and she was thankful when Spencer signaled that he had saved her a chair beside him. She passed along the row and sat down.

The murmur of voices stopped abruptly as DCI Tyler walked in. He was wearing a short-sleeved white shirt and tie, which, by the creases, looked as if he had just taken it out of the packet. Behind him was shorter man who was slightly overweight, but with a square jaw and iron-grey hair, which gave him an air of toughness. Jane recognized him as Edward Walker. He was the Detective Chief Superintendent controlling four sections – their station included – and he had a formidable reputation. An old-fashioned copper who had worked his way from the ground up, Walker was known to take a hard line with his officers and was famous for his rigorous interrogation technique.

Tyler waited as the female clerk carried in a jug of water and plastic beakers, then poured a glass of water for himself and one for Walker. Three chairs remained empty beside them.

'I doubt he needs an introduction, but this is DCS Walker. He'd like to say a few words before the briefing begins.'

Walker eased off his jacket, placing it carefully on the back of his chair. He had heavy-lidded eyes and, Jane thought, there was almost a thuggish quality to him. When he spoke, there were still traces of a cockney accent.

'Right, I'll make no bones about it. This murder inquiry is at a standstill. I am in no way pointing blame at any one of you gathered here, but I have taken the unprecedented step of bringing in three very accomplished detectives who have, for the last twenty-four hours, made themselves privy to the entire investigation to date. We are very fortunate as one of the officers was here in London from the famous FBI training academy in Quantico. He is an accomplished criminal psychologist and an expert profiler.

'As you are all very well aware, this case has created a lot of press interest, and some of it not very welcome. I want to reiterate the warnings you have been given not to be drawn into any dialogue with reporters. I am also taking this opportunity to inform you that due to recent and ongoing health issues,

Detective Inspector Timothy Arnold has taken a lengthy leave of absence and will be replaced.'

Spencer nudged Jane. He was about to whisper something when there was a knock on the door. Tyler pushed his chair back and crossed to open the door. It was not theatrical in any way, because everyone gathered was tense and felt as if any one of them could be removed from the inquiry. The first man who entered was a thin, wiry detective with jutting cheekbones, his blond hair cut short, almost military style. He wore an expensive-looking suit and a blue shirt with white starched collar and cuffs.

'This is Detective Inspector Lucas Miller, who will be replacing DI Arnold,' Tyler announced.

Miller nodded acknowledgement and sat down beside Walker.

Tyler then ushered in the second man. He had red hair, pale, watery blue eyes and ruddy cheeks that gave him a boyish quality, but he had a muscular physique, as if he worked out. He was wearing what appeared to be an off-the-peg, grey single-breasted suit with a cream buttoned-down shirt.

'This is Detective Chief Inspector Jack Collins,' Tyler said. 'He handles serious organized crime cases.'

'He spends a lot of his time abroad on investigations, but as you can see, he never manages to get a sun-tan,' Walker chipped in.

Jane peered over the shoulder of the officer in front of her to get a good look at DCI Collins as a ripple of laughter went around the room.

Finally, standing patiently in the doorway, was the man who Jane had heard called Harry Belafonte. He was a tall, handsome black man and, unlike the two previous detectives, he was not wearing a suit. He had on a black turtleneck sweater and a fashionable jacket with dark trousers.

'Welcome to Senior Special Agent of the FBI, Harry Bellamy,' Tyler said with a grin.

Bellamy gave a relaxed smile to everyone as he took the remaining seat, pushing it back to accommodate his long legs.

There was a pause as Walker turned towards Lucas Miller, who gave a brief nod and stood up. He made a quick adjustment to his pristine white cuffs and began.

'Reading the statements, I felt it was imperative that we get a clearer idea of who the victim was. From all the conflicting statements, he comes across as a man of many contradictions. On the one hand, he's an exceedingly successful, respectable theatrical agent. On the other, he's a masochistic sexual pervert. On the one hand, he's well-liked, with an impressive list of clients. On the other, there seems to have been numerous people with grievances against him. Now, grievances about mismanagement are, in my estimation, rarely powerful enough to be the motivation for such a brutal, vicious murder. Which is why we're hoping my associate from the FBI can help us with a possible profile of the killer.'

He turned to acknowledge Bellamy, before turning back to the expectant faces in the room.

'I want to start with the person who has been most frequently described as having a motive, but we know very little about.'

Spencer leaned closer to Jane. 'Maybe we didn't bother digging too deeply because he committed suicide six months before the murder!'

Miller glanced towards them and asked Jane and Spencer to kindly move to one side so he could screen the pictures on the white wall behind them.

The room waited patiently as Miller prepared the slide projector, with the boxes of slides already in position beside it.

'This man is Sebastian Martinez.' Everyone turned to the wall as the machine clicked and a picture of a handsome, slender, Spanish-looking man appeared.

'Martinez was a very talented theatre set designer, whose work was much in demand. He was also addicted to cocaine and was a promiscuous homosexual. Martinez had accrued a number of awards and was possibly at the peak of his career when the accident occurred: A leading soprano fell from a balcony during a performance.'

There was a mild titter in the room, which was quickly stilled as Miller glanced coldly towards the offenders.

'Martinez was sued for producing an unsafe design. He counter-sued, blaming the opera company, but he lost the court case. His drug addiction subsequently began to spiral out of control. Charles Foxley was his agent, and he had encouraged him to counter-sue. At the same time, the famous director Zeffirelli had approached Martinez to design a film set. Martinez borrowed a significant sum from Charles Foxley to help with his spiraling costs. But by now two further complaints had emerged and Zeffirelli's offer was withdrawn. Martinez blamed Foxley for his financial ruin. Foxley attempted to help Martinez by purchasing his flat and apparently did everything in his power to keep the deal with Zeffirelli. Everyone has stated that Foxley bought the property for way below its asking price, but as he had already loaned a substantial amount to Martinez, he refuted the claim. There were heated arguments as Martinez began insinuating Foxley had ruined his career.'

Miller turned off the slide projector.

'The reason I felt it was necessary for you to be aware of this is that Foxley, contrary to what has been claimed, did try to protect his client, and after Martinez committed suicide, Foxley was never reimbursed for the money he was still owed.'

He paused and gestured for some water. He took a few sips before continuing.

'The point is, we have to be very careful dealing with people in this business. We're dealing with actors and people who sometimes lie for a living. Sometimes they'll tell very convincing stories, and we have to be on our guard against swallowing them hook, line and sinker. Which means, I'm afraid, that right now we still have no definite suspects.'

Across the room a red-haired officer leaned forward. 'Unless, like Dracula, Martinez came out of the grave to do it!'

There were a few guffaws around the room, but from his expression, Miller did not seem to appreciate the joke.

'Thank you for your attention,' he said coolly.

Miller sat down as Jane moved her seat back in position next to Spencer. She now felt that all the hours the pair of them had spent interviewing, along with most of the other detectives gathered in the boardroom, had basically been a waste of time. Before anyone asked any questions, DCI Collins stood up.

'I have been working on Mr. Foxley's finances. Gaining access to his accounts at Coutts was a time-consuming and frustrating process, but we know the dent in his finances during the period he bought Martinez's flat was considerable. He was then very generous in his divorce settlement. Although he earned considerable sums, he paid substantial amounts in alimony to his wife, on his own mortgage and on the property he handed over to her. He had no substantial savings, but often withdrew two to three thousand pounds per week in cash, which we assume he was spending at Mandy Pilkington's. I believe Foxley was also spending money on drugs, but we haven't found where he was purchasing them.'

Spencer stood up. 'We're still waiting on the toxicology report from the postmortem.'

Collins nodded and gestured for Spencer to sit down. 'I suggest we make further inquiries with all the agents in the company to discover if his drug use was common knowledge, and if anyone else there uses drugs recreationally. Mr. Foxley did have considerable earning power but it appears he was living above his means.'

He glanced towards Jane, who stood up.

'We have information that Foxley was an obsessive gambler on the horses, sir. On one credit card alone, he owes ten thousand pounds. Also, his will stipulates that his wife inherits his shares in the business.'

Collins tapped the table with his pen. 'We need to clarify just how the agents plan to run the company without him. Apparently clients are leaving in droves, but we need to confirm if there was a possible monetary motive.' Collins closed his notebook and looked around the table. 'I have to say that I have not come across a compelling one as yet; a motive, that is. Like him or dislike him, Foxley was a major part of this company and was able to secure, even in the last months before his death, two exceedingly big artists.'

As he sat down, Walker poured some water for him and topped up his own beaker. The last one to speak was Harry Bellamy, he stood up and gave a slow look around the room.

'OK. I'm afraid that due to the little time I've had, this will be a rough sketch until I've gained further access to all the evidence, specifically to go through the diary. This is vitally important, in my opinion, for what it doesn't say. We are presuming the dates and times of "family matters" refer to visits to Mandy Pilkington, but this can only be confirmed once we know just how much money the victim was paying out to her.

'Charles Foxley was a successful and outgoing man, someone able to deal with big stars and powerful movie company executives. He therefore must have had a great deal of self-confidence. But the flipside of that was his secret visits to a dominatrix. He liked to be abused, humiliated and whipped. The obsessive need for this constant flagellation – sometimes twice in one day – must mean self-hatred was deep-rooted in his psyche. This is an important area we need to uncover in his background. As I said, I have had very little time to familiarize myself with the case to date and will obviously have a lot more to say in due course. But my instinct tells me that this could be a key element in the investigation.'

He paused and removed a small notebook from his pocket. He glanced through it and then put it back.

'But we are, at this point, without a motive for the killer. So what do we know? The killer is almost certainly male, because of the strength needed to lift and carry the victim to the bathroom, slit his throat and then drag him to the bedroom for the disembowelment. And Foxley was himself a strong, athletic man, so it was unlikely he was overpowered by a female. That said, there is only one clear footprint in the victim's blood and DS Lawrence has determined that it was a size six Adidas trainer, which could suggest that a female was at the scene.'

A murmur of interest went around the room.

'Then there are the handcuffs. If we consider the possibility that the killer brought the handcuffs with them, that suggests they knew about his predilections. So we must ask ourselves, did the victim know his assailant? Did he allow entry to the killer because he knew him? The blunt force occurred to the back of his head, close to the front door. The blow would have made him semi-conscious, then two further blows followed and he was dragged to the bathroom.'

Bellamy flicked through a few pages of his notebook. 'The weapon used for the disembowelment hasn't been found. Which strongly suggests the killer knew Charles Foxley and went with the sole purpose of committing murder.'

Bellamy glanced around the room and then sat down.

There was a weighty silence as Detective Chief Superintendent Walker got to his feet.

'You will all now be given your assignments. Weekend leave will be cancelled and half of you will be working late or early shifts each day.' He gestured to the three detectives sitting next to him. 'My associates will remain at the station for discussions on moving the investigation forward. Some of you will be assigned one-on-one sessions. That's all for now. Thank you for your attention.'

Tyler opened the door for Walker and the others to leave. He looked around the faces in the room as he listed the officers required to remain at the station. Jane and Spencer were among them. He left the door open as he walked out.

The canteen ran out of hot meals and were now making sandwiches as the detectives waited to have their one-on-one sessions. There were a few disgruntled moans; some of them, like Jane and Spencer, had been on duty since early morning. The meetings scheduled were taking place in two bare interview rooms, in Tyler's office and in a corner of the incident room where DI Arnold's now empty desk was.

Jane saw Spencer heading into an interview room with Bellamy. She wished she had been allocated him, but instead she was instructed to meet with Lucas Miller in Tyler's office. It was now after nine p.m. Miller had a large bound paper notebook and beside it there were stacks of Jane's official reports. He gestured for her to sit down, and it felt as if she was back in school. Miller had a habit that she recalled an unpleasant geography teacher shared: when he looked at you, he didn't meet your eyes but focused on your forehead.

'I've been reading your report, Tennison. It's very interesting. I also now have the warrant to search Justine Harris's house in Barnes. As you live near Baker Street, I will collect you at 8:30 a.m. sharp.'

'Yes, sir.'

'The reason I'd like you with me is that I have read your interview with Mr. Foxley's ex-wife.'

'I see.'

'So can you explain the reason you thought the warrant was necessary?'

'I felt that, with her mother present, along with her friend George Henson, she was not being very forthcoming. She was also present at the victim's flat.'

'I know that,' Miller snapped.

Jane swallowed, then continued. 'I just felt that, with the information regarding the small shoe-size footprint, we should search her house.'

Miller gave a disparaging wave of his hand. 'That should have been done a long time ago.'

'Yes, but I don't know if you are aware, sir, that Ms. Harris attempted suicide. We were therefore delayed in interviewing her.'

'Yes, yes,' he said curtly. 'Now tell me, do you believe it was a deliberate delaying tactic and her suicide attempt wasn't serious?'

'She had to have her stomach pumped, and you know she had attempted suicide on two previous occasions.'

'Yes, well, obviously she isn't very good at it,' he said sarcastically. 'Now, I'd like you to take me through the entire interaction with her, if you wouldn't mind.'

Jane nodded. 'May I get my notebook, sir?'

'Yes, by all means. May I just say, Sergeant Tennison, that your reports are very thorough. They often contain inconsequential information, as if you are not really aware of what is important in an investigation.'

Jane felt even more as if she was in school. But Miller was ruder and more intimidating than any teacher she had ever had. As she went through her notes of the interview with Justine Harris, he didn't make a single encouraging or positive remark. To the contrary, he made her feel as if she were a rank amateur. He even made a very uncomplimentary remark about women gaining promotion too early.

She was finally released to go home and was told that Spencer was still being grilled by Bellamy. It had been a long time since she had felt so depressed. She wished she had someone to lean on, but it was too late to call her parents or her sister. She was also starving. She decided to have fish and chips and, without thinking, drove straight to the place that Dexter had taken her the first time she had been with him. She often wondered where he was and how he was doing, but she had listened to all the advice she'd received to stay clear of him.

And yet here she was, not even admitting to herself the possibility of seeing him. Dexter had real style and had showed genuine heroism when she had been involved in the bombing. He had also made her more sexually aware than any of her previous lovers.

She stood in line and ordered cod and chips with salt and vinegar. After Miller's grilling, she was feeling at a low ebb, so much so that she wanted to cry.

'Well, well, well, if it isn't Jane Tennison.'

Suddenly, there he was. He looked as handsome as ever, and a little bit sun-tanned. A bit like Steve McQueen, she always thought, with the same vivid blue eyes.

'Oh, hi!' Her voice caught in her throat. 'I've been working late and the canteen was closed, so I thought I'd come here. I've made this quite a regular stop.'

It sounded lame, even to her, but he grinned.

'Well, they do sell the best fish and chips in London. Are you taking them out?'

As there were only a few tables inside and they were occupied, it was obvious she would not be eating in the shop. But before she could answer, her chips were rolled up in a newspaper and put into a brown bag. She fumbled to get her purse but Dexter already had his wallet out.

'That's very nice of you, but it's not necessary.'

'I know it's not necessary, but it's good to see you.' He leaned forward and kissed her cheek as he put a five-pound note on the counter. 'Cod and chips for me, too.'

Jane hurried out and was so annoyed with herself she almost threw her fish and chips onto the passenger seat of her car. What a fool! She knew she must be flushed, her cheeks red with embarrassment.

It took only ten minutes to get back to her flat in Malcomb Street. She had just locked the car and was heading to the front door when Spencer appeared. He had a takeaway bag and a bottle of scotch tucked under his arm. Given the circumstances, he was the last person she wanted to see.

'Spence . . .'

'I'm sorry about this, Jane. The wife's kicked me out. I've got us a burger.'

'D'you want to stay the night here?' Jane asked without enthusiasm, as she unlocked the front door.

'Just for tonight. I had a bloody nightmare session with that fucking Harry Belafonte lookalike. He's a sarcastic bugger. He questioned virtually every fucking thing I've written in every fucking report. I felt like saying to him that from the little I know about so-called fucking profilers, he should have been sitting down with Paul Lawrence and the pathologist, questioning the bloody forensic scientists.'

Jane laughed. 'I felt the same way with Miller.'

She unlocked the front door.

'You know one of the things in my report that he picked on? My fucking description of that Mandy Pilkington's security guy. He tapped my report with his pen and said, "What is this?" You know me, Jane, I just put in brackets: "Looks like Odd Job from *Goldfinger*". It's a pretty good description of him.'

As Spencer passed her and went into the hall to go up the stairs, Jane was about to shut the main front door and thought she was imagining it for a moment as she heard the deep vibrations that could only come from a Porsche. She was right; it was Dexter slowly driving past her flat. He glanced towards her as she looked out of the door and he gave her the lopsided smile that she loved so much, but he didn't stop. He couldn't have been heading home, as it was the wrong direction. If Dexter had been intending to drop by, seeing her with Spencer had obviously made him change his mind.

She closed the door and trudged up the stairs to her flat, where Spencer was slumped onto the stool in the kitchen, heaving for breath. 'Bloody hell, three floors and those stairs are steep!'

She got two glasses and he poured them both large ones. They were both exhausted, and so hungry that they ate mostly in silence – she ate her fish and chips and Spencer consumed both burgers and chips, and in the end had three large glasses of scotch.

Jane only had a small two-seater sofa and her own double bed. There was no way she wanted Spencer in bed with her so she put the cushions from the sofa on the floor, took a pillow off her own bed and blankets from the cupboard.

'Don't worry, I'll be gone early to get a change of clothes.'

While she was trying to find a toothbrush for him in the bathroom cabinet, he lit a cigarette.

'You know what, Jane? I think maybe my time is up. You and me have just been given the crumbs of the case to investigate. And the way Bellamy spoke to me was the last straw. Do you ever think back to those days with Bradfield?'

She was taken aback. 'Don't go there now,' she said softly.

'I do go there a lot, Jane. You know, after his death, I was drinking way too much. I was well looked after, I admit that, but I never really got over it. I loved that man.'

'We all did,' Jane said. She didn't want to talk about it, so changed the subject. 'How's your band doing?'

He shrugged. 'I'm getting a bit long in the tooth to be schlepping out to bars and pubs. The truth is I've lost interest in it.'

'I think you're just tired,' Jane said.

'Yeah, I'm tired because we were sent off to the agency and hung around to get the bloody diary an entire morning, and then it felt as if I was being accused of doing fuck all.'

Jane stood on tiptoe and gave him a hug. 'I feel the same way, Spence, but maybe we are both just tired. Look, I need to get some sleep.'

'OK,' he said. 'I'll finish my cigarette, have a drop more to drink, and if you are sure I can't keep you company in your bed . . .'

'Goodnight, Spence.'

From her bedroom, she heard him moving around the kitchen. The combination of seeing Dexter and Spence bringing up Bradfield had made her feel sad. She had experienced so much since those early days when she was fresh out of the training academy. Hackney seemed such a long time ago. Having worked in equally tough areas like Peckham, and then with the Sweeney, she felt, like Spencer, that she was going backwards through no fault of her own. After the grueling interview with DI Miller, it was almost as if she was back at square one.

Jane found sleep out of her reach. She couldn't hear any movement from Spencer and began to toss and turn. It started to feel like a low-level panic attack. She had to force herself to breathe deeply in an attempt not only to relax but to stop the traumatic memories flooding back, but she kept on hearing Spence say to her, 'He didn't make it . . . he didn't make it . . . he didn't make it . . .' The words kept echoing in her head, bringing back the terrible aftermath of the explosion in the bank vault when DCI Bradfield had been killed, along with her good friend Kath.

In many ways, like Spencer, she had never really got over the tragedy. She had forced herself to suppress her true emotions, but it felt as if they were now surfacing uncontrollably and she couldn't stop the tears. She bunched the sheet up in her hand, forcing it against her mouth, afraid that she would be heard.

Eventually, after what seemed hours of tossing and turning, she fell asleep.

CHAPTER ELEVEN

Jane, in her eagerness to get to bed, had not set her alarm. She had never really needed it as she was always awake at 6 a.m. anyway. So she couldn't believe it when she heard the banging on her bedroom door, and Spence shouting that it was 8 a.m. She sat bolt upright, then had to lie straight back down again as her head was thudding.

'Is it OK if I have a shower?' Spence asked loudly.

She cranked herself upright again. 'Yes, go ahead.'

She had to sit on the edge of the bed for a few minutes before she was able to get herself together. She took out a suit from her wardrobe, gathered some clean tights and underwear and laid everything out on the bed. She pulled on an old terrycloth robe and headed out to the kitchen, desperate for a black coffee and a couple of aspirin. By this time it was 8:10 a.m. She was confronted by a dripping Spence, with her bath towel wrapped around his waist.

Jane realized she didn't have time for a shower and went into the bathroom, carrying her cup of instant black coffee, to get the aspirin from the bathroom cabinet. A short while later Spencer shouted that he was going and would probably see her later.

Before brushing her teeth Jane had to wipe the steam left by Spencer from the mirror, then she quickly applied some make-up and hurriedly went back to her bedroom to get dressed.

Spencer's head was thudding as he went down the staircase. He opened the front door as a police patrol car drew up and DCI Lucas Miller stepped out from the passenger side. He gave Spencer a cold stare. Spencer quickly pressed Jane's doorbell to give her a warning signal.

Jane was pulling on her tights when the doorbell rang. She picked up the intercom and said that the front door was open, assuming that Spence must have forgotten something. She went back to the bedroom, swearing as she noticed a ladder in her tights. She tore them off and was searching through her underwear drawer for another clean pair when her bedroom door opened.

'Good morning, Tennison.'

Jane whipped around in disbelief.

'I'm a fraction early as I wanted to have a quick chat with you before we headed to Barnes,' Miller said.

'I'm so sorry, sir, I'll be two minutes . . . ' she blurted out, quickly shutting her bedroom door.

Miller walked into the kitchen and looked over the discarded hamburger cartons, the open bottle of ketchup and a crumpled newspaper still stinking of fish and chips, alongside an empty bottle of scotch.

Dirty crockery and cutlery was piled high in the sink. Miller backed out of the kitchen with a look of disgust on his face and walked into the small sitting room, stepping over a large, damp bath towel. Spencer had at least put the cushions back on the sofa before he had left.

As Miller went back into the small hallway, Jane opened her bedroom door. She was wearing a suit, a clean white shirt and a pair of black tights. Miller glanced at her. It was 8:25 a.m.

'I'll wait downstairs in the car,' he said brusquely.

Jane went into the kitchen and saw what a tip it was. She was mortified that Miller had seen it like that. Her headache had now been replaced by a terrible feeling of nausea. She quickly rang her mother to say that she had been so caught up at work that she hadn't done any laundry or cleaning, and asked her mother to use her spare keys to help her out by doing some housekeeping.

Jane swiftly mixed herself a glass of Andrews Liver Salts. It was now just after 8:30 a.m., the actual agreed time Miller said he would collect her.

Miller was sitting in the rear of the patrol car, with a uniformed driver up front. He didn't attempt to open the car door for Jane to get in but stared straight ahead as she bent down to the passenger window.

'Shall I get in the front, sir?'

He shook his head and gestured for her to sit beside him in the back. As she climbed in and shut the door, the driver turned on the ignition.

'Detective Tennison, I am not one to interfere in officers' private lives but I think, considering the status of this inquiry, it was perhaps not a good idea to fraternize with an officer on the team, whom I happen to know is married.'

Jane was speechless. She was considering how she should answer when Miller flipped open his leather briefcase.

'Subject over and done with,' he said curtly.

'Actually, sir, I don't think it is. I am aware that DS Gibbs is married. He did not get released from the station until late last night and his wife told him he wasn't welcome to return home, so he asked if I could put him up for the night. He is a friend.'

'Whatever,' Miller said, as if he had absolutely no interest in what she had just said. He adjusted his cuffs. This time he was wearing a pink shirt with white collar and cuffs, and a Metropolitan Police-issue blue and white striped tie. His suit was neatly pressed, with pristine creases in the trouser legs.

'So,' he said. 'We have this chap, wearing monogrammed slippers and taking care of the deceased's pack of dogs, apparently living with the ex-wife. Is that right?'

'Yes, sir. Apparently he is a highly regarded producer and director. DS Gibbs has seen a number of his films,' she added wryly.

Miller waved his hand. 'Yes, yes, I know what he does for a living. I just wish to prepare myself for the possibility that he will be there at the Barnes property.'

They drove in silence as they headed towards Hammersmith, fortunately going against the incoming traffic into the West End. Miller made detailed notes in a leather-bound notebook before snapping it closed and placing it between them on the back seat. He tugged again at his immaculate white cuffs.

'Let me explain the way I like to conduct interviews, Tennison. You are to be an observer. I don't in any way condone the "good cop, bad cop" attitude. I like to question, and re-question, until I get answers. I would like you to remain silent and if and when I give you an instruction to do something, I expect you to carry it out immediately.' Miller gave a strange half laugh. 'Perhaps it will be a learning curve for you.'

Despite his obnoxiousness, Jane forced herself to keep her emotions under control, refusing to allow her anger to show.

As they turned into Vine Road, Miller leaned forward and tapped the driver on the shoulder.

'I'd like you to cruise past the property, do a U-turn, then head back. Take it nice and slow.'

The driver did as instructed, finally turning into the wide gravel driveway and parking behind Justine Harris's Mercedes. Miller waited for the driver to get out and open the rear passenger door for him, but he made no attempt to assist Jane out of the car. She followed him to the front door and stood slightly behind him as he rang the bell. Jane saw him touch the knot of his tie and, even though he was holding his briefcase, he once again adjusted his shirt cuffs.

They heard the sound of dogs barking for a few moments before the door was opened by George Henson, who was dressed casually in corduroy trousers, T-shirt and cashmere cardigan, still with the monogrammed slippers.

'If you'd like to go straight into the drawing room, I will inform Miss Harris that you're here. She's just putting the dogs out into the back garden. Unfortunately, we're having to care for three of them now.'

Henson opened the door and stood back while they passed him to go into the drawing room.

'Do you need a coffee, tea or anything?' he asked.

Jane immediately thought a strong black coffee was just what she needed.

'No, we're fine,' Miller said, walking into the room.

Henson paused in the doorway. 'I believe you have a warrant, is that right? Does that mean you wish to search the house?'

Miller nodded. 'In time, yes.'

'Oh, well, I won't be a minute.' Henson shut the door on them.

Jane looked around at the large, comfortable drawing room. It had highly polished parquet flooring and an expensive-looking oriental carpet. Two well-worn four-seater sofas faced each other, with a low, glass-topped coffee table between them, stacked with numerous magazines, journals and art books. There was an ornate marble fireplace with logs neatly piled either side, and the embers of a previously lit fire in the grate, and a grand piano positioned in front of the bay windows. There appeared to be silver-framed photographs on every available surface.

Jane sat anxiously on the edge of the sofa while Miller moved around the room, looking at each photograph in turn. There were wedding photographs alongside christening photographs, as well as various pictures of the couple at premieres, Foxley dressed in black tie with Justine looking glamorous on his arm. There were also photographs of her in various plays, framed posters from her film and TV work, and in a small glass-fronted cabinet were a number of BAFTA awards. Jane couldn't help thinking how different it all seemed from the austerity of Foxley's flat.

Miller stood admiring the piano. 'If I'm not wrong, this is a Steinway.'

At that moment the door opened and Justine Harris walked in holding a mug of coffee. She was wearing a pair of old, worn jeans, flat ballet shoes and an open-necked man's shirt. She wore no jewelry or make-up, and her long hair was caught up in a large clip. She had the most beautiful bone structure, but she was exceptionally pale. Jane had the same feeling she had had the first time she had seen her, that there was a vacant look in her eyes. It made her wonder if she was using tranquilizers.

Miller glided towards her with his hand outstretched. 'I'm DS Miller,' he began, then, to Jane's astonishment, he went on, 'I just want to say what an admirer I am of your work. I'm very grateful for the time you're giving us.'

Justine smiled briefly in reply, then walked past him to sit on the sofa next to Jane.

Miller placed his briefcase beside him on the sofa. 'Do you mind if I use a tape recorder?' he asked.

'I don't suppose I do,' Justine replied, sipping her coffee.

'It's just a precaution in case I forget something. I am sure you are very used to press conferences and being recorded.'

She shrugged her shoulders. 'Not for quite some time.'

'I'd like to start by asking . . . may I call you Justine?'

Jane caught a little lift of her eyebrow.

'Please do.'

'Well, Justine, could you tell me what you were wearing when you went to your husband's flat?'

She tilted her head. 'I can't really remember . . .'

'It is rather important, Justine.' He leaned forward. 'You see, we have to exclude you from the investigation. At the same time we are aware that there was considerable friction between you and your husband and there is a possibility that two people were involved in his death.'

Justine sipped her coffee, frowning, as if trying to make sense of what he had just said. 'I was wearing jeans, similar to these, a T-shirt and a camel-hair coat.'

'Are those clothes here, Justine?' he asked.

'Yes, my coat is in the closet in the hall. I think my jeans and T-shirt have probably been washed.'

'What shoes were you wearing?' he asked.

She sighed. 'Good heavens. I think I was wearing either these shoes, or maybe a pair of trainers. I can't really remember.'

'And are those trainers also here?'

'Yes, I think so.'

'We need to know if you got bloodstains on your shoes when you entered the flat. Do you recall noticing any stains on your clothing or shoes?'

Justine shook her head. 'Of course not. I was too distressed to. I suppose you are aware of what happened to me?'

'I would like you to tell us about it, if you would,' Miller said encouragingly.

'I was obviously in a terrible state . . . I drove home. I couldn't think straight. I was so shocked and I really only meant to try and calm myself down. I remember pouring a glass of whisky and taking a diazepam that I had been prescribed for anxiety, but I couldn't stop shaking and crying. I went upstairs to the bedroom. I just desperately wanted to block it all out of my mind . . . to not see his body. I took some sleeping tablets; I don't even recall how many I took. I tried to come downstairs and that's where George found me – at the bottom of the stairs. I must have fallen as I had bruises on my arm and thigh, but I don't remember. George called an ambulance and I was taken to St Mary's.'

There was a pause as Miller flicked through his notebook.

'On the two previous occasions you had attempted suicide, did you use the same tablets?'

She leaned back on the sofa. 'Those incidents were some considerable time ago. The first time I took Librium, which are sleeping tablets. I did not intend to take my life. I just wanted to sleep because my then-husband was discussing the divorce and it was becoming unbearable.'

Miller tapped his notebook. 'Did you write a note?'

'No, I called my mother. I was very upset and I was concerned about my daughter Clara, who, at that time, was at home. It was my mother who found me.'

'And the second time?' Miller asked.

Justine rolled up the sleeves of her shirt. 'I did this,' she said, revealing two large scars on her wrist. 'I just couldn't take it anymore and by then I had found out about my husband's perversions. I was frightened he would try to move back into the house, but in actual fact it was Charles who came and found me in the bathroom.'

'Did you write a note that time?' Miller asked.

'I phoned Charles at his office and told him that I was never going to see him again.' She rolled her sleeves back down. 'You have to understand, being married to Charles was like living in a nightmare. Beneath all the charm and bon viveur, he was a deeply angry and disturbed man.'

At that moment the door opened and Toots, the dachshund, trotted into the room. George Henson held firmly onto Jack, the Jack Russell cross, by the scruff of his neck.

'I'm sorry to interrupt, but Stick has got out through the back-garden hedge and he's wandering around on the common!'

Justine stood up. 'There was no need to bring the other two in here. Take them into the kitchen and then go out and look for him. He usually makes his way directly across the road. If you take the dog whistle he should come back. Unless . . . ' She turned to Miller. 'Do you mind if I go and get the dog?'

Miller stood up and switched off the tape recorder. 'Yes, I'm afraid I do mind.' He looked over towards Jane, pointing at her with his pen.

'Tennison, perhaps you could go and assist Mr. Henson?'

Jane followed George down the wide hallway with Victorian mosaic tiles and into the kitchen. He shut the door behind her.

'It's as if I have nothing fucking else to do apart from look after these dogs,' he complained. 'She won't hear a word against them. They piss and shit everywhere, and as for this Jack Russell, he's managed to eat his way through the legs of two stools. God forbid that you should leave a shoe out. He'll have it buried in the garden in minutes.'

Jane waited while he pulled on a jacket and fetched a lead, taking in the large farmhouse-style kitchen, with a white stove, fitted pine cupboards, and a big pine kitchen table with matching chairs and cushions. There was even a row of costly copper pans hanging on the wall. There was a warm, family atmosphere in the kitchen, with its fridge magnets and childish drawings pinned to the wall – so different from the designer one in Foxley's Kensington flat. It was easy to see why Foxley would find it hard to leave this house.

* * *

Spencer was in a car with DCI Collins, on their way to interview Foxley & Myers' accountant, John Nathan.

'Make sure you pay attention and take proper notes,' Collins told him. 'I read your description of Mandy Pilkington's security guard, Ahmed Farook, looking like Odd Job from *Goldfinger*. All very amusing, but why didn't you mention that he had a bloody police record, even though the offence occurred a considerable time ago?'

'Miss Pilkington gave him a very strong alibi,' Spencer argued. 'On the afternoon of Foxley's murder he was at her property, verified by two witnesses, and later in the evening he was driving a client. I did put this in the report, sir.'

'You cannot cut corners, Detective Sergeant Gibbs. It's standard practice to check out the previous convictions of people you interview and put the details on the descriptive form.'

Spencer nodded, taking it on the chin. He knew he had made a mistake, and after being demoted, he couldn't afford to make another one.

* * *

Once Spencer and Collins were seated in Nathan's office, Spencer immediately started taking notes, listening attentively to every word as Nathan outlined the financial structure of the company.

'Mr. Foxley owned fifty-two percent of the company, and Mr. Myers owned the rest.'

'So tell me about the other agents working in the agency,' Collins said. 'How do they get their percentage?'

Nathan cleared his throat. 'The other agents all have their own clients and pay ten percent of their income to the company for the privilege of working under the umbrella of the company name.'

Collins sucked in his breath. 'Ten percent? Nice little earner for doing nothing. So can you give me a breakdown of all the agents' earnings?'

Nathan looked nervous. 'I don't think I can divulge personal earnings.'

Collins leaned forward and spoke in a low tone. 'Nathan, I am leading an investigation into a brutal murder and as there is a possibility the motive was financial, you have no option but to provide all the information I require.'

He leaned back in his chair and glanced towards Spencer, indicating with a finger and thumb for him to keep making notes.

Spencer nodded. It was going to be a long morning.

* * *

It took Jane and George Henson twenty minutes to track down the whippet cross, and when they found him he had a dead squirrel in his mouth. It took them another fifteen minutes to restrain him, get the kill out of his mouth and drag him across the road and back into the house. He smelled dreadful.

'There's no way I'm going to wash him again, whatever he smells like,' Henson said.

Having wrenched the squirrel from his mouth, Jane was now more concerned about getting herself clean. Henson showed her into a downstairs toilet, which also acted as a cloakroom. She washed her hands, noting the expensive gardenia soap, then dried them on a thick white towel. She was just about to return to the drawing room when she noticed various coats hanging up, as well as a row of wellington boots. One of the coats was a ladies' camel coat, and the hem had what looked like dark bloodstains on it. Jane inspected the coat carefully but did not remove it.

As she stepped back through the doorway, Henson almost knocked into her.

He lowered his voice. 'I need to know exactly what's been happening in the drawing room. You have to realize Justine is an exceedingly fragile woman. I need to know if a solicitor or someone should be with her.'

Jane eased the door closed behind her and gestured towards the kitchen. 'Could we talk in there?'

Henson nodded, opening the kitchen door carefully so none of the dogs would escape.

'I understand your concerns, sir. But it's vital DI Miller gets all the information he can from Ms. Harris, given that she was present at the murder site.'

'I suppose so,' he said grudgingly. 'I'm sorry – would you like a coffee?'

Jane's head was throbbing. She needed a coffee.

'Yes please.' She reached into her bag and took two paracetamols from a blister pack and quickly popped them in her mouth.

Henson plugged in a fancy-looking coffee percolator. 'Black or white?'

'Black, please,' Jane answered.

She watched as Henson opened a cupboard, took out two mugs and a sugar bowl, and then went to the fridge to get some milk. He was very obviously at home in the kitchen. The dogs were huddled in their various baskets and there was a pungent smell rising from the filthy whippet cross, Stick.

'Can I ask, do you live here with Ms. Harris?'

He glanced towards her and gave her a half smile. 'You have to understand that I've known Justine for twenty-five years, ever since I first employed her when she was a young actress. I rent a bedroom here and use a small box room in the eaves as my office. I actually have a cottage in Kent and an apartment in Manhattan, and my two boys – well, they're twenty-four and twenty-two now – live with their mother in Los Angeles. I work from here when I have an edit in the West End, but I made sure I was never present when Justine's ex-husband appeared.'

He poured two coffees, placing one in front of Jane and then perched on a stool beside her.

'I am always here until Abby, Justine's cleaner, arrives. I don't want her to be left on her own.'

Jane took a sip of her coffee. 'Did Mr. Foxley stay here frequently?' she asked, trying to appear casual.

He shrugged. 'To be perfectly honest with you, I would say he spent more time here than he did in his own flat. Even though I loathed him, I didn't think it was my business. I just made sure that when he was here, I was not.'

'Were you ever represented by Mr. Foxley?' Jane asked.

Henson shrugged his shoulders again. 'It was a very long time ago, but that's when my dislike for him began. He was representing me in a big deal with a Hollywood studio who were very keen for me to write the script. Foxley made all sorts of promises, and then suddenly told me there was no deal, even though I'd written a script. Then two years later a film came out based on my script. We had a very unpleasant argument with a two-faced bastard at the studio who denied ever receiving my original draft. In those days, to even launch a plagiarism legal action would have cost around a quarter of a million. One lone writer could not take on a major studio. So I left Foxley, but I remained friends with Justine. I could tell you about numerous other writers whose careers have been screwed by Foxley working hand-in-glove with Hollywood studios. They call it the white envelope, where scripts are passed on without writers' names attached.'

The doorbell rang and the two dogs leapt up and started barking furiously. Jane could see the Jack Russell had been curled up on a pair of socks. Henson bent down and snatched up the socks angrily.

'This bloody dog steals socks, shoes, you name it. Goes into the laundry room, picks them up and usually buries them in the garden.'

Jane finished her coffee. 'I should go back into the drawing room.'

The doorbell rang again and she skirted around the door as the whippet tried to get through. As Jane hurried along the hallway she could hear Toots, the other dog, barking. Justine opened the living room door and the dachshund charged out. Justine picked her up and opened the front door.

'Abby! Come in, come in.'

A young Filipino girl came in carrying a bag of groceries.

'I'm so sorry, Ms. Harris, I didn't think I should let myself in as there is a police car in the drive.'

'That's all right. Can you take Toots and put her with the other dogs?' She turned to Jane. 'I presume you found Stick?'

Jane replied, 'Yes, it took quite a while. He'd been chasing squirrels.'

Justine shook her head. 'He is so badly behaved. My concern was he would get out onto the railway line.' She turned towards the kitchen. 'I'll come back directly.'

Jane turned and walked into the drawing room. Miller glanced up at her as he was labelling a small cassette tape and inserting another in its place in his recorder.

'I'm sorry it took so long, but the whippet got into the clearing opposite the house and it was a while before we could catch him.'

Miller ignored her, concentrating on his cassette player.

'I think I should tell you, sir, that after I came back with the dog, I needed to wash my hands, and I went into the cloakroom. There is a camel-hair coat in there with clear bloodstains on the hem and on one sleeve.'

Miller nodded and checked his watch. 'Well, I'm not finished here, so go out to the patrol car and get some evidence bags and start looking in all the rooms upstairs.'

Jane went to the door. 'I think Mr. Henson wants to leave now that Abby, the cleaner, is here.'

'Really? Well, I need to talk to him. I can do it here or at the station, whichever he prefers.'

Henson appeared behind Jane. 'I would prefer to do it here and now. I'm going in to edit a new film, so whatever you need to know, I can give you half an hour. In order not to waste my time, perhaps you should know that on the night of Charles Foxley's murder I was at my home in Kent all day. I had two guests for lunch and did not know what had happened until Justine called to tell me she had seen her ex-husband's body. I came to be with her straightaway. I can give you the names of my guests if you wish to confirm this.'

Miller nodded to Jane. 'Could you please shut the door? Thank you, Mr. Henson, this is very helpful. Please do sit down.'

Jane went out to the patrol car. In the boot of the car were evidence bags of all shapes and sizes. She started searching for a very large one to put the camel-hair coat in.

* * *

As Nathan outlined more about the agency's finances, Spencer could not believe the earning levels of some of their clients, to say nothing of the twenty percent cut their agents were getting. He was amazed that actors he hadn't heard of could be paid six-figure sums. Often their pay for a few days' work was twice his monthly salary. And it was becoming clear that Charles Foxley had been a major earner himself.

Myers had an influential list of clients, too; Emma Ransom and Laura Queen were almost equal in their earnings, and the next biggest hitter was Daniel Bergman.

Collins tapped the table. 'One thing you haven't told us about yet: Simon Quinn's modelingagency.'

Nathan stood up and crossed over to a cardboard box, removed a file and returned to his desk.

'This is a fledgling company Mr. Foxley was in sole charge of. No one else was interested, to be honest. The name of the company was KatWalk, with a K not a C. It was used to provide models for runway, magazines, fashion shoots and events.'

Nathan flicked through the documents in the file. 'The company is in its infancy and although Mr. Foxley injected a considerable amount of money, it was not making a profit. The only person on a salary was the young Simon Quinn. However, Foxley had agreed a one-year contract with him, so although the other agents here are not interested in the venture, Quinn is still on the payroll.'

Collins stood up abruptly. 'OK, thank you for your time, Mr. Nathan.'

Spencer followed him out. It was a relief to leave the hot, airless little room.

'I need to take a leak,' Collins said.

Spencer directed him across the landing to the cloakrooms and was about to go down to the car to wait for him when he bumped into Julia Summers hurrying out from the annex, carrying a large portfolio. She was wearing a very short mini skirt and a pink V-neck Ralph Lauren sweater. Her blonde hair hung loose without her Alice band and she had heavy eye make-up.

Spencer nodded and smiled.

'Oh, hello,' she said.

'Are you still working here?'

She gave a small frown. 'Yes, I am, but mostly with Simon. I'm just taking these photographs through to reception. Do you think you could take the chairs back from Mr. Nathan's office because we're interviewing some models this morning?'

She scurried away as Nathan came out of his office, carrying the two chairs.

'I think those chairs are wanted by Mr. Quinn,' Spencer said.

Nathan placed them down against a wall and said, 'Well, he can come and get them.' He returned to his office and shut the door.

Spencer heard a shriek coming from Daniel Bergman's office. The next moment Bergman shot out.

'Do you want to see me?' he snapped.

'No, I don't. I've been in with Mr. Nathan.'

'I have had a fucking awful morning,' Bergman went on, as if he hadn't heard. 'You cannot believe what I have had to deal with. I fought tooth and nail to get this piece of shit the part, and now he's on the set complaining about unrealistic dialogue. I tell you, the only unrealistic thing about it is that he got the fucking part in the first place. He's been shoveling so much coke up his nose that his septum ruptured and now he sounds like he's talking underwater. I now have to go all the way to Elstree—' He stopped and gestured at the two chairs that had been placed against the wall. 'Who put these chairs here? This is supposed to be an empty corridor.'

Spencer pointed towards Simon Quinn's office. 'I think they were meant for the models.'

Bergman, his hands on his hips, started bellowing, 'Simon! Simon!'

The young man instantly appeared from his annex.

'You know we do not have chairs left in the corridor. If anyone is early for a fucking meeting they are going to be sitting out here eavesdropping. Just get them out!'

Bergman was about to go back to his office when Spencer tapped his arm. 'I'd like to ask you a personal question. We know that Charles Foxley used cocaine. Is there anyone else in this agency that you are aware of who uses it?'

'Are you accusing me of using cocaine?'

Spencer put both hands in the air as if to apologize.

Then Bergman moved closer. 'I think perhaps you should talk to Emma Ransom.'

He then turned on his heel as Simon Quinn scurried over to pick up one of the chairs. He was wearing a skin-tight black T-shirt with an Iron Maiden logo under a stylish leather waistcoat. Quinn picked up one of the chairs as Julia Summers came out carrying another one.

'You can't leave them in the corridor. He's already having a fit about them. We need to put them up by my annex.'

'There's three girls already waiting in reception, Simon.'

'Just let them wait there until I have the chairs sorted. The fashion editor from *Teen* magazine hasn't arrived yet.'

Spencer offered to carry a chair and followed Julia along to the end of the corridor. Simon nodded his thanks.

'Just go back to reception and keep the girls busy,' he told Julia. 'And make sure we've got all their portfolios and latest photographs.'

Spencer looked into Simon's office. It had actually been created from part of the corridor, with floor-to-ceiling partitions that were covered in photographs of some stunning young-looking girls. His desk was stacked with so many files they looked in danger of collapsing. Simon was obviously in an anxious state as he ran his fingers through his spiked hair.

'Do you need to talk to me? Because I think I'm the only person who hasn't been interviewed. But now is *not* a good time. I've got to find a girl that looks fifteen as these teen magazines sell to twelve-year-olds. And they want them to look tanned as the shoot is supposed to be on a Mediterranean cruise.'

'I've been told business isn't that good.'

Simon pursed his lips. 'Who told you that? I'm doing the best I can, but it's like the blind leading the blind. Julia brings in all her posh friends who have never been on a catwalk in their life, never mind had a photo session. I'm finding it all very difficult.'

Spencer smiled. 'Well, I'm sure if we need to talk to you we can come back at a more convenient time.'

As Spencer headed back down the corridor, a woman tottered past him in high wedge-heeled shoes. She was wearing a turban headscarf, dark glasses and a red jacket, which appeared to be covered in gold buttons. She left a waft of musky perfume as she brushed past him, pausing by Bergman's open door.

'Hello, darling, we must have lunch some time,' she called out, before disappearing into Simon's annex.

Spencer was just passing the doors to the reception area when Julia Summers appeared, ushering three girls ahead of her. Two of the girls had white-blonde hair and fake tans, and the third was exceedingly tall and thin with red hair. All of them were clutching their portfolios. Spencer remembered Simon saying the models for this shoot needed to look young, but to Spencer, even with their faces caked in make-up, they looked like children.

* * *

Jane was checking the rooms upstairs, first looking through Clara's bedroom, which was a young girl's paradise. The large canopy bed had drapes in a beautiful pink and silver fabric, and there was a pale pink fitted carpet, stained in certain areas, most likely, she imagined, from dog pee. There were rows of girls' toys, and a shelf full of Barbie dolls still in their boxes. The night-light had dolphins around the shade, and the small bookcase beside it was full of children's classics. There was even a pink-tiled en suite with a collection of expensive-looking bath soaps, moisturizers and talcum powder. The fitted wardrobes contained tasteful young girls' dresses and shoes, and the dressing table had frills that matched the bed canopy. On the wall were numerous photographs of Clara with a little white pony.

The next room was a family bathroom containing shelves of soft towels and bottles of bath salts and perfumes beside a whirlpool bath. The cabinet had no pills or medication but was filled with moisturizers and oils.

As she came out onto the landing, George Henson was standing at the top of the stairs.

'At least I haven't bumped into you again,' he said smiling. He gestured to a room up on the next floor. 'If you want to search through my office, I will give you a code as I keep the door locked. My bedroom is next to it. I just need to get myself some shoes and a jacket.'

Jane followed Henson up the stairs and onto the next landing. He went to the end of the landing and tapped a code into the panel, which opened the door.

'My office . . . help yourself.' Henson went into the next room.

As he'd described, George Henson's office was really a box room. There was a filing cabinet, shelves full of scripts and film posters on the walls. His desk was an old pine table. Jane moved around the small room, recalling that two of the posters were films Spencer had pointed out to her at the agency's office. There were stacks of stationery, a typewriter and various notebooks. Rather incongruously there was an electric kettle with a jar of instant coffee beside it and two clean mugs. Henson appeared in the doorway now wearing an expensive-looking jacket and clutching a briefcase.

'I'm going to shoot off. If you shut the door behind you it will relock.'

He hurried down the stairs, then stopped and looked back up at Jane.

'Look out for Justine, will you? As I said before, she is very fragile. I've asked Abby to call me if she needs me to return.'

Jane nodded. 'Of course.'

Henson's bedroom was not much larger than his office. There was a single bed with a white duvet and pillows, and a comfortable-looking leather armchair. The fitted wardrobes contained two pairs of trousers, a couple of shirts and some loafer shoes. The monogrammed slippers that she remembered were beside the bed. It really did appear that he used the Barnes property as a stop-off residence when he was working in London. On the bedside Jane noticed a number of classic novels next to a small white portable TV set.

She closed the door and went back down the stairs to look in the master bedroom. Pushing open the door she was astonished at the size of the bay window-fronted bedroom. It had a thick, pale green fitted carpet and one of the largest super-king-sized beds she had ever seen, with an ornate carved headboard. It was draped in a green satin canopy with a selection of green silk and velvet throw pillows. The large windows had silk white and green striped drawback curtains, and a chaise longue was also covered in the same fabric.

The artwork on the walls were Erté fashion magazine copies, and the whole room had a feminine elegance about it. Fitted wardrobes covered two walls and Jane looked enviously at the shelves of pure cashmere sweaters, sorted by color and folded as if on display at Harrods. One wardrobe contained evening wear and furs, and the other had a selection of shirts, jeans and trousers.

Jane put on some latex gloves, then knelt down to check through all the shoes stacked neatly at the bottom of the wardrobe. As if thrown randomly into the mix was one white Adidas trainer, left foot, size six. It was quite well-worn and she checked the sole for bloodstains but found none. Jane immediately placed it in an evidence bag. She searched the wardrobes in the hope of finding the right shoe but couldn't locate it. The laundry basket only contained underwear and a night dress.

The en suite bathroom had tiles that matched the color of the carpet. Unlike the family bathroom, this was very modern and had two wash basins, a sunken bath and an elegant glass-fronted shower.

Beside the basins there were toothbrushes, toothpaste and face cloths. Jane discovered some standard Bic disposable razors, but not a cut-throat one. There were medications in the mirror-fronted bathroom cabinet and she took out her notebook to list the names of all the prescriptions, including Nembutal, Librium and Valium.

There were also herbal menopause capsules, migraine tablets and an entire shelf of vitamins. Jane shut the cabinet, frowning to herself. Apart from the medication and the trainer, there was nothing in the master bedroom that could possibly be relevant to the investigation.

She went across the landing towards a door leading to the other bedroom, leaving the evidence bags on the floor beside her handbag as she opened the door. Nothing could have prepared her for what was inside. The size of the room was on a par with the master bedroom, but it was very dark as the heavy red velvet curtains were drawn. The velvet color matched a thick fitted carpet and there was an overpowering musty odor.

Jane eased herself further into the room, trying to accustom her eyesight to the darkness while she searched for a light switch. When she turned it on, an elaborate chandelier lit up the room, revealing a large double bed that looked as if someone had just thrown the sheets aside. A crumpled duvet lay half on the bed and half on the floor. To the left of the door was a bank of recording equipment, stereo equipment, and the biggest television screen Jane had ever seen. The room had floor-to-ceiling bookcases, which held hundreds of audio tapes and video cassettes. On the bedside tables were open bottles of Perrier with some dirty glasses. A half-empty bottle of whisky stood on the floor next to the bed. Jane bagged the bottles for fingerprint examination to see if Foxley's, or those of anyone as yet unknown to them, were present.

It felt very eerie, as if at any moment the occupant would walk in. Jane looked in one of the wardrobes, which contained men's evening clothes, an array of expensive suits and shoe racks full of loafers and ankle boots. Another wardrobe was completely filled with pristine cotton shirts and on the shelving units were underwear, sweaters and socks. Dirty clothes had been thrown aside on the floor beside the bed, including jeans,

T-shirts, scuffed trainers and dirty underwear. There was nothing bloodstained, but she bagged the pillow and bed sheets to be examined for pubic and head hairs that didn't match Foxley's. She then looked at the desk. There were many rolled-up bank notes and she knew from previous work that they more than likely had been used to snort cocaine. There were small packets left conspicuously on the desk, along with stacks of scripts and more dirty drinking glasses. She took the bank notes and glasses and bagged them for fingerprint analysis at the lab.

The search was beginning to make her feel nauseous as it was obvious that this was where Charles Foxley had spent a lot of his time. Jane began to open the drawers in the desk, removing documents and photographs to sort through. She found some hardcore pornographic magazines with men and women having sex; from the writing, she guessed they were from Germany, though she knew they could be purchased in the seedy porn shops of Soho. She heard the sound of laughing. It made her jump and she hurried out of the room onto the landing. She could hear Justine's voice, accompanied by her high-pitched girlish laugh. Jane moved silently down the stairs and stood outside the drawing room listening. Justine was recounting a funny anecdote that had occurred on a movie set.

She doesn't sound very fragile now, Jane thought wryly.

She returned to the master bedroom to collect the bags of evidence. There was still no sign of an end to the discussion in the drawing room, so after some hesitation she knocked and opened the door. Miller glanced up at her, clearly irritated, with a large photo album on his lap. Justine was sitting with her feet up on the coffee table, smoking a cigarette. She turned in surprise as Jane entered.

'Are you still here?' she asked.

Jane nodded and looked to Miller. 'Would you like me to remain here? Or shall I return to the station?'

He glanced at his watch. 'Good God! I didn't realize the time. We should be leaving.' He put the tape recorder in his briefcase and stood up. 'I can't tell you how much I appreciate the time you have given me, Ms. Harris. You have been very accommodating and I'm sure what you told me will be very helpful. And if we need anything further, I hope you will agree to see me again?'

Justine stood up and flicked the ash of her cigarette onto the carpet. 'Yes, of course. Actually, I've rather enjoyed our conversation. I think it was beneficial for me too.'

Jane couldn't believe it. It was as if she had interrupted a couple of friends having afternoon tea together.

Justine went over to an ashtray and stubbed out her cigarette. 'I feel so bad. You haven't been offered any refreshments.'

'That wasn't necessary,' Miller said.

'I have made a list of all the items I have removed and placed in evidence bags,' Jane said, tearing a page from her notebook and handing it to Justine, who barely glanced at it. Jane looked to Miller before turning back to Justine. 'Would you mind if I asked you a personal question?'

Justine gave one of her soft laughs. 'Well, that is very sweet of you, my dear, but Lucas and I have been discussing personal things all afternoon, and I can't believe there's a question I haven't already answered.'

Miller gave Jane a quizzical look as she referred to her notepad.

'Ms. Harris, I noticed that your husband's bed appears to have been slept in quite recently. It would help if you could clarify when he last slept here.'

Justine shrugged. 'Oh God, I'm trying to remember. Maybe a week or so ago? I have already told you he was a frequent visitor, but please do not imagine for a moment that I continued to have a sexual relationship with my ex-husband.'

Miller appeared eager to leave, but Jane wasn't finished.

'Also, I know you have a young Filipino cleaner working for you. Does she also do your laundry?'

'My laundry?' Justine started to sound irritated. 'Yes, she does my washing. We have a very good machine.'

Jane held up her pencil. 'I'm sorry, I meant the bed linen?'

'Oh, well, that's all sent to the laundry.'

Jane persisted. 'Including your ex-husband's?'

Justine sighed. 'Yes, I suppose so.'

Jane closed her notebook as Justine approached and touched her lightly on the arm.

'I hope I've answered all your questions.'

'Yes, you have, thank you,' Miller said with an unctuous smile, ushering Jane towards the door.

Jane nodded her thanks. 'Mr. Henson said that if you need him, you are to call him.'

Justine walked them to the front door. She watched Jane and Miller get into the patrol car, then closed the front door. She stood there, her hand still on the door, as if frozen.

Then she suddenly started screaming.

'You two-faced little shit in your fucking pink shirt! You cunt! You bastard!'

She closed her eyes and took two deep breaths.

More calmly, she said to herself, 'You fooled him ... you fooled him completely. You are *such* a good actress ... you are *so* clever.' She smiled. 'He really has no idea.'

CHAPTER TWELVE

The return journey to the station was tense. Miller asked exactly what Jane had removed from the house and she passed him her notebook, where she had duplicated the list given to Justine Harris. He flicked through the pages and held it over his right shoulder to pass it back to her.

'Take everything to the forensic lab and get them working specifically on the blood and drugs. DS Lawrence will forward them to Toxicology.'

Jane put the notebook back into her bag. 'There was something odd about the bedroom that Charles Foxley had been using,' she said. 'There was a dank smell to the room, as if he had only left the bed that morning. I did remove the sheet and a pillowcase for traces of human hair, and a number of items for fingerprinting—'

'Yes, yes. I can read!' snapped Miller.

There was a long pause before Jane spoke again.

'Unless his ex-wife had been sleeping in the room? She may have been using the drugs, which, from the rolled-up bank notes, I'm certain was cocaine.'

Miller did not respond. He tapped the driver on the arm. 'I want you to drop me at the station, then take DS Tennison to the laboratories in Lambeth.'

Jane would have liked to ask him how his interview with Justine Harris had gone, but decided it was not worth getting another reprimand.

* * *

DS Gibbs and DCI Collins had spent an hour with Tyler, discussing the finances of Foxley's agency.

Collins gestured to the documents they had accumulated. 'With regard to the list that James Myers gave to DS Tennison and DS Gibbs, the inquiries to date have come up with nothing.'

Tyler sifted through the documents. 'Dear God! It's unbelievable! This eighteen-year-old actress is earning for six weeks' work more than I will in a lifetime.'

Collins shrugged. 'That's showbiz for you, sir! There was one area that was financially insecure and that was this new venture Foxley started up about nine months ago. A young lad, Simon Quinn, is running KatWalk and contracting sports stars for promotional photographic work. But it's barely covering the costs of the boy's salary, and Foxley had been putting in money in the hope that they could turn it around.'

Tyler sighed. 'Anything else?'

Spencer raised his hands. 'I know we're still waiting on the toxicology results from the victim. Based on his manner and the pace he seems to be working, I suspect Daniel Bergman might be using cocaine. I took the opportunity to put it to him, and he denied it, but he inferred Emma Ransom may possibly be a user.'

Tyler tapped the table with his pen. 'Well . . . ' He hesitated. 'Let's wait for the toxicology report to come in from the lab, then we can go back and have another interview with her.'

Collins stood up. 'That's me done, Lenny. I need to get a flight to the Bahamas and get my sunglasses out. In my honest opinion, I don't think the motive for this murder was money. As I said, Foxley was a big earner but the others were catching up. Only one person benefits from Foxley's death, and that's his ex-wife.'

* * *

DCI Tyler had yet again been caught driving into the station yard by three journalists. He had already radioed in to say he was arriving so that the double gates would be open, but he was forced to wait as one camera flashed in his eyes and another journalist shouted to ask if there was an update or any news.

Tyler put his hand on the horn and blasted it continuously, shouting at them to get away from his car. The gates opened and he drove inside.

Tyler was now in a foul mood as he made his way towards the incident room. It was becoming a daily occurrence with the persistent group of press waiting at the gates into the station yard. Even though he gave the station prior warning of his arrival, the ineptness of some of the probationary officers never ceased to amaze him.

Entering the incident room, he looked over to the team who were all at their desks, then went straight into his office and slammed the door shut behind him.

Miller's head appeared over the partition, then quickly disappeared. He was using the departed DI Arnold's coveted corner desk and had acquired a further screen around it for privacy. He was working with the FBI agent Harry Bellamy, who was listening intently to the tapes Miller had recorded during his interview with Justine.

As the tape was turned on and off, Jane was working at her desk and could clearly overhear. It was making it hard for her to concentrate as Bellamy constantly asked Miller to replay a section of the tape, stopping, rewinding, listening. The two men had been closeted together for almost as long as it had taken for the interview. It was coming up to five p.m. when they finally went in to discuss their conclusions with Tyler.

Jane gestured to Spencer, asking if he would like a cup of tea, and together they went up to the canteen. As they waited in line for their tea and a fresh cheese sandwich for Spencer, Jane was holding the empty tray.

'I suppose you know about the Adidas trainer, the one found in Justine's wardrobe?' Spencer said. He moved along the line to the cashier, picking up two Kit-Kats. 'Apparently DS Lawrence is almost certain it would be a match to the bloody right foot-print they lifted from the murder scene.'

Jane carried their now-full tray to a table.

'It's a bit ridiculous, isn't it? I mean, why keep one trainer and not the other? Why not get rid of them both?'

'Reality is, Spence, there were bloodstains all over her coat, too. Everyone knows that she was at the murder scene and she could quite easily have stepped in the blood while she was there.'

'Then why did she get rid of the blood-stained trainer?' Spencer asked.

Jane shrugged. 'I don't know. It was all quite weird at the house. Everything seemed really normal at first. In the draw-ing room, the lovely kitchen, in the master bedroom . . . then I opened the door into the room Foxley must have been using and it was horrible. What was really freaky was that it was as if he had just tossed the duvet back. There was an indentation on the pillow and in the mattress, as if he had just got up and left. I asked her when her ex-husband had last been there and she couldn't give me an exact date.'

Spence drained his coffee cup. 'Well, she may have been sleeping in there. He's been dead four days now, which brings me to no weekend leave.'

'How's everything with your wife?' Jane asked.

'She hasn't changed the locks, but we're supposed to be sitting down to talk to the in-laws tonight. So, it's either going to be "pack your bags", as they bought the flat, or try and make us go to marriage counselling.'

'Are you prepared for that?' Jane asked.

'Counselling? Yeah, I don't mind. Right now I could prob-ably use some. I'm in two minds about my career. That Collins bloke is very thorough, used to discussing finances and knows what he's doing. I sat in on the interview with the accountant at the firm and I felt like a spare prick at a wedding.'

Jane looked around the canteen and leaned closer. 'Have you heard what exactly happened with Tim Arnold?'

'I heard that he was out watering the window boxes at the front of the station, stepped back to admire his blooms, fell off the pavement and a cyclist ran him over.'

Jane shook her head. 'Ha ha. Very funny. I heard he was with the guv at the murder site and complained of feeling ill. I think Tyler had just about had enough of poor old Tim's stomach ail-ments and there were a few unpleasant words.'

Jane was about to get up and order another coffee when Gary Dors came into the canteen. 'The guv has asked for everyone to be at a briefing at six p.m.,' he said after spotting them.

Jane hurried from the canteen and returned to her desk to finish off her report. She was printing out copies when the FBI agent came and stood beside her.

'What is your opinion of Justine Harris?' Harry Bellamy asked softly.

'My opinion?' Jane replied, confused.

'Yes, what do you think of her?'

'Well, I have talked to her on two occasions and found her to be very pleasant and quite helpful, but I couldn't really give you an honest opinion as I haven't spent enough time with her.'

Bellamy turned and leaned against the side of the printer, his hands in his pockets. 'That's all you've got to say?'

'Yes. I really haven't spent enough time with her to give a fuller assessment. I do know from conversations with the peo-ple at her ex-husband's agency that she had a temper and could be very difficult. But, as I said, she seemed very amenable considering the appalling situation.'

Bellamy nodded. 'Well, good luck. I have to return to Oxford tonight. But I've given DI Miller a character study from the tape recordings.' He moved away slightly, before turning back to Jane and looking down at her. 'You may find my conclusion interesting.'

Jane stacked the papers from the printer. 'Oh, yes?'

He nodded. 'I'm aware that in the UK, criminal profiling is not seen as particularly relevant, but eventually time will rectify that. In my estimation it is, and will continue to be, essential in all murder investigations.'

He walked away with a smile Jane thought a little arrogant.

By the time she had filed the report, then passed a copy to one of the clerks to give to Tyler, it was almost time for the briefing in the boardroom. On her way there she bumped into a disgruntled-looking Spencer.

'I hope this bloody briefing won't take long. I need to get home for my crisis meeting with the in-laws.'

Their conversation was cut short as the officers began to fill the seats around the boardroom table. DI Miller walked in and sat at the far end, with his tape recorder and neat array of tapes. He proceeded to pass round the table the typed-up transcripts that a secretary had worked on since his return to the station. He glanced at his watch with a frown. The last to arrive was Tyler, who was beginning to look jaded and clearly needed a shave. He sat down next to Miller and nodded to the young DC to shut the door.

'Right, we'll make this as brief as possible. As you may be aware, we have already lost the very helpful DCI Collins and the FBI agent Harry Bellamy, who have both assisted our investigation to date. We have had a report in from the laboratory, and although tests are still being carried out, they are certain that the one trainer brought in by DS Jane Tennison is the left size six that will match the right bloody footprint. But we are still testing the bloodstains on the coat owned by the ex-Mrs. Foxley. We have confirmation that the cocaine brought in is of a very high quality. There is also a residue of cocaine on three rolled-up twenty-pound notes. The drinking glasses brought in from the deceased's bedside table are being tested for prints. The video cassettes are being reviewed, but they are all hard-core porn, along with pornographic magazines. We are also, at this time, checking through the many documents brought in by DS Tennison, which were removed from a desk drawer in the deceased's bedroom. We will be able to give further details on the various receipts and on a small leather-bound notebook, but not until tomorrow. I would now like you all to read the transcripts and pay attention to DI Miller as he walks you through each section.'

Jane and Spencer had to share a transcript between them as there were not enough to go around.

Miller, Jane noticed, had changed his shirt and was now wearing a fresh blue shirt without the usual white collar and cuffs.

'First, before I begin to take you through the tape of my interview, one of the most important questions I needed to ask the ex-Mrs. Foxley was: did she recall any incident, or time, in her ex-husband's life that would have given him such a propensity for his use of prostitutes, and in particular why he chose to be humiliated and beaten by obese women? This is her reply.'

Everyone in the room waited, even though they had the transcript in front of them.

The tape began: '*I was unaware that Charles ever had any sexual perversions. He was always a considerate husband, even though early on in our marriage I had to be the main breadwinner.*'

There was a soft, girlish laugh, her voice sounding breathy and young.

'You see, you may not be aware but I was at one time very well-known. I was working on a successful television series – I was actually the star. My husband was feeling insecure at the time because he was basically unemployed. I introduced him to my then-agent, who was a very dear man. He agreed to take Charles under his wing and train him to be an agent. As I said, I was very well-known, and to help my then-husband's career, I asked him to be my agent.'

They all listened as Miller fast-forwarded the recording. Jane noticed that he never included his voice – he was only playing Justine's answers – while on the transcript they had the questions.

'Did your then-husband find the situation difficult to deal with?'

'Yes, I suppose he did at times, but then he began to take over the agency and was acquiring more and more clients to represent, and he decided to open his own agency. I financed him again and I think it was around this time that he started to become argumentative. He was never physically abusive towards me, but I left him. I had an affair with an actor who was starring with me in a film. I regretted it, but then Charles actually chose to represent him.'

It slowly began to dawn on Jane that Justine Harris talked in different voices. Her high-pitched laugh, when she mentioned anything about her relationship with her husband, was breathy, like someone imitating Marilyn Monroe. But at other times, specifically when she was asked about the gaps in her successful career, her voice became more strident and snappy – denying that there had ever been any lulls that had not been her personal choice. When referencing herself there was always a slightly aggressive tone. She continually repeated that she had always made the choices to have any breaks, because her husband was becoming successful and no longer needed her financial support.

They carried on listening. When asked if her husband was faithful to her, Justine's voice changed again. She sounded child-like as she said in a sing-song voice that she herself had often been a very naughty girl. This had driven Charles to become obsessively jealous.

Everyone in the room was astonished at the sound of Justine giggling, seeming to enjoying repeating how much her infidelity had tortured her husband. She said it made him insanely jealous and he started stalking her. On one occasion he threatened her lover, who ended up throwing the weeping Charles into a swimming pool, fully-clothed. Foxley was humiliated by the experience.

Miller exchanged one tape for another. They listened to Justine's ability to switch effortlessly from being shamelessly promiscuous to a doting wife. She used a warm, maternal voice as she explained in detail how everything in their lives stabilized when she became pregnant. She made the choice to give up her career and take care of her daughter and her husband, who then formed the partnership of Foxley & Myers.

They continued to listen for another half an hour as Justine described their happiness in buying their wonderful property in Barnes, and how much their beloved daughter meant to them. She then discovered that Charles was using prostitutes, and even described an occasion when he had been with a prostitute who had later been found murdered. He had been terrified that he would be exposed in the press, and Justine had protected him by giving him a false alibi.

Miller turned off the tape. 'We know someone else was convicted of the murder, but it's interesting that Justine seems to have a compulsion for repeating how she had protected her then-husband.'

Miller looked around the table. 'Does anyone have any questions? If not, I'd like to give you the appraisal that the FBI profiler put together after analyzing the tapes.'

Miller waited a moment, then carried on. 'Justine Harris had a number of psychiatric problems, evidenced by the medication she was taking, the suicide attempts, and her stays at the Priory. She clearly has a manipulative side to her. Although she has attempted suicide three times, in each instance she made sure that someone would find her. She has benefitted financially from her ex-husband's will, inheriting not only his shares in the agency but also the property in Barnes and the flat in Kensington. In the interview she discussed her ability as an athlete and spoke of being a proficient tennis player and skier. In my estimation, at almost five foot ten, she appears to be a very fit woman.'

Jane was surprised when Spencer raised his hand. 'Do you mean that Justine Harris was physically capable of the murder of her husband?'

'In my estimation,' Miller replied curtly.

'So, she is suspected of hitting her husband over the head,' Spencer continued, 'dragging him to a bathroom, cutting his throat, then lifting him and dragging him to the bed—'

Miller held up his hand, interrupting him. 'We have still not been able to determine if there was more than one person involved.'

'Yes sir, but what I'm finding it difficult to come to terms with is that if she had committed this murder and left the premises knowing he was dead, would she have returned several hours later, when we had discovered the body?'

Miller looked unimpressed. 'It could be that returning to the scene provided a way of explaining the bloodstains she already had on her clothes.' He looked around the table. 'Anyone else?'

No one responded.

Tyler checked his watch. 'OK, we'll reconvene at eight tomorrow morning. We need to get all the results back from the laboratory, but the consensus is that our prime suspect is now Justine Harris.'

* * *

Jane was giving Spencer a lift to Shepherd's Bush so that he would be in time to meet his in-laws.

'You were quite impressive in there, Spence.'

'Yeah, well, he did his best to cut me down to size. I think he's a right prick.'

'I agree,' Jane said. 'And don't forget, I had him all day. Tell me, do you think Justine could have done it?'

Spencer shook his head. 'I think they're barking up the wrong tree. From what I've heard she doesn't sound very likeable, but I think she's probably just a woman with a lot of problems. There's something else too.'

Jane pulled up at a red light as Spencer continued.

'It's the dachshund. If she had organized someone to kill Foxley, would she really have taken the dog and left it there? Or, if he had the dog and she did the business, wouldn't she have taken the dog with her? It was the dog that raised the alarm to the neighbor.'

Jane's head had started thudding. 'Well, she's got all three dogs now. I don't know ... I honestly don't think we have enough evidence.'

She dropped him off and headed home. There was no thought of fish and chips or Dexter; she just wanted to have a good night's sleep. But as tired as she was, she made a mental note to tell the team doing house-to-house calls to check the garden at Justine's Barnes property. She remembered George Henson telling her that Jack, the Jack Russell cross, often stole things and buried them in the garden.

She was just about to step into the shower when her phone rang. She decided not to answer and leave the caller to go through to her answering machine. It clicked on.

'Hi, Jane. This is Elliott. I was just wondering—'

Jane picked up the phone. 'Hello, Elliott. I've just walked in.'

'Oh, hi, Jane. Look, I'm sorry if we got off on the wrong foot the other morning. I'm not used to training females.'

'Oh, I'm an exception to the rule, am I?'

'I treat you no differently, even though you are a very attractive woman.'

Jane was completely taken aback and not sure how to take his compliment.

Elliott continued. 'I have a session booked at the Milton firing range in Gravesend. It's a military and MOD police training center, and I think you'd really benefit from learning how to shoot at moving targets.'

Jane was in two minds whether to ask him how he had found out about her situation with the Sweeney. If Dabs had not been talking to him, then she needed to know where Elliott had got the information. But in the end she didn't have the strength.

Elliott gave her the address. 'And make sure this time you're at the club by six forty-five.'

CHAPTER THIRTEEN

Jane was determined not to be late and as a result had given herself double the time she would need. She had fetched her tracksuit out of a washbag, and as before, she put her towel in her overnight bag along with a fresh skirt, shirt, jacket and court shoes, ready for work at the station. She headed out towards Marble Arch and then Horseferry Road. She drove through Lambeth, across Westminster Bridge and on to the New Kent Road, eventually getting on to the A2 slip-road towards Dover.

It was quite a complicated route, and she missed one turning before finally finding the appropriately named Shooters Hill Road, before joining the B262 towards Gravesend. Eventually she found herself on a narrow road with high fences and a barred gate at the end with a small guard box and an armed uniformed Ministry of Defense police officer inside. As she pulled up by the gate Jane checked her watch and was pleased she was fifteen minutes early, though she wished she'd had something to eat and drink before she left home as her stomach was rumbling. She opened her glove compartment and took out a packet of Polo Mints, and had just popped one in her mouth when she saw Elliott, wearing a black tracksuit with the hood pulled up and carrying a metal briefcase. The MOD officer came out of the hut and had a brief conversation with him. Elliott walked over.

'Do you have your ID with you?'

She opened her handbag and passed it to him. He went back to the MOD officer, showed him Jane's ID and signed her in as a guest. Returning to the passenger side of Jane's car, Elliott opened the door and got in beside her.

Following Elliott's instructions, Jane turned right onto a narrow tarmac lane until they arrived at what looked like a warehouse. There were numerous white-painted parking spaces but no other vehicles and Elliott instructed her to continue towards a glass-fronted door with a keypad beside it.

'Is this used for training Met and Kent police officers as well?' Jane asked as they got out of the car.

'No,' he said simply.

Jane pursed her lips, determined not to be riled by him. She collected her handbag, locked the car and followed him to the entry door. There was a long corridor with various safety notices and rules and regulations in glass-fronted frames screwed into the wall. Elliott moved quickly along the corridor, then opened another coded door at the far end.

'OK, we are going to go down to the indoor moving-target range. We have the facility for half an hour before the troops come in.'

Jane followed him down the staircase to a long room, with wooden sections that looked like shops but with no glass in the windows. The only furniture in the room was a bare wooden table and two old chairs. She noticed a switchboard at the side of the entry door, which had eight green push button knobs, which she assumed was for controlling the moving targets.

Elliott pushed back his hood and lowered the zip on his tracksuit as she placed her handbag down on one of the chairs. He opened his briefcase, then took out a handgun and a box of bullets.

'You are going to be using this Smith & Wesson snub-nose revolver, which fires .38 caliber rounds. It's got a lot more kick to it than the .22 you used last time.' He carefully placed the gun and bullets on the table and, with his hands on his hips, gave Jane a sideways look. 'Have you been practicing your breathing?'

'Yes, I have.'

'Good. Now, I want you to pick up the gun and, with both arms outstretched, exactly as you would if you were aiming at a target, move around the entire perimeter of this range. Get the feel of the gun and your surroundings, keep moving and continually look to both sides of your body as well.'

Jane picked up the revolver and checked that it was empty. Elliott gave her a nod of approval. She extended both arms and carefully positioned her hands and thumbs in the correct way. Elliott watched with his arms folded as she began to walk around the room.

'Keep the gun up,' he barked. 'And look to the sides.'

Her muscles were already aching and she found it hard to maintain the shooting position and, at the same time, walk and turn without losing her balance.

'Keep steady. Concentrate!' he shouted.

By the time she returned to the table, her arms felt like lead weights and it was a relief to put the gun down. At that moment, the door opened and an official-looking man wearing army combat fatigues walked in and approached Elliott.

He looked at his watch. 'You've got fifteen minutes before the MOD police need the range.'

'We'll be ready to go in a couple of minutes,' Elliott said.

The man nodded and went and stood beside the green-buttoned switchboard.

Jane waited to be introduced, but Elliott just went over to the door and switched on a red light.

'OK, we are up against it a bit time-wise, but let's see what you can do. What's going to happen is you will do a walk round the building as you just did, only this time the targets will pop out in front of you from both the left and right sides of the range. You will have some targets that pose a threat and innocent bystanders that don't, with a split second to decide if you shoot or not. It is also imperative you keep on the move.'

Jane could feel her heart begin to thump. Even more so when Elliott loaded the gun with five bullets and said there wasn't a safety catch on it before handing it to her.

'So, I just press the trigger when I see the first target?'

'That's depends on what the target is,' he replied. 'The primary method double-action revolvers use to prevent accidental discharges is in the trigger press. Unlike other firearms, these triggers offer more resistance and take a hard squeeze to fire.'

Jane gritted her teeth and took a deep, slow breath to calm herself. Elliott instructed her to take position at a small cross six feet in front of the table.

'Shouldn't I be wearing ear protection?' she asked.

'No. I want this to be as real an experience as possible,' Elliott replied.

Jane wanted to remind him she knew what it felt like to be shot at after her near-death experience on the Flying Squad.

She took some more deep breaths, trying to control the panic she felt, and then he quietly said from behind, 'Take your time. When you hear me shout "go", you start moving forward down the range. You only stop when you hear the Klaxon sound.'

Jane nodded, holding the revolver with her finger on the trigger, ready for the life-like targets to appear.

He shouted 'GO!' and, as Jane edged forward, a target appeared in one of the mock shop doors. She felt an instant urge to fire, but quickly realizing the target was a uniform police officer, held back.

'Keep moving,' Elliott shouted as the target retracted back behind the door.

Suddenly to her left another target appeared – a man with a shotgun. She steadied herself and firmly squeezed the trigger. The sound of the gun blast was deafening and the recoil made her hands instantly jerk upwards. No sooner had she fired than the target retracted and another one sprung out on her right side. She turned and instinctively fired again, this time more able to control the recoil, but her heart sank as she realized the target in the window was an unarmed young female. As the target retracted, she turned and looked at Elliott, who was glaring at her.

'Keep fucking moving,' he shouted as another target – this time a man with a handgun – popped up.

Jane's ears were ringing and she had difficulty hearing him. She hesitated before firing and the target retracted, followed by the sound of the Klaxon. She returned to the table, carefully removed the two unfired bullets and placed them and the gun down on the table.

'We have to vacate the area now,' Elliott said as he put the gun and remaining bullets in his gun case.

'I shot an innocent bystander, didn't I?' Jane said, feeling disheartened.

'The range supervisor will have a look at the targets and let us know the results. In the meantime, let's have a coffee.'

'Right now, I feel like something stronger than a coffee,' she sighed.

Elliott ushered her out of the shooting range and she followed him down the stone corridor and up a flight of stairs to a small anteroom. Inside were worn cloth chairs, a couple of low coffee tables and a corner bar that had a coffee and tea-making machine and a few chipped mugs. Elliott placed his weapon case down and gestured for her to sit.

'Did I hit that woman?' she asked, sitting on one of the chairs.

'Be patient, we'll get the results in a few minutes. Black or white?'

'White, please.'

'Sugar?'

Jane didn't usually want sugar, but she felt she needed some. 'Yes.'

Elliott brought the coffees over and they had just sat down when the door opened and the range officer wearing the military fatigues walked in carrying two of the targets. He went straight to Elliott and handed them to him, again totally ignoring Jane, before leaving the room.

'Looks like you hit two of the targets.'

'One's the woman, isn't it?'

He turned the target to show her. 'Well, if it's any consolation, she'll survive. You hit her in the shoulder. You didn't shoot the police officer and you hit the target with the shotgun in the throat, so that would have incapacitated him.'

'I can't believe I missed the last one,' Jane said, shaking her head.

'You lost your concentration when you thought you'd hit the woman, and that slowed your reaction time as well. If I'm honest, and it was a real-life situation, the last target could well have shot you because your reaction was slow.'

'I'm sorry. I feel like I've let you down,' Jane said sadly.

'Hey, stop feeling sorry for yourself,' Elliott replied. 'Beginners always make mistakes. But the good ones move on and learn from them. Compared to some officers I've seen on a range, you did well.' Elliott looked at his watch. He glanced at Jane and, for the first time since she had met him, he smiled. She was astonished to see how it lit his whole face, revealing a completely different side to him. 'The most important thing, Jane, is you remained calm and didn't panic.'

She actually flushed. 'Thank you very much.' She noticed for the first time that he had a slight accent. 'Where are you from?' she asked.

He gave another one of those smiles. 'Oh, you detected a bit of the Dorset burr. But I've been a long time away from there.'

'What do you do exactly?' Jane asked.

He gave a slight shrug of his shoulders. 'I'm head of security at a customs office in Southampton.'

Jane intuitively knew he was lying. 'Really? And that means you get access to this place?'

He leaned back in the chair. 'Well, you know, we have a lot of problems with illegal weapons being brought in all over the UK, so I'm on secondment in London at the moment.'

'But were you at one time in the police?'

Again, he took her by surprise as he stood up and laughed. 'This is a bit of an inquisition, isn't it, Jane? Next you'll ask me if I'm married.'

Jane stood up. 'No, Elliott, I was going to ask who gave you all the information about my situation in the Sweeney. I asked Dabs if it was him, but he said he hadn't spoken to you. My concern is that my career could be damaged by defamatory gossip.'

He turned towards her, but she wasn't intimidated this time, even though he was a big man. 'Dabs is a good guy, and he didn't say anything derogatory about you, Detective Sergeant Tennison. Neither will I. I have a personal interest in your situation, and, just so you know, I'm not married. Now, I've got a meeting at Customs House in Billingsgate, so I need to get you out of here.'

* * *

When Jane got to the station she was disappointed that she would be deskbound, with the job of matching dates and names from Foxley's diary with the small notebook she had removed from his bedroom. She was also instructed to reconcile his finances, as Foxley had made a multitude of cash withdrawals in the seven months prior to his murder. They were now looking into the possibility that drugs were involved. It would be a long and tedious morning for her, but Spencer seemed to be in high spirits.

'You're looking like a happy bunny this morning,' she observed. 'I see you've got your favorite tweed suit out of moth balls. Nice tie, too. What are you up to?'

Spencer grinned. 'I'm going to interview two movie actors about Charles Foxley. One lives in a posh place in Hampstead and another not far from home.'

Jane signed out the diary and the small leather-bound notebook.

'How did it go last night with the counsellor?'

Spencer laughed. 'I reckoned counsellors were all a load of wankers, but this one was rather nice, with a great pair of pins. The overall feeling was that we should talk more, which is all we seem to bloody do. Anyway, it seems she wants to start a training course so she can teach yoga, which her father agreed to pay for, and hopefully that'll calm her down. So it's onwards and upwards.'

He walked off, whistling to himself.

* * *

Two hours later Jane was still working on listing the names from the notebook to compare with those in the agency diary. There were frequent references to 'KW' alongside the Premiere Hotel or the Ritz Carlton. These were often accompanied by ringed numbers of three and six, but she couldn't match any of these with the diary entries and she had not found any reference to drugs or cash payments.

She was relieved to see DS Lawrence arrive for a meeting with Tyler. He stopped by her desk.

'I've checked the list of medications that you compiled from Justine Harris's bathroom cabinet. Seems the lady is taking a cocktail of prescription drugs for an array of mental issues. We are pretty certain that the trainer you brought in, although the left foot, is the make and size of the one that made the bloody footprint. And we did some tests on the coat and I'm certain it will match the victim's blood group. You also brought in some of the bedding from the victim's bed – I wasn't sure why you had included that.'

Jane shrugged. 'I just found it very strange that, although the victim had been dead for a number of days, the bed looked as if it had only just been slept in and nothing had been disturbed in the bedroom. That's why I also brought in the dirty drinking glasses.'

Lawrence checked his wristwatch. 'Well, we've got a lot of prints, and the guy checking them out is pretty certain they were left by the victim. However, I did find two things of interest: caught in the pillowcase was one long blonde hair, and there was also some staining and another hair on the sheet. We are using a UV light test that will establish the presence of semen.'

'You know she is being earmarked as a suspect.' Jane said. 'What do you think?'

Lawrence smiled. 'I'm not paid to think, sweetheart, I'm paid for forensic evidence. I only deal with the crime scene, so I'm not privy to all the evidence, and I can't make a proper judgement about her involvement. What about you?'

'I think if she did kill Foxley, she didn't do it alone.'

DCI Tyler opened his office door and gestured for Lawrence to join him. He turned to Jane.

'Just had a bloody complaint from a neighbor at the victim's Barnes property. Apparently the Jack Russell is causing havoc in her pigeon coop.'

* * *

Spencer reckoned the three-story property in Hampstead was worth quite a few million. When he rang the doorbell, a young Chinese man opened it and asked to see his identification. He was polite, asking Spencer to wait and not closing the front door again, but nevertheless leaving him on the step. He returned within a couple of minutes, ushering Spencer along the polished pine floor of a corridor lined with modern art. He opened a double door at the end of the hall, gesturing for Spencer to follow him inside. It was an astonishingly beautiful, light, airy room with floor-to-ceiling sashed windows overlooking a manicured garden. Beyond the garden lay Hampstead Heath.

The room was sparsely furnished with a soft six-seater leather sofa and two matching armchairs. There was a block wood coffee table with the obligatory array of expensive design books and a large bricked fireplace with logs stacked on either side. There were steel-rimmed bookcases on every wall. Spencer was offered a drink and accepted a glass of chilled water, being told that Mr. Francis would join him shortly.

Left alone, Spencer moved from one bookcase to another, skimming through the titles until Mr. Francis entered the room. He was very handsome, and at six foot, as tall as Spencer, wearing a pristine white linen shirt with pale green corduroy trousers and leather slip-on sandals.

'Do sit down, detective . . . ' He hesitated, putting his hand out as if he could not remember Spencer's name.

'Detective Sergeant Gibbs, sir.'

'Yes, of course. And you're here in connection with the awful murder of Charles Foxley. I don't think anyone has really come to terms with how this will affect not only their careers, but their lives. He was such a genuine and well-liked man.'

Spencer took a sip of the chilled water and then, unsure if he should place it on the table, held onto it awkwardly.

'Perhaps not by everyone, though. Do you know anyone who had a grievance against Mr. Foxley?'

Francis crossed his legs, leaning back against the leather armchair. 'Well, obviously in our business there will be people who have petty grievances, some more than others, but I am not aware of anyone wanting to harm him. He could be a pain in the arse, but there weren't many people better than him at packaging.'

Spencer adopted what he thought was an intelligent expression. 'Packaging?'

'Yes, in simple terms you are making a package. If you have the star, producer, director and writer, and they are also your clients, that is a package. Charles was making major headway in packaging his clients for big film projects.'

Spencer nodded, still not too sure about what it all meant. 'And these packages are lucrative?'

Francis laughed. 'If the movie's successful, you're talking millions. Charles was leading the way with two or three big-money deals.' Francis sprang to his feet. 'Come into my office and let me show you some of the posters.'

* * *

Jane had been working with the help of one of the female clerical staff trying to trace all the cash withdrawals Foxley had made, and see where the money had ended up. She had already estimated that his visits to the brothel could have cost between £250 and £600 a week, but even if he was sometimes going three times a week, that still did not make a dent in the amount of cash he was withdrawing. She was becoming frustrated and about to break for lunch when DC Tony Johnson came to her desk.

'There's someone in reception who I think you'll want to see. She asked for DI Miller but I told her he was not available.'

Jane sighed. 'Well, who is it?'

'Justine Harris.'

Jane jumped to her feet. 'I'll use the public interview room at the front of the station, next to the front counter. I'll go in there and you bring her into me, all right?'

Jane grabbed her handbag and made her way to the interview room.

The room contained a small desk and chair, with another hard-back chair against a wall, and some filing cabinets. It was private, and that's what Jane wanted. She ran a comb through her hair and adjusted her shirt collar as Johnson ushered Justine Harris in.

Jane was taken aback. Justine was wearing a black beret with a black trench coat and was carrying a small leather clutch bag. Even with no make-up on she looked stunning. She waited for the door to close before she held up a manila envelope.

'Um, the little detective in the pink shirt asked if I had any photographs of Charles that might be useful, and also if there were any living relatives. At the time, I honestly couldn't recall anyone. Have you heard?'

Jane was slightly flustered. 'Have I heard what?'

'They are releasing Charles's body for the funeral, which I'm arranging for Monday.'

Jane just nodded, inviting Justine to sit down.

'I really don't have long as I have a hair appointment,' Justine said, perching on the edge of the chair. 'I just wanted to give the little detective the name of someone I remembered – Eunice Small. She's very elderly but she was his aunt. I haven't had any contact with her for many years, but when I found her number I called her. I am only inviting family members to be present at the funeral.'

Justine stood up abruptly and waved the manila envelope again. 'I've also got a couple of photographs I found; whether or not they will mean anything to you, I don't know . . . '

She adjusted her beret, tilting it a little more to the right. 'Now, I really must go. These diva hair stylists like to keep you waiting, but God forbid that you are ever a minute late.' She placed the envelope on the desk and then opened the door before Jane had a chance to assist her.

'When will I be able to put the flat on the market? Obviously the carpet will have to be replaced, but I would like to sell it as soon as possible.'

Jane felt wrong-footed. 'Um, I'll have to talk to my superior and let you know.'

Justine nodded. 'There is another thing that you may or may not be interested in. After the funeral, I have every intention of allowing the agents to buy me out.'

She closed the door behind her.

Jane sat back down at the empty desk. She wished she had not been so unprepared. She would have liked to have seen Justine's reaction if the hair discovered in the bed was verified as hers.

*　*　*

Spencer was starting to get slightly bored as Francis talked him through all the movie posters, outlining the plots and how successful each one had been.

'What you have to understand is, these are all independent movies. Charles had Max Summers brought in for all these projects. He is a major financier who worked with his brother running a film production company in New York.'

'Were they all financially lucrative?' Spencer asked.

'A number, I would say, but after the advertising expenditure, they were mostly just covering the initial budgets. The latter films were very successful and Max Summers' brother then did a major deal with two of the big studios.'

He paused by a framed poster of *With Dawn Comes Love*, featuring Francis wearing a thirties slouch hat. There was a large black marker-pen cross over the glass.

Spencer nodded to the poster. 'What happened there?'

Francis shrugged his shoulders. 'That's a reminder for me to always ensure I have a good lawyer check my contract. The poster was just promotional, but I was going to star in it. It was at the time the scandal broke about Rock Hudson, and it all became a bit unpleasant when the leading actress refused to work opposite me.'

Spencer frowned. 'I don't understand.'

'The American company had invested in it, and although it never really became much of a big deal in England, I was replaced. As it turned out, the film bombed and I know Charles lost a bundle. It was a while before he got another independent film rolling as the money men were pissed off at losing a fortune.'

Spencer was still confused as he tried to recall the scandal surrounding Rock Hudson. He suddenly caught sight of a poster on the opposite wall promoting a television series. It had a younger-looking Francis next to Justine Harris.

'That's Justine Harris, isn't it?'

'Correct,' Francis said. 'But it was a long time ago. It was a big Granada television production at the very beginning of my career.'

'Did you know her well?' Spencer asked.

'Yes, I knew her. She was also quite young.' He laughed. 'She was very promiscuous, even in those days. I'll tell you a very funny story. We were on location in Cornwall, because the series was a poor man's version of a Daphne du Maurier novel. I wouldn't suggest that it was plagiarizing *Rebecca* but it had a very similar theme. Anyway, we were all on location and living in various hotels. Justine was in a rather upmarket B&B that had an elaborate terrace with an abundance of roses climbing up to a small balcony.' He chuckled. 'It was all quite sad, I suppose. Charles was desperate to find out if she was shagging one of the actors – not me, I hasten to add! – so he started climbing up the terrace and got caught on the thorns and fell down, screaming his head off. Justine was furious and said he was stalking her. He later claimed that he was just doing it for a joke and was even

seen drinking in the local pub with the offending actor. I have
a feeling he soon after represented him, which is typical. Even
though Charles had made a fool of himself, he still managed to
get a new client out of it.'

Spencer laughed politely. 'Thanks for your time, Mr. Francis.
It's been very interesting – and helpful.'

The truth was, he was keen to leave. The glamour of the film
business was definitely starting to wear off.

* * *

Jane briefed Tyler on Justine Harris's visit before they sat down
to go over her notes on Foxley's diary and notebook entries.

'As you can see, Mr. Foxley was withdrawing large cash sums
almost every week. Two to three thousand pounds every time.
I made a list of the fees that Mandy Pilkington could have
charged him. But even if he was also buying a substantial
amount of drugs, there's about twenty-five to thirty thousand
pounds in cash I can't account for. I even costed the dog walker,
and also double-checked the gambling debts. Foxley used his
credit card with the bookies and the costs of the social events,
lunches and dinners are on his business card, so obviously he
was not using this cash for those things either.'

Tyler frowned, running his finger down the columns of figures. 'Maybe blackmail?'

'Yes, sir, that could be possible. The most obvious person
would be Mandy Pilkington.'

Tyler passed the list back. 'Well, we'll need to check this out
on Monday. I want you and Spencer back at the agency to question Emma Ransom about her drug use, to follow up Daniel
Bergman's tip-off she used cocaine. We need to know how
heavily involved Foxley was in drugs and specifically who his

dealer was. We will also need to have one or two of us visible at the funeral on Monday.'

He picked up the envelope that Justine Harris had given Jane. It was torn and had stains on both sides. He carefully withdrew the photographs.

'Did she explain anything about these?'

Jane shook her head.

The first photograph was of a young, blond boy wearing a yellow sweater, knickerbockers and long socks. Jane presumed the photograph was Foxley as a child. There was a black and white photograph of a young teenage boy, equally blond, and behind him was a poster of Junior Wimbledon league tables. He was wearing white shorts and holding a tennis racquet. Another photograph showed what appeared to be the same boy, aged about fifteen, in a rowing team. Lastly there was a black and white photograph of a plump woman with a lot of make-up and what looked like bleached-blonde hair, wearing a frilly blouse with a large pearl necklace and drop earrings. Her wide eyes looked distinctly angry.

Jane could sense Tyler's tiredness and exasperation that the photographs were not moving the investigation forward.

'I don't know what she thinks she's playing at,' he said finally, pushing the photographs to one side.

* * *

Spencer was sitting in Marcus Welby's comfortable home, enjoying a very nice cup of espresso coffee. Welby was a good-looking man in his late thirties. He had seemed genuinely distressed about the death of Charles Foxley and told Spencer that Foxley had engineered his career after meeting him at a performance of a Noël Coward play at the National.

'Even though I had been with my then-agent for quite a few years, Foxley was very persuasive. He promised me that if I left my agent, I would quickly feel the benefits. He said I should be doing more film work. And that's exactly what happened. I'm now working six months of the year in Los Angeles and I'm about to sign a contract for a big TV series after a successful pilot. And before you ask, that's where I was when Charles was murdered: Hollywood.'

'What about people with a grievance against him?' Spencer asked.

'Most people liked him, but of course you have to be a tough operator to be successful in this business. Charles was known for stealing clients. He was blatant about it.' He shrugged. 'I would say my former agent had reason to be bitter, but, like I say, that's the nature of the business.'

Spencer drained his coffee and placed the mug down on the coffee table. 'Would you say that, more recently, Foxley's ability to package films was what made him successful?'

Marcus looked surprised. 'So, you know about packaging? Well, Foxley had fingers in a lot of pies. By being an agent handling stars, and also having the other agents like Emma under his umbrella, it was easy for him to pick and choose the right talent. Foxley was clever, but he wouldn't know a great script unless he was told about it. He was predominantly a talent spotter. Charles was brilliant at using people like Max Summers; he even employed Max's brain-dead daughter to keep him happy.

'Max and his brother Ivor were a formidable duo. They were the money men and tough operators. I know they bombed badly on one movie that lost them all millions, but Charles managed to persuade them to finance an independent movie based on one of Shakespeare's plays. From being just an arthouse favorite it became an extraordinary success, winning the Golden Globe and God knows what else.'

Spencer tapped his notebook. 'That must have been a huge financial boost for Foxley.'

Marcus gave a slight shrug of his shoulders. 'Well, it certainly *should* have been. Somewhere around then, I think, there was a fall-out with one of the brothers regarding money.'

* * *

Jane had just replaced all the diaries, notebooks and financial information in the property lock-up when the news came in that an officer had discovered a right-footed, blood-soaked Adidas trainer in the garden of Justine Harris's Barnes property.

Although this new development caused a ripple of interest among the assembled officers, there were no blood drops on top of the shoe, eyelets or laces, so no evidence that Justine had been present when the murder took place.

Tyler was more interested in the four photographs Justine Harris had brought in, which he was now pinning up on the incident board. The name 'Eunice Small, Foxley's aunt' had also been added.

Tyler loosened his tie. 'There'll be a briefing later this afternoon, but I know people are worn out, so I'm thinking of only retaining a skeleton staff for Sunday, and everyone else can have the day off.'

There were muted cheers as he returned to his office.

Jane was just clearing her desk when Spencer called in. She told him that they may be given Sunday off, but that it was likely they would all be wanted for an early briefing on Monday morning.

'Did you find anything I should add to the board?' Jane asked.

'Yeah, we need to investigate Max Summers, a film financier with his brother Ivor, who lives in New York.'

Jane jotted down the names in her notebook as Spencer continued.

'Remember we interviewed Max's daughter, Julia? She was the ditsy girl who had Foxley's diary at her home.'

Jane tapped the pad with her pencil. 'Interesting . . . Maybe her daddy wanted to look at something in it. You need to double-check that the guv doesn't want you in, Spence.'

'OK, will do.'

Jane replaced the receiver and crossed to the incident board, picking up the marker pen. She wrote the two financiers' names and then drew an arrow from them to the young girl who had worked as a secretary for Charles Foxley.

CHAPTER FOURTEEN

As usual Jane woke at six a.m. She took a long bath and then called her parents, asking if they could have lunch. They were delighted.

On her way, Jane bought a large bouquet of flowers for her mother, to thank her for cleaning her flat and doing her laundry. When she got there, Jane managed to relax for the first time in a while; nobody discussed the murder and the Sunday newspapers were left unread. The Charles Foxley case was clearly no longer front-page news.

Jane was carrying a bowl of her mother's terrific roast potatoes to the table, and as she placed it down, Mrs. Tennison pointed to Jane's hand.

'Where did you get that from?'

Jane flinched. 'What?'

'You have a nasty bruise by your thumb.'

By now, the bruise between her thumb and forefinger from firing a gun had become even more prominent.

'It's nothing. I caught it on the typewriter.'

'How do you get a bruise like that from a typewriter?' her mother asked.

'Well, I was lifting the typewriter from one desk to another,' Jane lied.

'Oh, I see.'

By the time they had finished lunch and Jane had asked all the necessary questions about her sister and the grandchildren, the obligatory queries about her private life began, but since she didn't really have one, for once they were easy to deal with.

Jane returned home, washed her hair and, with the clean sheets her mother had laundered, made up her bed before hanging up her suit for the following day. She felt better for some time away from the case, even with all her mother's questions.

As she lay in bed after watching some TV, she started thinking about herself. She began to realize that her life was almost entirely bound up in her work; the only area that was different was the sessions with Elliott. She felt that not only had she improved her shooting, there was also some progress in their relationship.

She got up and poured herself a stiff whisky. She then opened the kitchen cutlery drawer and found the crumpled pack of Marlboro cigarettes. Sitting with the whisky and a cigarette, she began to play over in her mind the conversation she'd had with Elliott. What had he meant when he said he had a personal interest in her situation?

Jane inhaled deeply. It didn't make sense. Why would he have any interest in her? She asked herself whether she would ever find him attractive. She topped up her glass and took another drag of her cigarette. She had liked his smile when it suddenly appeared. But then, the more she thought about it, the more she knew that something didn't quite make sense. The only person who perhaps could answer her questions was Dabs. And even though she knew she shouldn't, she got off the kitchen stool and went to call him.

'Hello?' It was Joan, his wife, and she sounded anxious.

'Joan, it's Jane, Jane Tennison. I'm sorry it's rather late. I just wanted to have a quick word with Dabs if he's there.'

'I'm afraid he's not, dear. He is out at York Hall at a charity boxing event. I don't know what time he will be in, but do you need him to call you?'

'No, thanks, Joan. Sorry to bother you.'

Jane hung up, instantly regretting the call and thinking that she'd sounded drunk, but the whisky had given her Dutch courage, so the next person she called was Elliott. The phone rang and there was no answer.

* * *

Jane was in the canteen eating scrambled eggs on toast and drinking coffee when a disgruntled DC Dors came in. He limped over to join her, carrying his tray.

'That bloody dog should be put down. You have no idea how much stuff we found buried in the garden. Then we had this woman screaming her head off because the little bugger had a pigeon in his mouth.'

The canteen was filling up as everyone knew Tyler had called for a very early briefing. All the officers involved in the investigation were supposed to be present. Through mouthfuls of his full English breakfast, Dors complained how he'd thought being sent to Justine Harris's property would be a welcome break from the perpetual onslaught of pickpockets.

'They didn't tell me I'd be digging up her effing garden all afternoon, and then I get attacked by that bloody Jack Russell.'

Jane found her scrambled eggs a little watery, so put them to one side.

'Still, you found the bloodstained trainer,' she said affably.

'I didn't, it was one of the other blokes. I found a beautiful velvet slipper, though – man's, embroidered.' He ate a large mouthful of egg and bacon, as a spruced-up Spencer appeared with a bowl of cornflakes. Spencer picked up a spare chair from the next table and joined them.

'I've had a big breakthrough,' he said, pouring the sugar shaker over his cornflakes.

'Is it to do with those two financiers?' Jane asked.

'No, no, no, nothing to do with the bloody investigation. One of the blokes in our band taped one of our jam sessions and sent it in to Sony Records. He called me on Saturday night to say that we might have a deal. You could be looking at a recording artiste.'

Jane smiled warmly. 'That's terrific, Spence! I really hope you get lucky.'

DCI Tyler, with a tray of eggs and bacon, was passing and paused. 'What are you hoping to get lucky about, sergeant? I hope it's a bloody arrest for our case.'

'No, sir, just something connected to my band.'

It was quite unusual for Tyler to join any of the team for breakfast, but he sat down at the adjoining table and asked Dors to pass the HP sauce.

'Before we start the briefing this morning, Charles Foxley's body was released from the mortuary to the funeral home and the coroner has released him for burial. This will take place at Putney Crematorium at midday today. His ex-wife has requested there be only family members. She has only disclosed the funeral time to me to avoid any press, photographers, etc. However, I myself will be going, and Jane, I'd like you to accompany me.'

'Yes, sir.'

Spencer was munching his way through his bowl of corn-flakes and waved his spoon. 'We've organized a warrant and will be at Mandy Pilkington's home this morning.'

Tyler looked unhappy. 'She should have been identified as a suspect as soon as we knew about her business, even more so since a handcuff was attached to Foxley's wrist. I'm sure you are all aware that I've been rapped over the knuckles because her premises should've been searched earlier and pressure put on her because she is running an illegal brothel.'

Spencer wanted to make it clear that he had brought the details to the attention of everyone, but as DCI Collins had already given him a ticking off, he felt it would be wise to keep his mouth shut.

Tyler pointed to Spencer with his knife. 'I want you, Spencer, to accompany DI Miller on the search. Because of the delay, if there was anything of value to the investigation, she has had plenty of time to get rid of it.'

'Yes, guv.' Spencer stood up, keen to make himself scarce before any other accusations could be thrown at him.

* * *

Florence Harris had arrived in a chauffeured Mercedes with dark tinted windows, hired from her local Ascot luxury car company. She was accompanied by Clara, her granddaughter, and two large designer shopping bags. Clara was wearing dungarees and a thick sweater, her hair held back in two plaits.

The driver opened the boot and removed one suitcase. The dogs barked furiously as they waited for the front door to open. Eventually George Henson, after bellowing for the dogs to be quiet, let them in.

Florence dropped the shopping bags to hug him. 'I'm so glad you're here, dearest. Could you just check that the car is what she would want? There aren't many of this model with blacked-out windows in Ascot. You'd think there would be loads of them with all the races. Anyway, go and see if it's OK, otherwise we'll have to order another one.'

The dogs continued barking from the kitchen as George looked out through the window. 'I'm sure it'll be perfect,' he said.

Justine appeared at the top of the stairs with a towel wrapped around her hair, wearing an old dressing gown. 'Did you find a coat for Clara? She has to have one of those coats with a black velvet collar and little black velvet buttons.'

'For goodness' sake, Justine, I said I would get the coat, and I've got it. And we got a lovely dark navy cashmere dress with a little white collar for her to wear.'

'That's good.' Justine looked down at her daughter, who stood forlornly with her head bowed, holding her grandmother's hand. 'You can wear white tights and your black patent-leather shoes.'

'They're too small.' Clara pouted.

'Nevertheless, you will be wearing them.' Justine turned away, stopped, then leaned over the bannister. 'George, will you be a darling and give them some food to shut them up? I've got a man out in the garden, putting in a proper fence so that Jack can't get out again. The next-door neighbor is driving me mad just because he killed one of her pigeons. Oh . . . ' She turned back to her mother. 'I found some old photographs in the garage. The detectives were asking for photographs of Charles's family or something. You won't believe it, but I found Eunice's phone number.'

'Who is Eunice?' Florence asked, removing her coat.

'Eunice Small. God knows how old she must be now, but she's still alive, apparently. She was Charles's aunt. Anyway, I told her about the funeral. Whether she'll be at the crematorium I don't know.'

'I don't recall meeting her,' Florence said.

'Well, it doesn't really matter. I have to go and do my hair. Clara, go up to your bedroom and ask Grandma to wash your hair. I want you looking beautiful this afternoon.'

Florence sighed and gently drew the child towards her. 'You don't have to make yourself look beautiful, because you already are. And you'll only have to wear the shoes for a short time – crematorium services are always very short.'

Clara's washed-out blue eyes looked up at her grandma. 'Will I be able to see the coffin burn?' she asked.

'Oh, no. A curtain will close as it goes into the furnace. When my father went in, it only took a few minutes. I always think it's such a waste of money, buying an expensive coffin. I used to think that they took them out first, but I was assured they never did.'

George closed the kitchen door, having thrown a handful of biscuits in to quiet the dogs. Overhearing their conversation, he looked at the pale-faced child but knew it was not his place to say anything comforting. As far as he was concerned, he'd be perfectly happy watching Charles Foxley going up in flames.

*   *   *

At the station the briefing continued, as one by one the officers involved in the investigation gave their updates. Some of them had made inquiries at two tennis clubs, asking about Charles Foxley. They reported that he was an infrequent player but exceptionally strong. He appeared not to socialize with any other members, always arriving with associates of his he brought in as guests. Another officer had been investigating Foxley's gambling and said that it was unusual for him to delay payment, but he was a very frequent gambler who sometimes lost heavily.

There was a lot of information to communicate, and it ended up being a lengthy meeting. Eventually it was Spencer's turn to discuss his report, focusing on the two financiers, Max and Ivor Summers, and explaining how they had backed a number of projects that had been packaged by Charles Foxley and sustained substantial losses from two independent movies. He explained that he and DCI Collins had met with the company accountant and that the separate account for Foxley & Myers' independent film section was now showing strong profit, although it had suffered serious losses over a two-year period.

DCS Walker raised his finger. 'When you say that Foxley had major financial problems two years ago, how much would you say he was in debt?'

'Well, sir, the way Foxley handled these losses was by ploughing a lot of his commission from his clients back into the company to keep it afloat. So he was very adept at moving money.'

Walker nodded. 'What do we know about these Summers fellows?'

Spencer pulled at his tie again. 'Their parents were originally from Prague but the brothers were brought up in New York. One is a major property developer and helped finance the other's independent film company.'

Walker nodded and gestured for Spencer to sit down. 'We should investigate both of them.'

Two more officers detailed the results of their interviews with various actors represented by Foxley, but none of them had said anything negative about him.

Finally it was Jane's turn. She went into some detail about her work on Charles Foxley's financial records, and the contents of his desk diary from his office and his personal notebook. She also repeated that she had been unable to reconcile as much as £30,000 of his cash withdrawals and her suspicion was that he may have been being blackmailed, but they had not yet organized another interview with Mandy Pilkington. They had also not identified anyone who could be his drug dealer and nobody had confirmed that Foxley was actually a drug user. But Jane felt it was imperative that they continue that line of inquiry.

Jane was closing her notebook when Spencer nudged her. She looked up and DCS Walker pointed at her.

'From what you've just said, Tennison, you think that our victim was potentially being blackmailed. Do you think that it could possibly be drug-related? Have you any other thoughts?'

Jane cleared her throat. 'It could be drug-related, or it could be that he was being blackmailed because of his visits to Mandy Pilkington.'

Walker nodded. 'I don't really buy that. If he's paying through the nose to a dominatrix, why would she kill the golden goose? Ditto your drug dealer.' He slowly stood up. 'You've all been very diligent, but not one of you has brought to the table a possible motive that I can support. That said, we will be interviewing Mandy Pilkington, and DI Miller will be leading on that. I think there's a consensus that his ex-wife, Justine Harris, may have been involved – possibly with at least one other person. But at this point we don't have enough evidence to arrest her.

'I now suggest we bring in George Henson, because I think we need to go back to square one. That's it, everyone. Thank you for your attendance.'

There was an air of gloom as Tyler and Walker left.

Jane overheard one of the officers talking quietly to another. 'I say Walker is going to pull half the team off, and replace Tyler . . .'

* * *

Jane was at her desk when DI Miller, wearing yet another of his blue and white shirts, was leaving with Spencer to go to Mandy Pilkington's house in Clapham. She had agreed to be interviewed but had used her ill health as a reason for not being brought to the station.

As Spencer passed Jane, he whispered out of the corner of his mouth, 'I'm looking forward to this.'

Shortly after they left, DCI Tyler, wearing a dark coat over his suit, came out of his office and signaled to Jane that they should leave for the funeral. Jane was wearing a neat black suit with a white shirt. She carried a black raincoat over her arm.

On the way to the crematorium Tyler was quiet, staring through the window as he sat next to the driver.

'We got a lot of stick at the press conference earlier,' he said quietly. 'I've honestly never known anything like this.'

Jane was unsure what to say. It didn't feel as if he was talking to her, but then he turned his head and asked if she had contacted Eunice Small.

'I did try, sir, but there was no reply.'

'That'll be another waste of time . . .' He turned back to stare through the window.

There was a long pause before he spoke, and again, he seemed to be talking to himself.

'Seven days and we still don't have a solid motive or a suspect.' He turned to look back at Jane. 'Is it the ex-wife?'

Not waiting for an answer, he turned back again to stare through the window.

'Did she hate him that much? He spent almost every weekend living with her in the house that she got in the divorce. It just doesn't make sense. She doesn't need money. Was it maybe because she couldn't have him?'

'I don't know, sir. I think we have to uncover what made Charles Foxley feel compelled to be regularly beaten by a dominatrix, and have sex with obese women. We know his ex-wife was promiscuous and he was humiliated over and over again by her. Her mother told me that they could not live together, but they could not live apart. I think they may have had an obsessive love-hate relationship.'

'Yes, yes . . . I read the reports. But this goes beyond a love-hate relationship, sergeant. Harry Bellamy warned us last week that it was something more.'

The conversation ended as they arrived at Putney Crematorium. One minicab was parked outside the building. There were no other cars.

Tyler and Jane walked towards the crematorium entrance.

'Be typical if they gave us the wrong bloody time,' he said.

When they reached the arches in front of the door, a cleric was standing holding a prayer book.

'Charles Foxley's service?' Tyler asked, looking rather embarrassed.

'Yes, it will take place in Chapel One at midday.'

Tyler glanced at his watch. It was 11:55 a.m.

'We might as well go in.'

Just as they were about to enter, a hearse drew up with a white coffin and a small wreath of white tea roses on top.

Jane and Tyler went into the empty chapel. A plinth waited for the coffin. They sat to one side, at the rear.

Four men in black mourning suits carried in the white coffin and placed it on the plinth. They bowed and walked back down the aisle. After a few moments a small woman in a rather old-fashioned high-shouldered fur coat entered. She was carrying a large handbag and wore a silk scarf knotted under her chin. She looked nervously towards Tyler and Jane. She was heavily made-up, with a lot of mascara, and her red lipstick ran in tiny rivulets around her lined mouth. She seemed to hesitate, as if unsure where she should sit. Eventually she chose a center row and sat in the middle.

There was a camera flash, then two or three more, and then the sound of piped music – 'Where Did Our Love Go?' by The Supremes – at high volume. As the song began, Justine Harris, wearing a black Chanel suit, her hair loose and shining under a silk veil, walked slowly down the aisle. She was followed by her daughter Clara, wearing a black coat with, as requested, black velvet collar and buttons, white stockings and patent-leather shoes. Her hand was held by her grandmother, Florence Harris, who was equally elegantly dressed in black with a wide-brimmed black straw hat. Finally, George Henson, who was carrying a flash camera.

They took their seats in the front row as the vicar closed the doors and walked slowly up the aisle to stand by the lectern. With perfect timing, the music stopped. Jane didn't need to look at Tyler because it was obvious that neither of them could quite believe what they were seeing, and judging from her bewildered expression, nor could the elderly woman in the old-fashioned fur coat.

The service was astonishingly short. After the vicar had said a few words of prayer, Justine stepped up to the lectern. She lifted her veil dramatically.

'I am here, our daughter is here, and my beloved mother, to say farewell to you, husband, father and son-in-law. There will be a public memorial service but we are here today just to say goodbye. May God embrace His son and give him peace.'

She turned and stepped towards the coffin, leaning forward to kiss the top. She held her hand out and her daughter joined her and stood on tiptoe to kiss it as well. Then, bizarrely, Justine picked up the small coronet of tea roses and placed it on her daughter's head. They then walked back down the aisle and her mother briefly nodded towards the coffin as the curtains slowly began to close. Henson glanced towards Jane and Tyler, nodding briefly in acknowledgement. Then it was over.

By the time Tyler and Jane had left the chapel, the family had already been driven away in the chauffeured Mercedes. The vicar excused himself as he had another service to oversee, but it was quite obvious that he was somewhat taken aback by what he had just witnessed.

Jane and Tyler were about to head towards their car when Jane felt a touch on her arm.

'I have never in my entire life known anything like that. That wasn't a funeral service! I've come all the way from Brighton – well, Hove, really – by train, then a minicab from the station.'

Jane knew immediately who it was.

'Are you Eunice Small?'

'Yes, dear, and I've come all the way from Brighton. I never expected her to be nice to me, but she just ignored me, unless she didn't know I'd come all this way. I'm eighty-two.'

Jane turned to Tyler. 'I would very much like to take Miss Small for a cup of tea.'

He nodded.

Jane slipped her arm into the crook of Miss Small's. 'Or would you prefer to have some lunch?'

'Well, I would like something to eat as I've come all this way. I didn't know whether to get up and touch the coffin or not. I've never known anything like it, but then that Justine never liked me. I'm a bit worried because I'm paying waiting time to the minicab.'

Jane assured her that she would cover the taxi fare and would take her to a very nice restaurant near Victoria Station.

* * *

Spencer, unlike Jane, hadn't worked alongside DI Miller and was taken aback by his uncommunicative manner during the journey to Mandy Pilkington's. Spencer had tried to make conversation but was curtly told that he had read all his reports and that he should just listen intently and, when directed, make notes. He had no intention of wanting to share any interrogation and disliked any form of interruption.

Spencer shrugged. Fine by me, he thought.

For the rest of the journey he stared through the window as Miller flicked back and forth through his small notebook, occasionally jotting down a note.

As soon as the patrol car drew up outside the ordinary-looking terraced house, Miller double-checked that his little tape recorder was working and that he had spare tapes and new batteries ready for the interview.

They got out and Miller removed the search warrant from his jacket.

It was only when they approached the front door that anything about the house looked unusual. Behind the net curtain the window was barred, and the front door had three separate large keyholes, suggesting a heavy-duty lock. The bell push gave a low buzzing noise rather than the usual ring. They waited patiently as they heard the locks on the door being undone and then the sound of a bolt at the top of the door being released.

Spencer was standing behind Miller, so couldn't see his expression when a middle-aged man dressed in fishnet tights, a maid's outfit and a cheap nylon wig opened the door.

'I'm DI Miller and this is DS Gibbs,' Miller said curtly.

The man nodded. 'Miss Pilkington is waiting for you in the parlor,' he said in a tremulous voice.

Nothing in the hall gave any indication of the services being provided. There were some framed pictures of tourist attractions such as the Tower of London, Buckingham Palace and Windsor Castle. On a small side table was a display of plastic flowers.

The man dressed as a maid knocked on the door and in the same quivery voice announced them. The room wouldn't have looked out of place in any other house on the street: a shag-pile carpet in fawn, two matching sofas, a standard lamp and a brick fireplace with an electric coal fire. Above the fireplace was a large fake Constable painting in a heavy gold frame.

It was only Mandy Pilkington herself who made it extraordinary.

She sat on one of the sofas, virtually taking up the entire length of it. She had severely bloated legs that contrasted with her tiny feet, which were encased in red patent-leather shoes. Her kaftan-style floral dress was frilled around the neck and she had four strings of different-colored pearls around her neck. She had clearly once been very pretty, but she now seemed to have a tiny face almost swamped by an enormous head of dyed blonde hair. Her small hands were full of sparkling rings, with bright crimson nails that matched her crimson lipstick. There was nothing doll-like about her eyes, however. Although large, there was a hawk-like gaze in them as she waved her tiny hand for them both to be seated.

Spencer perched on the arm of the opposite sofa as Miller put his briefcase down on the glass-topped coffee table. He handed over the warrant and waited as Mandy skim-read it and handed it back.

'You are most welcome to peruse every room at my home for as long as you like. You may take anything that you want or feel might be necessary. I give you carte blanche.'

She had no trace of an accent; in fact, if anything, she sounded well-educated. She then folded her tiny hands over her bulging stomach as Miller opened his briefcase.

'Would you mind me taping the interview?'

'You can do whatever you like, dear,' she said.

Miller clicked on the recorder. He spoke quietly, saying his rank, the date, time and location, and that he was accompanied by DS Spencer Gibbs. He then pressed rewind and listened to make sure the machine was recording, before continuing.

'Miss Pilkington, I am aware that you have already been interviewed in connection with the murder of Charles Foxley, but I would now like to ask you specifically about his payments as one of your clients.'

Mandy dug her hand into the seat beside her and drew out four sheets of paper held together with a paperclip.

'I thought you might need these. I have been as diligent as possible, because the client you refer to had been visiting my establishment for a period of eighteen months.'

Miller had to stand up to reach over and take the papers. He glanced at them as he sat back down on the sofa, flicking from one sheet to the other.

'I don't want to play games with you, Miss Pilkington. If I wanted to, I could have you arrested for running a brothel where serious acts of perversion take place.'

Miller's words had no effect on her whatsoever. She tossed her head and laughed.

'I give a good service to people who need it. You may not be aware that I am a qualified psychotherapist and in many cases what you refer to as perversion is an acceptable form of therapy. I have the documents to prove it. My business is entirely legal—'

Miller interrupted. 'I am certain a High Court judge would find your explanation for what is in fact a brothel less than convincing.'

She gave another high-pitched laugh. 'Listen, sweetie, I've had more High Court judges before me than you've had hot dinners, and I don't think you know what you're talking about. I have never had a complaint or an arrest, and none of my staff has either.'

Miller smiled coldly, as if he was enjoying himself. Without referring to any notes, he began listing all her previous convictions for soliciting, along with the dates, going back twenty years. He even recalled the various aliases Mandy had used. He obviously expected a reaction, but she simply waved her hands, saying that she had been young and abused by her pimp and had been rehabilitated during a prison sentence.

She pointed a tiny finger at him. 'People like you have no notion of the hardships a homeless fourteen-year-old girl can be subjected to. I have been an honest hard-working woman since I was married. I pay my taxes and if you want to threaten me, I know my rights and I will call my lawyer.'

Miller gave a dry laugh. 'I can have you out of here faster than you could pick up the phone. You don't seem to understand,

Mandy, I am investigating a vicious, brutal murder and right now you are a suspect. I am going to ask you some questions and if I do not get direct answers, I will waste no time in having you dragged out of this house.' At that point the door opened and the maid entered with a tray of tea and sandwiches.

'Thank you, Gregory. Put it down on the coffee table and we will help ourselves. In the meantime, would you please make sure the kitchen floor is washed and all the glasses in the main cabinet polished. When Farook comes back after walking the dog, he is to put him in his cage. I don't want these gentlemen scared that my Doberman might attack them.' She giggled. 'Then tell Farook to make sure the Jacuzzi's been emptied and cleaned – and make sure there's no trace of Vim left. There are no more clients expected today, so he can go home after that.'

Gregory gave a little curtsy and scuttled out.

'He's such a dear man. He lost his wife a few years ago and finds solace in house-cleaning. I think he's always had a bit of a fetish as he brings his own costume.'

Miller declined tea on behalf of himself and Spencer, so Mandy poured herself a cup then filled a little plate with tiny squares of cucumber sandwich. She eased her bulk back into the chair, balancing her plate on her stomach as she sipped her tea.

'Right, dear, shall we continue?'

At this point, a small button on the tape recorder blinked to indicate the tape had run out.

CHAPTER FIFTEEN

Jane and Eunice Small were sitting at a small table for two in the corner of the restaurant. Jane had paid the taxi fare and although Eunice had murmured that she should really pay, Jane had insisted. Eunice seemed very impressed with the Rubens Hotel and the fact that it was so close to Buckingham Palace, saying that as a young woman she had been outside the gates and seen the Queen driving past. Eunice thought the à la carte menu looked rather expensive, but Jane encouraged her to choose whatever she fancied. In the end, they both ordered roast beef followed by apple turnover.

Jane was taking it slowly, as she had a lot of questions for Eunice and didn't want to overwhelm her, so she just let the old lady talk at her own pace.

'I don't think Justine expected to see me there, to be honest. Which isn't surprising as I haven't spoken to her for what must be more than ten years.' She frowned and shook her head. 'No, that's not right. I remember we did have a conversation when their daughter was born, but I think Justine felt I was rather common.' She shrugged her shoulders and gave Jane a sweet, twinkling smile. 'It never bothered me, though. I often thought about Charlie, but he never made contact and so I just got on with my life, really.'

Eunice explained that her brother, Reginald Small, was Charles Foxley's father. She provided a concise family history, saying that her brother had been an employee of a mining company and had married Melody, who had been only eighteen and had had dreams of becoming a model. Melody was extremely pretty with wide green eyes and thick curly auburn hair. She was also very slender and could definitely have had a career as a model. After she married Reginald, they moved to South Africa.

At this point the waiter brought their beef and asked if they would like some wine. They both declined and Jane asked for a pot of tea.

Eunice ate like a bird, cutting up her food into tiny slices and making sure she had a little roast beef, a little carrot and a little slice of roast potato on her fork before dipping it into the gravy. She took a mouthful, chewed carefully, then continued.

'When Melody got pregnant, she didn't want to continue living in Johannesburg. She said she had never really been happy there and so she came back with my brother. I truthfully believe that to begin with, they were very happy, but, because his work required him to spend time in Africa, they were often apart for lengthy periods. I'm not accusing Melody of any infidelity, but I think she was bored. Then poor Reg got some awful illness, malaria-related, and never really recovered. He left Melody a reasonably well-off young widow with two young boys.'

Jane placed her cutlery together on her plate and glanced at her watch as Eunice continued eating. She bent down to pick up her bag, placing it on her knee.

'You said two boys?' Up to now no one had mentioned Charles Foxley having a brother or, for that matter, ever having had a different surname.

'Yes, dear, two boys. Tommy and then, four years after dear Tommy, Charles.' At that point Eunice carefully placed her knife and fork together and patted her lips with a napkin.

'Where does the name Foxley come from?' Jane asked.

'That was Melody's second husband, Sean. He was in property development. I always thought he was rather pompous, but Melody would never hear a word against him. He took on the responsibility of the boys and they assumed his surname.'

A waiter came to remove the plates, then brought their dessert with a pot of tea.

Jane continued, tentatively. 'You are obviously aware of what happened to Charles and that I am part of an ongoing investigation, but this is the first I have ever heard of Charles having a brother, Tommy. What happened to him?' Jane asked.

Eunice folded her napkin and dabbed her eyes.

'He was the mirror image of Melody, you know, with big green eyes and the same glorious red curly hair. He had such a bright personality, everyone loved him.' She sighed. 'He could sing, he could dance. Charles was always in his shadow. No one could ever compete with this beautiful boy – he was so good at school. He'd inherited my brother's brain, you see.'

Jane waited while Eunice took a careful bite of her apple turnover, then put her spoon down.

'He was nearly twelve and for no reason at all he began to have periods where he found it difficult to breathe. Melody was absolutely distraught. These episodes would come out of the blue for no apparent reason. Eventually he was diagnosed with severe asthma. It made poor Tommy quite fragile. He had been such a sporty and physical little boy, playing football, cricket, as well as his dancing. One thing that seemed to really trigger it was laughing. He had one very bad attack and Melody rushed him to A&E. From then on the little soul always had an inhaler in his pocket and would say, "Don't make me laugh, please don't make me laugh." Because of his condition he was always the focus of everyone's attention – even more than before. I think Charlie tried in every way possible to get some attention for himself, but no matter what he did, he always came second.' She dabbed at her eyes again. 'And then it happened.'

Jane waited.

'I know he never meant it to happen,' she said sadly. 'They were in their bedroom and Charlie had been told to look out for his brother and always to make sure he had his inhaler. You have to remember that Tommy was a few years older. Anyway, Melody heard the boys fooling around and Charlie was tickling his brother to make him laugh. She was heading up the stairs, shouting for them to stop as she heard Tommy start laughing, and the next moment, he was having a terrible asthma attack . . . This time they couldn't save him.'

Jane leaned forward in her chair.

'Melody swore Charlie did it on purpose, because he was jealous. She was even more sure of this after she found the inhaler hidden under the bed. She beat Charlie savagely, screaming at him that he had killed his brother. It was horrible. The neighbors found Charlie, black and blue, hiding in their garden. Melody never recovered and began to gorge herself. She hardly left the house. It was tragic to see her look so awful.'

Jane called for the bill, then showed Eunice the photographs that Justine had given to her at the station.

Eunice peered at them with a sad expression. 'The little boy in uniform is Thomas and the one holding a tennis racquet is Charlie.'

When she saw the photograph of the rowing team, leaning across the oars of their skiff, she patted it with her hand.

'Charlie won so many awards, you know, but no matter what he did, it was never enough for Melody. I don't think she ever kissed or held that child again.'

* * *

Mandy's coffee table was now stacked with photo albums, and each album was filled with images of the girls working for her. Charles Foxley's preference was for obese women, and they had nicknames like Big Betty, Fat Fanny and Heavy Helen, and they were the ones he requested for his weekly visits. Mandy was candid in describing exactly what took place during his sessions. He would be stripped down to his underpants and tied to a leather horse by his wrists, then whipped. It was all very professional, she assured them. They never drew blood, and the whip often left no mark. It was more the swishing sound that the clients liked. After the whipping, he would be taken to a waterbed, but would never have full sex with the women. He would ejaculate between their breasts, often while having his buttocks slapped.

'Why do you think Foxley subjected himself to this treatment?' Miller asked.

Mandy shrugged. 'My clients tell me what they want. It is not my job to find out why. If a well-known aristocrat likes to wear nappies, drink milk from a large baby bottle, and becomes sexually excited when he poos in his nappy, that's his business. My job is to make sure they are satisfied and that they pay the fee. And they're not all what you would call perverts. I even have one poor soul who has been crippled since a young age after contracting meningitis. My driver collects him and returns him home. All part of the service.'

'Very commendable, I'm sure,' Miller said sourly. 'So far, Miss Pilkington, you have refused to name any of your clients.'

'Yes, dear, and I will continue to refuse. I will get legal representation, if necessary, to ensure my clients are protected, as I signed a non-disclosure agreement with each of them. You can get any High Court judge you like involved.'

Spencer couldn't hide his smile. The more she spoke, the more he warmed to her. She certainly had no fear of DI Miller.

'When was the last time you saw Mr. Foxley?' Miller asked.

She rolled her eyes. 'That lanky young man perched on my sofa arm was here when I gave all the details. Charles Foxley came here on Monday at lunchtime. He usually arrived by taxi at around one p.m. He would have the session I just described to you and then he would pay. I've shown you my receipts: it's two hundred and fifty pounds per session. One hundred goes to the girl and then smaller amounts go to the cleaners, who wipe down the waterbed and the other equipment, and also the masseuse. The session would usually take about three quarters of an hour. He would either have a taxi waiting for him or we would order one when he was ready to leave. I have to say, when he arrived he was often tense and anxious, and by the time he left you could see that he was more relaxed. He usually showered and sometimes even shaved . . . and he was always polite. On that Monday – the Monday that the tragedy happened – he came as usual and left as usual. I saw no difference in his manner.'

Miller pulled at his tie. 'How much did Mr. Foxley tell you about his business?'

She gave an exaggerated sigh, her huge breasts rising and falling. 'Listen, sweetheart, do you really think a man shitting in adult nappies wants me to know his profession? He was always well-dressed and polite, but I had no idea he was a big theatrical agent.' She tossed her head back and laughed. 'If I had known, I would have introduced him to a young actor I have here, who gets up to all kinds of things in a rubber suit.'

Miller abruptly stood up and switched off his tape recorder. 'I'd like to see the rest of the premises now.'

Mandy shrugged. 'I will have to ask Gregory to show you around – I can't get up and down those stairs – but help yourself. As I mentioned earlier, I have no clients today.'

She made no effort to get up and show them out. As they left, Spencer saw her popping the remaining little sandwiches into her mouth.

Whatever DI Miller felt as he moved from room to room, he showed no reaction. Mandy's bedroom was next door to the lounge and contained an enormous double bed with a frilly valance, a duvet covered in pink cartoon figures and pink nylon frilled pillow slips. The shag-pile rugs were rose-colored and even her dressing table had pink frills surrounding the perfume bottles and make-up. The fitted wardrobes contained numerous kaftan-style gowns.

As he showed them the large, well-equipped kitchen, Gregory was polite, verging on deferential. In the basement there was a dungeon-type room, as well as a 'nursery' room with a giant baby's cot, rag dolls and enormous plastic bottles with rubber teats. A third room had an array of whips, rubber matting and an old leather pommel horse, which looked as if it had come from a school gymnasium. The upstairs bedrooms were fitted out for various fetish and sex games, and in the bathroom was a huge Jacuzzi, which Miller muttered must be illegal.

The wardrobe on the landing contained a selection of rubber suits. Gregory pointed out that each one would have cost at least £200. In the wardrobe drawers, instead of underwear and ties, there was a selection of handcuffs. Some were lined with fur, some with velvet, but none of them matched the set of handcuffs found on their victim. Miller made a few notes and occasionally muttered into his tape recorder, before they headed back downstairs into the hall.

As a man came out of the kitchen, shutting the door behind him, they could hear the low growling of a large dog.

'You are?' Miller asked.

'Ahmed Farook, sir. I'm Miss Pilkington's chauffeur and security guard.'

'I believe you know Mr. Foxley's dog walker.'

Farook nodded. 'Eric Newman? Yes, sir, I know him. Not well, but he did a good turn for me when I needed someone to walk Miss Pilkington's dog, Bruno.'

'Have you ever walked Mr. Foxley's dogs?'

'No, sir, I just walk Bruno. To be honest, I don't like little dogs.'

'Did you know Mr. Foxley?'

'No, sir.'

'So when clients come into the house, you don't interact with them?'

'No, sir. Madam would not approve. I just look after her car, I do her shopping, tidy around the garden and clean up when necessary. I do my job and don't ask questions.'

'But you do collect one of her clients, don't you, then take him home?'

'Yes, sir, but only him. He is disabled and I have to carry him from the car upstairs. I then wait and return him to his care home.'

Miller made a note. 'Are you married?'

Spencer saw Farook now had a sheen of sweat on his upper lip and forehead. 'Yes, sir.'

'Does your wife know what kind of a job you do?'

'My wife knows I work as a driver and I do security. I never discuss what madam does.'

Miller paused. 'Could you tell us exactly what you were doing on the night of Mr. Foxley's murder?'

Spencer stood patiently to one side. They had asked Mandy Pilkington the exact same question. She had clearly stated that Farook had been in her presence that afternoon and that he had collected one of her clients, who was a disabled young man.

'That afternoon I collected the disabled young man, then, as far as I can recall, I was at the house helping Miss Pilkington. In the early evening I went to collect another one of her clients.' He shifted his weight from foot to foot. 'I cannot give you his name or his address. It is a rule of the house.'

Miller turned without thanking him. Gregory already had the front door open and Spencer smiled and thanked him before following Miller down the path and back to their patrol car.

Miller gave him a sidelong look as they got in. 'My God, that woman . . . like a beached whale.' He shuddered.

Spencer did not reply. He had rather liked Mandy in the end, but he thanked God he would never be a part of her world.

* * *

Jane walked Eunice slowly arm-in-arm towards Victoria Station to catch her train back to Brighton. A thought occurred to her.

'Did Justine know about Thomas?'

'I don't know, dear. She never mentioned it. I know Charlie never went to his grave, but then I hardly saw him in the past ten years or so. I think it might have been because I'm a reminder of the past. Truthfully, when he first met Justine I think he was happy for the first time in his life. She was so beautiful. I don't know what happened, but on one occasion he did tell me she was cruel.'

They got to the platform, Eunice still tightly gripping Jane's arm. 'I may be speaking out of turn, but I've always thought that Clara has no real similarities to our side of the family.'

Jane nodded. 'Well, sometimes family resemblance skips a generation.'

Eunice released her hand. 'Maybe . . . I suppose I shouldn't gossip.'

Jane saw her safely onto the train. She was concerned about having taken so long out of the station, but she also felt she had gained valuable insight into Charles Foxley's sad need to visit establishments like Mandy Pilkington's. She also began to think about what Eunice had said about Clara.

The truth was, Jane suddenly realized, she did look a lot like George Henson.

* * *

The team had gathered in the incident room. They had already lost a number of officers and no longer needed the much larger boardroom. DCI Tyler was sitting to one side and the officers were sitting at desks or perched on them. Miller, his shirt-sleeves rolled up, stood with a ruler indicating different items on the incident board as he talked them through the timeline they had so far verified for the Monday morning. They knew that Foxley had been to the agency as usual that morning and had then left for a session at Mandy Pilkington's.

'Although she refused to give us the names of the clients who were booked in that day, we do have names and contact numbers of the women, and specifically the woman who was paid for by the victim.' He turned to the officers. 'She's known as Big Betty, and she does have a record for soliciting over a number of years. We now have clarification of how much Foxley paid for his so-called treatments.'

He explained that Mandy had kept a meticulous diary with exact appointment times, concerned about one client crossing over with another, in case they were recognized.

'The last appointment on that day was at half past five when her driver, Farook, collected and dropped off a client, whose name and address we do have; he is a disabled man who requires the chauffeur to carry him to and from the car. He is usually there for an hour and Farook then collects him and delivers him home. In reality, there is a pretty watertight alibi for Miss Pilkington and her driver; however, we'll need to verify the times with the disabled client to see if he can confirm that he was at the brothel on the Monday.'

Miller turned again to face all the officers and described how he and Spencer had been showed around the brothel by a large hairy man in fishnet tights and a maid's outfit.

'As we left, Mr. Gregory Barker gave us his business card in case we needed him to make a statement. He normally works in the city as a solicitor.' He smirked as he pinned the card onto the board.

Jane slipped into the incident room, hanging her coat over her desk chair and giving a nod of apology to Tyler. He gave her a non-committal glance, but Miller couldn't resist pointing his ruler.

'Well, I'm glad we are joined by DS Tennison. So, we know where our victim was up until he left Mandy Pilkington's. But we do not know where he was that afternoon until three p.m. We have a statement from the dog walker, Eric Newman, who was unable to contact Mr. Foxley at his office but called in at his flat. Although he did not enter the premises, he said that Mr. Foxley appeared to be his usual self and asked him to keep the dogs overnight.'

Miller raised his hands and waved the ruler. 'We do not know what occurred after that. All we know about is the upstairs neighbor hearing incessant barking from the dog that had been left behind. Not very helpfully, she said "it could have been at five p.m. or even later".'

He moved along the incident board and pointed to the post-mortem details.

'We have an approximate time of death but, as you know, the pathologist always gives a fairly wide spectrum and believes the victim was killed in the early evening of that Monday. This could mean anywhere between five p.m. and nine p.m. I have ruled out Mandy Pilkington as a suspect because he was a regular and lucrative client for her.'

DCI Tyler stood up. 'We still have no motive. However, I believe DCI Collins will be making inquiries into the financier Max Summers and his brother Ivor in the US.' Tyler looked around. 'Have we any further developments from anyone?'

Jane put up her hand just as the young DC Tony Johnson stood up.

'I have just switched surveillance on Justine Harris's Barnes property, sir. She is still there with her daughter Clara, her mother and George Henson. The only time Ms. Harris left the property was at three p.m. when she got into a local minicab. I left my partner and followed her to Wardour Street in the West End. She went into Paramount House, presumably to Foxley & Myers, while I remained outside the premises. She came out after three quarters of an hour and hailed a black taxi, which I subsequently followed back to the Barnes property.'

Tyler nodded. 'Make sure those details are on the incident board.'

By ordering surveillance, it was now clear that Justine Harris had been the prime suspect.

Tyler turned towards Jane. She cleared her throat before opening her notebook.

'I do have what I believe is new information regarding Charles Foxley's visits to Mandy Pilkington's establishment.'

Jane succinctly repeated everything she had been told about Foxley's brother Thomas and how his aunt, Eunice, felt that Foxley suffered from a guilt complex that had tortured him for most of his life. Jane further explained that Eunice was uncertain whether Justine knew about Thomas.

'However, she did hint at something else, which might be relevant. She questioned whether Clara was Charles Foxley's daughter.'

Tyler held up his hand. 'So did she suggest who the father was?'

'No, but I wondered if it was possibly George Henson.'

There was a murmur from around the room – but it wasn't because of what Jane had just said. She turned around to see everyone was looking at DS Lawrence, who held up an *Evening Standard* as he made his way towards the incident board. On the front page there was a photograph of Justine Harris holding her daughter's hand with the headline: *Widow of famous theatrical agent says a final goodbye.*

Jane sat down. She suddenly remembered that when she had seen Justine coming into the crematorium, there had been the flash of a camera – and George Henson had been holding a camera when he walked down the aisle towards the coffin. The front-page photograph had to have been taken then because Clara had left the chapel wearing the rose-bud coronet.

Lawrence removed his coat and placed a large cardboard evidence box on the desk nearest to the incident board. He opened the box and removed a sheet of paper.

'I have here, way ahead of the usual time, a toxicology report on our victim. He had a very high level of cocaine in his nostrils and airways, and there was a residue of amphetamines. But although we did find a large quantity of vitamins at his flat, we did not find any amphetamines or cocaine. However, a quantity of amphetamines was discovered at Justine Harris's house.'

Jane realized there was more to come because Lawrence appeared to be very pleased with himself. He then withdrew the blood-stained camel-hair coat from the box.

'Although we cannot yet confirm an identical match, the blood stains on Ms. Harris's coat are the same blood group as the blood of our victim. The same goes for the trainers. But that's not what I wanted to share with you.'

He then held up the camel coat and put his hand in the right pocket. 'We discovered this crucial piece of evidence while testing for the blood.' He withdrew, in a plastic cover, a parking ticket. 'This ticket is for Justine Harris's car and was timed at 5:15 p.m. on the evening of the murder. The car could have remained there longer and it could have been parked there earlier, but it is confirmation that Justine Harris was at the victim's location the day he died. The ticket was issued in Onslow Square.'

The room almost erupted. This was the piece of evidence they had all been desperate for because it meant Justine Harris had lied.

Tyler held his hands up for quiet. 'Right, the surveillance will continue on Justine Harris's house. Then I want Justine Harris and George Henson arrested for the murder of Charles Foxley and brought in for questioning. But it's imperative that the child's grandmother be present to take care of her daughter and the dogs.'

After finishing her report Jane was called to DCI Tyler's office. 'You've screwed up badly, Tennison. When you removed the coat from the property it was your job to search the pockets. Let this be a lesson for you.'

Jane flushed with embarrassment.

'You can go now.'

She nodded, utterly crestfallen.

*   *   *

It was after ten p.m. when she let herself in and hurried up the three flights of stairs to her flat. She wanted to scream, because it didn't matter that Lawrence may have covered for her. She had made a major error.

She had a glass of wine and lit a cigarette from her emergency packet, which was getting worryingly depleted. Then she dialed a number, and even before it was answered she knew she would regret it.

Dexter's answering machine clicked on and Jane left a message to say that she just wondered how he was and if he would like a drink, but she realized how late it was so she would call again another time. She hung up, furious with herself, but at the same time relieved he hadn't answered.

When the phone rang a few minutes later she was reluctant to answer it, but it turned out to be Spencer.

'Well, you certainly fucked up, Jane, but I think your friend Lawrence must have got you out of the shit somehow because you and I are on the arrests at seven tomorrow morning.'

'Thank you for that vote of confidence,' she said glumly.

'I'm with Tyler, and you're going in with the pink-shirted mighty midget. It's a covert operation, no paddy wagon or blue lights flashing. It's about time we got a result.'

Jane tried to match his excitement, but was too busy worrying about the repercussions of her mistake.

CHAPTER SIXTEEN

Jane and DI Miller were in an unmarked car parked behind DCI Tyler and Spencer. It was 7:05 a.m. The two drivers got out and positioned themselves beside the cars, while the four officers gathered at the front door.

Tyler rang the doorbell and, after the usual cacophony of barking, the front door was opened by George Henson, eating a piece of toast.

'We'd like you to accompany us to the station for further questioning about the murder of Charles Foxley,' Tyler said briskly.

Henson stepped back with a frown and they trooped inside.

'We also want Justine Harris to accompany us for further questioning,' DI Miller added curtly.

'Dear God, how many more questions do you lot want to ask?' Henson asked testily.

'As many as necessary,' Tyler said. 'You are both being arrested on suspicion of murder.'

Jane watched Henson as Tyler cautioned him, and was astonished at how relaxed he seemed.

'Well, can you just wait a moment?' He started heading towards the kitchen.

'Please remain in the hall, Mr. Henson,' Miller snapped.

'All right, fine. I just want to talk to Justine's mother first.'

He opened the door to the kitchen a fraction, keeping the dogs inside. He told Florence Harris to call McDermott immediately and to go upstairs and tell Justine the officers needed to speak to her. Florence eased her way out of the kitchen, looking distressed. She explained that Justine was in the shower and

Tyler gestured towards Jane for her to accompany her up the stairs to the bedroom. Henson nonchalantly finished his slice of toast and asked if he could go and collect a jacket. Spencer was told to accompany him, and before any of them reached the top of the stairs, Justine appeared in a terrycloth robe with her wet hair wrapped in a towel.

'What is going on? I need to know what is going on. Why are you all here? This is outrageous,' she screeched.

'They've come to take us to the station,' Henson explained calmly.

Justine carried on screaming. 'You can't do this! You have no right!'

'Justine, listen to me. There is no need for you to panic, I am going to be with you.'

She stopped shaking and began rubbing her wet hair frantically with the wet towel.

'Listen to me, Justine, do not say one word to them, do you understand me? Not one word. Not until Darren McDermott gets there.'

Spencer and Miller ushered Henson out of the house.

Jane waited in the bedroom while Justine insisted on blow-drying her hair. Meanwhile her mother had returned to the kitchen to quiet the dogs. Eventually, Justine came downstairs, wearing the black raincoat she had previously worn over a turtle-neck sweater and a pair of white slacks. She was also wearing dark glasses. She was calm, but Jane could see she was trembling.

No one spoke on the drive back to the station. As Tyler's car drew up, the press were already gathering at the front. When they saw the car carrying Justine, they ran at it with their cameras flashing.

'How in the hell did those bastards get here so fast?' Tyler snapped angrily.

Two small interview rooms had been prepared with instructions to keep Henson and Justine apart and give them no opportunity to talk to each other. DI Miller was to lead the interrogation of Justine, and Tyler would take charge of the interview with George Henson.

Miller was keen to start, but before they could interview Justine, Tyler received a call from Darren McDermott's assistant to say that Mr. McDermott would be arriving at the station and that there was to be no questioning of his client Justine Harris until he had arrived. Tyler sighed with frustration. McDermott was one of the toughest QCs around and a very experienced operator. He was stunned that such an eminent lawyer should want to be present instead of his many junior lawyers. McDermott's assistant also said that his boss demanded to meet with DI Miller.

'Who the fuck does he think he is?' Miller swore.

'He's a heavy hitter,' Tyler told him. 'We'd better have all our ducks in a row when he gets here.'

Justine was given a cup of coffee and taken into the interview room. A uniformed officer remained with her until McDermott arrived.

Jane took the opportunity to go into the canteen and get some breakfast. The news that the infamous QC McDermott was representing Justine Harris was spreading like wildfire. Considering that no charges had yet been brought, his attendance sounded a bit heavy-handed.

George Henson remained nonchalant as he was offered refreshments in the second interview room, replying pleasantly that he would love a coffee with milk and sugar. DI Miller and Spencer sat at the desk in front of him. Miller repeated his caution and Henson laughed.

'My, my. This really is serious, isn't it?'

Miller opened a pristine new notebook and then set beside it his own personal one. Spencer sat with his pencil poised ready to take notes.

'Could you tell us where you were on the night of Charles Foxley's murder?' Miller began.

Henson gave an exasperated shrug. 'I have been asked this numerous times, and I have clearly stated that on that Monday evening I was at my cottage in Kent, entertaining three friends at dinner. I have given their names, and I believe they have been questioned. They will explain that I was there all evening and did not leave my cottage until late the next afternoon, when I received a distressed call from Justine after she had seen her ex-husband's body. How many more times do you need me to explain this?'

Miller took the cap off his fountain pen. 'We need, Mr. Henson, to verify those alibis. After questioning your three friends, they all explained that a lot of alcohol was consumed that evening. Although you were the host, they could not be one hundred percent sure that you were indeed with them the entire evening.'

Henson threw his hands up. 'Oh, bollocks to that! I absolutely admit that I was two sheets to the wind, but as you could easily have worked out for yourselves, I do not own a car and the last train, I believe, leaves for Waterloo at 10:30 p.m., so how do you think I could have got to Charles Foxley's flat? If I had hired a taxi the fare would have been astronomical, and you detectives would very easily discover the identity of the taxicab if I had used one.'

Miller pursed his lips. 'I now want to ask you about your relationship with Justine Harris. How long have you known her?'

'For God's sake! I don't know, maybe twenty-five years, maybe more . . . '

'And you frequently stay at her property in Barnes?'

'Yes, I have told you that and have explained that I work from there. I rent a bedroom and a small office. It's just a peppercorn rent – Justine is a very generous soul and is aware of the costs of me commuting back and forth to the West End.'

'So you rent a couple of rooms at Ms. Harris's home and have done for many years?'

Henson waved his hand in the air. 'Dear God. I have not always rented there, nor have I always worked there, but after her divorce she kindly asked me to stay.'

'So you were very familiar with her husband, Charles Foxley?'

'I don't know what you mean by "familiar". I detested him. He was an obnoxious man, and I had very little time for him – particularly recently as I believe he was getting out of control, or his drug abuse was. I know Justine was fearful as he would leave packets of drugs open in his bedroom. I had little or no interaction with him, and in all honesty, I would have liked to thrash him.'

'Did you?' Miller asked quickly.

'No, I did not, probably due to the fact that he was a very fit man and could likely have beat the living daylights out of me.'

'But he must have found your closeness to his wife, now his ex-wife, disturbing?'

'He probably did,' Henson said.

'When was the last time you saw him?' Miller asked quietly.

'Probably a week or so before he was killed. I saw him pulling up outside, with his bloody dogs, and I made my escape.'

'And how did Justine feel about that?'

'What, about his bloody dogs or that I escaped?'

'That you allowed Charles Foxley to stay at his ex-wife's property even though you did not approve.'

'Dear God! It was not a question of me approving; he would just turn up, whether she liked it or not.'

'Are you the father of Clara, Justine's daughter?'

Miller leaned back in his chair and folded his arms. 'Well, I don't know who suggested that, but I can tell you unequivocally that I am not Clara's father.' He smiled. 'DI Miller, I can categorically state that I could not have fathered Clara because I had a vasectomy after the birth of my second son. He is now in his twenties, so I suggest you do the maths.'

Spencer had to hand it to Henson, he had answers for everything.

Henson then leaned forward and his tone became more serious and even emotional. 'All I have ever done is care for Justine deeply for many years. She is one of the sweetest, most generous and, at one time, the most talented of people. As someone who adored her, I had to watch as Charles Foxley caused her such pain and anguish. Sadly, no matter what I said or what any of her friends said, she would always side with him. In my opinion, she could see the darkness in him and ultimately felt pity for him.'

Miller wrote a few sentences in his notebook, trying to look as if he was still in control, but the truth was, the interview had been a disaster. He hoped Tyler was having better luck with Justine Harris.

* * *

At 8:15 a.m. Darren McDermott was in his Bentley waiting for the station yard gates to be opened to allow him entry. There were still two persistent journalists hanging around, but the rest of the paparazzi had left. A uniformed officer led him into the station, where DCI Tyler was waiting.

Jane was at her desk and watched as Tyler greeted him. Tall and elegant, McDermott was wearing an immaculate charcoal-grey overcoat with a black velvet collar over a grey suit. He was slightly tanned, with thick, iron-grey curly hair. He didn't look to either side or acknowledge anyone as he followed Tyler into his office.

Spencer came out from interview room two and joined Jane at her desk.

'What's going on?' she asked.

He shrugged. 'Henson's more than likely going to be released without charge after Miller's interviewed Justine.' He then turned and nodded towards Tyler's closed door. 'What's going on in there?'

'A big-time QC called Darren McDermott has arrived. I think he's here to represent Justine Harris.'

Spencer frowned. 'He's a bit of a heavy hitter to come in as a brief for her.' Spencer looked at Tyler's closed office door again. 'How long are they going to be in there?'

'I don't know,' Jane said.

Spencer leaned close, grinning. 'I have to say, Henson made DI Miller look a right twat.'

'What about him fathering Foxley's daughter?'

Spencer shook his head. 'He had a vasectomy after his second son, and even had the surgeon's number if we wanted to call to verify it. You know something, I quite like him.'

DI Miller walked in. 'Well, I'm glad you do, Detective Sergeant Gibbs, and if you have nothing better to do but stand around here gossiping, you can make yourself useful and do something for me. Go and speak to the agent who knows about Foxley's drug use.'

'Emma Ransom?'

'Yes. We just heard Henson confirm that Foxley's drug habit was getting out of control, so we may be looking for a drug dealer.'

'So you don't think Justine is involved?'

Miller pursed his lips. 'I never said that. She is the only one to benefit from Foxley's death, so I haven't changed my mind yet.

But she now has Darren McDermott acting for her, so we might not get anything out of her.'

* * *

Spencer took the Underground into the West End and was heading into Paramount House as a young girl was hurrying down in the other direction. She was so intent on holding tightly to an envelope that she didn't see him and they bumped into each other, knocking the envelope flying. It was filled with banknotes. She hurriedly snatched at the fallen money.

'You should watch where you're going,' she said, brushing herself down.

She was still stuffing the money back into the envelope as Spencer headed up the stairs. The two receptionists, Rita and Angela, greeted him like a long-lost friend and went straight into gossip mode.

'You aren't gonna believe what happened here. She comes in and goes ballistic, screaming and shouting! It was very unpleasant, wasn't it, Rita?'

Rita nodded. 'We couldn't believe it when the same day we saw the *Standard* with her picture at his funeral. She must have come straight here. We couldn't believe that anyone would do something like that.'

Spencer shook his head sympathetically. 'Is Emma Ransom available?'

'She's over on the other side talking to Mr. Nathan,' Rita told him. She leaned over the reception desk conspiratorially. 'Bit of a feeding frenzy going on here . . . Not too sure what it's about, but it's connected to the black widow.'

Spencer crossed the landing to the other offices. John Nathan's door was firmly closed but Spencer could hear Daniel Bergman's voice, so walked over to his open door.

'It has nothing to do with me. I am having no part of it. If you want the truth, nobody in this agency can be bothered running after poxy models that don't have a hope in hell of making a career. That part of the business is running on empty.'

Spencer then heard the high-pitched, whining voice of Simon Quinn.

'But I'm contracted for another six months and we owe three girls. Without Mr. Foxley, I don't know who to ask to tell me what to do.'

'I am not a fucking agent for fucking underage bimbo models! Right, now I've got better things to be doing than listening to you blubber all over my desk. Fuck off.'

A tearful Simon Quinn scuttled out of Bergman's office. He looked up at Spencer.

'I don't know what I have to do. I've asked him, and I even asked Emma. I've got all these girls on my books and I've got no petty cash to pay them. Now I don't even know if *I'm* going to be paid. They are all complete bitches on the other side.'

Spencer followed the agitated young man to his small cubicle office, which was lined with photographs of all the young models. Quinn grabbed some tissues from a box, blowing his nose.

'I don't know if the premiere is going ahead or not. No one is telling me anything. I just don't know what to do.'

At that moment Emma Ransom came in behind Spencer.

'I've been told you want to speak to me?'

Spencer turned and smiled. 'Yes, if I can just have a few minutes of your time.'

'We'd better go over to the other side,' Emma said, moving ahead of him.

Unlike Charles Foxley's office, Emma's was remarkably clear. There were already two step ladders placed against the wall closest to Foxley's vacated office.

'There's been a lot of discussion going on about who will get Charles's old office. It's the biggest space and James says he should have it. Daniel said he should have it, but neither Laura nor I really care. I'm quite happy here and so is Laura. The agents can get so vicious! To be honest, I can't even go in there.'

She sat in her swivel desk chair, turning slowly from side to side as Spencer sat in a leather and chrome chair opposite.

'We've been discussing a memorial service but no one really knows what to do. We haven't been told if anyone has been arrested.'

She cocked her head to one side and he noticed she was wearing the same clothes she had on the previous occasion – a grey sweater with black trousers. Her face was still devoid of make-up.

'We have made no arrest as yet,' Spencer said.

'Dear God, it's been a week, hasn't it?' she said, continuing to swivel around in her chair.

Spencer nodded. 'Tell me about Justine Harris's visit to the office.'

'No one was expecting her. She marched in unannounced and demanded we all meet in James's office. He was exceedingly put out because she went and sat behind his desk. We all had to gather in front of her like school children.' Emma did two more swivels before she sat still, folding her arms. 'She wants us to buy her out as Charles owned the majority of shares in the company. She said that unless we buy her out, she will consider selling Charles's shares to another theatrical agent. Our fear is if James doesn't step up to the plate, we all might have to go and hawk our clients to other agents.'

'Must be quite a nerve-racking time for everyone,' Spencer said, nodding sympathetically. 'One more question, Miss Ransom. I don't want to name names, but we have been told that you were privy to Mr. Foxley's drug abuse.'

Emma plucked at a bobble on her cashmere sweater. 'I don't know where you got that from.'

'Look, we're not interested in your personal drug use, but if you supplied Charles Foxley with cocaine, we will require you to disclose the dealer.'

'Are you inferring that I supplied Charles with drugs?'

'I simply need to know who Mr. Foxley scored his drugs from.'

'Oh my God.' She opened a drawer and took out a small packet of tissues. 'This is terrible; I think I should have a lawyer present. I assure you that, beyond Charles offering me a line or two, I have never physically scored drugs in my entire life.'

'Where did he get them from?' Spencer asked.

She took another tissue from the little packet and blew her nose. Spencer waited.

'I don't want to get you into trouble, Miss Ransom, but if we discover that Mr. Foxley was killed due to his association with a drug dealer and you've withheld information from us, it could have severe repercussions for you.'

Emma burst into tears. 'This is just terrible.' She dabbed at her eyes and blew her nose. 'Of course I knew he was doing cocaine; everyone here knew that. But I swear to God, I have no idea where he got it from.' She thought for a moment. 'I know who said something to you – it was Daniel, wasn't it?'

Spencer stood up. 'Thank you for your time. I'd appreciate it if you would contact us if you recall any information that would be helpful.'

He walked out of her office and headed back down the corridor. Bergman was in reception, complaining loudly as Rita handed over a bundle of scripts.

'Nobody has told us anything, Mr. Bergman. Julia Summers isn't in and she would be the one to know.'

Bergman looked at Spencer. 'It's beyond belief what's going on here. We've had a movie premiere cancelled, and Ivor Summers is flying in, and no one seems to know what's going on. This business is enough to drive you insane!'

Spencer decided there was no point in asking further questions of Daniel Bergman.

As he left the building, Emma Ransom was tipping the contents of a small plastic container into the toilet and flushing it away. As she came out of the cubicle, Laura Queen walked in.

'Are you all right?' she asked.

Emma shook her head. 'That policeman has just asked me if I knew who was supplying drugs to Charles. I know it was Daniel who said something. He is such a slimebag. How the hell would I know where Charles scored from?'

Laura shrugged. 'I doubt if he would be using street dealers. With his money and his contacts he wouldn't need to take the risks; you know how paranoid he could be.' She put her hand on the cubicle door and hesitated. 'I doubt very much if anyone he scored from would want to murder him. You know how he could straighten himself out when he needed to. Right now we all need to get our acts together because that bitch of an ex-wife could ruin us all. I don't know about you, but I've lost a few clients already, and now they've put his latest movie on hold and it might not even get a premiere here.'

Laura went into the cubicle and shut the door. Emma looked at herself in the mirror, suddenly wishing she hadn't flushed it all down the toilet.

CHAPTER SEVENTEEN

Darren McDermott and DCI Tyler had been closeted in his office for over an hour.

While the team waited to see what was going to happen next, Jane was told to remove all of Justine's coffee cups from interview room one and went up to the canteen to get a tray, shaking her head in irritation. There was a probationary officer on duty outside the interview room and she gave him a brief nod of acknowledgement, tapped on the door and walked in. A second uniformed officer, who had spent half the morning on duty, raised an eyebrow as Jane placed the tray onto the cluttered table. Justine was sitting crossed-legged, smoking a cigarette, her chair pushed away from the table.

'I've just come to clear the coffee cups, Ms. Harris.'

Justine looked up but made no effort to acknowledge her; she behaved as if she had never seen Jane before.

Stacking the array of canteen mugs and plastic beakers, Jane picked up the ashtray full of cigarette stubs. As Justine was still smoking, Jane tipped the stubs into one of the coffee mugs and placed the ashtray back in front of Justine, who immediately flicked the ash from her cigarette onto the floor.

When Jane returned to her desk, McDermott was being ushered out of Tyler's office and into the interview room so he could confer with Justine. Tyler was looking ragged. He walked over to Jane's desk.

'Can you organize some coffee and sandwiches for myself and DI Miller, Tennison? Oh, and you will not be required in the interview of Ms. Harris.'

Jane now really felt she was being punished for her mistake over the camel-hair coat.

A uniformed officer came into the incident room to say that McDermott and Justine Harris were now ready to be interviewed.

The young DC Gary Dors looked over to Jane and spoke in a whisper. 'He's got everybody running after him, it's beyond belief. You'd never get this if it was just the station brief handling the interview. Just shows you what money can do.'

He quickly returned to typing up a report about a handbag snatch as DI Miller and Tyler left the room to begin the interrogation.

A few moments later DCI Collins walked into the incident room, asking to speak to Tyler, but when told he was not available, he crossed over to Jane's desk. He looked slightly sunburnt as he had white sunglass marks around his eyes.

'Is there any update on Max and Ivor Summers?' he asked.

Spencer wandered over. 'I heard from one of the agents that a film that was due to be released in the UK has been withdrawn. I believe Ivor has flown in from New York.'

Collins smiled. 'Well, that's good. I can catch two birds with one stone. Although I quite fancied a quick trip to New York.'

* * *

In the interview room the atmosphere was tense. DI Miller had his notebook open and his fountain pen placed in the middle of an empty page. DCI Tyler was sitting slightly back from the table, his tie loosened. Justine had taken her trench coat off and was sitting with her head bowed, her hair partly covering her face and her hands clasped together in her lap.

Darren McDermott was the only one who looked comfortable. He had removed his fashionable overcoat to reveal a Savile Row suit that probably cost a large part of the annual wages of the detectives sitting opposite him. He wore a chunky gold Rolex watch, a prominent signet ring and heavy gold cufflinks.

When he spoke, his voice oozed confidence. 'Your so-called evidence implicating my client in the murder of her ex-husband seems to amount to the fact that she inherits his shares in the theatrical agency. This is nonsense. She is already a wealthy woman. In addition, she was receiving substantial alimony payments from Mr. Foxley, which depended on the continued health of the business, which in turn was dependent on his expertise. The suggestion of her gaining financially from Mr. Foxley's death is patently absurd.'

Miller picked up his fountain pen. 'Mr. McDermott, we have been told by your client herself that she fully intends on selling her late ex-husband's flat. We are also aware she has every intention of selling his shares in the agency. Whether or not you agree that she will benefit from his death is neither here nor there.'

McDermott had very deep-set, dark eyes with heavy eyebrows. This made it difficult to read his expression, but it was as if Miller had not spoken. He looked at Tyler.

'We can also dismiss the fact that you have a shoeprint left at Mr. Foxley's flat that forensics have now matched to my client's trainer. At no point did my client attempt to hide anything. On the contrary, the left trainer was found in her wardrobe, in plain sight, while the right had been removed by one of the dogs and buried in the garden. Surely if it was her intention to hide what you believe to be crucial evidence, she would have done so more effectively. And in any case, the shoeprint was obviously made when she appeared at Mr. Foxley's flat and she saw her ex-husband's body.'

He gave Tyler a half smile, as if he found it all rather amusing.

'The same goes for the bloodstains on my client's coat and any fingerprints that were found at the scene, given that she was a frequent visitor. It has also been inferred that my client was in a sexual relationship with George Henson, and they were involved in this horrific act together.' He chuckled, as if at the absurdity of the idea. 'This is preposterous, and equally preposterous is the suggestion that Mr. Henson is the father of my client's daughter, Clara.'

Justine turned towards McDermott, who gave her an encouraging nod. Justine kept her eyes fixed on her hands folded in her lap.

'I first met George around twenty-five years ago. I was eighteen. He was an actor, like me, and we did a production of *Miss Julie* together.' She laughed nervously. 'George was not a very good actor, so eventually he turned to scriptwriting but it was many years before his first film script was accepted ... ' She trailed off and McDermott took over.

'Shortly after meeting Mr. Henson, my client became very successful, starring in a long-running television series. This made her financially secure and she was able to support Mr. Henson. In return, he ensured that Ms. Harris was offered the leading role in a major film. They have maintained a close friendship ever since.'

Miller felt they were losing control of the interview, and tried to switch tack. 'How did you feel about your ex-husband?'

'I had been very happily married to him. But the pressures of his success began to change him.'

Miller persisted. 'But you still allowed your ex-husband to take up residence in the property you had been awarded in your divorce settlement?'

McDermott decided to intervene. 'I'm sure you're aware that Charles Foxley and my client had joint custody of their daughter, Clara.'

Miller tapped the table with his pen. 'I am sure that was a very amicable arrangement, but their daughter was away at boarding school much of the time. The weekends we know Mr. Foxley spent at the previous marital home were frequent and often when their daughter was not there. Whether or not your client' – Miller glanced towards Justine, who no longer had her head bowed meekly, but was staring at him with a look of fury – 'continued, as we believe, to have a sexual relationship with her ex-husband after the divorce—'

'That is not true!' Justine snapped.

'Ms. Harris, we have forensic evidence taken from your ex-husband's bed in your home: a long, blonde hair, which matches yours. We also have possible semen stains on his sheets.'

Justine looked apoplectic. McDermott reached out and clasped her forearm, but she pulled away from him. Before she could say anything, Miller flipped over his notebook.

'When did you last see your ex-husband, Ms. Harris?' He placed his hand over a plastic wallet to ensure that neither of them sitting opposite could see what it contained.

'My client has clearly stated that she had not seen Charles Foxley for a considerable time, at least a week and a half before his death,' McDermott said evenly.

Miller was starting to enjoy himself as he leaned back in his chair. 'I would just like Ms. Harris to clarify exactly when she last saw her ex-husband alive.'

Justine clenched her hands. 'I had not seen him for at least a week, maybe more. And I have also told you' – she jerked her head disdainfully towards Miller – 'that the reason I went to the flat that awful day, and I had to witness the horror of it all, was because I had received a concerned call from his dog walker—'

'So, just to clarify,' Miller interrupted, 'you are claiming that you had not seen your ex-husband for over a week before you arrived at his flat on the Tuesday, just as the police were cordoning off the scene of crime?'

'Yes!' she snapped.

Miller slowly passed the plastic wallet across the table so they could both see the parking ticket inside.

For the first time, McDermott looked nonplussed, while Justine looked equally bewildered.

'Mr. McDermott,' Miller began. 'That is a parking ticket issued at 5:15 p.m. on the Monday. It shows Ms. Harris's vehicle registration number and gives the parking meter location as being twenty yards from Mr. Foxley's flat. We traced the parking meter attendant. He was unable to determine how long Ms. Harris's vehicle had been parked there, but when he came to the meter the time had expired, so he issued a ticket. He was also unable to confirm when the vehicle was driven away.'

A muscle twitched on the side of McDermott's jaw, as though he was gritting his teeth. 'I asked for full disclosure of the evidence you've gathered, and there was no mention of this parking ticket.'

Miller smiled. 'I'm sorry, I was not privy to the meeting as I was still making inquiries regarding this ticket. As you must realize, Mr. McDermott, this parking ticket proves without doubt that your client has lied to us.'

There was a moment of silence while McDermott considered how to respond, then Justine suddenly let out a guttural scream of rage as she hurled her body across the table and started clawing at DI Miller's face. She managed to grab hold of his tie, dragging him towards her so he fell face-down onto the table. Still holding tightly to his tie with her left hand, she began to punch his head with her right hand, all the while screaming, 'No! No! NO!'

Completely unnerved, McDermott was slow to react. But Tyler managed to get hold of Justine's arm and haul her away. She attempted to bite his hand, then fell to the floor, frothing at the mouth as her legs kicked out in some sort of fit.

Tyler rushed to the door and called to the custody sergeant: 'Get a doctor – quick!'

*   *   *

Jane was at her desk when Spencer hurried in to tell her that Justine Harris had attacked DI Miller. Miller appeared in the incident room with a bloodied handkerchief held to his face, his nose bleeding profusely. He went straight into Tyler's office, instructing Jane to get him a cup of tea and some paracetamol.

Justine Harris had been taken into the small medical room by the canteen, accompanied by McDermott and the station doctor.

By the time DCI Tyler entered the incident room, calm had been restored. Jane asked him if he would like a cup of tea and told him that DI Miller was in his office.

Tyler ran his fingers through his hair. 'Christ almighty . . . is he all right? We're going to need one of the girls from the canteen to clean up in interview room one. Yes, I could murder a cup of tea, although perhaps that's not quite the word I should be using.'

The canteen was busy as Jane, together with a young probationer, collected a bucket, mop and disinfectant to take to interview room one. There was a congealing pool of blood on the table and some spattering on the floor, which they dealt with quickly, returning the bucket and mop to the canteen.

When she got back to her desk, Spencer was shaking his head in disbelief. 'She only jumped across the table and punched Miller on the nose!'

Jane couldn't help but smile; she had felt like doing that to Miller many times herself.

'It's serious, Jane. She might have busted his nose. He's gone to the hospital for a check-up, while that smarmy QC is sitting upstairs with Wonder Woman. Apparently she's perfectly all right and wants to continue with the interview.'

Jane shook her head in disbelief. 'She's not going to be charged? Are you serious?'

'That's what I've been told.' Spencer turned as Tyler came out of his office wearing a clean shirt. He took Jane to one side.

'I need you to accompany me, but if you're concerned about it, I'll get Spence. I just feel that having another woman in the room might keep her calm.'

Jane was anxious not to show how eager she was, but immediately opened her desk drawer to take out her notebook. She couldn't resist giving Spencer a raised eyebrow as she knew he would have loved to be in on the action.

They went back into the disinfectant-doused interview room one. Tyler gave Jane a brief rundown of exactly what had occurred and where they had reached when Justine had lost control. He was clearly still quite shaken.

'She was like an animal – and strong: she lifted DI Miller off his feet and right across the table.' Tyler chewed at his bottom lip. 'I don't know whether it was the right thing to do not to prepare Mr. Smooth Operator for the parking ticket, but Miller wanted an element of surprise . . . and we certainly got that! She was totally out of control.'

'Well, she used to be a very successful actress; you don't think she could have been acting, do you?'

Tyler shrugged. 'If she was, I don't know what she thought she could accomplish by doing something that crazy.' He folded his arms.

'Well, it's given her some time to think,' Jane replied.

There was a knock on the door and a uniformed officer appeared. 'They're on their way, sir.'

Justine appeared to be a completely different character. She was composed and straight-backed, politely thanking McDermott when he pulled the chair back for her to sit down.

'Thank you for agreeing to see me again,' she said, turning to Tyler with a demure smile. Again, she ignored Jane, keeping her focus entirely on Tyler, who now read her her rights for the second time.

If McDermott had been shocked by Justine's previous behavior, he didn't show any sign of it now. Once again, he took immediate control of the interview.

'My client now wishes to explain why she lied. I also hope you will accept her apology for wasting police time. You have to understand that she was simply trying to protect her daughter and had not realized the importance of the timeframe.' He held his hands out, palms up. 'She desperately wants to apologize for her earlier behavior, but you must understand that she suffers from a number of challenging mental conditions that need to be controlled with medication.'

Justine lowered her eyes and smiled sadly, and Jane wondered which of them, Justine or her QC, was the better actor.

McDermott turned towards Justine. It should have been Tyler asking her to explain the parking ticket, but he seemed tongue-tied as McDermott resumed.

'Justine, I want you to tell them why you were parked at a meter close to your ex-husband's flat. But if you feel that at any time you are unable to continue, then I advise you to request the return of the doctor, as you are here on a possible serious charge and could be forced to remain in custody.'

Tyler knew he was right. If Justine could not give an acceptable answer then she could be charged.

She looked towards McDermott, as if for permission to speak, and he gave her an encouraging nod.

Tyler leaned forward slightly. 'Did you, Ms. Harris, go to your ex-husband's flat in Onslow Square on that Monday afternoon?'

Justine looked over to McDermott again.

'Just explain exactly why you were there at that time,' he encouraged her.

She bowed her head again and began twisting her fingers. 'After the divorce, Charles began to make things difficult because we had joint custody. I had fully agreed with him that he could, when Clara was home from school, stay at the house. In reality, some time before we even divorced, we were sleeping in separate bedrooms, but over the past year it had become unbearable. It wasn't just when Clara was at home for the weekend; he was making it permanent and would simply turn up and often be abusive. These occasions began to form a pattern. He would be unpleasant towards me, although he was never physically abusive: he would scream and rant, then start sobbing like a child, begging me to forgive him.'

'Were you aware of his sexual deviances?' Jane asked.

Justine took an intake of breath and looked up. 'Yes, of course I was. How could I not be? It wasn't something that just occurred overnight. It went on for years and years. Even in those instances when I was so naive and caught him out going to prostitutes, he would react by weeping and crying like a child. He blamed his mother and said that she had been cruel and had never loved him. In answer to your question, I did know about it but I didn't know the lengths he was going to in the latter part of his life. I had even suggested to him that he should see a psychiatrist. But to someone like Charles, that was an insult to his intelligence. Our tempestuous relationship had been a rollercoaster for so many years and I found it excruciatingly difficult to deal with him. I gave up my career for him. I financed him when he first began as an agent. But the more successful he became, the more I felt he despised me.'

Tyler coughed. 'Could you please just answer the question about the parking ticket?'

'I am getting to it,' she replied, with a hint of annoyance, as if a member of the audience had interrupted one of her performances. Once again, Jane could see a different character appearing. She no longer held her hands demurely in her lap but was gesturing expressively.

'Fine, if you don't want all the details.' She sighed dramatically. 'I had always refused to clean his bedroom in the house. I have a cleaner called Abby and she would occasionally wash his bed linen and do other bits of laundry, but in the last few weeks I wouldn't allow her to do anything for him. I just wanted him to leave me alone.' She put her hands down flat on the table. 'He appeared not to accept the fact that he didn't actually live there. If he had a premiere to go to, his clothes were left at the house. He blatantly ignored the fact that I didn't want him using my home. On that Monday, I had had enough. Abby called me up to his bedroom. On his bedside table he had left small plastic bags of cocaine. There were more bags on the dressing table, just casually left there. The room smelled of body odor and Abby was quite distressed as she had also found pornographic magazines left lying around. I decided that I would go and tell him that if he didn't leave me alone, I would sell the house and move away. There was no point in me changing the locks, he would just have broken a window. Charles was aggressive and obsessive, especially where I was concerned. I drove to Onslow Square and had to drive around three or four times before I found a parking meter. I was scared.'

Jane held her hand up. 'Could I ask you, Ms. Harris, as it was in the afternoon, how did you know Mr. Foxley would be at home?'

Justine hesitated. 'I called him. First I rang the agency, and they told me he wasn't there. Then I called his flat and spoke to him. He opened the door and he was holding Toots, the little dachshund. He was immediately wary, asking me why I was there. I tried to remain as calm as I could and we went into the kitchen. I told him that he had to stop coming to the house and that he had left drugs in his room, which at any time Clara could have taken. At first he did his usual denial, but then when I told him that I was serious, he became belligerent and accused me of being to blame for everything. I was quite used to his accusations as he had been jealous throughout our entire marriage. The reason I did not disclose that I had seen him was because when I saw what had happened to him, I did not want to be involved. That was the sole reason that I lied.'

Tyler looked over to Jane. Justine sat back in her chair as though the interview was now finished.

'So you just left, after you say that he became belligerent and made accusations against you?' Jane asked.

Justine nodded. 'Yes . . . when he was like that there was no point in trying to reason with him, so I left.'

'You have said that your ex-husband was never physically abusive towards you. Were you scared of him? Particularly that afternoon, when you told him that he was no longer able to stay at your house?'

Justine made an odd movement, twisting her body, as if she was trying to escape from something.

'He had threatened me,' she said finally.

'Did he threaten you that afternoon?' Tyler asked.

'If you have been listening to what I'm saying, it must be obvious, isn't it?'

McDermott straightened up in his chair. Justine was flexing her hand and curling it into a tight fist. He leaned towards her.

'Now is the opportunity for you to tell them exactly what happened, Justine. There is no need for you to protect his reputation now.'

She sighed and made a slight hissing sound, then bowed her head and spoke softly, so she was barely audible. 'I hit him.'

'Could you repeat that, please?' Tyler asked.

'I HIT HIM!' she almost shouted. She took a deep breath before continuing. 'He threatened me and said he would call someone to throw me out. I decided that it was pointless talking to him. He was becoming agitated, so I walked down the hallway to let myself out. I did not plan it, it just happened. There was a cricket bat, which he always kept by the front door. I knew he was going to try to stop me leaving. I picked it up and I swung it. I think it caught him on the side of the head and he lost his footing and hit the wall. He started crying and, as always, began begging me for forgiveness, but this time – and this was the first time – I did not feel an overriding sense of pity for him. Instead, I said something that I have never said to him before. Charles had a terrible guilt complex, which was the seed of his self-hatred. He believed that he had killed his brother, Tommy. I had always reassured him that it wasn't his fault, but I told him that I knew he had hidden Tommy's inhaler and deliberately provoked an asthma attack. I then repeated what his aunt Eunice had told me.'

Jane looked up sharply, recalling Foxley's aunt Eunice telling her that she had not seen Justine for many years.

'It was at Clara's christening. I think she felt ashamed because of her humble background, and it's true that Charles had behaved appallingly towards her. Anyway, that was when she told me about what he had done to his brother. She also told me that his mother had blamed him and had eaten herself to death. She was grossly overweight when she died. I never told him that I knew. Whenever he became hysterical, it was almost as if he was reverting to being a child, slapping himself in the face, screaming, "It was not my fault, it was not my fault," but I think his mother always blamed him and he had been consumed by that knowledge all his life.' Tears streamed down her face. 'I drove home and was terrified that he would come after me. When he didn't turn up, I called him, but he didn't answer.'

Tyler had been taking notes, and now held up his pencil. 'Ms. Harris, could you just describe to me again how you struck Mr. Foxley with the cricket bat?'

She closed her eyes and sighed. 'Well, I just told you that I thought he was coming after me. I just picked it up and I swung it.'

'Where exactly did you strike him with the cricket bat?'

She touched the right side of her head. 'I almost missed . . . It was just a sort of glancing blow.'

'Did it draw blood?'

'No, I don't think so. As I said, I almost missed him.'

Jane made a note and passed it to Tyler. *Bat had handle rope: no prints. Blunt force was to the back of the skull.*

Tyler glanced at Jane's note. 'So, Ms. Harris, after you had struck Mr. Foxley with the cricket bat, what did you do with it?'

Again, she shrugged her shoulders. 'Well, I just threw it aside because he was still standing. I thought he was going to try and stop me, and that is when I ran out. The following day, when I still hadn't heard from him, I was worried that I might have really hurt him and that was why I went back to his flat. Then . . . I saw his body.'

Tyler nodded. 'So you went home. What time did you call Mr. Foxley?'

'It must have been about nine p.m.'

Tyler made a note. If Justine was telling the truth, they now had a solid timeframe for the murder. Foxley was alive at 5:30 p.m. but did not pick up the phone at nine p.m., presumably because he was already dead.

After a few more formalities, Justine was released from custody and McDermott offered to drive her home. He also agreed that her passport would be retained; she would not be allowed to leave the country with the possibility of an assault charge against her.

It had been a long day. Jane watched from a window in the ladies, which overlooked the car park, and saw McDermott guiding Justine into the passenger side of his Bentley. He tucked a blanket around her before closing the door. Tyler was standing to one side and she watched as the two men shook hands before McDermott got into the driver's side and drove out of the police yard.

* * *

Tyler came back into the incident room and stood by the board, writing up the time and date that Justine had been released from custody, while Jane sat at her desk typing up her report of the interview. Part of her did not want to believe Justine's story because she always seemed to be acting. But she couldn't help feeling that she was also a genuinely tortured woman.

Tyler looked as if he had the weight of the world on his shoulders as he slowly moved along the incident board, which was now taking up almost the entire length of the room. He looked back to the expectant faces of the gathered officers.

'We're back to square one,' he said.

CHAPTER EIGHTEEN

The next morning Jane had showered and blow-dried her hair in plenty of time so she could have breakfast at the station. Before getting in the shower she had put in a call to Elliott, but there had been no reply. She decided to try again before leaving, but got the same result. However, when she got down to the front door, her mail had been delivered and there was the acceptance of her membership for the rifle club. There was a note welcoming her and suggesting she keep the enclosed card in a safe place. The card gave the code for the garage doors. She would be given the club door's entry code from the secretary because security was, at all times, uppermost in their minds.

Jane placed the card in her wallet and was now even more eager to have another session, preferably with Elliott; she realized, with a touch of surprise, that after their last meeting at Gravesend that she was beginning to rather like him.

* * *

Jane was at her desk when Miller walked in with two pads of cotton wool in his nostrils. There was also a red-purple bruise around his right eye. The young detectives quickly smothered their sniggers as Miller approached Jane.

She looked up.

'We didn't find any drugs at Foxley's flat, but we know from the postmortem that he had a high quantity of cocaine and amphetamines in his system. I believe Justine Harris lied because we know from the search at her house that there was cocaine and amphetamines in his bedroom. I have every intention of arranging a further interview with Ms. Harris.'

'We know she knew her ex-husband was at home on the afternoon of his murder. Do you think Justine took him the drugs?'

Miller's mouth tightened. 'I would have thought, Tennison, that was obvious.' He crooked a finger for her to join him at the incident board. Miller pointed to the first day of the investigation.

'Sergeant Tennison, I want every date matched and every alibi reconfirmed.'

Jane's heart sank. The amount of work Miller had just dropped in her lap would not only be time-consuming, but she would be desk-bound for a lengthy period.

Miller headed towards Tyler's closed office door and, almost as an afterthought, turned back to those gathered in the incident room, catching DC Gary Dors putting two fingers up his nostrils.

Miller snapped, 'You think this is funny? Don't think for one second that I am finished with Justine Harris. If I had my way, she would've been put in the cells for what she did to me.'

He went into Tyler's office, slamming the door behind him.

* * *

DCI Collins was wearing another ill-fitting suit. His sunburnt face had at least paled slightly but Spencer found it amusing that the outline of his sunglasses was still obvious around his eyes. They were in a gilt elevator in St James's, heading up to the fourth floor of an elegant seventeenth-century building. There had been considerable modernization in the lobby but the impressive plaster panels and honeycomb ceiling indicated that, at one time, this vast building had been a palatial private home.

Exiting the lift on the fourth floor, they stepped into a thickly carpeted corridor lined with oil paintings. They headed towards a large open area. In the center was a modern half-circular desk, with a variety of telephones and an electric typewriter. Sitting behind it was a woman in her late forties who resembled Wallis Simpson, the mistress and subsequent wife of the Duke of Windsor. She was wearing a black fitted jacket, with a large white collar and white cuffs. Her black hair looked dyed, with wings of white either side.

DCI Collins approached her and introduced himself and Spencer, saying they had an appointment with Max Summers. She opened a large leather-bound diary, looked down the page and then gave a casual glance at a small gold wristwatch.

'Please take a seat and I will tell him you are here.'

They sat on a long red couch, looking around at the opulent room complete with a huge chandelier. It was a further five minutes before the austere receptionist picked up one of the telephones, listened for a moment, then replaced it.

'Mr. Summers will see you now.' She swiveled in her desk chair towards two beautiful polished wooden doors, at least ten feet high.

The enormous office, with another huge chandelier, had the same thick maroon carpet but with floor-to-ceiling bookcases lining the walls and a bay window that looked out onto a large garden. In front of the window was one of the biggest desks Spencer had ever seen, in dark mahogany with lion claw feet and ornately carved legs. It was completely bare except for three telephones. The leather desk chair was empty. The two men were standing rather awkwardly in the middle of the room when one of the bookcases suddenly opened and an Alfred Hitchcock lookalike, with bulbous eyes and prominent jowls, came into the room, from what appeared to be an en suite bathroom. He gave a brief nod.

'Must have eaten something last night,' he grunted.

He sat down heavily in the desk chair and indicated for them to take a seat. Both the chairs were at quite a distance from the desk. Collins took the initiative and pushed one closer to the desk, and Spencer did the same. Max Summers opened one of the drawers and opened a packet of indigestion tablets.

'What do you want from me?' he asked.

Collins leaned forward. 'We are investigating the death of Charles Foxley—'

Summers interrupted him gruffly. 'I know that, but I don't understand how I can be of any assistance. I did business with the man, but I have no idea why he was murdered. I never mixed with Mr. Foxley on a social level, apart from when we were organizing a premiere, but then my brother Ivor handles that side of the business.'

'You had considerable investments in Mr. Foxley's independent film projects,' Collins said.

'That is correct, but to be honest with you, my brother is the creative one. He runs the film company, and I have always taken my brother's advice in terms of investing in film projects. It was after I was approached by Mr. Foxley for an investment that I suggested he meet with my brother – that's how their relationship began.'

Spencer noted that he had small hands with polished nails folded over his protruding stomach.

'Your business, Mr. Summers, is predominantly in property development?'

'That is correct. I also own a number of high-end restaurants and apartments. The movie business isn't really my thing.' He pursed his lips, emitting an odd, high-pitched giggle. 'To be perfectly honest, I'm being constantly told off for falling asleep at premieres of the films my brother produces. But my wife loves all the glitz and glamour of these occasions.' He gestured towards a large silver-framed photograph on the wall. 'That's my wife, taken at last year's Oscars.'

Both Spencer and Collins turned. Summers' wife looked very glamorous herself, and at least twenty years his junior. She was also considerably taller than him, wearing a couture gown with her slender arm resting on her husband's shoulder. Before they could remark on the photograph, one of the double doors into his office suddenly opened. Without having to be introduced, it was obvious from their physical resemblance that this was Max's brother.

'I can't wait any longer, Max . . . I gotta get back to New York to organize the locations and cinemas. It's a huge damned pain in the ass.' His guttural New York accent was a stark contrast to his brother's smooth English vowels.

Max stood up from behind his desk and held his hand out towards the new arrival. 'This is my brother, Ivor. These gentlemen are here from the Metropolitan Police.'

Collins stood up to shake Ivor's hand. 'I'm Detective Chief Inspector Collins and this is my associate, Detective Sergeant Gibbs.'

Ivor was clearly considerably younger than his brother, with a full head of dark hair that looked as if it might have been dyed. It was swept back from his broad face, which was not yet as jowly as his brother's. He was oddly dressed in a loose denim shirt with grey pinstriped trousers and two-toned shoes.

'They are here about poor Charles Foxley,' Max said.

Ivor raised both hands. 'My God, that was shocking. Hard to believe. Even harder to believe you haven't yet caught the bastard who did it. I'm telling you, if this was New York, they would've got him by now. If you want to know where I was when it happened, that's it – New York.'

Max nodded. 'And I was at a big charity dinner.'

Ivor perched himself on the edge of his brother's desk. 'It's caused a major headache for us, I can tell you. The reason I'm here is because we'd organized a big premiere at Leicester Square with a ton of publicity. I'm gonna have to cancel everything. I'll tell you, though, we're going to dedicate this film to Charles Foxley.' He gave a short, barking laugh. 'It'll probably be the best credit he ever got in his life.'

'That's unnecessary,' Max said scowling.

His brother guffawed again. 'Look, I don't mind admitting it. I've said it often enough. Charles Foxley was becoming a liability. You give some people a little success and it goes to their fucking heads. Half the time he would make out as if he had produced, directed and written the damned movie, never mind spent millions of dollars in promotion. He had a big ego, all right. But I have to give credit where credit is due: he had a stable of very bankable actors, and he had three other agents who were also able to bring names to the table, along with well-known directors and writers. But if it hadn't been for my expertise, Foxley wouldn't have had the first idea of how to package a movie.' He laughed again. 'I've got to hand it to him, though, he did learn fast, but he tried to undercut us and the movie turned out to be a flop, and it was my brother and I who lost the big bucks.'

The meeting continued for a further half an hour as Collins asked about the financial stability of both their companies. To Spencer, their wealth was jaw-dropping. Although he found both men obnoxious, he couldn't help but be impressed. Eventually, Ivor said he needed to go and deal with some of the formidable costs they would incur by cancelling the premiere of Foxley's last movie.

As Collins and Spencer stood up to leave, Spencer turned to Max. 'How's your daughter, Julia?'

It was just an afterthought, but Max visibly tensed.

'Why are you bringing her up?' he snapped.

'No reason – it's just I met her at the agency.'

Max immediately relaxed. 'Well, she isn't there anymore. She was only there as a favor because these young teenage girls don't have a brain in their head. When she got two O-levels she thought she was Einstein. Takes after her mother . . .'

He glanced at the photograph of his wife but, before he could say anything further, his desk phone rang. He waved a hand dismissively at Spencer and Collins as he picked up the phone and they made their way out.

* * *

Jane had Foxley's work diary on her desk alongside his personal notebook. She had been cross-checking all the dates and timings but there was no indication where the cash, which Foxley withdrew almost every week, was going. The assumption had always been that he was paying a drug dealer, and Spencer had noted on the incident board that the drug squad should be brought in to get heavy with the agency in case one of the agents was the dealer, but there was still no actual evidence.

As Jane was checking through the money trail, she crossed to Spencer's last memos on the incident board. He had written: *KW possibly being closed, no finances.* Jane hurried back to her desk. Checking through her notes, and comparing them to the diary, she noticed that there were several references to KW over a period of time. The initials were often accompanied by names of hotels, such as The Ritz, The Dorchester and The Grosvenor, and there were odd numbers beside them. She then thumbed through the main desk diary in an attempt to match the dates. On four matching dates there had been heavy use of whiteout, blocking out information.

She looked across to Gary Dors, who was thudding out a report on his typewriter about a recent robbery. His use of whiteout was infamous.

'Gary. Do you know how to lift whiteout off a page? I mean, it's water-based, isn't it?'

He picked up his ever-present whiteout bottle and squinted at it. 'I suppose . . . It's a bit like a paint, isn't it?'

'I was just wondering how to ease it off from paper to see what's written underneath.'

Dors shrugged. 'If I were you, I'd experiment – put a few brushes on a blank piece of paper and let it dry. Then see if you can get it off if you wet it. But you better not attempt to do it on any important document because it could destroy the paper.'

'Thank you for that expertise,' Jane said, deciding she wouldn't attempt it. Then she had a thought: the forensic lab sometimes used ESDA, an electrostatic detection apparatus, along with oblique lighting. She remembered that the machine allowed the visualization of obscured writing without damaging the document.

Spencer came in eating a sandwich.

'My God, the Summers duo are something else. DCI Collins reckons Max is worth over a billion and God knows how much his brother is worth. But both have a confirmed alibi for the night of the murder. That said, they've got enough money swirling around to hire someone. Then again, a professional hitman doesn't usually disembowel his victim and slit their throat. That really is what you'd call overkill.'

Jane was only half listening and tapped him with a pencil. 'You know you put KW on the incident board?'

'Yeah, it's KatWalk, the modeling agency Foxley was running. Mostly, from what I can suss out, it was financed by Foxley himself, as none of the other agents appeared to have any interest in a bunch of unknown teenage models and ex-footballers.'

Jane flicked through the pages of her notebook. 'Do you think it is possible that's where Foxley's cash was going? I'm still missing sixty-odd thousand. I've highlighted this over and over again and keep being fobbed off with the idea it was being used for drugs.'

'That's a shit lot of drugs,' Spencer said.

'Maybe we need to pay another visit to the agency,' Jane said.

'Christ, I'm wearing the carpet out there. Who do you need to talk to now?'

'Simon Quinn. We should ask if he can tell what all the numbers mean, and explain about the hotels.'

When they approached him with their request, Tyler was unenthusiastic.

'You don't think we should wait for the drug squad to have a crack at them?' he asked Spencer.

Spencer looked skeptical. 'I honestly don't think there is major dealing going on in the agency, guv. I mean, they may do a couple of lines here and there but Justine Harris has said that Foxley could straighten himself out when he needed to. So it doesn't sound like he was a complete addict.'

Tyler sighed. He was looking ragged. 'OK. Fine. But don't waste too much time on it.'

Tyler had had a tough morning and although the chief superintendent hadn't mentioned anything to the team, he knew that he was probably going to be replaced. The worst scenario would be if he was replaced by DI Miller. They had an unpleasant argument when Miller suggested that they had been too lenient on Justine. He had become angry, saying that he wanted to have Justine charged with assault of a police officer because when he had gone for an X-ray on his nose it turned out to have been broken. He didn't care if she was represented by a big hitter like McDermott. It had taken considerable time for Tyler to talk him down.

Justine Harris's alibi had been confirmed and Tyler had released her on police bail, pending further inquiries. She could be charged at a later date with the assault on Miller, but that wasn't enough for him.

'It's not over with that woman,' he said theatrically as he left the office. 'Before I'm done I'm going to prove she's a murderer.'

CHAPTER NINETEEN

The team were all processing the day's duties. Jane had put in yet another call to Elliott but received no reply. She returned to making a list of what she and Spencer would need when they went to the agency.

The double doors into the incident room banged open as DI Miller, now with tape across his nose and a nasty black eye, came in wearing a grey peaked cap. There were a few mutters of 'Afternoon, sir' but everyone kept their eyes averted.

Miller went to his corner desk and removed his trench coat and cap. Jane could see from her desk that he was using a small hand mirror to check his appearance. She turned as one of the double doors into the incident room opened and McDermott walked in, this time without his velvet-collared overcoat, but wearing an elegantly tailored pinstripe suit and carrying an expensive-looking leather briefcase.

As Jane stood to acknowledge him, he gave a curt bow of his head.

'I think DCI Tyler is expecting me.'

Before Jane could put in a call to him, Tyler opened his office door. Miller hurried over, and McDermott gestured for him to go ahead of him into the office.

I'd like to be a fly on that wall, Jane thought to herself.

'Come in, please,' Tyler said cordially.

McDermott opened an expensive monogrammed leather notebook. He declined coffee or tea, feeling it imperative they quickly come to an agreement.

'Gentlemen, firstly let me say that any assault charge against Ms. Harris would not be appropriate. It's a matter of record that she has psychiatric problems for which she is on medication, and I do not think it advisable that she be brought back into the station for further questioning. That would clearly be detrimental to her health.'

Miller couldn't believe what he was hearing.

'Well, I can tell you, Mr. McDermott, that interviewing Ms. Harris has been detrimental to *my* health. But we still have a number of unanswered questions and Justine Harris still remains a suspect in the murder of her ex-husband.'

'I am very aware, Lucas – may I call you Lucas, Detective Inspector Miller?'

Rather taken aback by McDermott's pleasant tone, Miller nodded.

'Lucas, you have an impressive career and are a very well-regarded officer. I also agree Ms. Harris needs to be re-questioned, but my primary concern is for her wellbeing. I am asking if you would, in this instance, agree to interview Ms. Harris at her residence.'

McDermott continued before Miller could answer.

'Obviously time is of the essence; I am able to delay meetings at my chambers and could be with you for a meeting with Ms. Harris at midday today.'

Tyler glanced at Miller and gave a small nod, encouraging him to agree.

McDermott closed his notebook. 'I do think, Lucas, it would be perhaps advisable if Detective Sergeant Tennison accompanied you. It would, I am sure, be a calming influence on my client.'

'Let's do it now,' Miller said curtly.

'I do apologize, Lucas, but I am due to have a meeting with the Chief Justice's department, so if you could make it for midday, I would be most grateful.'

Miller hesitated for a moment, then gave a small shrug of his shoulders. 'Twelve it is then, Mr. McDermott.'

*　*　*

Spencer came over to Jane's desk. 'Come on, the car's waiting.'

Jane stood up 'You just missed McDermott. Apparently he's talked Miller out of pressing assault charges but he's now agreed to another interview with her and I'm to be present. Midday at her home.'

'We better get a move-on, then,' Spencer muttered.

Sitting in the rear of the patrol car, Spencer was hungover and irritable. 'I'm sick and tired of interviewing the same people over and over again. What are the chances we'll come up with anything new this time?'

Jane could feel her temper rising. 'Well, if you'd told me the KW initials stood for KatWalk, we could have done this before.'

'If you had asked I would've told you. I put it on the incident board.'

'Yes, I know you did!' she snapped, turning away to look out of the window.

Spencer yawned and scratched his head. 'You know they were talking about going back to Mandy Pilkington and interviewing her again to get the personal details of all her clients. If she doesn't play ball we'll put a uniformed officer outside her address 24/7 and they'll speak to every man who comes and goes from the address. That will soon destroy her business.'

Jane sighed. 'That's all a total waste of time. I'm the one that has been working on this bloody timeframe. According to her, the clients listed for that day were in the morning, our victim mid-afternoon and another client after him. The only client whose name she gave, together with his address, was the disabled man. From her timeline, he is the only one that was there at her brothel from five thirty onwards, until he was collected by Farook and taken home. I suggest you don't waste time and just interview him.'

'Terrific, I'm sure a guy with no legs could've got over to Foxley's and gutted him. Now that's what I call a waste of bloody time.'

Jane was now really angry. 'Maybe you should spend more time on your day job, Spence, instead of worrying about whether or not your band has secured a record deal.'

Spencer glared at her. 'For your fucking information, Tennison, Sony Records turned us down. Happy now?'

Jane felt bad for snapping at him but didn't have time to apologize as they drew up outside Paramount House.

The first agent they went to see was Daniel Bergman, who was sitting at his desk eating a bagel and drinking coffee. 'My God, it feels like you two are moving in here. Now what do you want?'

Jane took out her notebook. 'We have some questions about entries in Charles Foxley's diary.'

Bergman reached over as she passed him her neatly typed page of queries.

'I now know KW stands for KatWalk,' Jane said. 'But what about the other references?'

He picked up a paper napkin, wiped his mouth and opened his desk drawer to pull out his personalized desk diary.

'Right, I can't be one hundred percent sure, but . . .' He flicked the pages in his diary. 'I would say the references to hotels are when a film premiere is taking place. There would be a number of press launches, cast and crew, and then, usually after a premiere, they would have a champagne buffet celebration.'

'So these were all movie premieres?' Jane asked.

Daniel continued flicking through the diary. 'Yes, I'd say so. I may have been at a couple. I mean, they weren't all Foxley's independent premieres. You know Ivor Summers has quite an impressive film company.'

Spencer leaned forward. 'What do you make of him?'

Daniel scrunched up the napkin and tossed it into a waste bin. 'Well, let's say I wouldn't like to argue with him. He's a heavy hitter.'

'Would you say the Summers brothers are untrustworthy?' Spencer asked.

Daniel laughed. 'I would say that is putting it mildly. I know for certain that Charles was becoming disenchanted with them.' He gestured to various film posters in his office. 'Charles was getting packages together, but with the last projects there was a lot of ill-feeling about how the brothers were taking the lion's share. He brought the actors to the table, the script, writers, director; but I know when they won an award at Cannes, Charles's name wasn't even mentioned.'

Daniel's phone began ringing.

'Do you mind if I get to work? If there is anything else I can help you with, feel free to ask.'

He picked up the phone and his usual abrasive tone was instantly replaced with a syrupy cooing. 'Oh, my darling. I just have to congratulate you. What a brilliant performance.' He put his hand over the receiver and rolled his eyes. 'She was fucking dreadful,' he whispered. 'If you don't mind, I'd like some privacy.'

Spencer and Jane went back down the corridor and turned right, heading towards Simon Quinn's office. The small cubicle room was in complete disarray. There were stacks of ten-by-eight photographs on the floor, and many of the framed photos had been taken down and were leaning against the wall. His desk was piled high with files and more photographs while he was on his hands and knees, putting things into a large cardboard box beneath his desk. As they entered, he sat up and hit his head on the edge of the desk, swearing.

Jane stepped over photos of the young, beautiful girls and asked if he could double-check some dates, which she needed to confirm were connected to KatWalk. Simon was wearing a

T-shirt emblazoned with 'Kiss', with the white, ghoulish face of Gene Simmons on the front.

He looked at the two typed pages Jane handed him. 'Oh shit, I don't know. I'll have to have a look at my ledger because I can't remember who we sent and who we didn't.'

Jane moved closer to the untidy desk. 'I don't understand. What do you mean by "who we sent"?'

'Well, models, of course.'

'But these were film premieres?'

'Yes, they were, but the boss was often asked to supply some really glamorous girls – "arm candy", they call it.'

Spencer was standing with his hands in his pockets, looking around at the upturned photos of the young models.

'They weren't asked to serve drinks or anything like that,' Simon continued. 'It was usually a good gig, as all the press photographers were there and some of these girls would give their right arm to get their faces in the paper. When there was a star actor who didn't have anyone with them, we'd organize it for the girls to accompany them on the red carpet.'

Jane took back her notes. 'So the numbers six, four, three – were these the number of girls at the premieres?'

'Yes, I would think so, but it was always organized by Mr. Foxley. You have to understand that this was his sideline. None of the other agents were interested.' He shrugged. 'Not that anyone in this effing place shows any interest now he's not here. In fact, I've not even had my wages paid. No matter who I ask, I'm given the cold shoulder. I know we were losing money, but we'd only been up and running nine months or so. Without him, as you can see, it's finished.'

Spencer bent down, looking through the photos of the gorgeous young girls. At first he was unsure what he was looking for, then he straightened up.

'The girls you supplied for these events – did they get paid?'

For the first time, Simon seemed uneasy. He looked away before shrugging his shoulders.

'Well, they were given expenses, of course, and in some instances they were paid to get glammed up. But on the whole, as I said, they were very eager to be seen.'

Spencer nodded. 'You didn't quite answer the question. On top of the expenses, and on top of maybe buying a designer gown, were they also paid to go to these premieres?'

Simon was sweating. 'You're making it sound sleazy. I can assure you it wasn't. I don't know what you've heard, but all the girls were very well cared for. They had taxis home and there was nothing untoward about the evening.'

'Thank you very much.' Spencer nodded to Jane for them to leave.

Jane couldn't quite see what direction Spencer was going in, but looked at her wristwatch and knew she needed to go if she wanted to get to Barnes for midday.

As they headed down the stairs, Spencer paused.

'The last time I was coming up these stairs, one of the teenage models was hurrying down and was so intent on keeping hold of a wad of cash she had in an envelope, she knocked straight into me and everything spilled out.'

Jane pursed her lips. 'Why haven't you brought this up before?'

'To be honest, I didn't really see the point.'

They walked out onto the pavement.

'Well, there is a point, Spencer, particularly if Foxley was paying for these models to be a lot more than arm candy. I've been trying to figure out where the shedload of cash Foxley was withdrawing each week was going. I suggest you get back there and put some pressure on young Mr. Quinn.'

CHAPTER TWENTY

In reception, Rita took a call from DC Gary Dors, asking to speak to DS Tennison. She held the line and put a call in to Simon Quinn's phone and was told that both Spencer and Jane had already left the building, missing Spencer's return across the corridor.

Spencer tapped on Simon Quinn's door.

'What is it now?' he asked petulantly.

Spencer walked into the room. 'I just need to straighten out a few things.' He looked around and saw a stool, which had a stack of models' photographs on top. He picked them up and placed them on the edge of the already cluttered desk.

'I have answered every single question. I just don't know what you want from me.'

Spencer took out his notebook and leaned over the desk to remove a pencil from a jar. 'It is just to satisfy my boss. You stated that the models were hired to be – and this is your description – "arm candy" for various premieres, which were not necessarily Charles Foxley's movies.'

'Yes.'

Spencer made a show of flicking from one page to another, but there were actually no notes written on them.

'So you say you paid for these girls to have taxis back and forth, and for evening dresses. How much would you say that would cost per girl?'

'I don't know, it depends where they lived. I mean, if they had a flat in Hampstead and were going to the Odeon in Leicester Square, we would have to book a taxi there and back.'

'So what would you say was the usual outlay for cash for taxis? I presume you paid them cash?'

Simon sighed. 'Yes, cash. They would come in the day after with their receipts and that's how we paid them.'

'What about the evening wear?'

Simon sighed again. 'Well, sometimes they would hire an evening gown. We aren't talking Valentino or Yves Saint Laurent. They just had to look glamorous.'

'So, on these occasions, the girls would come in with the receipts for the clothes the next day?'

'Yes. On a couple of occasions the hire company refused to take the item back due to a drink being spilled or a torn hem, something like that.'

'So how much would you say you were forking out for these glamorous clothes you wanted the girls to wear?'

'Well, it varied, but on average I would say around two hundred pounds. Sometimes they included shoes and an evening bag. I mean, some of these girls were pretty savvy, you know. It wasn't as if they didn't jump at the chance. As I've already told you, sometimes the star of the movie needed an escort, so the girls couldn't wait to get the gig.'

Spencer made quite a show of writing down figures and totting up the amount. 'So, shall we say when six girls were required to attend one of these first nights, you're looking at a thousand pounds, maybe fifteen hundred payout?'

Simon shook his head, 'No, no . . . it would have been more like five or six hundred.'

'Do you have these receipts?' Spencer asked quietly.

'You must be joking. Look at the state of my office! Do you really think I can put my hands on any of the receipts? Besides, they would be handled by Julia to give to Foxley.'

Spencer nodded thoughtfully. 'Did you ever have any problems with these girls?'

'What do you mean, problems?'

'Well, did any one of the girls complain or say they felt they were being taken advantage of? I mean, you said there were a lot of movie actors, producers and directors.'

'They couldn't wait to get there. Most of them were aspiring actresses and, as I have said before, the girls were almost fighting each other to be given the job.'

'You didn't actually answer my question. Did any of these girls ever make a complaint that perhaps they might have been forced into providing sexual favors?'

'I don't understand what you mean.'

'Mr. Quinn, I have put it as plainly and politely as possible. I am asking you if these young girls, I would say some of them under-age, ever felt obliged to go further than being simply "arm candy".'

Quinn shook his head. 'I can honestly say that I never had to deal with anything like that. I am sure that if there had been any instances of wrong-doing, Mr. Foxley would have dealt with it personally.'

'Do you know if any girl was ever paid extra?'

Quinn's face was now glistening with sweat, his cheeks flushed. He plucked a tissue from a box to wipe his forehead.

'I'm not getting involved in any of this. I only just started to work here recently, so I can't tell you what may have gone on before my time. I did hear a rumor that one girl had caused a lot of problems, but I don't know who she was.'

Spencer held up his pencil. 'Wait a minute. You heard about a girl causing problems? What do you mean by "problems"?'

'Oh Christ! I was just told that there had been a problem. I think she was young and immature and I was told afterwards to make sure that any of the girls we sent to these first nights were given strict instructions: if anyone made an unwanted approach, we encouraged them to leave immediately and then they should report back to Mr. Foxley.'

Again Spencer held up his pencil. 'So what you're saying is Mr. Foxley knew that he was sending these girls into a situation which could easily end up with the expectation of sexual favors?'

Simon had to wipe his face again. 'I am not getting into this because it had nothing to do with me. When I was told that they needed six girls, or four girls, for a first night, I would call them up. As I keep on saying, they were eager to accept. These girls hoped to get discovered at these events: there were photographers, journalists ... A number of times these girls were photographed and got onto the front page of the top gossip papers. I mean, they were encouraged to mingle with the cast and crew, and therefore had every opportunity to meet directors and producers at these parties. But Mr. Foxley was often there to personally supervise the girls.'

Spencer flicked through his notebook again. 'These parties, as you just said, would take place before the film began and afterwards at certain top hotels like The Ritz, The Savoy, The Dorchester?'

'Yes, yes. The producers spared no expense on these events.'

'So often a lot of these people involved with the movie would be staying at the hotels?'

'Yes, I suppose they would.'

'Can I take you back to the girl you said was a problem? Can you give me any indication what that problem was?'

'No, I can't! I wasn't working here at that time. You have to understand this is a fledgling company, which now, due to the circumstances of Mr. Foxley's death, is no longer functional.'

Spencer turned back to the notes he made with Jane in the accountant's office. 'So, KatWalk was making losses from the moment it was opened, is that right?'

'Yes, because we had to get the girls on our books. So Mr. Foxley ran the company at a loss until he felt we could begin earning. I had also booked a number of sportsmen for advertising purposes.'

'Can you give me the names of the girls you know were at the last premiere? I recall the last time I was here I saw a very tall red-haired girl who appeared to be carrying an envelope stuffed with money, a lot more than I would say would cover a taxi and a hired gown.'

Quinn stood up, pushing his chair back. 'I don't remember. As I said earlier, you should contact Julia Summers. Perhaps she can give you a name.'

'Come on, Simon. She looked like a model: red hair, wearing high-heeled shoes and carrying an envelope bulging with cash. All I want is a name.'

Quinn gestured to the mounds of photos boxed up and stacked in heaps around the room. 'If you want to go through all the photographs, you're welcome.'

Before Spencer could say anything, Quinn had pushed past him and into the corridor. Spencer looked around the room. He doubted that he would be able to remember the girl that clearly but, nevertheless, he picked up the stack of photographs and began to sift through them. He took out his notebook, jotting down the names from the back of the photos. He noticed they all had a cross in the corner. A memo on top of the stack read: *No longer clients, no further booking.* He put them aside and picked up a box from the floor.

* * *

Jane walked to Piccadilly Circus and caught the Piccadilly Line to Hammersmith. She then hailed a taxi to take her to Justine Harris's house in Barnes. By the time she got there it was almost noon. Parked in the drive was Justine Harris's Mercedes, but there were no other vehicles.

Jane walked to the front door and rang the bell, thinking perhaps that DI Miller had been dropped off. She could hear a telephone ringing. No one answered the phone or came to the door. Jane checked her watch again and walked back to the gate, which had been left open. She stood on the pavement, waiting as she saw Justine heading towards her, coming out from the copse and starting to cross a field not far from the railway line. She was wearing a slouch hat and an old overcoat and had all three dogs. Stick, the whippet, and Jack, the Jack Russell, were on leads, while she carried Toots, the dachshund, under one arm.

She was about ten yards away when she saw Jane and gave her a friendly wave, still holding the two dogs' leads. As she approached Jane, she smiled and said they should go in the back way as she needed to wipe the dogs' paws down and feed them. Justine appeared to be relaxed as she unlocked the back door to go into the rear garden, pointing out to Jane the new fencing that had been erected to keep the dogs from escaping, and in particular to prevent Jack from attacking next door's pigeons.

She laughed as she let the dogs off the lead. 'I'm sure the poor woman's deluded. Half her precious pigeons were wild and just took up residence in the pigeon loft when they felt like it.'

Justine ushered Jane into the kitchen as she kicked off her muddy boots and left them outside. The dogs all bounded about outside for a while before they followed the women into the kitchen.

'Take a pew,' Justine said, indicating the breakfast bar with high stools. She then began to prepare the three bowls of dog food. At the same time she filled the coffee percolator and moved gracefully, almost like a ballet dancer, around the kitchen. Jane had never seen her so amicable and so relaxed. She checked the time again but didn't feel that it would be a good idea for her to mention the imminent arrival of DI Miller. She wondered if perhaps he'd been delayed in traffic or was being driven to the house by Darren McDermott.

Justine finished feeding the dogs and washed her hands carefully in the sink before taking down coffee mugs and putting out milk, sugar and a plate of biscuits, then sitting down beside Jane.

'I have been very busy,' she said brightly. 'I forced myself to make notes and think very clearly about my every move on the Monday before I went to visit Charles. Now, I know that you found a parking ticket from when I parked outside his flat, but I thought it would help if you also knew exactly what I had been doing before that.'

She poured coffee for them both and Jane added milk to hers. Justine got up from the breakfast bar and went over by the draining board to pick up two sheets of notepaper.

'Do help yourself to a biscuit,' she said as she sat down again. 'Now, on Monday morning I made a big decision.'

Suddenly Jane began to feel uneasy.

'Where are your mother and Clara?' she asked.

'Mummy's taken Clara to buy some groceries. It's quite a walk, but she felt it would be good for Clara to get some exercise.' She squinted at the notepaper. 'Now, I just said that I had made a decision that morning. I talked it over with George because I was anxious and I knew it was not going to be easy. This is where I have been untruthful because I know what I did was very wrong.'

Jane sipped her coffee, waiting.

'Aren't you going to ask me what I did?' Justine said, smiling.

'Yes, of course, if you want to tell me.'

'Well, I went into Charles's bedroom and when I was searching his desk drawers, I found lots of little plastic bags of cocaine. I knew what it was because I've always known he used it. I planned to go to see him at his office, but when I called, they told me he was not available. It was lunchtime and I knew exactly where he would be.' She glanced at Jane. 'I knew he would sometimes see these dreadful women during a lunch break.' She gave one of her high-pitched laughs. 'Apparently he would sometimes go to this brothel several times in a single week. One could ask where got the energy from, but then he was very athletic.'

'So, when you found out he wasn't at his office, what did you do?'

Justine shrugged. 'Well, I planned to wait until he returned to the office.'

Justine continued to calmly explain how she had put everything in her handbag and left the house to go to Kensington. She parked in the Harrods car park but said she had more than likely thrown the ticket away. However, she was sure that the security cameras would be able to confirm her arrival and departure time. She then went into Harrods and went up to the accounts floor as her account was outstanding and she settled it by cheque. While she was there she asked to use their telephone.

Again, she assured Jane all this could be checked out because of the time she paid off her account. They allowed her to use one of the phones at the accounts desk and she called the agency but was told that Charles was not there. She then made a second call, this time to his flat. When he answered, she just replaced the receiver. By the time she collected her car from the car park, it was almost three p.m. Knowing Charles was at home, she decided that she would go through with her intention of telling him that he was no longer welcome at her home. If he persisted, she was going to sell the house and see a lawyer to discuss custody of Clara. She could then provide evidence that he was a drug user and that their daughter was not safe in his company.

Jane glanced at the clock in the kitchen. It was already half past twelve, but she didn't want to stop Justine as she was still calm and giving Jane new and valuable information.

'I knew Darren McDermott would handle the custody hearing. He's a very experienced and respected QC; he is also a close family friend.'

Jane nodded. 'He certainly seemed to be very solicitous of your welfare.'

Justine laughed. 'You have no idea just how caring he is. I am sure she won't mind me telling you this, but he was once my mother's lover. She was an exceptionally beautiful woman then.' She tossed her hair back. 'I've always been told how fortunate I am to have inherited her looks. McDermott was deeply in love with her for many years.' She shrugged. 'Anyway, I digress . . . Where was I?'

Jane sipped her coffee and had another uneasy feeling as Justine used a finger to go up and down the page of her notes.

'Right, now then . . . I can't give you the exact time I found a parking space. I didn't know how long I was going to be there so I put in some change and I thought that it would be enough because it was about 3:45 p.m. My intention was to go and tell him exactly what I was going to do, then leave. I went in, and he seemed surprised to see me. I said we needed to have an adult conversation because I had reached a decision not only for myself, but for Clara. He laughed but when I continued to tell him my intentions, he said that even if I attempted to get full custody, he would be able to prove that I was mentally unstable. At that point, I opened my handbag and told him I could prove that he was a cocaine addict and that he was also stuffing himself with amphetamines.'

Justine picked up a pencil and began to scribble on the page as she described how he had laughed and told her that he could consume any amount of drugs and still functional normally. He tipped out the contents of the cocaine packet and used a bank note to snort up a line in front of her.

'"There, you see," he said to me. "You don't stand a hope in hell of ever getting rid of me, and if you attempt to stop my access to Clara, I will have you certified."' Justine's eyes filled with tears.

'He would drive me mad like that because he could be vicious and cruel, but then he would become like a child, needing me to care for him, and that's why I always forgave him. But on this occasion I waited because I was hoping the combination of what I put into the cocaine would quiet him down.'

Jane held up her hand. 'What did you mean by "combination"?'

'I crushed up my sleeping tablets and mixed it with the cocaine.'

Jane looked up from her notes. 'When you went to see him at his flat, do you remember what he was wearing?'

Justine screwed up her face. 'Well, I think he was wearing his jeans, because he almost always was, his sneakers and a white shirt – in fact, rather an expensive one, with one of those priest collars, not a button-down – and he wasn't wearing a tie.'

Justine got up from her stool, fetched the coffee pot and refilled their mugs.

'I left the flat and, as you know, the parking ticket shows that I was fined at five fifteen p.m. I drove from Kensington straight home and I have only just remembered that when I got there, Abby, my cleaner, was waiting. I had forgotten to pay her on the Friday. I asked if she could come with me to the nearest cash machine and I withdrew enough to pay her wages and for me for the rest of the week. When we returned, Abby finished some ironing and left. I then went to bed.'

Jane could hardly believe it. If everything Justine was saying could be verified, she had an alibi for the time of her ex-husband's murder.

Justine picked up her coffee mug and smiled. 'Perhaps we could sit in more comfort in the drawing room as I'd like a cigarette.'

* * *

Spencer had grabbed himself a sandwich and a coffee to eat at his desk and was intending to write up a report of his interview with Simon Quinn. As he walked into the incident room, he was surprised to see DI Miller.

'Aren't you supposed to be interviewing Justine Harris, sir?'

'Yes, but not until three p.m. That pompous twat Darren McDermott has put the meeting back because he has an urgent situation at his fucking chambers. He should be collecting me any minute.'

Spencer put his coffee down and checked the time. 'Hang on a minute, sir, did anyone talk to Tennison? The last time I saw her, she was on her way to meet with you at Justine Harris's home.'

On the other side of the room DC Dors put up his hand. 'Guv, I put in a call to the agency to speak to Tennison but I was told you had both already left, so I presumed someone must have got in contact.'

Spencer glared at him. 'You fucking presumed? What the hell is going on here? She left around eleven thirty this morning and was getting the Underground to be sure she got to the interview for midday. Has anyone been in touch with her? I mean, does this Justine bitch know the meeting isn't going ahead until three p.m.?' Spencer turned his attention to Miller. 'Tennison has gone to see her, and you, of all people' – he pointed at him – 'know what Justine Harris is capable of doing.'

Miller looked as if he was about to give Spencer a dressing down, then reined himself in. 'Get a patrol car and get straight over there. In the meantime, call the house and see if Tennison is there. And then contact Barnes police station and ask them to get over there urgently and check on Tennison's safety.'

Spencer ran down the stairs two at a time, banging the door out into the yard. He collared one of the uniformed drivers and got the keys to drive, shouting at him to inform DI Miller he was on his way to Justine Harris's.

* * *

Jane followed Justine into the drawing room, carrying her fresh cup of coffee. She could see from the clock on the mantelpiece that it was already ten to one. She thought she should call the station to check what was happening. Just as she was about to ask if she could use the phone, she noticed a large white envelope on the coffee table. It had been sealed shut with Sellotape and had a pink ribbon tied around it. In large loopy writing on the front was the word 'Mummy'.

Justine frowned and untied the ribbon. 'This is odd,' she said, crossing over to the mantelpiece. She stared hard at the envelope in her left hand as she patted along the mantelpiece with her right hand. Then to Jane's horror Justine held up a silver dagger. 'I bought this in a bazaar in Morocco when I was filming there three years ago,' she said, waving it in the air. 'The blade's terribly sharp, so I always keep it high up here on the mantelpiece, out of Clara's reach.'

Jane pushed her back further into the chair as Justine continued to wave the dagger around. She could feel a rising sense of panic and tried to take some deep breaths unobtrusively as Elliott had taught her.

Justine quickly slit open the envelope, slicing through the Sellotape. She looked up at Jane as she placed the dagger back in its sheath and tossed it towards her.

'Have a look, it's really beautifully carved.'

Jane felt swamped with relief as she held the ornate dagger. Justine sat on the edge of the sofa opposite her, smiling broadly.

* * *

Spencer, with sirens blaring and lights flashing, drove as if he was competing in a Formula One race: at top speed, sometimes on the wrong side of the road, other times mounting the curb to avoid traffic. He was heading for the Hammersmith Bridge but there was no possibility of him overtaking the line of traffic crossing the bridge in single file. As he reached the traffic lights he shot through the red light and overtook vehicles heading towards the right-hand turn for Barnes. Any ill-feeling he had had towards Jane over the situation with the models had dissolved; all he was concerned about was her safety.

* * *

Justine pulled out two letters from the envelope. The first one was on lined notepaper and written in a childish scrawl. She read it then placed it to one side and unfolded the second letter.

'My God, how could she do this?'

Jane looked at her questioningly.

'It's from my mother. Listen to this: "Dear darling Justine, I am sorry for the subterfuge, but for a while I have felt this is not the atmosphere for Clara to be living in. I am constantly on edge and worried for her, and also for you. I have therefore decided to take my granddaughter home to live with me in my house. This is for her benefit and I will be talking to her headmistress about these arrangements."'

Justine glanced across at Jane with an empty look on her face, and then back down at the letter.

'"I have contacted dear George and he will hopefully be with you shortly."'

The telephone rang and Justine stood up and crossed to the drawing-room door, yanking it open. She picked up the phone, screamed 'Fuck off!' then slammed the receiver down. When she walked back into the room, her whole demeanor had changed. Her eyes were wild and she was grimacing as if she had eaten something sour.

'I knew that would be my mother. That bloody two-faced, interfering woman . . . The stupid cow has been wanting to take my daughter for years and now she thinks she has the right to move her out of my home – my daughter's home. Well, I won't let her get away with it.'

Jane eased herself forward in the seat. 'You know, Justine, perhaps it might be for the best at the moment. You are going to be re-questioned this afternoon and maybe your mother is just trying to keep Clara away from anything upsetting.'

'My mother is a complete bitch. She was always more glamorous, better educated and more sophisticated than me. She's been competing with me my entire life and now she has taken away the only thing that makes my life worth living.'

Jane watched as Justine went over to the mantelpiece and began patting along it with her hand again, knocking over an ormolu clock and a china figurine.

She turned to Jane. 'Where is my knife? Where is my knife?'

Jane didn't dare get up. She had slid the dagger down the side of the chair cushion and now watched as Justine became more and more uncontrolled. She was moving in rapid, jerky steps, backwards and forward. Jane knew she had to calm her but she didn't want to give Justine the opportunity to find the knife.

Jane reached for her coffee mug. 'Justine, you are one of the most beautiful women I have met in my life. When you came into my office, I said to myself you reminded me of Faye Dunaway.'

Justine seemed to heave for breath.

'It was that film . . . you remember that film? What was that film called, Justine?'

'*Bonnie and Clyde*,' Justine said, nodding. 'I've been told that before, you know, that I look like her, but I gave up my career when I got married. My mother always told me that I should have never even considered marrying him.' She gave one of her strange high-pitched laughs. 'Probably because she wanted him for herself . . . That's how she was, my mother.'

Jane desperately wanted to get her off the subject of her mother. Although Justine's movements were no longer as jerky, she was still pacing. Jane wanted to buy time to enable her to get out of the room. She slowly stood up, certain the knife was well hidden, and kept up deep, steady breathing to maintain control.

'Do you have any photograph albums of when you were acting? I'd love to see pictures of the productions you were in.'

'Oh, please, don't be so patronizing,' Justine sneered. 'I'm sure you have no interest in my career. I have explained to you that I had nothing to do with my ex-husband's murder, but I don't think you believe me. You're just like everyone else. You don't believe everything I remembered about where I was and what I did. Just as I was beginning to trust you. Now you're trying to convince me that I look like a movie star just to calm me down. What you don't understand is, I could have been a star.'

The sound of the police siren cut through the room. For a second the noise distracted Justine and she turned in a panic towards the window. The siren came closer, along with the blue flashing light, then the front door was being hammered. Spencer screamed out for Jane. She was now in a position to make a run from the drawing room into the hall, as Spencer kicked out the stained-glass panel in the front door. He reached in to open it then ran towards her. There was a look of such relief on his face that it was almost comical.

'Christ, Jane, are you all right?'

She was so thankful to see him that she almost wept. 'I'm fine, but Justine is out of control. She's in there.'

'You just stay where you are.' Spencer walked cautiously into the drawing room. Justine was sitting at the piano.

'I'm going to play you my favorite piece. I achieved Grade Eight when I was seven.' She began to play the 'Moonlight Sonata'.

Spencer stopped in his tracks. He looked over to Jane, who was standing in the doorway.

She said, very quietly, 'There is a silver sheathed dagger down the side of the cushion in the armchair opposite the sofa.'

Spencer moved further into the room as Justine continued playing. Spencer retrieved the dagger and returned to join Jane in the hall, shutting the door behind him.

The dogs had been barking frantically from the moment Spencer had hammered on the front door. He put a call into the station to say that DS Tennison was with him at the Barnes property and they would be waiting there with Justine Harris until DI Miller and Darren McDermott arrived.

Spencer went into the kitchen and placed the dagger in a plastic bag he found in a drawer.

'You think this may be the weapon used to disembowel Foxley?'

Jane shrugged. 'It's possible. Lawrence should check it for any blood residue.'

Spencer found a dustpan and brush to sweep up the broken glass from inside the front door.

Justine stopped playing the piano just as DI Miller, accompanied by Darren McDermott, arrived.

CHAPTER TWENTY-ONE

McDermott went in to sit with Justine. She was calm but tearful, repeating to him that her mother had taken Clara and that was the reason she had become so upset. Meanwhile, Jane sat with a very tense DI Miller in the kitchen. He was reading Justine's account of where she had been on the Monday afternoon of the murder and kept on glancing irritably towards the dogs, who had returned to their respective baskets.

He tapped Justine's list. 'Do you believe all this? Don't you think it's strange that she didn't say this in the interview at the station?'

'Well,' Jane said, 'she has made it very clear that we can double-check everything. It gives her quite a strong alibi if we take the time of death to be early that evening.'

Miller shrugged. 'More legwork. I, for one, still don't believe a word she says. Now, about this knife. Did she threaten you with it?'

'No, she used it to open a letter. I think it's sharp, though.'

Miller turned as the dogs got out of their baskets. McDermott had entered the kitchen.

'I think we should both go and talk to her now. She has explained to me that she was distressed due to the letter from her mother and wanted me to apologize to Detective Sergeant Tennison if she behaved erratically.'

Jane and Spencer left together in the patrol car. On the way back to the station, he told her he had already been reprimanded by DI Miller for driving to Justine's and that more than likely they would be presented with a bill for damages to the door. Jane told him not to worry about it: if there was any query, she would emphasize the fact that she had been genuinely fearful and was relieved when he came to her rescue.

She smiled at him. 'It did feel like a rescue, Spence, and I really appreciate the fact that you drove over here. I'm sorry if I was a bit terse with you earlier.'

He patted her knee. 'You were right about KatWalk. I think we might have a development on that front.'

During the rest of the drive back to the station, Spencer filled Jane in on the interaction with Simon Quinn and the fact that he had been unable to identify the model he had seen on the steps of the agency with an envelope full of money.

'I got the girls' contact details form the back of the photos. I'm telling you, Jane, I was shocked how young some of them were. But the person we need to question about the girls is Julia Summers. I think she knows all about it. I reckon these so-called models were being exploited for underage sex.'

*　*　*

When they got back to the station, Jane typed up the report of her meeting with Justine, underlining that there should have been measures to ensure her safety when there were concerns about Justine's mental state.

It was coming up to 5:30 p.m. and Spencer decided to contact Michael Langton, Mandy Pilkington's disabled client and the only one they felt could give a timeframe regarding the afternoon of Foxley's murder. Spencer spoke to a Mr. Alistair Jones, the caretaker at the care home. He was told that Mr. Langton was not available until the next day as he was undergoing treatment. Spencer clocked the time and wondered if his treatment was at Mandy Pilkington's. Alistair Jones said he would be available at ten the following morning.

After he finished his report he went over to Jane's desk and said he was going home, suggesting that she should do the same. Although she had dismissed the whole incident with Justine as being nothing serious, he knew that she had been shaken by it.

'Thanks, Spence, but I'm fine. I just need to finish my report.'

Twenty minutes later, as she was about to leave, Gary Dors came over.

He explained that he'd contacted the forensic laboratory with regard to removing the whiteout and had been told their equipment had been taken to check a fault so they wouldn't be able to examine the pages until the following day

'But,' he said, looking pleased with himself, 'I've figured out how to lift whiteout off a page. You use a wet cloth and just keep dabbing gently until it's almost gone and then if you hold the page up to the light, you can sometimes see what's written underneath.'

'Thanks, Gary, but I'd rather let the lab examine it,' Jane said.

'That's OK,' he said. 'I just feel bad about being the one who was supposed to contact you with the time change. What I should've done is radio the driver, but I didn't think of it.'

'Never mind, Gary, what's done is done.'

He said goodnight and left the incident room, which was now ominously quiet. The noticeboard would be filling up tomorrow with all the new information from the visit to Justine's.

Jane couldn't resist going to the property lock-up and taking out Charles Foxley's diary. Frustrated that she wouldn't get the lab results until tomorrow, she decided not to waste any more time, and put in a call to the agency to find out Julia Summers' home phone number.

Rita answered the phone. 'She doesn't work here no more, I'm afraid. She's now working for her father. I've got an office number there and also a home number if you want it.' There was a pause. 'Look, I'm sorry about the mix-up earlier. I told the policeman who called that you and the other detective had left but I didn't see he'd come back.'

Jane told Rita not to worry, then called Julia Summers' father's office. She was told, rather curtly, that Julia was only working a few hours a day in the postal section and was not available until the following morning.

Jane tried Julia's home number, which was answered almost straightaway.

'Is that Julia?' Jane said. 'My name's DS Tennison. My colleague and I talked to you at the agency? We have a few more questions for you, I'm afraid.'

'Oh, I see. I suppose you could come this evening, if you like,' Julia replied, without sounding very enthusiastic. She gave her home address as a mews in Queen's Gate. 'I'll only be there until seven, though, because I'm going to the theatre.'

'Thank you, Julia,' Jane said. 'I'll be with you shortly.'

Jane put a note on Spencer's desk to say she had gone to see Julia Summers, and also made a note in the station diary.

As she left the station, she passed Tyler in the corridor.

'I heard about your problems with Justine this afternoon. If you want to talk, I'll be in the office early.' He nodded to her and went back to his office.

It didn't take long for Jane to drive from the station to Julia Summers' house. The mews was directly behind Queen's Gate. Jane reckoned at one time they had been stables or staff quarters for the elegant houses. Julia's address was at the end of the mews, where there were two bicycles chained up against a railing beside a notice saying: *No bicycles*.

Jane rang the doorbell and waited. After three attempts the front door was eventually opened and Julia Summers, with her hair in giant rollers and wearing a terrycloth robe, appeared, looking surprised.

'Good heavens! I didn't think you would be here so quickly.'

'I'm sorry, but as you mentioned you were going out to the theatre, I thought the sooner the better.'

'Oh, absolutely. Do come in.'

The two-story mews house had a small narrow staircase. There was one large combined drawing and dining room, and a neat, compact kitchen. The interior was well decorated and furnished, but the place was a tip. There were old newspapers and food cartons everywhere, and clothes strewn on all the furniture. There were also a number of dead plants, and Jane could see dirty dishes stacked on all the surfaces in the kitchen.

'Do you want a cup of tea or anything?' Julia asked.

Jane shook her head and removed a large bundle of underwear from a chair to sit down.

'Sorry about the mess,' Julia said, waving her hand vaguely around the room. 'I don't have a cleaner anymore. She left without saying a word. I'm going to advertise for someone else but my roomie is just a student and hasn't got much cash. She always accuses me of being untidy but a lot of this is hers. My father would have a fit if he came in. But I don't see why I have to clean it if it's not all mine.'

Jane nodded, trying not to look as appalled as she felt. 'Absolutely.'

Julia perched on the edge of a cluttered sofa, slowly removing one large roller after another and shaking her silky blonde hair loose. Jane opened her briefcase and took out her notebook with copies of the pages that she had taken of the desk diary before she left.

'I wonder if you could help me with this, Julia. There are a number of pages that have a lot of whiteout covering what was written underneath. I've listed the dates and I wonder if you could tell me what was originally there and explain why it was blocked out.'

'Oh gosh, I can't remember. I mean, I know why I used whiteout but I can't really recall exactly what was written before, just that I was told not to put it in the agent's diary.'

'What were you told not to put in?' Jane asked.

'Well, when I'd been told there was a film premiere, you know, a first-night party for cast and crew, I was told by Mr. Foxley they would like four models, or sometimes two or six. So I had begun to write it down in the diary because I had been told to let Simon Quinn know what was needed and the location of the event.'

'So when did you use whiteout to block these out?'

'Ummm . . . ' Julia looked up to the ceiling. Jane felt she could almost hear the little wheels turning in her head. 'Do you mean when was I told not to put them in the diary anymore?'

'Yes.'

'Well, I suppose it was when I used the whiteout.'

Jane was beginning to lose her patience. 'When were you told to whiteout out what you had written in the diary?'

Julia began to chew a fingernail. 'I can't remember the exact date, but I think it would be a few weeks before that terrible thing happened.'

'You mean the murder of Mr. Foxley?'

'Yes, that's right, but it might have been a month or so before. He was quite hard to work for, you know. He did most of everything in his head, and Emma oversaw his appointments and made sure he was where he should be. But he was always late and had to be reminded of everything. She would call him before all his meetings to remind him and—'

Jane held up her hand. 'Yes, yes. Could you just tell me when Mr. Foxley instructed you to whiteout out any reference to the number of models required for premieres?'

'Oh, gosh . . . ummmm . . . he was horrible to me about it and he made me cry. I keep trying to remember the exact time, because as I just said, he rarely made any reference to the diary. He would come in and tell me to tell Simon he needed four girls for three nights at The Dorchester for the cast and the crew, and—'

Jane closed her eyes. 'When did Mr. Foxley tell you to delete all the references to the models hired to go to these first nights?'

'It might be eight weeks ago? Maybe less. He had come in very early for some reason. As I just said, he hardly looked at the diary, because it was Emma who always reminded him. But on this occasion he was standing by my desk, flicking through the pages, and he said to me, "Who told you to put these bookings in?" and I said to him, "No one, Mr. Foxley, but when you tell me to organize it with Simon Quinn, I write them in the diary. I thought that is what I was supposed to do!" He swore at me; in fact, he did more than swear. He threw things around the room and told me I was to get some whiteout and block out every reference I had made to models in the diary. That KatWalk and the sports agency had nothing to do with the main Foxley & Myers agency, and as such there was never to be any reference in the diary.'

Julia dug into the pocket of the terrycloth robe and took out a tissue. She began sniffing.

'He was so horrible to me; I didn't know what to do. He told me I only got the job because of Daddy and if I messed up again he would throw me out. My father can be equally nasty to me, but I was happy working with Mr. Foxley ... until then.' She blew her nose. 'That's why I used almost two bottles of whiteout.'

'But Simon Quinn always had a record of how many girls were needed?'

'Well, he was supposed to, yes.'

'I understand that you also introduced some of your friends to the modelling agency. Is that correct?'

She nodded.

'How did your friends find working for KatWalk?'

'Well, they didn't really work as proper models, you know. They didn't have any experience. Lots of them went to have photographs done, but they really all agreed to do it because they wanted to go to the premieres.'

'How did they find mixing with all the movie actors and directors?'

Julia shrugged. 'I don't know. I mean, I don't think they lasted very long. They didn't really have to work, so they did it as a one-off, you know.'

Jane wrote a few things down in her notebook and, without looking up at Julia, she quietly asked, 'Can you tell me about the situation which became very difficult with the modelling agency?'

Julia crossed her legs and began to kick one foot up and down. 'I don't know about that.'

'I think you do,' Jane said, looking at her.

'OK, I don't honestly know who it was or what happened, but there was a situation that was complicated. All I do know is something happened in one of the hotel bedrooms and Mr. Foxley was in a fury about it. The reason I know that much is because my father also seemed to know something, but I was not told what had happened. I even asked one of my friends if she knew anything.'

'What's her name?' Jane asked quickly.

'I don't see any point in me telling you her name as she doesn't work for the agency. She's just a friend.'

'All right then, just tell me what your friend told you.'

'Um, it was a while ago; in fact, a long time ago. She had hired a dress and was told to mingle. She didn't actually have to hire a dress as her family are very rich. Anyway, she had too much champagne and she thought she was just being very friendly to one of the producers; he told her that if she came up to his room at the hotel and was very nice to him, he could give her a part in his next movie.'

Jane leaned forward. 'Go on.'

Julia began to shift in her seat, flushed with embarrassment. 'He wanted her to do something to him.'

'Julia, we're both grown-ups. Tell me exactly what he wanted her to do.'

'He wanted to have sex with her and do dirty things. When she refused, he threw her out. She just left.'

'Then what happened?' Jane asked, her patience almost at breaking point.

'Mr. Foxley gave her a lot of money and apologized and said he was appalled at what happened and hoped she would never talk about it.'

Jane sighed. 'So that's one incident you know about. What else do you know about that you haven't told me?'

Julia shook her head. 'I don't know any more than what I just told you. I hadn't worked there very long and I don't think I should have told you about Annalise anyway. Oh God, now I've told you her name. I need to call my father about this. I'm really worried now because I don't think I should be talking to you.'

Jane snapped her notebook closed. 'Thank you very much for your time, Julia. You have been very helpful. Don't be concerned about your friend Annalise. I won't be contacting her.'

As Jane left, Julia slammed the front door behind her. She was certain Julia would be on the phone to her father in seconds but she didn't care. She had a feeling the case was about to take a new turn.

* * *

Jane was at her desk, typing up her report on her visit to Julia Summers, when a thought struck her. She called Spencer at home and his wife answered.

'Oh, sorry if I've interrupted dinner, it's Jane Tennison. Could I have a word with Spence?'

Spencer came to the phone. 'My God, what is it now? We just had a takeaway delivered and I'm halfway through a bottle of wine. Don't say I have to come in.'

'No,' Jane said quickly. 'I spoke to Julia Summers and I just wanted to ask you something about the models in Simon Quinn's office.'

'What about them?'

'You took down a lot of names, didn't you?'

'Yeah, I don't know how many. The girls' particulars were printed on the back of the photographs but I haven't typed up my report yet.'

'Can you recall if you saw the name Annalise?'

'Anna who?'

'*Annalise*. I'm not sure how it's spelled.'

Spencer sighed. 'I honestly can't remember. To start off with I was looking through a stack of girls they were no longer booking, so I then started on another stack. I remember there was a Yasmin in the obsolete file, but I was really looking for the red-head I saw with the envelope of money, and I didn't find her.'

'OK, thanks. Sorry to bother you. Enjoy your takeaway.'

'You do know we have a seven a.m. briefing tomorrow? I'll come in early to bash out my report. Did you get anything from Julia Summers?'

Jane was hesitant. 'Maybe, maybe not. I'll see you tomorrow.'

As she replaced the phone, Tyler came out of his office and looked at her, shaking his head. 'You're becoming a permanent fixture here, Tennison. I have you down as off-duty.'

Jane packed up her bag. 'Yes, sir. I just wanted to finish a report.'

Tyler folded his arms. 'Anything I should know about?'

'I'm not sure, sir. I need to do more work tomorrow.'

He nodded. 'Well, you get off home. There's a briefing at seven a.m. That's for all the team.'

Jane filed her report and left the station. By the time she got home, it was after 10 p.m. She made herself some cheese on toast and finished a half bottle of wine from the fridge. She had one message blinking on her answer phone. It was Dexter. 'Hi, I was just passing by and wondered if you fancied a bite to eat?'

Jane replayed the message and realized it had been made earlier in the evening. It was too late to return his call. She felt quite pleased about it, though, and promised herself that the following evening she would call him back. She went into the bathroom and was just reaching to turn on the bath and empty some relaxing bath salts into it when her phone rang. She rushed to pick it up, thinking it must be Dexter.

'Hello?'

'Jane, it's Dabs. Just checking in. Sorry if it's a bit late. But Joan said you called a couple of times and I was just a bit concerned that something was wrong.'

'No, nothing wrong. I was actually just going to tell you . . . ' She hesitated to mention that her relationship with Elliott had really moved on. Instead, she told Dabs that she had received her membership card for the rifle club.

'That's good. You probably won't get the main door code until the next time you go.' He gave a soft laugh. 'You have to memorize the number and if you write it down you have to eat the paper. Security, you know.'

'I've been trying to contact Elliott. I'd like another session with him, but he never answers his phone. I wondered if you had a work number for the customs office he works from?'

'No,' Dabs said quickly. 'Look, don't do that. Leave it with me. He might be in Devon if he's not still in London. I'll get him to call you.'

Jane hung up the phone and went back to the bathroom. After a long, luxurious bath, she lay down on her bed, replaying the brief phone call with Dabs in her head. She couldn't quite put her finger on it but it felt like Dabs was hiding something. She sighed. Maybe Elliott was married. Typical! She put Elliott out of her mind and made herself concentrate on what she needed to do the following morning. She'd told Julia Summers she wouldn't try to contact Annalise, but that was exactly what she was going to do.

* * *

Jane had a thudding headache the following morning. She didn't bother making herself breakfast but drove in early to the station to get a coffee and scrambled eggs in the canteen. She took two aspirin and, even though she didn't feel hungry, forced herself to eat the eggs. Her headache persisted. At 6:50 a.m., Spencer joined her, carrying a full English breakfast and a mug of tea.

'Sorry about last night,' he said, banging down his tray. 'I've been working nights on and off and it was just going to be a nice evening at home with her. You didn't spoil it, though; the takeaway was terrible. Soggy chips and an overcooked kebab.'

Jane sipped her coffee. 'Did you finish your report?'

He nodded, his mouth full. 'Yeah, yeah, yeah . . .'

'Did you come across the name Annalise?'

'No, sorry. What's so important about this Annalise?'

Jane pushed her half-eaten scrambled eggs away. 'It's just a possibility, but she'd been hired for one of the premieres and something bad happened. Julia didn't actually mean to give me her name and was reluctant to tell me about it. I just have this feeling that we might be on to something.'

Spencer shrugged. They had no time to discuss it further as the briefing was about to begin. They left the canteen and walked down to the incident room. This time there were even fewer officers than for the last briefing. DI Miller was already sitting with his pristine notebook and sharpened pencil at the ready as

Tyler, looking haggard, sipped from a large mug of black coffee. Tyler kicked off the briefing by explaining how crossed wires had led to Jane going to Justine Harris's house on her own. He glanced towards Jane and nodded his head.

'However, we were in the end able to question Ms. Harris, and she attempted to clarify her movements throughout the day Charles Foxley was murdered. These details are to be checked out and verified. We are still not able to pinpoint the exact time of death; the pathologist has just given us a three-hour window from five thirty to eight thirty as rigor mortis had occurred within that time. There is still the possibility that Ms. Harris is a suspect.' He frowned. 'I can certainly vouch for her physical strength. She has admitted giving Mr. Foxley drugs, and claims that when she had not heard from him, she became concerned, and that was the reason she returned to his flat the following day. As we are all aware, the blood on Ms. Harris's coat and on her trainers is a match for Mr. Foxley's, but there's nothing to prove the bloodstains weren't acquired at the scene when police were there.'

Miller turned a page in his notebook. 'We have confirmed that Ms. Harris has been committed three times, first at age thirteen, a couple of years later at fifteen and then again at twenty-five. Her diagnosis is schizophrenia and she is on medication. Notes attached to her medical records describe her dysfunctional behavior and violent mood swings.'

'With that diagnosis, I'm surprised her daughter wasn't taken into care,' Jane remarked.

Miller shrugged his shoulders. 'Perhaps social services were never made aware of it. Maybe you could now tell us about the dagger found at Ms. Harris's home.'

Jane flicked back through her notebook. 'The knife had been placed out of sight on a marble mantelpiece in the drawing room. Ms. Harris explained that it had been put there for the safety of her daughter. The blade's eight inches long and very sharp. The knife is being examined for traces of blood, which could be matched to the victim. But it's unlikely to be the missing weapon used to disembowel the victim as that appears to have been a serrated-edged knife.'

She was about to sit down when Miller pointed his pencil at her.

'You spent some considerable time at the agency. Is there any further information you gathered we should be made aware of?'

'We know Foxley was withdrawing a large amount of cash – two to four thousand pounds every couple of weeks – and even after taking into account his visits to the brothel and his drug use, there's a substantial amount of cash unaccounted for.'

Miller interrupted her. 'Do you think he was being blackmailed?'

Jane shook her head. 'I have not identified anyone who might have been blackmailing him.' She gave a sidelong look to Spencer but he had his head down, doodling in his notebook.

'Anything else?' Miller asked.

Jane hesitated. 'At this time I don't have anything I feel would definitely be relevant to the investigation, but . . . I have found out that Mr. Foxley used the models from his KatWalk agency to act as "arm candy", as Simon Quinn put it. These young girls would be taxied to and from the events and were enabled to hire expensive evening wear. Obviously the more glamorous they looked, the more press photographs there were. The girls were ambitious and some hoped for a career as an actress.'

Miller looked around the table and then back to Jane. 'So where does this leave us? I can't see the point, Sergeant Tennison.'

Jane flushed. 'At the moment, sir, I don't really have evidence to back it up, but I think these girls may have been paid money for sexual favors.'

Miller gritted his teeth. 'And where, if this is true, is the connection to our investigation?'

'I'm attempting to find that out, sir.'

'Charles Foxley had his throat slit and was then disemboweled, for God's sake. I cannot see what paying young models to be "arm candy" could possibly have to do with it!'

There was an embarrassed pause as everyone glanced down at their notes. Eventually another officer was asked if he had verified with the Harrods car park if they retained lists of the vehicles that used their facility. The briefing continued for a further hour as they churned over the information they already had.

When it was over, the detectives given new assignments filed out. Jane and Spencer sat at her desk. He thumbed through his notebook showing all the names of the models he had written down.

Spencer checked his watch. 'I have to go. I have an interview with Michael Langton. I think it's going to be another dead-end. I doubt very much that the poor bloke will be able to give us any new information.'

After Spencer left, Jane sat thinking for a moment, then decided to try to cut some corners. She called the agency, hoping Rita would answer. She was in luck.

'Oh, 'ello,' Rita said. 'We aren't officially open yet, but I always come in early because I have to sort the mail.'

'I just wanted to ask you, is it true that KatWalk and the sports agency is closing?'

'Yes. It's been on the cards ever since *you know what* happened. No one else really wants to take it on. They're all quite snooty about it. Only handle famous people, not skinny, hopeful models.'

'I need a big favor,' Jane said. 'There's a young model, Annalise, who I really need to contact. It's very important. I believe she was a friend of Julia Summers.'

Rita remained silent, so Jane had to push a bit harder. 'It is very important, Rita, and I'm wondering if you could possibly get me her address and contact number? I think she was no longer being booked as a model . . . It would be very helpful to the investigation.'

'All right,' Rita said eventually. 'Let me have a look. There's boxes of documents for shredding and Simon Quinn was supposed to come in and organize it, but he had such a hissy fit the last time he was here, claiming he hadn't been paid and that he was going to take somebody, anybody, to a tribunal. So the KatWalk office has been left in a total mess. I'll call you back.'

CHAPTER TWENTY-TWO

Jane was working on updating the incident board when her desk phone rang.

'Sorry for taking so long to get back to you,' Rita said, 'but Simon's office was in such a state it was hard to know where to start. There are photographs scattered all over the floor and piled up on his desk, and he's left no invoices or lists of clients. None of the girls were in alphabetical order, and to be honest I was just about to give up when I realized I was standing on it! I mean, I didn't recognize her – I didn't know any of the girls – but I saw her name. It's Annalise Montgomery. And there's an address and phone number.'

Jane jotted down the details. 'Thank you so much, Rita.'

She dialed the number and someone with an accent she couldn't identify answered the phone.

'I'm from the Metropolitan Police,' Jane explained. 'Can I speak to Annalise Montgomery's mother, please?'

She was kept waiting for about a minute before a woman with a very posh voice came on the phone.

'Hello, this is Penelope Montgomery.'

Jane told her that she would appreciate it if she could interview Mrs. Montgomery and her daughter Annalise, but that she didn't want to disclose the nature of the matter over the phone. She hastened to say that Annalise was not suspected of anything of a criminal nature. Mrs. Montgomery asked for more details, and Jane, again being as diplomatic as she could, said that she needed to see them face to face regarding an inquiry she was working on.

'I still think I need to know more,' Mrs. Montgomery insisted.

Jane realized she needed to take a different tack. 'It's in connection with the murder of Charles Foxley.'

There was an audible gasp. 'You'd better come over, then.'

After she'd taken down the details, Jane replaced the receiver, giving it a small congratulatory tap.

* * *

When Spencer arrived at the care home in Wandsworth where Michael Langton was a resident, he was pleasantly surprised to find that it didn't have that awful old-people's-home smell of stale food and disinfectant. There was a fresh feeling to the wide reception area. It had two comfortable chairs and a small desk with a phone and typewriter, plus a high stool. There was no one present when he walked in. There was a neat board with directions to the kitchen, dining hall, activities room and day room. There was also a second board with a list of names and room numbers. Spencer headed towards the kitchen and drew a wide sliding door open. A pretty young black girl was cooking, stirring a big pot on the stove, and when she turned to Spencer, he noticed she was wearing leg braces and was missing half an arm.

'Hi, I'm sorry to bother you. I'm looking for a Michael Langton. I'm Detective Sergeant Spencer Gibbs.' He showed her his ID.

'I think you'll find him in the activity room. If not, he'll be in his room. Shall I find him for you?'

'No, no, I'm fine, I can have a look myself.'

Spencer left the kitchen and pulled the door closed. He noticed that the reception and corridor were extra wide to accommodate wheelchairs. The wide door with the *Activity Room* sign on it had a door knob very low down. He opened the door and looked in. The room was large and airy, with floor-to-ceiling windows looking out onto a garden. There was a half-size table-tennis table, a lowered table-football table and four easels with half-finished canvases alongside tables containing oil paints and brushes. The only occupant of the room was seated in a high wheelchair fitted with a hydraulic lift device to enable the occupant to move up and down. He was painting using a brush in his mouth. Although incomplete, Spencer could see it was an astonishing, vibrant image of two horses jumping a fence. Pinned to the canvas was a photograph.

'I'm sorry to interrupt . . . '

Spencer watched as Michael Langton turned his head and very carefully used his mouth to put the paint brush into a jar of turps, then turned the chair around by using the stump of his right arm. He was a good-looking man. Probably in his late thirties, he had a square jaw with high cheekbones and very dark thick-lashed eyes. His reddish hair was wiry and cropped close. At one time he must have been at least six foot, and he still looked very athletic, with wide shoulders tapering down to his waist. His legs had been amputated just above the knee and he had no left arm, only the stub of his right arm. He was wearing a tartan shirt and army fatigue trousers folded up under his knees.

It was rare for Spencer to be taken aback, but Michael made him feel guilty for wanting to question him. But Michael showed no embarrassment whatsoever, smiling broadly.

'I suggest that if we want a bit of peace and quiet, detective, we should go to my room. Or we can go next door. It's a sort of hospitality area for when guests are visiting as some of the rooms are not really designed for groups of people.'

Spencer smiled. 'I'm very impressed with this place. It looks like a lot of thought and care has gone into it.'

'Believe you me, it has. I don't know how long it took to be converted from an oldies' home, but Wandsworth Council are really one of the best councils for disabled people. A lot of us here are on benefits so we don't cost them too much.'

Spencer pointed to the easel. 'I like your work too. That's pretty good.'

Michael nodded towards his painting. 'I must say, horses are quite difficult. I've done a lot of pets, cats and dogs. But this is for one of the resident's sisters – she's a show jumper. I'm not doing very well with the hooves . . . and that feeling of getting the horse jumping forward, that's hard, too.'

'It looks good to me,' Spencer said. 'We can go wherever's most convenient for you – next door or in your room?'

'Let's go to my room,' Michael said. He turned the chair so Spencer was behind him. 'This is the only tricky door in the whole place.'

Spencer was impressed by his ability as Michael opened the door and moved the chair through. He followed him down the corridor to a small lift. The young girl he had seen in the kitchen walked past.

'Hi, Mikey,' she said. 'Do you need some tea brought up?'

'No thanks, darling, I've got my coffee percolator.'

'OK.'

The lift only just accommodated Michael's wheelchair and Spencer. They went up to the second floor and Michael led the way along a wide corridor to a room at the end. In the breast pocket of his tartan shirt, he had a wide stick with a rubber end attached to it, which he jabbed into a keypad. The door opened.

'Come in,' Michael said as he moved ahead of Spencer, replacing the stick in his pocket with his mouth.

The room was quite small, with a single bed by the window. The bed was quite high off the ground, with a very thick mattress. There was a chair, a chest of drawers, a wardrobe and a desk with a typewriter. The furniture left very little space in the room. Michael eased his wheelchair beside the bed and Spencer sat in the chair. Michael nodded to the typewriter.

'That's electric. I can't tell you what a time-saver it is for me. I'm writing my second novel. The first one I had to learn how to rewind the ribbon and it was a bastard to do. Now, brilliant! Anyway, I'm sorry, I can't remember your name.'

'Spencer Gibbs, I'm with the Met Police.' Spencer was still feeling uncomfortable, perhaps because Michael was so confident. The walls were lined with photographs of a wedding, a rowing team, Michael playing cricket in full whites, and numerous photographs of him with who Spencer presumed were his family. He'd surrounded himself with memories of when he was an able-bodied young man. Above his bed was a photograph of a very beautiful blonde girl that caught Spencer's eye.

As if reading Spencer's mind, Michael gave a soft laugh and said, 'Would you like me to give you a who's who? The girl who looks down on me every night was my fiancée, then you have my brothers and sisters, and of course you have me, before.'

'How long have you been disabled?' Spencer asked, feeling awkward.

'Nearly twelve years. I was in Dubai on holiday and just felt unwell. I stayed put, saw out the holiday.' He gestured to the blonde girl. 'I was with my fiancée. By the time I got back home I had a raging fever and went into hospital. They thought it was sepsis; in fact it was, combined with meningitis. You fall unconscious and then . . . ' Spencer waited as Michael shook his head. 'You end up like this, but some are worse off. It took me many years before I began to live again, and I only found living bearable if I didn't see my family or my fiancée. I had a lot of therapy. Now I do what I can to help kids like me, so I'm writing a lot of lectures and painting. But you'd be surprised how difficult it is to maintain normality in my head.'

'You seem pretty normal to me.'

Michael smiled ruefully. 'That's because I'm putting on an act for you. But sometimes I can't do it anymore. And sometimes I go into a really dark place. I used to go there much more often than I do now, because one of my therapists gave me a name: Mandy Pilkington. She gave me a part of my life back, something I had never believed possible. I suspect that is why you are here.'

Spencer realized what an intelligent man Michael was. He hadn't broached the subject of Charles Foxley's murder, or the fact they had been making inquiries at Mandy Pilkington's, but somehow Michael had figured it out. Spencer began to suspect that Michael was enjoying second-guessing him.

Spencer explained that he was trying to establish a tight timeframe because they knew that the afternoon of the day he was murdered, Charles Foxley had also been using Mandy Pilkington's establishment. He asked if Michael had ever met Foxley or knew who he was.

'I read about him in the papers, obviously. I mean, it was front-page news for a time so I knew he was some high-powered theatrical agent or film producer, but I never saw him in the flesh. Old Mandy is very careful about protecting her clients' privacy. I personally wouldn't give a shit, but I dare say some of them would not like it known that they could be found in nappies or dressing up as Mae West, or whatever. But I go there for straight sex and I also use the Jacuzzi, sauna and get a massage. Often' – he cocked his head to one side – 'if this is of interest to you, I can have two girls. It may be costly, but it's worth every penny. Like I said before, to feel normal is quite tough. But when I come back from there I feel fucking marvelous.'

Spencer cleared his throat. 'You are collected from here, is that right?'

'Yeah, it's quite a problem with the wheelchair in a normal taxi getting in and out. But Mandy organized transport from day one. I'm ready and waiting, and Farook is always on time. Farook is as strong as an ox, because I'm quite heavy. He lifts me into the back of Mandy's car. He takes good care of me. We get to Mandy's and he lifts me out and carries me into her house and up the stairs. Farook undresses me, even though I don't really need it. He's the one who gets me ready, then I have the fun and games.'

'On the Monday that you know Charles Foxley was murdered, can you tell me what time you went to Miss Pilkington's? And did you see Charles Foxley when you were there?'

Michael frowned, and for the first time he seemed irritated. 'I just told you, I have never seen him or met him. I also told you that Mandy doesn't like her clients meeting each other. She does it for a reason, to protect our privacy, all right?'

'Yes, of course, I'm sorry. So this was your normal time?'

'I was collected at five p.m., my usual collection time.'

'And what time did you leave Miss Pilkington's?'

Michael frowned, then he pursed his lips. He started to speak, then stopped. There was a slight sarcastic smile when he replied.

'I don't wear a watch, for obvious reasons. So I'm trying to piece together the exact time for your investigation.' He leaned back in his wheelchair and moved slightly from side to side with eyes closed. 'OK, on that Monday, the pick-up was at the usual time. I remember I asked for the waterbed, and I also asked for a particular girl who I've had sex with before. She often brought another girl, and so at that session I had two girls on the waterbed, then I was massaged, ah . . . ' He gave a strange chuckle. 'You should try it; these girls really know what they are doing.'

Spencer smiled. 'Thanks for the recommendation. Do you remember what time you got home?'

'As I just said, I had quite a lengthy session – a full hour. There was only one thing that was different. I always need Farook to bring me down the stairs and put me in Mandy's car. I remember now that I did have to wait a considerable time for him that day. So it may have been anywhere between six thirty and seven p.m. He was apologetic and seemed out of sorts. Anyway, he took me to the car as usual. I remember I asked if he was OK, and he didn't answer. He was never very chatty anyway, but he asked . . . ' He paused.

Spencer waited.

'Listen, I don't want to get this guy into trouble, all right, because he's a very decent bloke. He's hard-working, he's an honest family man, and if he earns the odd extra quid here or there, that's not my business. But . . . he asked if I needed anything.'

'What do you mean by that?'

'Sometimes he would supply me with a bit of coke and, like I said, I don't want to get this man into trouble – not to mention me; I'd be out of here if they found out, it's strictly against the rules – but sometimes I got a few tabs.'

'Are you saying he was actually dealing stuff to you?'

'God, you do like me to repeat stuff to you three or four times, don't you? I just told you. He never pushed it, it was just that occasionally he had a bit of gear, he knew a few people . . . I'm not a regular user, and as I said I don't want it ever getting out as it could cause me a lot of problems.'

Spencer nodded. 'OK. Can you be a bit more specific about what time you got back to the care home?'

Michael sighed in irritation. 'Maybe some time after seven? I can't be more specific than that.'

'Did you see Farook at all between him bringing you to Miss Pilkington's and then taking you home again?'

Michael gave a barking laugh. 'No! I had a lot more on my mind. How it usually went is, he would wait outside or be sweeping up, doing odd jobs. He was a full-time employee.'

'So you didn't see him between 5:30 p.m. and the time he collected you?'

'There you go again, asking me to repeat myself. No.'

Spencer stood up. 'Thank you very much for your time, Michael, I appreciate it. I'm sorry if I've made my questions repetitive. I'll show myself out.' Spencer opened Michael's bedroom door.

'Look, I hope I don't get him in trouble. He's a lovely man with a beautiful daughter. His wife is very religious and I probably shouldn't have said what I said.'

Spencer nodded but didn't reply. Like Jane, he had a gut feeling that he was getting closer to something, he just didn't know what.

*　*　*

The Montgomery house was in Notting Hill Gate, just off Ladbroke Grove. Jane could see it had to be worth millions. It was a four-story Georgian property with pristine white steps and a black front door. The windows had beautifully decorated window boxes and beside the front door were two ornate planters. When she rang the door, a maid answered wearing a black dress and neat white apron.

'I'm Detective Sergeant Tennison.' Jane showed her ID card.

The young girl glanced at it, stepped back and ushered her into a hallway lined with elegantly carved mirrors. She was shown into a drawing room with silk drapes, an enormous white marble fireplace and another elaborate mirror. The carpet was so thick it felt like she was sinking into foam.

Two huge sofas dominated the room and between them was a glass-topped coffee table stacked with art books. Jane waited for at least five minutes before a petite woman entered wearing a smart tailored suit and a white blouse with a large bow at the neck. She had silky hair, cut short in a page-boy style, and wore flawless make-up. She walked towards Jane with her hand out.

'I'm Penelope Montgomery.' Jane shook her hand, introducing herself and again showing her ID card.

'Do sit down.'

Jane had been rehearsing how she should broach the subject and had decided the best way was to be as direct as possible.

'Firstly, thank you very much for seeing me at such short notice. I appreciate it. I'm part of a team investigating the murder of Charles Foxley.' There was no reaction. It was as if Mrs. Montgomery knew what was coming and had rehearsed her response. 'I believe your daughter Annalise was at one time employed as a model at Mr. Foxley's modeling agency, KatWalk?'

Mrs. Montgomery crossed her perfect legs and pulled at her tight skirt. 'My daughter is not a model. She is only seventeen and is hoping to go to art school. As for being employed in a professional capacity as a model, that is simply untrue.'

'There must be some confusion. We have a professional photograph of Annalise from the KatWalk agency's files.'

Mrs. Montgomery pursed her lips. 'No, I'm afraid that is not right. Annalise did have some photos taken by a professional photographer for her fifteenth birthday; in fact, if you turn and look at the piano, there is one over there. But they were not for professional purposes. She was just a teenager celebrating her birthday.'

Jane was slightly nonplussed. She got up and walked over to the baby grand piano. Sure enough, there was a photograph of a beautiful young girl in a heavy silver frame.

'It's a lovely photo,' Jane said. 'Is it possible for me to speak to her? Is she here?'

'I'm afraid it is not possible to talk to her. Anything you need to ask, you can ask me.'

'Do you know Julia Summers?'

'She's one of Annalise's school friends. They used to know each other quite well.'

'Are they still friends?'

'My daughter has lots of friends. It's hard to keep track sometimes. But I believe they parted company. You know how teenagers are.'

'Did your daughter go to any of the film premieres that Mr. Foxley's company organized?'

'I very much doubt it. I wouldn't think they were at all suitable. In any case, her father would never have allowed her to stay out late for such a thing. So, no, I don't think my daughter would ever have gone to a film premiere. It is not the world she mixes in. As I said, she is hoping to be an art student. She's working on her portfolio.'

'So, does she live here with you?'

'Yes, she does.'

'But she's not at home now?'

'I think I made it very clear to you that I do not think it is necessary for you to speak to my daughter. I have clearly stated she wasn't present at any premiere.'

'Did she know Charles Foxley?' Jane persisted.

Mrs. Montgomery uncrossed her legs and began to clasp her hands nervously. 'I'm aware of the terrible thing that happened to him. I mean, it's been in all the papers. It's terrible. But I have never met him and I'm sure Annalise doesn't know him. I really don't understand why you are persisting in asking me questions I can't help you with.'

'Mrs. Montgomery, I think there may be some questions that only your daughter can help me with. I understand you're being protective, but I simply want to ask her a few questions.'

'There is a reason I'm guarded about my daughter. She is suffering with anxiety. I may appear over-protective but it is a necessity. Annalise has been depressed and we have been very concerned about her wellbeing. If my husband was here, I think he would refuse to even allow this conversation to continue.'

Jane had been making notes but she now snapped her notebook closed and pulled the elastic band around it before placing it back in her handbag.

'I'm sorry if I've upset you. But as I said, this is a murder inquiry.'

Mrs. Montgomery stood up abruptly. 'I really would like you to leave now. I am not going to answer any more questions. If you do wish to speak to me, my husband or daughter, then we will arrange legal representation.'

Jane stood up. 'I'm sorry you feel this way. I would hate to have to subject either you or your daughter to being brought into the station to answer questions when it could be very easily accomplished here.'

Mrs. Montgomery's voice increased in volume. 'I am not saying another word. I want you to leave now, please.'

Jane persevered. 'If your daughter is at home, why won't you let me talk to her?'

'Get out of my house!' she almost screamed.

The maid rushed into the room.

Jane held up her hand. 'There's no need for you to get upset. I'm leaving.'

Mrs. Montgomery and the maid followed. As Jane got to the door, the maid stood back and the front door opened. A tall, austere-looking man in an immaculate pinstripe suit with granite-grey hair walked in holding his briefcase out for the maid to take.

'I got here as soon as I could, darling. What on earth is going on?'

Mrs. Montgomery started crying. 'This woman's a police officer. She's asking questions about Annalise and that man, Charles Foxley,' she said between sobs.

Mr. Montgomery took his wife by the shoulders and kissed her cheek. 'Go and sit down, darling. Just do as I say – go and sit down and get yourself a drink.'

He turned to Jane. 'Who are you?'

She took out her ID card. 'I'm Detective Sergeant Tennison.'

'Well, Detective Tennison, you'd better come into my office.'

He walked down the hallway without waiting for Jane, opening a polished mahogany door. He stood to one side and gestured for her to go in. He closed the door and walked over to a carved desk, indicating for Jane to sit in the chair opposite him.

'Now, Detective Tennison, why don't you tell me why you are here? You have obviously upset my wife. I'd like to know everything that's been said and everything she has told you.'

Jane repeated their conversation almost word for word. He listened attentively, frowning.

'Can I just get this clear, Detective Tennison? You wish to question my daughter regarding your investigation into the tragic murder of Charles Foxley? Firstly, I cannot see any connection. I am aware that my daughter was at school with Max Summers' daughter, and I believe they have remained friends. I am also aware of Max Summers' financial affairs, not that I am a close friend in any way, but I have been in business with him on various investment opportunities. However, I was not connected with, and had never met, Charles Foxley. Regarding the real reason you are here, I think it would be prudent if you could get to the point, as I suspect there is some kind of agenda that you have not yet mentioned.'

At that point his desk phone rang. He excused himself and answered it. He listened for a brief moment, then apologized, saying that he would need to take the call but would make it quick. Jane watched him closely as he spoke in fluent German to the caller, appearing to be discussing some transfer of funds and the tax implications. He exuded relaxed confidence, and although on first appearances he seemed austere, he was in fact a rather good-looking man. Jane caught herself musing that of late she had also found the middle-aged Darren McDermott very attractive and at one time she had even considered DCI Tyler to be rather handsome. She wondered why she was feeling attracted to more mature men. She certainly wasn't interested in having a father figure – on the contrary, what she really needed was to get laid.

'Sorry about that.'

Jane was startled out of her reverie.

'As I was saying, could you please get to the point? I have no intention of allowing my wife and daughter to be interviewed at a police station.'

Jane hesitated. Montgomery stared directly at her.

'I feel certain that if I was allowed to have a private conversation with your daughter, this need not be taken any further,' Jane replied.

'You must understand that she is still a minor. I insist on being present when you talk to her.'

Jane shifted in her seat, becoming slightly embarrassed. She knew that their daughter had lied to them and that if she could talk to Annalise herself, that might not have to be revealed.

Montgomery leaned back in his desk chair as Jane cleared her throat.

'I believe that your daughter's friendship with Julia Summers may have led to the situation I am here to talk to her about. Miss Summers was working for Charles Foxley's modelling agency. We know for certain that at one time your daughter was on their books—'

'Absolute rubbish! There is no possible way I would ever allow my daughter, who has only just turned seventeen, to do that. There has to be a mistake. She has never expressed any desire to be a model, although she is an extraordinarily beautiful girl.

She is academically very bright and is determined to go to art college.'

Jane persisted. 'She may not have admitted to you, or to your wife, that she had sent her photograph and particulars into the KatWalk agency. But we do have evidence that her photograph was with the agency. I am here to make inquiries about an incident that may have occurred relating to her work there.'

He pushed his chair and stood up. 'Please wait one moment.'

He walked out and Jane heard him call out for his wife. She could then hear fragments of their conversation: 'Annalise has been silly . . . she's lied to us . . . No, I think it would be best for her to come down and talk to Detective Tennison.'

Ten minutes later Montgomery returned to the room and sat down. 'Annalise will be joining us in a moment. I would like you to be completely honest with me, Detective Tennison. It is very distressing that our daughter has lied about this modelling thing, but I need to know, before she comes to talk to you, the consequences of any connection she might have to your investigation.'

Jane took her time considering how she should phrase it. 'Your daughter is not a suspect in our investigation and I have no reason to think she has broken the law, but I believe she knew the victim and may be able to assist our inquiries.' She made it sound as official as she could, but the truth was she was on a fishing expedition that had not been sanctioned by anyone.

There was a light knock on the door. Jane had seen the photograph of Annalise on the piano, but she was far more beautiful in the flesh, and if she looked like a model, it wasn't the Twiggy type. She was at least five foot eight, with quite broad shoulders. Even though she was wearing a baggy tracksuit, it was clear she had a voluptuous figure.

'Now, don't be frightened, darling, just come in and sit down,' Mr. Montgomery beckoned.

Annalise, head bowed, shuffled into the room.

Mr. Montgomery fetched a hardback chair for his daughter to sit down. He rested his hands on her shoulders and lightly kissed the top of her head. 'Everything's all right. I'm not angry, and nor is your mamma. Just answer Detective Tennison truthfully and there will be no repercussions.'

Annalise had thick, wavy, strawberry blonde hair that fell below her shoulders. She kept her head bent forward so it was hard for Jane to read her expression.

'Hello, Annalise. Now, can you tell us about Julia Summers and how you got involved with KatWalk?'

Annalise had a very soft voice with a slight lisp. 'Well, Julia told me that it was sort of a joke and that if I gave her a photograph and my contact details, she would take it into the agency.'

Annalise hunched her shoulders, bending further forward and hiding her face even more.

'I mean, I didn't want to be a model . . . Besides, I'm not even the right shape for a model, but Julia said that wasn't the point. She told me that if they liked me I could be at a premiere with lots of stars and producers and directors. She said it would be great fun, and that there were cast and crew parties – but the best part was that I would be allowed to buy an evening gown and they would provide a taxi to take me there and bring me home afterwards.'

She glanced up at her father with tears in her eyes. 'I'm sorry I lied, Daddy. I told Mummy I was going to be staying at Julia's, at her mews house, because one of the other girls had also been chosen and we were going to get dressed together there. A friend was doing our hair and make-up.'

Montgomery remained silent. Jane could see that Annalise appeared to be getting very distressed. So far there had been no reason for this – she had simply lied, as teenagers do. Then Annalise began sobbing, speaking incoherently and repeating over and over that she was very sorry and had not dared tell them because she had lied about the modelling agency.

Jane leaned forward and gently laid her hand on Annalise's shoulder, drawing her chair closer.

'Listen to me, Annalise, you're not going to be in any trouble for what happened, but I need to know the truth. I think it will actually be a big relief for you when you don't have to keep it a secret any longer. And whatever happened, there's nothing for you to be ashamed of.'

Mr. Montgomery handed his daughter his pristine white handkerchief and she wiped her eyes and blew her nose. She slowly sat upright.

'There was . . . a man at the premiere who gave me champagne and then he asked if I'd like to go to his hotel room. He said he was a producer and was casting for a big Hollywood movie and he thought I might be just what he was looking for.'

Jane nodded. 'Do you remember the man's name?'

Annalise shook her head.

'Can you describe him to me?' Jane asked quietly.

'He was late forties, maybe fifty. Not very good-looking and fat.'

Jane smiled encouragingly. 'Go on.'

Annalise began twisting the handkerchief in her lap as she explained that after another glass of champagne – which made her feel dizzy, so maybe the man put something in it – he had sexually assaulted her. It did not get to the point of rape, although he had stripped her clothes off, but Annalise began screaming and he got scared that someone would hear her, so he told her to get dressed and get out.

She had taken a taxi straight home. She saw Charles Foxley as she was hurrying through the hotel lobby. He saw that her make-up was smudged and she'd been crying, and he hailed a cab for her.

Before Jane could stop him, Montgomery banged his hand on the desk. 'Did you tell him what had happened?' he yelled.

Annalise shook her head. 'No, Daddy, I just wanted to get back to Julia's. I was also worried because my dress had been torn and it cost so much money.'

Jane could see Montgomery's anger in his face as he tried to keep it under control.

'When I got back to the mews, Julia was so kind and really looked after me. I told her what happened and she stayed with me until the other girl came home. The other girl, Tanya, had a wonderful night. At least that's what Julia told me . . . ' She hesitated, chewing her lip.

Jane kept her voice soft and leaned in close to Annalise. 'You have been really brilliant, Annalise . . . but there is more, isn't there? Can you just tell me what happened afterwards?'

'If whoever it was dared come after you, by God, I'd strangle him!' Montgomery shouted.

'No . . . No, Daddy . . . NO!' Annalise shrieked.

'Go on, Annalise,' Jane soothed.

'Tanya told me that she knew about another girl, and that she had gone into the agency to confront Charles Foxley because she was underage, too.'

'Did you go and see Charles Foxley?' Jane asked.

After a lengthy pause, Annalise slowly nodded. 'He was very upset and asked if I would keep it private and tell no one. If I agreed he had a present for me. He gave me an envelope with fifteen hundred pounds inside it.'

'Dear God!' Montgomery exclaimed.

Jane sat back in her chair. There was no need to ask Annalise to make a formal statement because Jane knew now that these sums of money that Charles Foxley had been paying out were to the young girls. She had gotten what she came for. Even though it had caused the young girl distress, she was certain it was a good thing she'd now told her parents and was hopeful that they'd be understanding.

Montgomery ushered Jane out of his office and down the hallway. Annalise followed.

Jane turned. 'That was a horrible experience for you, Annalise. Thank you for being so honest with me.'

'I'll no doubt get it from Mother, but I have kept it secret for so long. And,' she laughed softly, 'I've never been able to wear the Cartier gold bangles I bought with the money.'

'Do you recall the name of the film that you were due to see?' Jane asked.

Annalise shrugged. 'I think it was called *The Slave Trader*.'

CHAPTER TWENTY-THREE

Jane couldn't wait to get back to the station. She had just parked her Mini when Dabs drew up alongside her car. He got out, leaving his Mini station wagon double-parked and the engine ticking.

'Listen, what time do you get off tonight, Jane? Elliott needs to have a session with you.'

Jane locked her car. 'I'm off-duty at six thirty, unless something crops up. But I don't have my tracksuit.'

Dabs waved a hand dismissively. 'You won't need it. Just get to the rifle club as soon as you get off-duty. He'll explain everything.'

Before Jane could ask anything, Dabs had hurried back to his car and driven off. She headed into the incident room, not giving any more thought to the odd interaction she'd just had. Instead, she sat at her desk to begin checking the list of models who had been involved in Foxley's promotional events. As she had diary notes going back for the past nine months, indicating when the girls were required, it would mean a lot of interviews to determine which girl had suffered the same abuse as Annalise. One of these girls, she thought, could have had a lover, a father or brother who could have been enraged enough to murder Charles Foxley.

Spencer was finishing his report on the meeting he had had with Michael Langton and was eager to pass on the information he had gained, particularly the fact that they now had a suspect for who had been dealing drugs to Charles Foxley. He went over to Jane's desk and suggested they go have lunch in the canteen. Jane was equally keen to pass on her findings after interviewing Annalise. They both ordered a rather stewed shepherd's pie and baked beans, and a cup of coffee.

'OK, Spence, you go first.'

As he shoveled down his shepherd's pie, smothered in HP sauce, he described how much he had admired Langton and how impressed he was with the care home. He went into a lengthy description of how Langton used a typewriter, how he painted using a brush held in his teeth and, for a man with his horrendous disabilities, how he somehow still projected a strong and confident demeanor. Spence had really liked him and understood the importance of his visits to Mandy Pilkington, which in his own words were often the only times he felt normal.

Spencer heaped sugar into his coffee, as Jane listened.

'Go on . . . What did you get?' she asked.

'You're not going to believe this. Langton admitted that on occasion he took cocaine, but insisted that he was not an addict, just an occasional user. And—'

Jane had a mouthful of shepherd's pie on her fork, holding it inches from her mouth as she waited for him to continue.

'Ahmed Farook is his dealer.'

Jane dropped her fork onto her plate. 'You're kidding me.'

'Nope.'

'My God. We never even considered him! But it makes sense. Foxley, a regular client needing a regular supply of coke, or whatever. Did you get anything else?'

Spencer told her about Langton's visit to Mandy Pilkington's on the afternoon of the murder, and how he'd had to wait for Farook to take him home again.

'Langton was dressed and ready to leave. He was expecting Farook to be on the landing to help him down the stairs, but he wasn't there, which was odd as he was rarely late. Eventually Farook turned up at about quarter to seven and apologized for keeping him waiting. Langton said he appeared to be agitated and unlike himself. What do you think?'

'Well, we've obviously got enough to bring Farook in for questioning regarding the drugs and we could get a warrant to search his house and his car as well. But are you also putting him in the frame for the murder?' Jane asked.

Spencer shrugged. 'I've not thought that one through yet. What would be his motive? If Charles Foxley paid him on a regular basis for drugs, why kill the hand that feeds you? However, they could have had a fall-out. Foxley might have got another supplier or refused to pay him.'

Jane frowned. 'But Farook had the time, between say 5:30 until six p.m., to commit the murder?'

Spencer nodded. 'I suppose. But it wasn't exactly quick: you've got the blows to the head, slitting his throat, then the disemboweling, plus the time needed to clean himself up afterwards . . . ' He looked at Jane expectantly. 'OK, your turn.'

Jane briefly described her interaction with the Montgomery family and only went into more detail when she explained that Annalise had been sexually abused by someone connected to the film *The Slave Trader*.

'She does look older than she is, but when the sexual assault occurred, she was only sixteen. We have Julia Summers as a friend, introducing her to the modelling agency.'

Spencer nodded. 'Yeah, I remember when we first went there. I can't recall who it was, but they mentioned that Julia Summers often brought in her posh girlfriends.'

'Well, I would say Annalise fits that description – they're very wealthy. But after the incident, she had run off to Julia Summers' place. When she told her what had happened, another of the girls, Tanya, said that it had happened before and that she should complain to Foxley. Guess what happened then?'

Spencer grinned. 'Surprise me.'

'Charles Foxley paid her fifteen hundred pounds to keep her mouth shut. If I go through the diary, how many times did one or other of these young girls get physically abused? I have a feeling that a few of them may have been onto the fact that they could make money, and maybe even exaggerate what had happened. I think that this could be where all that unaccounted-for cash went.'

'My God, he was a sleazebag,' Spencer said, rubbing his head. 'Don't tell me we're going to have to go through all those girls again?'

Jane drained her coffee and sighed. 'We can perhaps cut a few corners by bringing in Julia Summers and maybe putting the frighteners on her. She has to know why she was blocking out the information in Foxley's diary.' Jane glanced at her watch. It was already 4:30 p.m. 'I think we both need to go and talk to Tyler.'

Tyler eventually came out of his office at 5:15 p.m., looking tired and in need of a shave. He was accompanied by an irate-looking DI Miller, who glared at Jane as he returned to his corner desk.

Tyler glanced over at Jane. 'You wanted to see me?'

'Yes, sir. DS Gibbs and I would really like to have a briefing with you regarding a few things we've come up with today.'

He glanced at his watch. 'Do you want to go into the boardroom? I'm sick of the sight of my office, but I have to be out of here shortly as one of my kids has got an abscess on his tooth. But we could do with some good news after the tests for blood on Justine Harris's dagger came back negative.'

'I'll organize some coffee, sir,' Jane said.

'Good idea,' Tyler sighed, returning to his office.

'Did you get that, Spencer?' Jane looked over to Spencer as he was finishing typing his report.

'Yep. And I'll have a ham sandwich.'

By the time Jane got back to the boardroom with a tray of coffee and a plate of surprisingly fresh ham sandwiches, Tyler was already glancing through her report. He reached out for a coffee and gave her a grateful smile as she passed him a sandwich.

'What's your gut feeling, Tennison, after that interview with the Montgomery family?'

'I seriously think, sir, we need to find out how many girls were paid off when they complained about the sexual abuse, and how many were actually fully aware of what was expected of them. Max and Ivor Summers must have known what was going on.'

Tyler raised his hand. 'Just a minute, Jane. To put an already depleted team of detectives onto yet another vast investigation into God knows how many young girls ... I'm not sure it's moving this inquiry forward.'

Jane pursed her lips. 'I hate to disagree with you, sir.'

'OK, I suggest you bring in Julia Summers and hopefully she will give you the names of any other girls who were paid off by Foxley. But we need to tread very carefully. Her father, Max Summers, is a very influential man.' As he finished his sandwich, he turned to Spencer. 'Right, Gibbs, let's hope you've got something more solid.'

'Maybe, guv. So far we've been unable to identify the drug dealer who was supplying Charles Foxley. But I now have a name – we've had him in our sights before as he's Mandy Pilkington's driver – Ahmed Farook. I was given his name by one of her regular clients, a Michael Langton. I don't think he's a major drug dealer, and I doubt if Foxley owed him enough money to warrant him being considered a suspect in his murder.'

Tyler leaned back in his chair and stretched his legs out. 'Not much of a motive, though. I mean, Justine Harris admitted bringing in drugs to give to her husband. Christ, she even admitted to hitting him over the head with a cricket bat! And this had to have been around 5:30 p.m., so your window for Farook to commit this murder is even narrower. But we've got fuck all else, so let's bring him in tomorrow. And bring in Julia Summers as well.' Tyler stood up. 'Right, that's it for tonight.

Thank you both, and see you in the morning.' He walked out, yawning.

Spencer scribbled in his notebook then turned to Jane. 'I didn't actually have Farook down as the fucking killer. I just thought he might have dealt Foxley some drugs. I'd forgotten about Justine Harris saying she took them to him.'

Jane stood up, suddenly exhausted. 'Listen, I don't know about you but I'm going to take off. In the meantime, you'd better do some homework on Farook.'

Spencer nodded. Jane had already left when he started flicking through his notes. He had a habit of not writing things down when he was interviewing as he found it distracted the person he was talking to. But he always wrote things down afterwards and he had trained himself to have excellent recall. As he flicked through his notes of the entire interaction with Langton, he suddenly stopped. Scrawled halfway up a page was Langton's reference to Farook being a very kind man with a religious wife and a beautiful daughter. Spencer snapped the notebook shut and hurried out of the boardroom to see if he could catch Jane, but she was gone.

* * *

Jane arrived at the rifle club at 6:45 p.m. She used the code to open the garage gate, drove in a few yards and then got out and closed the gate. There were a few vehicles in the car park, but she didn't see Dabs's car. She rang for the entry door into the club to be opened as she still didn't have the code. She had to wait a few minutes before the locks were electronically drawn back and the heavy iron door was opened. Elliott was wearing another one of his tracksuits and had a woolen hat pulled down low on his face.

'Thanks for coming,' he said, stepping aside for her to pass him. She followed him down the corridor and then entered the club where Vera was serving coffee to a handful of members, but Elliott had his hand in the small of Jane's back, ushering her immediately to the shooting range. He opened the door, gesturing for Jane to go ahead. He then clicked on the red light for no admittance. She was beginning to feel tense as well as slightly annoyed.

'Well, this is all very confusing,' she said as she placed her handbag down on a shelf in one of the stalls.

He gave a small shrug and smiled. 'I will keep this as brief as possible, but the most important element is I need to know if I can trust you.'

Jane needed to take a deep breath because she found the situation so uncomfortable, particularly when Elliott put his hand against her diaphragm and told her quietly to breathe deeply.

'Get your fucking hand off me. I don't know what game you're playing, but I've had enough,' Jane snapped.

'No, you have not,' he said firmly. He nodded to a hardback chair against the stone wall at the end of the stalls. 'Sit down.'

Jane was wary, but she did as he asked. He then picked up another straight-backed chair and placed it in front of her, sitting astride.

'You must be aware of Operation Countryman.'

Jane nodded. 'Of course. I doubt there's a Met officer who isn't.'

'So you know that since 1978 there's been an investigation into corruption targeting the Flying Squad. Although there have been major arrests for corruption, fraud and bribery, not one Flying Squad officer has as yet been charged and convicted.'

'Well, maybe that's because there wasn't enough evidence, or the allegations were false,' Jane retorted.

'No, it's because Countryman has faced massive obstruction from the Met's senior management as well as the lower ranks. Their offices at Camberwell police station were broken into in an attempt to steal incriminating documents and evidence, forcing them to move to Godalming police station in Surrey, outside the Metropolitan Police District.'

Jane leaned forward. 'You said you wanted to find out if you could trust me. Well, I don't trust you. I want to know exactly what is going on.'

'Fair enough. I'm a Dorset detective working undercover on Operation Countryman.' He reached into his pocket and showed her his police ID.

She had to control her breathing just as he had taught her. 'Have I done something wrong?'

Elliott smiled, shaking his head. 'Absolutely not, Jane. On the contrary, I'm hoping that you are going to be able to assist me in arresting a senior Flying Squad officer who had, until recently, remained under the radar.'

'Who?' she asked quickly.

'I'll come to him in a minute. We believe he was involved in the £175,000 payroll robbery at the *Daily Express* newspaper, and the £225,000 robbery outside Williams & Glyn's Bank. Then a £200,000 payroll robbery at the *Daily Mirror*, where a security guard was shot and killed.'

'You think he committed the robberies?' Jane asked, genuinely shocked.

'Not directly, but he was involved in the planning and took a cut of the proceeds.'

Jane thought for a moment. 'Those three robberies all happened before I joined the Flying Squad.'

'I'm aware of that. We have made some headway in attempting to track down the proceeds of the three robberies I mentioned, but we are having problems with tracing the cash from a more recent one.'

Jane licked her lips. She couldn't think why Elliott was telling her all this. It was beginning to frighten her.

'Everything we're discussing has to remain strictly between us. You must not repeat any of it to anyone. Do you remember the bent lawyer involved in the Shoreditch Security Express robbery?'

She nodded. 'Anthony Nichols. He helped the Ripley brothers and two others plan it. He also murdered George Ripley's stepson, Carl, and got sent down for life.'

'I heard that it was some very neat detective work on your part that led to the arrests and the recovery of the guns and money from the Shoreditch robbery.'

Jane relaxed. But she still didn't understand what Elliott wanted.

'Are the Ripley brothers and Nichols connected to the bent officer you're after?'

'Yes and no. We were working on turning Nichols into an informant, but it's proving difficult. He wants a reduction in his prison sentence and early parole. And, in any case, his evidence could be easily challenged and discredited in court. So we're looking at other ways to arrest and charge our man. That's where you come in.'

'Is Dabs involved?' she asked.

He laughed. 'No, not at all. Dabs is doing some important ballistics work for me, but that's all.'

Jane could hardly say the name, and almost whispered it. 'Is it DCI Murphy?'

Elliott made a gun with his hand and pointed it towards her. 'I'm going to need you to help me bring him down.'

* * *

Returning to her flat, Jane poured herself a large tumbler of whisky. She then lit one of the cigarettes from her stash and thought about what Elliott had told her. Apparently Nichols' cellmate had asked to speak to Operation Countryman officers and revealed that Nichols had been boasting about a 'bent cop' on the Flying Squad who had tipped him off the night Jane was working undercover as a waitress at a wedding, where Nichols and the Ripley brothers were finalizing details for the Shoreditch robbery. Nichols had not revealed the police officer's name, but Countryman were almost certain it was DCI Murphy he'd been talking about.

She took a drag of the cigarette. 'That two faced-bastard,' she said to herself.

At the time, she had suspected that Nichols recognized her. She shook her head and almost laughed, remembering how she had gone to Murphy, afraid she could have blown the undercover operation. Now she knew she would do all in her power to help arrest and convict him.

The phone rang. It was Spencer.

'Do you want to know the latest?'

'Just tell me, Spence.'

'OK, here you go: Farook has a teenage daughter called Yasmin. And guess what?'

'She was on your list.'

'Correct. I mean, I don't know how many Yasmins there are in the world, but it's a fucking big coincidence. The thing is, if Farook is our man, we mustn't tip him off.'

'Did you take Yasmin's phone number down when you listed her as one of the girls?'

'No, that's when I realized that they were no longer clients and were not on their books, so I tossed them aside. The rest of the girls' names I took from a stack left on the desk.'

'Who gave you the name Yasmin?' Jane asked.

'I talked to Michael Langton. I had to wait an hour before he came out of his therapy session.'

'How did you get around to asking about Yasmin?' Jane asked.

'I was going through my notes, and I had written down that Michael Langton had said that Farook was a lovely guy, very religious, with a very beautiful daughter. But he didn't give me a name.'

'You didn't bring that up at the meeting with Tyler,' Jane replied curtly.

'For Christ's sake! It was only when I was going through my notebook afterwards, and it just triggered something that I thought I should check out.'

'So what did you say to Michael Langton?' Jane asked.

Spencer sighed irritably. 'I just thanked him for seeing me and said that I was checking into something and asked if I was right that he had mentioned Farook had a daughter. He came straight out with it and said he had never met her, but he knew her name was Yasmin. I'm not stupid, I didn't keep on at it and quickly changed the subject, all right? Is that OK with you, Jane?'

'Sorry, Spence. This could be a huge breakthrough. But I don't think there's anything we can do tonight. I'll be back in the station first thing.'

'OK, I'll see you then.'

Jane replaced the receiver. Surely it was too much of a coincidence. But then coincidences do happen. She took another slug of whisky, feeling energized. She went over to her briefcase to look at one of the leaflets Harry Bellamy had left in the incident room. It listed the locations and times of his lectures. Bellamy was at Liverpool and she reckoned he might still be there. She called the contact number on the leaflet, which was the box office line for bookings. It rang for a considerable time before it was eventually answered. Jane asked if Mr. Bellamy was still lecturing and was told that he had just finished. She then gave her name and home phone number, saying that it was urgent that Mr. Bellamy contact her that evening. Replacing the receiver, she lit her second cigarette of the night.

It was a while before the phone rang. She knew it was Bellamy by his deep-toned voice. He obviously recalled who Jane was, even though she had not given her rank.

'Are you all right?' he asked.

'Yes, I'm fine, and grateful to you for returning my call. I need to run something by you. When you gave a talk in the incident room, there was something you said, which I wondered if you could just clarify for me? You said that you doubted the murder of Charles Foxley had been committed by someone connected to his work because the atrocities were rage-driven, so that would rule out, for example, the designer Sebastian Martinez, suggested as a suspect by DI Miller before we learned Martinez had killed himself six months prior—' Before Jane finished, Bellamy was laughing.

'That DI Miller is an interesting man. The night before we were brought in to give a briefing, I had shown Miller my notes and had handed him my slides. I didn't realize he would take it upon himself to actually use them! But that's par for the course, I guess. My intention was to highlight that there is a difference between rage motivated by revenge and simple anger. That kind of rage can become obsessive and involve inflicting as much pain as possible – which is why I did not believe the murder had been committed by someone close to Foxley, or even in his industry.'

Jane had grabbed her telephone notepad and was scribbling as fast as she could. 'Can you give me an example, Mr. Bellamy, of the type of person capable of committing that kind of act?'

Bellamy covered the mouthpiece for a moment and Jane could hear him talking to someone, saying that he wasn't going to be long.

'I'm sorry . . . Right, because the disembowelment was accurate, he might have been a butcher and able to gut animals. I recall that the weapon used in the disembowelment was never found, but the cut-throat razor was left at the scene. I do not think that this was a spur of the moment act but preplanned. I do not believe it was a female, but a man driven by rage at what he considered a betrayal for which he was exacting a horrific punishment.'

'Thank you for your help. I'll say goodnight.' Jane was grateful to Bellamy for calling her immediately after his lecture, so she ended the call, even though she could have asked further questions. Right now she needed to look deeper into Farook's background.

CHAPTER TWENTY-FOUR

Jane was surprised to see that Spencer was already at the station when she arrived at 8 a.m., looking very smart in one of his favorite tweed suits with a pristine white shirt and floral tie. He beamed at Jane as she took off her coat.

'On your desk, Sergeant Tennison, you will see copies of Farook's criminal records. He's had a couple of assault charges, but I'm still trying to check the electoral register and so far it's a blank. If he is a foreign national he wouldn't be registered to vote.'

Jane glanced down the record sheet. 'Well, it appears he can certainly handle himself. What about previous employment?'

Spencer shrugged. 'I'm coming up with a blank. I've no idea how long he's worked for Mandy Pilkington, and I've got nothing on the housing register either.'

'But there has to be . . . unless the property is in his wife's name, and maybe he's never voted. People can stay undern the radar, you know. What about births, deaths and marriages?' Jane asked.

'Nothing. Maybe he's an illegal immigrant. I can go back and question Mandy Pilkington, but I'm edgy about tipping him off.'

Jane hung up her coat and said she was going to pop up to the canteen. As usual, Spencer asked her to bring him down a bacon sandwich and another coffee.

'You know, Spence, I sometimes feel as though I'm your personal waitress. How about you offering to get me a cup of coffee and a bacon sandwich for once?'

Spencer pushed his chair back. 'Yes, sarge! Do you want ketchup on your sandwich?'

Jane grinned. 'Yes please, and no sugar in the coffee.'

Spencer sauntered out as a couple of the team came in, among them DC Gary Dors, who had the worst haircut imaginable. Jane looked over to him.

'Gary, what possessed you to opt for the hedgehog style?' She laughed.

'Shut up! My brother did it. He's got himself a pair of clippers. I only wanted a bloody trim,' he replied.

Dors hung up his coat as two other officers came in to sit at their desks. Jane went back to checking through Farook's criminal record. She noted that he had spent time in Wandsworth prison ten years previously for assault. She put in a call to Wandsworth, not realizing the time: no one was available to assist her until the department opened at 9:30 a.m. Jane wondered if it was also too early to call Julia Summers and decided in the end to wait until she'd had her breakfast. Plus Tyler was not in his office to discuss bringing her in for questioning.

By the time Jane and Spencer had finished eating, the incident room was quiet but the appearance of DI Miller forced everyone to seem as though they were busy writing or typing, and even DC Gary Dors picked up the phone and spoke to a dial tone.

Miller walked to Tyler's office, knocking and opening the door at the same time. He turned.

'Guvnor not in yet?'

'He might be in the canteen,' Spencer replied, knowing full well that he wasn't.

Miller pursed his lips and went into the office, closing the door behind him.

'He shouldn't be doing that, you know. He behaves as if he's running the show, and if I was the guv, I'd give him a piece of my mind,' Spencer said.

He was almost overheard as the office door quickly opened and Miller asked Spencer and Jane to join him. They raised their eyebrows to each other as they trooped in. Miller had opened the file with their reports from the previous night.

'Well, you two have been busy, haven't you? Considering the snail's pace this case has been crawling along at so far, this all seems very interesting. I would suggest, Sergeant Tennison, that you bring in Max Summers' daughter, Julia, and waste no more time thumbing through stacks of these young girls' photographs. Let's put the screws on her.'

Jane chewed her lip. 'Er . . . DCI Tyler did warn us not to make problems with her father, Max Summers.'

Miller banged the desk with the palm of his hand. 'This is a fucking murder inquiry. If we upset any big-wig son of a bitch, so be it. I will personally take full responsibility.'

He turned to Spencer. 'Well, sergeant, you've certainly been pulling some rabbits out of the hat, haven't you? Let's see what Mr. Farook has to say for himself, shall we?'

Spencer was clenching his fists in frustration. 'I think it is imperative at this point that we do not tip him off, or that he even thinks we are going after him for dealing drugs. I think we should wait until we have more information about his background, in particular his family. We mustn't jump the gun.'

Miller stepped back from the desk. 'I don't like the way you're talking to me, Gibbs. Don't tell me how to do my job. We have to get a result, and my intention is to get that result in the fastest possible way. This means we re-question Langton at his care home or bring him in to the station to be interviewed. At the same time we arrest Farook and have him brought in for questioning. Meanwhile, I suggest that Tennison speaks to Julia Summers again. Most importantly – which should have already been done – do we know Farook's home address, and name of his wife and daughter? We don't actually know that the Yasmin from the modelling agency is Farook's daughter. She could actually be thirteen years old, yet we don't know, do we?'

'I've been checking births, deaths and marriages, but so far we've found nothing,' Jane said.

'Well, go back and look again. Somewhere there have to be records of where these people live, work and go to school.'

Spencer had controlled his temper but his fists were still tightly curled. 'Do you mind clarifying, sir, in exactly what order you would like everything to be done this morning? You have issued instructions for arrests and interviews, but could you tell us exactly how you want us to proceed?'

Neither Jane nor Spencer had noticed the office door opening. DCI Tyler had overheard the last part of the conversation. He could see, open on his desk, the files from the previous night.

'I'd like an update, please, DI Miller. Jane and Spencer, just wait in the incident room a minute.'

They walked out of the office quickly, feeling like naughty children.

As the door closed behind them, Spencer said quietly, 'Now's the time for him to show his mettle. If he doesn't get that little piece of shit by his scrawny neck and throw him out, I might just do it for him.'

They both returned to their desks, hoping to hear raised voices. Everyone gathered in the incident room continued working, but the hoped-for fireworks never came.

After fifteen minutes, Miller walked out. He was clearly angry. His lips were set in a tight line as he fetched his raincoat and carefully folded it over his arm. He didn't acknowledge anyone or say a word as he walked out.

Tyler beckoned Jane into his office. She stood at the side of his desk while he concentrated on her report, detailing her interaction with the Montgomery family, specifically with their daughter Annalise.

'I just need you to make something clear for me, Jane. Why focus on this young girl called Yasmin? Because we haven't had confirmation of Farook being her father, and right now we only have Langton's uncorroborated word he's a drug dealer.'

Jane nodded, but remained standing. 'I was acting on a hunch when I found out who Annalise was and, as I have written in my report, it was coincidence that when Detective Sergeant Gibbs listed some of the models working for KatWalk, he found the name Yasmin.'

Tyler looked impatient. 'You haven't actually answered my question.'

Jane thought for a moment. 'It was Edward Montgomery's reaction to learning about his daughter's sexual assault. He said that if he could have got hold of Charles Foxley he would have strangled him. Maybe Yasmin's father felt the same. We just need to find out who her father is.'

Tyler stood up. 'Right, no need to continue. Your job this morning is to re-question Julia Summers, and I will send one of the officers into the agency to bring back the photograph of this young girl Yasmin. I don't need to tell you we need to move quickly.'

'I've already put in a call to Julia Summers, sir, and she is at home.'

'Then I suggest you go there straightaway.'

Tyler walked over to Spencer. 'There will be two officers on round-the-clock surveillance at Mandy Pilkington's address and they can tail Farook from there to establish his home address and other places he visits. I have one officer prepared to time the journey from Mandy Pilkington's property to collect Michael Langton from the care home, drive to Charles Foxley's flat and back to Mandy Pilkington's. This is where we need the timeframe to be exact. There must be no signal given to Ahmed Farook that he is under suspicion.'

Spencer nodded. 'Yes, sir.'

'I want you to return to Michael Langton's care home and arrange transportation to accommodate his wheelchair. I want him to be brought to the station for questioning.'

* * *

Jane rang Julia's doorbell and waited. She was about to ring again when the door was opened, not by Julia but by a very tall, skinny, barefooted girl with giant rollers in her hair. She was wearing what looked like a man's shirt and was holding a bowl of cereal.

'Who are you?' she asked rudely.

'Detective Sergeant Jane Tennison from the Metropolitan Police,' Jane replied.

'Oh wow, is it about that parking ticket?'

'No, it isn't. I'm here to see Julia Summers.'

'You'd better come in then. She's in her bedroom.'

'And what is your name?' Jane asked as the girl closed the front door with her bare foot.

'Tanya Midhurst.'

She sauntered down the hall in front of Jane, calling out for Julia as Jane went into the untidy sitting room. Jane found it hard to believe that anyone could live in such a mess of discarded clothes, food cartons and empty wine bottles. Tanya went into the small, equally disgusting kitchen and put her cereal bowl on top of a pile of other dirty dishes in the small sink.

She loudly called out 'Julia!' again, then slipped past Jane and screamed out, 'Are you deaf?'

Jane was left sitting alone for a while, until eventually Julia, in an extraordinarily bright quilted dressing gown and fluffy slippers, walked in with a mug of coffee. She didn't look happy to see Jane.

'I don't want to talk to you because you've got me into an awful lot of trouble. You had no right to repeat what I'd told you. I've felt ill and I've not been able to go to work today because he is going to talk to my father, and my father has already threatened to stop my allowance. It's all your fault.'

'Julia, I don't have very long to talk to you, but what I do have to say is important.'

'Well, what I have to say is just as important,' Julia pouted. 'I asked you not to say her name and you did, didn't you? I'm no longer friends with her anyway but that's not the point. The point is her father got in touch with my father and has been telling him terrible things that I have absolutely nothing to do with. Now, this morning, I have to go and see him. You have no idea how angry he can get. The next thing I know I'll be sent off to some dreadful finishing school. Anything to get rid of me. And this is all because of you.'

Jane made every attempt to control her temper. 'Julia, I'm very sorry if I have inadvertently got you into trouble. The fact is, you could actually be in a great deal more trouble. I could be taking you into the station for questioning with regard to supplying underage girls for sexual favors in exchange for money.'

Julia's jaw dropped. 'I don't believe a word of what you're saying, and I don't know what you're accusing me of.'

'You could be accused of running a prostitution ring.'

Julia's face drained of color. 'I don't understand.'

'Let me try to make it clear for you, Julia. The modeling agency, KatWalk, would supply girls for film premieres, in many instances guaranteeing they would meet stars and directors. I believe some of the girls were under sixteen, but with promises of possible starring roles, these naive young girls were taken advantage of.'

Julia was heaving for breath as if she was having a panic attack.

'Take a deep breath, Julia, and just listen. If you are helpful to me now I may not have any charges pressed against you. I am aware you encouraged your school friends to join the agency, girls like Annalise.'

Julia stopped heaving for breath, but her hands were shaking so badly she had to put her coffee mug down on the floor beside her.

'And you know that Annalise was sexually assaulted, don't you? Now, all I want from you is the truth about a model called Yasmin.'

Julia was becoming tearful, shaking her head. 'I don't know her . . . I didn't know her. I'd only been working at the agency for about six months. Yes, I did encourage a few of my friends, one being Annalise, but all the other girls on the books were desperate to go to these premieres. I mean, they got designer clothes, they got jewelry, they got cars back and forth.'

'Were you also aware that they were being paid a considerable amount of money when, as in Annalise's case, they complained to Charles Foxley?'

Julia wiped her eyes with the cuff of her dressing gown. 'I don't know about that . . . I have no idea about that.'

'What do you know about Yasmin?'

Julia's voice rose higher. 'I don't know anyone called Yasmin. I only worked there for six months and I keep telling you I worked for Mr. Foxley. He told me what to do and I arranged his meetings. It was Simon Quinn who knew all the models.'

Jane turned in surprise as Tanya, brushing her long blonde hair, walked in.

'I knew Yasmin. She was one of the girls I worked with.'

Jane could feel her stomach tighten. 'Do you know her surname?'

'No, she just went by the name Yasmin. To be honest, I don't think she'd been with KatWalk for as long as I had. I just remember there was a situation with her.'

'What was the situation?'

'I don't know . . . something went on and then I never saw her again. It was at a premiere. It's got to be quite a long time ago because it must have been before Julia started work. I don't think anyone really knew what happened. All we were told was that she left the event at the hotel.'

'And you didn't know why she suddenly left?'

Tanya shrugged. 'No, but I remember something had gone on because Mr. Foxley was called by the hotel manager, but that's all I know. And I'd just like to tell you something: I overheard what you were saying to Julia, and I think you've got the wrong end of the stick. She really doesn't know the half of what goes on. I also don't think that poncy little twit Simon Quinn knows either. I was tipped off almost the first week I started work. I mean, I've only done a few photo shoots, but Mr. Foxley had a quiet word with each of us whenever we went to these functions.' She suddenly seemed distressed. 'Oh God, I feel awful. I don't mean to say anything against him because I know something terrible happened to him.'

Jane leaned forward. 'Tanya, you have been very helpful. I just need you to tell me a little bit more about Mr. Foxley having a quiet word with each of you – what were those quiet words?'

Tanya shrugged. 'He just said that we should realize we weren't there to pass out the hors d'oeuvres. We were there to enjoy ourselves and make sure that the stars, producers and whoever was important were also enjoying themselves. He said if any of them got over-familiar and we didn't like it, we were to politely reject their advances. On the other hand, he insinuated that if we didn't reject their advances, we would be very well looked after.'

'So, in these instances, when you say you were well looked after . . .'

Tanya ran her fingers through her hair. 'If we gave a blow job or allowed one of these so-called movie moguls to take us up to their hotel rooms, we knew there would be a big fat envelope waiting for us.' She giggled and said that she knew that a few of the girls often embroidered their activities, and in those cases Mr. Foxley was very generous.

'Do you know if Yasmin was paid money after that night she left early?'

Tanya rolled her eyes. 'She was very naive, and to be honest I don't think she had the slightest notion. I think she was a Muslim, wasn't she? But if anything did happen, she would have been paid a bundle.'

'When you say "paid a bundle", what kind of money are you talking about?'

'Well, it all depends what they had to do. Some of them might have done a blow job, some might have even had full sex . . . It could be anywhere between a hundred to a few thousand quid.'

Jane stood up. 'Thank you very much, Tanya, I appreciate your time. Julia, I do hope your father will be lenient with regards to Mr. Montgomery's visit.'

Julia didn't get up to see Jane out but Tanya went ahead to open the front door. She leaned towards Jane, keeping her voice to a whisper.

'She's a bit thick, but she's quite harmless. I hope to God her daddy doesn't cut her allowance because I can't afford the rent here.'

* * *

Spencer had checked that Michael was at the care home, but first he wanted to speak with the care home's maintenance and main care worker, Alistair Jones. He was a very affable, middle-aged ex-army officer who had suffered a severe leg injury in the Korean war. He lived on the premises in a small room at the top of the house and it was his job to do all the repairs, check plumbing and electrics, and supervise anyone using the kitchen. He had thinning hair, which he had oiled back and which ended in a little duck's tail at the back of his head.

Spencer asked if he could recall the Monday of the murder. Alistair immediately opened a large diary, saying his job meant that he was required by the council to make a note of everything and had to ensure all receipts were kept. He was very proud of his meticulous records. As he opened the diary, he explained to Spencer that he had to ensure the safety of a number of residents as they were very physically challenged. He went into detail about the problems they had with their small lift and that it was important to maintain it as so many people were dependent on it to get to their rooms.

Although Spencer was eager to get to the main reason he was there, Alistair was so helpful that he didn't want to pressure him. Alistair gestured to one page after another, listing therapy sessions, health visitors and family visits. He turned another page slowly, pointing out with a pen the neat lists of appointments alongside residents' names.

At last he got to the Monday in question.

'Right, here we are ... Monday. You want to know about Michael Langton?'

'That's right.'

'On that Monday I have him down for an art class. He is very good, you know – especially oils.'

Spencer nodded.

'He also had an appointment with the osteopath. I remember that clearly because he was having a great deal of pain from his prosthetic legs and they needed to be adjusted. They're handmade, but with Michael having no knee joint, there is always a question of his balance.'

'Five p.m. collection.' Spencer pointed to the diary entry.

'Yes, that's correct. He has a spa treatment three times a week.'

Spencer knew exactly what the 'spa treatment' was. Beneath Michael's appointment were numerous other appointments made for other residents. Spencer leaned in even closer.

'Do you have the time that Mr. Langton returned to the care home?'

Alistair looked down the page and said that he usually required arrival and departure times in case they need any assistance. But he had no time written down for when Michael Langton had returned as Michael didn't require assistance until bedtime. Then he needed to be bathed and undressed, usually at about 9:30 p.m.

'I have a feeling that Michael would have returned at about half past seven, or perhaps even before that,' Spencer suggested.

Alistair flicked through the diary. 'Yes, you're right. He usually does return about that time. About seven p.m. normally.' He pointed to a previous Monday in the diary.

Spencer frowned. 'Is there anyone else I can ask? I need to know exactly what time he got back on that Monday.'

Alistair seemed lost in thought for a moment, then patted the page. 'I remember. I wasn't here that night. Reason being I had to get to a vets' meeting. I don't need to arrange for anyone to help Michael after his spa dates as the chauffeur takes him back to his room.'

'So, if no one was here, Michael could just arrive home and go up to his room in the lift and no one would necessarily see him?'

Alistair nodded.

'OK,' Spencer said. 'Can you call through for Michael to come down? We've got a vehicle ready to take him to the station. It's nothing to be concerned about. We just hope Michael may be able to assist us in an ongoing inquiry.'

'Right you are,' Alistair said breezily. 'Whatever it is, it's his business. I'll go up and bring him down.'

Spencer waited by the lift gates and eventually Michael Langton, with Alistair, came down. Spencer tried hard not to show his surprise at seeing Michael wearing his prosthetic legs. Even though he was the shorter man, Alistair had a protective arm around his shoulders.

Spencer smiled broadly. 'Well, don't you look the business.'

Michael raised an eyebrow. 'You'll have to watch out I don't fall backwards. These bloody things are difficult to steer and the feet are locked.'

'Would you prefer to be in your chair?' Spencer asked.

'Hell no, it's taken me enough time to put these fucking things on. I need to look my best.'

There was a slightly uneasy moment when Spencer took over from Alistair and he and Michael walked very slowly towards the door. If Michael was in pain, he didn't show it. But the strain of moving each leg forward and getting into the van was clearly very difficult for him. He needed Spencer to help keep his balance.

'So, when are you going to tell me what this is all about, Spencer?' Michael asked once he was seated inside.

'My boss needs a few details clarified, but let's wait till we get to the station.'

Michael nodded. 'All right by me, mate. A day out is always a bonus because I don't have many. Oh, by the way, I'm halfway through that painting of the horses. I'm still having trouble with the hooves, but I've got their heads done now. You never know' – he grinned as he looked around the interior of the van – 'I might hire one of these one day and get me to a race course.'

Spencer laughed. 'Maybe I'll chip in with you and we can go together.' He knew he shouldn't have said it, but he couldn't help liking Michael, and admiring his energy.

* * *

When Jane returned to the station she was surprised to see a large blackboard had now been placed in front of the old incident boards. It was headed 'Operation Kingston' and listed the two surveillance officers in Clapham, and that Spencer was bringing in Michael Langton. There was a timeframe from the officer who had been instructed to drive from the brothel to the care home, return to the brothel, drive to Charles Foxley's address, back to the brothel and then back to the care home. The timings were all listed and underlined. Also added to the board was the latest contact address for Ahmed Farook. The clerical staff had made inquiries with the local councils and discovered that there was a high-rise council flat on the Winstanley Estate in Battersea which had been rented to a Farah and Ameer Fareedi, and there was a query regarding sub-letting to an Aiyla Farook, her husband and daughter Yasmin. They also pointed out that the estate was close to Clapham Junction, which made Farook's journey to Mandy Pilkington's only a short bus ride.

Jane was now able to add the information from Tanya Midhurst. As yet they had no photograph of Yasmin, but this was swiftly rectified when DC Gary Dors returned a short while later. He complained it had taken him so long as none of the photographs at the agency had been in alphabetical order, but eventually, with Rita's help, he had found a box marked 'no longer clients', and inside, a ten by six black and white photograph of a girl with her details printed in black felt-tip pen on the back: *Yasmin, aged 17, 5 foot 2 inches, 105 pounds*. No surname. When Dors showed Jane the photograph, she was struck by how very beautiful the young girl was. She went back to ask if the clerical staff could check the age of Farook's daughter Yasmin, feeling certain the girl was not seventeen.

* * *

Jane was in the ladies and could see the yard through the window. She watched as a van drove in through the gates and Spencer stepped out to lower a ramp. A man she presumed was Michael Langton was being helped out, and she was interested to see he was actually walking, albeit it with great difficulty. Spencer then wheeled out a rather old-fashioned-looking wheelchair.

As Jane closed the door behind her, DC Johnson appeared in the corridor and suggested that Jane should now join Spencer while Johnson went to the canteen.

Spencer was sitting behind a table with his notebook out and Michael Langton was in a chair opposite him, both prosthetic legs stretched in front of him. When Jane entered the room he was moving himself into a more comfortable sitting position. He was sweating from the physical exertion it took to maneuver himself, and Jane couldn't help noticing his body odor.

When she introduced herself, Michael smiled broadly. 'You must excuse me for not standing, but I've only just got my legs in a position to sit down.'

Jane smiled and remained by the door to hold it open as DC Johnson came in with a tray of coffees and a plate of biscuits. There was a moment when Jane was unsure how Michael could handle a mug of coffee, but Johnson had already provided two straws.

'Milk and sugar?' Jane asked.

'Yes to both, please,' Michael replied.

Jane leaned over and placed both straws into his mug of coffee. Spencer saw her hesitate to offer Michael the plate of biscuits.

'When you feel like one, Michael, I'll just aim it at your mouth.'

Michael grinned and Jane glanced at Spencer in surprise at his casual tone. She watched him flip open his notebook.

'I know you may think we have been through all this when we last saw you, but I now have to take a formal statement. I'll be writing down your answers and if there is anything you wish to query, just give me the nod.'

Michael nodded, then took a sip of his coffee through the straw.

'On the afternoon of Monday the seventh of April, you told me that you were collected from the care home by Miss Pilkington's driver, Ahmed Farook. Do you recall the time?'

'Yes, it was five p.m. That's my regular time.'

'I know that Mr. Farook then drove you to Miss Pilkington's property in Clapham. How long did the journey take?'

Michael thought for a moment. 'On that day there wasn't much traffic, but he doesn't go over the speed limit and is careful on roads with speed bumps. Shoot over one of those too fast and I'll be thrown out of my seat. He made sure I wore a seatbelt, too.'

'So how long did it take?'

'Well, as you know, I've got nothing to put a watch on, but I'd say twenty minutes.'

'So that would mean you arrived at Miss Pilkington's at around five twenty.'

'Yeah, I'd say that's about right. Farook then carried me up the stairs and helped me get ready for my session.'

'And you had booked for an hour session?'

Michael winced. 'I don't always have a full hour.' He glanced towards Jane. 'I don't want to embarrass the lady, but on this occasion I had two, er . . . therapists.'

'So your session would have been longer?'

'It might have,' Michael said.

'So, shall we say we are looking at about 6:30 p.m. when you were collected?'

'Yes, about that, because I also had a massage. Sometimes she includes them in the price. If your body is oiled and you are on the waterbed, there is a lot of cleaning up to do.' He looked at Jane. 'Sorry, but he wants me to be explicit.'

Spencer smiled. 'I don't necessarily need you to be too explicit, Michael. I'm really just interested in the time. If you could just think clearly about what time you were collected.'

Michael closed his eyes. 'I am trying to remember, because you know, Mandy is a bit of a stopwatch freak. If you go over your time Mandy doesn't like it – she doesn't like her clients bumping into each other. Not that I would have a problem with it. I remember the freak with the feather duster was around somewhere, but this wasn't like the usual routine.'

He took a long sip of his coffee through the straws.

'I was dressed, washed and brushed up like a newborn. Farook is usually ready and waiting for me, but now I remember that he wasn't there that day. Like I said, Mandy probably had someone else booked in for the waterbed, so I got myself to the top of the stairs and was able to push myself down and wait at the bottom. Farook then came in and took me back home.'

'Have you any indication of what time it was when you got home?'

'No idea, sorry. I do know that old Alistair wasn't around and Farook took me up in the lift and back to my room.'

'Did you see anyone in the care home as you came in?'

'No, nobody was around. Often at that time of night they will be eating in the dining room.'

'What does Farook usually do while you are at Miss Pilkington's?'

'I don't know, but he polishes that Mercedes of hers within an inch of its life. It's always immaculate. He uses this awful room spray in it – probably uses it after he drops me off as I can smell a bit,' he laughed.

Like Spencer, Jane was trying hard not to show her frustration. She sipped her coffee, desperately trying to think if there was any means of getting more detail from Michael.

'How well do you know Farook?' she asked almost nonchalantly.

'I wouldn't say I know him. Apart from the fact he is exceptionally kind and thoughtful. You have to understand my vulnerability when I need a man like him to carry me like a child, and to obviously know that I'm going there to fuck my brains out . . . Sorry,' he said, glancing at Jane.

'No need to apologize,' she said, noticing the flash of anger in Michael's eyes. Maybe he was angry at having to describe his dependency. 'You stated that Farook had a beautiful daughter. How did you know that?'

'He had prayer beads – they call them Tasbih – hanging from the rear-view mirror. When I asked him about them he told me they were a present from his beautiful daughter. But apparently Mandy disliked them and so he had to take them off. This was quite some time ago and we never really talked about her again.'

'Did Farook ever discuss Charles Foxley with you?'

'How do you mean?'

'Did he ever bring up his name with you?'

'I'm trying to remember. I think once he asked me something about him, but I've never met him. Ah, I remember now. He asked me if I knew Charles Foxley and if he was a very important film producer. I told him I had no idea, but if he needed to know he should ask Mandy, or better still, ask the old guy who dresses up as a maid. He seems to know everything that goes on in the house. I'm remembering it now because I had a laugh about it. Did you ever see that James Bond film?'

Spencer grinned. 'Yeah, I know what you are going to say. He reminds you of that villain, Odd Job.'

'Yes, absolutely. That's right. I asked Farook if he was after a part in a Bond movie. He got a bit serious and said no, he wasn't interested in anything like that. That's all, really. I can't remember anything else.'

Spencer flicked through his notebook. 'I know you won't like what I'm going to ask you now, and I have no intention of pursuing any kind of criminal charge against you. You admitted to me – and it is very important, Michael, that you tell me the truth – you admitted that on occasions you use cocaine.'

Michael pressed his body back into the chair and grimaced as if he was in pain.

'You also told me, Michael, that Farook gave you the drugs.'

'He didn't give them to me,' Michael said rather tersely.

'But he supplied you with them, didn't he?' Spencer said, trying to keep his patience.

'Look, I paid for it. It's not as if I was a frequent user; it just sort of came out of the blue once. Farook opened the glove compartment as it was a cold day and he often wore leather driving gloves. When he pulled them out of the glove compartment, some small plastic bags fell out. He was driving at the time, but he immediately pulled over. He kept the engine running and reached down to the passenger side. He was very nervous. There was also a large pill bottle that fell out when he picked up the plastic bags. He was apologetic and said they were for one of Miss Pilkington's clients. I said to him, "Looks like cocaine to me – is it?" Farook turned to me and said that he would appreciate it if I kept this to myself but if I was into stuff like that, he could supply me. He gave me a freebie. He tucked it into my shirt pocket when he carried me out of the car. It was very good quality. If you need to know how I know, I was quite a Jack the lad when I had all my limbs.'

It all sounded rather pitiful, and Jane could see that Spencer was finding questioning Michael about this uncomfortable.

'So how often, from that day, did Farook deal to you?' Jane asked.

'Listen to me: I don't want to get this man into trouble because I keep on saying he is genuinely a good guy. I don't know of any other man who would do what he does for me. He's not just strong, he has a good heart, and I don't want to get him into trouble or, God forbid, to lose his job.'

'Can you just answer the question, please, Michael?' Jane said.

'He'd sort me out when he collected me from my treatments.'

'Did he ever tell you about anyone else he was supplying drugs to?'

Michael shook his head. 'I have no idea. He never discussed it.'

'Thank you, Michael, you've been very helpful. As Detective Sergeant Gibbs said, we have no intention of pressing criminal charges against you. It's the timeframe we're interested in.'

Michael frowned. 'I can't for the life of me think I can tell you anything more. My God, you don't think Odd Job's got anything to do with it, do you?'

'We aren't here to joke with you, Michael,' Jane said firmly. 'On the Monday, when Farook collected you from Miss Pilkington's home, did you notice anything different in his behavior?'

Michael blinked, then winced as if he was in pain.

'Was he more talkative than usual?' Spencer asked.

'No, he was never what I'd call very chatty; in fact, he hardly spoke at all. There was only one odd thing, now I come to think of it.' He paused. 'When he carried me into the car, there was a full black bin liner on the floor beside my seat. He seemed concerned about it and, after he closed the door, he went around to that side of the car and took it out. He then opened the boot and put it in there. When he got back into the driving seat he said he was sorry but Mandy had asked him to dispose of some old towels and sheets. He was going to take them to the dog shelter but hadn't yet found the time.'

Spencer looked at Jane and closed his notebook, sliding it into the open file on the desk. 'Michael, can you recall whether Farook was wearing the same clothes when he collected you later as he was when he picked you up?'

Michael nodded. 'As far as I recall he was always wearing a rather ill-fitting suit that was too small for him.'

Spencer stood up. 'Do you have a contact number for him?'

'Not for him personally. I always make arrangements with Mandy.'

'I just need to go and have a few words with my guv, Michael, then I can arrange for you to be taken home.'

Michael laughed and said, 'How about launching one of those biscuits into my mouth?'

Spencer took a Bourbon biscuit and held it out like a dart before he gently put it into Michael's mouth.

Jane waited with Michael as he tried to move his legs straight, which was obviously a painful process.

'Would you mind helping?' he asked with a grimace.

He twisted his body around in the chair and Jane pulled each leg straight. She couldn't believe the weight of each of the legs. Although they straightened quite simply, the wooden feet, encased in brogue shoes, had no flexibility.

'Thank you,' he said, giving Jane a lovely smile, and like Spencer, she found herself falling for his charm.

* * *

Spencer went into Tyler's office and gave him an update on the interview.

'He still maintains the same exact time of collection and return to the care home. To be honest, guv, I didn't go into any depth regarding the murder, because he is obviously concerned about Farook losing his job. And if he was to contact Farook and tip him off that he has been brought here, I'd be concerned for Michael's safety.'

They walked out of the office together and stood in front of the chalkboard. They looked at the timings and Tyler pointed at the board.

'OK, Wandsworth to Clapham, one-way system, you can do that trip in fifteen minutes. If you go via the High Street, it's twenty minutes. Then he prepared Michael for his session, another ten minutes or so. From Clapham to Onslow Square, the murder site, you're looking at twenty-five to twenty-seven minutes. Back from there to Clapham is twenty-five minutes and then pick up Michael from Clapham and back to Wandsworth, we are looking at fifteen to twenty minutes. So, you tell me, where in that timeframe do you think he had enough time to commit the murder and clean up after himself, because after Langton we know we have him at Mandy's with her next client. At most, he's got twenty minutes unaccounted for, which isn't nearly enough.'

Spencer felt as if the rug was being pulled from under his feet, and he knew Tyler did even more. They already had on the board Farook's movements for that day. He had been tailed from the Winstanley Estate in Battersea where he traveled by bus to Mandy Pilkington's.

Tyler sighed. 'Farook did a grocery shop, drove her to a hair salon, returned her to the house, then made another trip to a petrol station and car wash. He's now parked outside the house eating a kebab. Now, I have two guys around the clock on this and I have search warrants for his flat, but if we're going to get a result, we need to find a connection with Charles Foxley.'

At that point one of the clerical staff passed Tyler a note confirming the name of Farook's sister-in-law as Farah Fareedi. Aiyla, Farook's wife, was her older sister, and according to a neighbor, there had been a young girl living there until four or five months ago. But no one had seen her since.

Tyler sighed again and continued. 'We have clarification that her name is Yasmin Farah Farook. They had made inquiries at local GP surgeries and, to date, none of the occupants of the flat are registered. It seems that the four-bedroom council flat was not allocated to Farook but to his brother-in-law.'

Spencer turned to Tyler. 'Did you see Jane's notes, sir? From that American profiler bloke? He said our killer might have some training as a butcher.'

Tyler put his hands on his hips. 'Jesus Christ, every time we think we have a break, it requires further investigation.'

'What do you want me to do with Michael Langton?' Spencer asked.

'Well, if you are concerned he is going to contact Farook and tip him off for dealing drugs, maybe that's just what we need,' he said.

'What?'

'We might need him to do just that. Let's see what happens.'

* * *

Jane had been trying to keep a conversation going with Michael until Spencer returned, but he seemed eager to leave. He sat, obviously uncomfortably, with his legs outstretched, and when she asked him about his family, he had been dismissive, explaining that his condition was too much for his parents. He looked away as he described his mother as somewhat over-emotional and, although no one could be blamed for his condition, she somehow decided that it was her fault. His father, on the other hand, had simply found it all too difficult to deal with. Neither of them understood his need to be independent. Michael shrugged his shoulders.

'I doubt if my parents would have approved of my extracurricular activities. I think their bridge circle would have refused to ever play a game with them again.'

Jane smiled. 'Before the illness struck, what did you do?'

'I was hoping to be a graphic designer, but I opted out of uni, did some backpacking in Australia and New Zealand. Then I went to Dubai as I was out of cash and my fiancée wanted to get married and have a family. She tried to persuade me to get back to London to finish my degree. My dad forked out for a flat in Wandsworth, not far from where I am now.' He laughed softly. 'Like all plans, mine truly went tits up.'

'I'm very sorry,' Jane replied, feeling this was an inadequate response.

Michael suddenly became very agitated and started moving from side to side in the chair. 'I need to stand,' he said, rocking backwards and forward. He then lurched upwards to stand unsteadily, almost knocking over the table. Jane had to quickly grab the edge to keep it upright. Spencer's open file slid off, and some of the contents spilled out across the table and onto the floor.

'I'm so sorry,' Michael said.

'Don't worry, it's fine,' Jane said as she bent down to pick up Spencer's notebook. Among the files were photographs of Charles Foxley, the photograph of Yasmin, and some copies of reports – but also pictures of the murder scene. As Jane quickly gathered the scattered papers from the floor, Michael was staring at the photographs spilled out across the table.

'I'm sorry, Michael, you shouldn't have seen these. They are obviously not meant for public viewing.'

He frowned. 'For God's sake, I'm not a child.'

Jane had intended to put everything back into the file as quickly as possible, but instead, even though she knew that it was unethical, she placed the horrific crime scene photographs out on the table. She could see that Michael was shocked by what he saw. She started explaining where each photograph had been taken: the bathroom, the bedroom . . . She then took the autopsy reports out of the file.

'We believe Mr. Foxley let his killer in, as we found no forced entry. He was first struck by a cricket bat and was possibly unconscious when he was dragged from the hall to the bathroom.'

She showed him the photograph of the disembowelment. Michael licked his lips and asked if she would help him sit down. It was at this point Spencer walked in. He quickly took in the fact the interview table was covered with items from his own file, and Jane was flushed as she said, 'I'm afraid that when Michael stood up the table almost fell over and your file tipped out. I tried to replace them as quickly as possible, but Michael insisted I show them to him.'

Spencer turned his back on Jane and rested his hands on Michael's shoulders. 'Are you all right, son?'

Michael nodded. 'Could you remove my legs? I'm not used to wearing them for so long, and sitting's difficult as the straps cut into my groin.'

Spencer turned to Jane. 'I think Michael would like another cup of coffee and I would too. Would you mind? Are you hungry, Michael?'

'I'll have a sandwich, anything going.'

By the time Jane returned to the interview room, the prosthetic legs were resting against a cabinet and Spencer had carefully folded Michael's trousers under his knees. He had a jacket around his shoulders with both arms pinned up and seemed far more relaxed.

Spencer stood up as Jane entered with the tray.

'Ah good, we have straws, Michael.' He put the coffee mug down in front of him. 'If you fancy me holding a sandwich out for you, just let me know,' Spencer said.

'No, thank you.'

Jane sat down beside Spencer. Michael watched Spencer demolish one of the sandwiches, then he took a sip of his coffee through a straw. 'I would appreciate it if you would treat me as an adult and tell me the real reason you brought me to the station,' he said quietly. 'This isn't about Farook giving me the odd snort or two, is it? And I don't think it's even about the fact he may have been acquiring drugs for Mandy. I reckon I'm not the only occasional user and I wouldn't be surprised if some of the girls did too. Mandy's always been a bit two-faced about her business being legitimate and her abhorrence of narcotics.'

Spencer opened his notebook. 'OK, I'll level with you, Michael. This investigation has been going on for a long time without us being able to identify a suspect – or even a motive. But recently we think we may have uncovered one.'

Michael glanced at Jane and then back to Spencer. 'You'd need quite a motive to do what was done to that man.'

'Yes,' Spencer agreed.

'Are you telling me Farook is a suspect? Because you keep asking me how well I know him. And what I know about his daughter. And you keep asking about his movements on that Monday. Is this why you are so interested about the times I was with Farook on the day of the murder?'

Jane leaned forward. 'We obviously questioned everyone who was associated with Miss Pilkington, which included all her employees. Mr. Farook gave you as an alibi for the time we believe the murder occurred. We also had witnesses saying that he was at Miss Pilkington's directly after he had taken you back to your care home.'

Jane was worried they were revealing more than they should about the investigation, but they had no choice now but to continue down the path they'd started on.

'Mr. Langton, we know that Charles Foxley ran a modeling agency and on his books were a number of young, impressionable teenage girls. Not only desperate to work as models, but willing to attend film premieres and other events where directors, producers and, in some cases, stars would be present. We know that in some instances these girls were underage. A few girls were aware that they would be asked for sexual favors and in some cases they were eager to please for the chance of stardom. Those girls who were willing to provide extra services were compensated by Mr. Foxley. I've talked to one of these young girls and I believe she was just one of many. Michael, have you ever heard any mention that Foxley was procuring young girls for older men?'

Jane sat back. Michael was listening intently but showed no reaction. Spencer opened his file and sorted through the various photos and documents before bringing out the picture of Yasmin. He pushed it across the table.

'Have you seen this girl before?'

Michael looked at the photograph, but made no answer. Eventually, after a lengthy pause, he bowed his head.

'I think that's Farook's daughter. I didn't lie to you before, because I have never met her, but he used to talk about her a lot. He said she was the jewel in his crown as she was stunningly beautiful. He told me that she had hair that shone like jet and felt like silk when he brushed it for her. You remember I told you about the amber beads hanging on the mirror and he told me they had been given to him by his daughter? I think I said to you that some months later they were no longer hanging and I told you that Miss Pilkington had asked him to remove them. That was a lie.' He chewed his lip.

'Please go on, Michael,' Jane said.

'He told me that his daughter had disrespected the family and had to leave. Farook never spoke of her again.'

'All right, Michael, I understand that you were trying to protect Farook—'

'There's more.' Michael took a deep breath. 'On that Monday, Farook collected me earlier than the usual five p.m., and I know it was just before 7:30 when I returned home because *Coronation Street* started not long after.'

Jane and Spencer looked at each other as the adrenaline kicked in. That gave Farook two hours unaccounted for.

'Farook asked me not to say anything,' Michael continued. 'He was worried he'd lose his job. As I've said, Mandy was a stickler for time-keeping, but Farook told me he'd just move the clock back; Mandy would never know because her last client was suffering from dementia and didn't know what time of day it was.'

Spencer pushed his chair back. 'We'll need you to write a witness statement detailing what you've just told us, but there will be no charges at present. We'll arrange for you to be taken back to the care home, but you must not contact Farook.'

Jane quickly left the room as Spencer started going through the statement with Michael. She was almost running when she entered the incident room, and there was a buzz of excitement when she informed everyone the entire timeline had changed.

* * *

Spencer was out of breath, having legged it up the stairs two at a time. When he burst into the incident room he could feel there was a new energy. Tyler had confirmation from the surveillance officers that Farook was at Mandy Pilkington's residence in plain sight, polishing the front windows of the house. He wanted the arrest to happen as soon as possible. Two unmarked cars were being sent, and the surveillance team would be moved on with a search warrant for Farook's premises.

Tyler grinned at Spencer. 'It bloody well took you long enough. He better be our man.'

CHAPTER TWENTY-FIVE

Spencer was in the first car with a plain-clothes officer, and DCI Tyler followed in a car with two more in uniform. Knowing that Farook had a history of assault, and that he was suspected of an extremely violent offence, they were taking no chances.

As soon as Farook saw Tyler and Spencer walking up the pathway, he gave them a polite nod.

'Ahmed Farook, I am arresting you on suspicion of the murder of Charles Foxley.' As Tyler continued giving him his rights, Farook dropped the sponge he was using to wash the windows into the bucket.

'Do you understand what I have just told you?' Tyler asked.

'I understand, sir. Is it permissible for me to wash my hands and put on my jacket?'

Tyler and Spencer entered the house with Farook and watched as he went into a small cloakroom, washed his hands, took off his overalls and took his black driver's jacket down from a peg. Spencer had already been briefed by Tyler on the need to keep Farook calm and was only planning to handcuff him if necessary. Eventually, Farook had combed his hair and buttoned his jacket, folding the towel he had used to dry his hands.

As they walked down the hall, the plain-clothes officer took Tyler's place as he went to Mandy Pilkington's room. Tyler tapped on her door, watching as the two uniformed officers led Farook to their waiting car.

'What do you want?' Mandy shouted.

'It's Detective Chief Inspector Tyler; I need to ask you some questions.'

'You are going to have to do it through the door as I'm washing meself down.'

'I need to know, Ms. Pilkington, if you gave Farook a plastic bag containing dirty used towels for a dog shelter.'

'I've already been asked this. I often gave them to my driver; I can't remember what date or when.'

Tyler tapped on the door again. 'Ms. Pilkington, I also need to inform you that we have just arrested your driver, Ahmed Farook. My officers will need the keys for your car to do an on-site examination and get it taken to the lab for full forensic checks.'

Mandy bellowed again. 'For Christ's sake, the keys are hanging up on a hook in the kitchen.'

Tyler turned to one of the officers, gesturing to him to go and collect the keys.

Mandy was in her bedroom, finishing applying a thick coat of make-up and removing rollers from her bleached hair. She heaved her body up and pulled on a massive floating kaftan with a frilled neck and cuffs. She slipped her tiny feet into satin mules and tottered to her bedroom door, pushing it open.

'I think this is fucking harassment. I mean, I can't remember when I gave Farook used towels for the dogs' home. Let me talk to Farook. He'll have a better idea.'

'Ms. Pilkington, I told you a moment ago, we have arrested your driver.'

'Well, that's bloody good for me, isn't it? How am I supposed to get about? What has he done?'

'Mr. Farook has been arrested on suspicion of murder. Please come to the station for further questioning with regards to your driver.'

'What? How do you expect me to get to the fucking station when you just arrested my chauffeur? Do you think I can fucking get myself into a taxi?'

Tyler had to step away from her to control his mounting anger. 'I will organize transport for you, Ms. Pilkington.' He backed away from her again as she jabbed at him with one of her painted fingernails.

'You are fucking destroying my business and if you think that man has done anything, you've got it all wrong. He's worked for me for years as a faithful employee. I'm going to get him a good lawyer because I don't trust you, or any copper, further than I can throw you.'

Tyler didn't reply.

* * *

Jane had been driven to the Winstanley Estate with the search warrant, and the two surveillance officers had radioed in to say they were waiting at the main entrance. When Jane joined them she asked if they knew how the arrest had gone and was interested to hear that Farook seemed to have been waiting for them. He had remained calm, and just asked to wash his hands and get his jacket.

The three of them went up in the lift to the fourth floor. The building was dilapidated and a number of flats were boarded up and empty, suggesting that it was soon going to be demolished. The lift smelled of urine and was covered in graffiti. Reaching the fourth floor, they stepped out onto a worn and stained carpet, and before they reached Farook's flat they passed two front doors that had been boarded up, with *No Entry* written on them. The front door of number 418 had been painted a deep blue. A note attached to the letterbox warned against circulars or newspapers. The mat in front of the door looked remarkably fresh and the area by the front door was also clean. The two officers stood beside Jane as she rang the doorbell. It was some time before the door was inched open, with a chain lock still attached. A woman wearing a full niqab peered through the gap, her face hidden. One of the officers held up the warrant.

'We have permission to enter your flat. This is an authorized search warrant from the Magistrates Court. Please allow us entry.'

The door was closed. Jane rang again and kept her finger on the bell. This time another woman eased it open, wearing a hijab. In faltering English, she asked what they wanted. The officer explained again and showed her the search warrant. She held her hand to take it but the officer told her that she had to allow them entry first. She looked hesitant. For a moment they thought she would shut the door, until Jane moved closer.

'Are you Aiyla Farook?'

The woman shook her head.

'I think you should know that we have every right to enter your premises. We can do it politely and respectfully, but if you refuse entry we will have to call uniformed police and break down the door.'

Again the woman hesitated, then slowly eased off the chain. Jane and the two officers entered the small hallway, and the woman stood in front of them with her hand out to check the search warrant. Behind her was the woman in the niqab.

'Are you Farah Fareedi?' Jane asked.

The woman continued to read every line of the search warrant. She then turned to the woman behind her and spoke in a foreign language, calling the woman Aiyla. She tapped the search warrant then passed it back to Jane.

'Is your husband Ameer Fareedi here?' Jane asked.

'No, my husband is at work.'

'We will need you both to sit with this officer while we search the flat. Anything we deem as evidence we will ask your permission to remove.'

Mrs. Fareedi repeated what Jane had just said to the woman they now realized was Aiyla Farook, their suspect's wife.

The two women went into the small but immaculate kitchen and sat on wooden stools as Jane and one of the officers began to look around the flat, while the other stood guard by the door. It was exceptionally clean, with only the bare necessities and very little in the way of furnishings. The floors had been painted white and only two rooms were carpeted. The first room they checked was a bedroom with two small single beds with iron bed frames, which looked as if they had possibly come from a hospital. Both had white linen, with the beds made up in army fashion. There was a small chest of drawers and a fitted wardrobe full of black gowns, suits and men's white shirts. The polished shoes were lined up beneath the garments. The contents of the drawers were equally neatly lined up with underwear, socks and white cotton night dresses. One drawer also contained men's silk pajamas.

A bookcase displayed numerous books of prayers and beads, with two silver-framed photographs of Farah and Ameer Fareedi. Neither of them were smiling; instead, both had a rather haunting blank expression. The black and white photographs looked old. A second bookcase contained a variety of university-level English, maths and history books bound in plastic to protect their spines and covers. Jane opened one of the books, and on the front page was the name Farah Fareedi in neat handwriting. Jane presumed she was home-educating herself.

They found nothing suspicious so went into the second bedroom. As Jane and the officer passed into the hallway, the dark eyes of the women stared out at them from the kitchen. This bedroom was larger, with a double bed, but with the same precise tight white sheets tucked under the mattress. Laid across it was a beautiful red embroidered rug and another similar-colored one was on the floor. This room had a larger dressing table with a mirror, and in a glass bowl were a few items of jewelry, beads and earrings. Inside each drawer were immaculately folded underwear, night shirts and extra bed linen.

The officer looking through the wardrobe could see by the size of the suits that they belonged to Farook. Most were well-worn, and the wardrobe had a musty odor. As in the other bedroom, they saw the lines of highly polished shoes as well as a number of small-sized black sneakers. Jane knew that this had to be the bedroom of Ahmed and Aiyla Farook. There was a bookcase full of school books, with many stacked on top of each other, the majority on the subject of English history. The photographs in this bedroom, again, had clearly been taken some time ago and both Jane and the surveillance officer recognized in some of them the portly figure of Farook. They walked slowly across the floorboards, to test if any were loose, but found nothing.

They went into the main sitting room opposite, which was clearly also used as a dining area. There was a four-bar electric fire with fake coals and a large shaggy rug placed over a worn green fitted carpet. There were two large three-seater sofas taking up most of the space in the room, and a small television set. There was a china cupboard containing a cutlery section and a glass section, with everything neatly arranged. But the overall feeling in the room was of decay and mold. A folding table was placed beneath the window with four dining chairs lined up against the wall. There was also another bookcase.

Jane was finding the total lack of warmth inside this bare flat disconcerting. There were very few pictures on the walls and no bric-a-brac whatsoever.

'You know, it feels as if this whole place has been stripped. I mean, we are looking at the bare necessities in every room.

Maybe they know this place is due for demolition and they have another place they are hoping to move to?'

The surveillance officer grinned. 'Well, it will just be the three of them now. He ain't gonna be back for a while.'

Jane was on her knees, checking the bottom drawer of a dresser containing a starched white tablecloth, white napkins, clean dish cloths and, in the drawer beside it, neatly folded pristine white towels. There were no photographs in this room, either, and when they lifted the carpet and the rug they found nothing beneath it. Jane felt as if these people were living in a prison, and she questioned whether they might have the wrong Yasmin. Could a teenage girl live in these austere surroundings? They had found nothing that gave any indication that Aiyla and Ahmed Farook's daughter had been living with them.

Jane stood up and took a good look around the room. Once again, as they passed into the hallway, the two women watched them closely.

The bathroom was similar to the kitchen. It was old-fashioned with green tiles and a chipped bath and wash basin. There were two mirrored cabinets, one containing shaving equipment, toothbrushes, and a plentiful supply of men's eau de cologne and men's deodorant. In the second cabinet were female moisturizers, bath salts and bath oils, but no make-up. Yet again, nothing giving any indication that a young girl had been living there.

Jane paused in the hall and went over to her briefcase, which she had left on the chair beside her handbag. She took out a copy of the photograph taken from the modeling agency. The two women continued to follow Jane with their eyes.

Jane asked Aiyla Farook if she had a daughter. Aiyla pressed her lips together and looked at the ground.

Jane turned to Farah Fareedi. 'Do you have a daughter?'

'Yes, I do. My daughter is with a relative.'

'What is her name?' Jane asked, stepping closer.

'Midilah.'

'How old is she?'

'She is nineteen and studying at South Thames College. She is a very clever girl.'

'Does your sister have a daughter?' She watched as Farah turned and spoke quietly to her sister. Jane took the picture of the girl they knew as Yasmin from the envelope.

'Is this your daughter?'

The total lack of expression from both of the women was almost disturbing. Jane repeated the question. 'Is this your daughter, Mrs. Farook?'

'My niece left to return home many months ago.'

'What is her name?' Jane asked.

'Yasmin.'

'Is this Yasmin?' Jane asked, showing the women the photograph. Again, neither showed any expression, and it was Farah who answered.

'Yes, that is Yasmin.'

Jane returned to her briefcase and put the photograph back in the envelope. They had one more room to go, a box room at the end of the corridor. Jane felt a faint trepidation as she opened the door, but was disappointed. This room had a small wood-framed single bed, with a bare mattress and two pillows without covers. There was a cheap chest of drawers, but each drawer was empty. When she went to open the door of the small, cheap wardrobe, there were wire coat hangers but no items of clothing. She was about to shut the wardrobe door when she leaned further in and moved the hangers aside. She could smell a light perfume. She knew that when Yasmin had been living here, this had been her room.

She turned and beckoned the officer to come and stand beside her. 'This is perfume, isn't it? Can you smell it?'

He sniffed. 'Yeah, I think so, but I couldn't tell you what it is.'

At the bottom of the wardrobe, just as Jane was closing the door, she saw the edge of a piece of white paper. She got on her knees and gently tried to ease the piece of paper out. Using a pen from her handbag, she eventually managed to prise open one of the boards on the bottom of the wardrobe and pulled out a folded piece of lined notepaper. She stood up, straightening the paper out. Written in neat, cursive pen were several lines.

Women have ird propriety, men have Sharaf honour. On another line was: *If a woman loses her propriety, it is gone forever.* She turned the page over and there was more writing. *Jordanian penal code.* Then, underlined: *Victim of rape stoned to death.*

Jane knew she had found something important, even though she didn't yet understand what it was, so she placed the note into a plastic bag.

Jane asked both women to leave the kitchen so the officer could search it. The women seemed ill at ease with Jane and the other officer in the sitting room. Jane was certain that Aiyla understood more than she let on and that Farah Fareedi was home-tutoring herself. She explained that Aiyla's husband had been taken into custody and that if they wished to contact the station or required someone to help them understand the process, they could call the number she gave them. Farah looked at the note and said she would speak with her husband Ameer and he would find out if her brother-in-law required a lawyer. Jane said he could come to the station and might be questioned.

Jane found it hard-going as the two women were so unresponsive, especially Aiyla, who had beautiful dark eyes that seemed completely empty. Farah was more intelligent-looking and had very expressive, long-fingered hands. She had gotten up and opened a drawer in a dresser to take out a small notebook and pencil and made notes of everything Jane was saying. Aiyla looked towards the kitchen as they heard drawers and cupboards being opened and closed. Jane looked directly at Aiyla and then leaned forward.

'Where is your daughter Yasmin?'

Until now she appeared not to have understood a word Jane was saying and needed Farah to translate, but she immediately became distressed at Jane's question. Farah quickly took her sister's hand and turned with an arrogant look to Jane.

'I told you, her daughter is home, she has gone to see family. She left many months ago.'

'Do you have any evidence of this?' Jane asked.

'Why do you require evidence if my niece decided to return to her family? It is our business and nothing to do with you.'

At this moment the officer appeared in the doorway. He gave a small nod for her to join him. In the largest cutlery drawer in the kitchen there was a wooden-framed knife block containing six razor-sharp carving knives, two with a serrated edge, and the blades slightly curved. As if Farah knew what they had found, she came and stood in the hallway and said that they were the property of her husband. He worked in a butcher shop and they were required for his work. Jane ignored her and gave the officer instructions to place all the knives, along with the block, into evidence bags.

Jane had now seen and heard enough. She was seriously concerned for Yasmin Farook.

* * *

By the time Jane made it to the interrogation room, Farook had already been questioned for an hour by DCI Tyler and Spencer. She was told Farook refused to have a solicitor and had, to all intents and purposes, been exceptionally forthcoming.

Jane had only just completed writing up her report from the visit to his flat when Spencer came into the incident room. She was quite surprised to see him as he went over to his desk to take out some aspirin from his drawer.

'How's it going?' she asked as he took the aspirin with a cold cup of coffee left on his desk.

'He's holding nothing back. He's admitted straightaway to murdering Charles Foxley. He was also determined that we understood Michael Langton had absolutely no idea why he had asked him to lie for him. And Mandy Pilkington was also unaware of his intentions.' Spencer shrugged his shoulders. 'He was almost freakily calm and claimed she'd been incredibly kind. She had taken him on years ago, despite his police record; he even went into great detail about his assault charge, which happened when he was working as a bouncer in a club. He insisted that he didn't intend to hurt the man but had been attempting to refuse him entry when the man had thrown a punch, which then led to a number of men ganging up on him. This was also mentioned by his defense at the time.'

Spencer looked at his watch. 'He's just having a toilet break now. I'm going to have to go back in. Tyler is very impressive, but he can't get him to implicate Mandy Pilkington in the drugs. It's the only time he became a bit agitated, and we both think it's vital we keep him steady.'

Jane handed Spencer the note in the plastic cover. She quickly described the interior of the flat, and explained that Farook's wife had not spoken English and his sister-in-law, Farah Fareedi, had dominated their conversation.

A uniformed officer came to the door of the incident room and signaled to Spencer to go back into the interview room.

'Spence, we really need to talk to him about his daughter, and perhaps have a quick moment with Tyler and show him what I found in the room I believe was her bedroom.'

Spencer had a quick look. 'I'm not sure what that all means, but I'll show Tyler anyway.'

Jane wished she could listen in to what was going on in the interview room, but she knew, like everyone else, she would just have to wait for the outcome.

At least they knew they had their killer.

* * *

Farook had been brought back by two uniformed officers. He remained calm, as if he was actually relieved to have offloaded the burden of his crime. He had accepted only a glass of water and sat facing the two empty chairs, waiting for Tyler and Spencer to return. Outside the door, Spencer showed Tyler the note.

'Not sure what it adds up to, sir.'

'So the daughter's not there,' Tyler said.

Spencer shook his head. 'According to Jane, she may have lived in a small box room, but it's been stripped bare and the note had been tucked into the bottom of a wardrobe.'

Tyler pursed his lips. 'Right now, the important thing is that he's admitted he did it. We just need him to tell us why, and to go through what happened in the flat, step by step.'

'Guv, Jane thinks it's got to be connected to his daughter.'

Tyler was losing patience. 'Right now, Spencer, I'm not interested in what she thinks. We have to go with the evidence we have to progress things further.' With that, he opened the interview room door and they both walked in.

Tyler repeated to Farook that he was still under arrest and read him his rights again. Once again he asked if he required a lawyer and Farook said no, even when Tyler told him that Mandy Pilkington had offered to pay for one. Farook, who rarely lifted his eyes to look either man in the face, stared down, clasping his hands over his belly like a Buddha. Spencer reminded himself that this tubby, congenial-looking man had the strength to carry Michael Langton up and down stairs.

Farook stared at his clasped hands in front of him. 'I've already told you that Miss Pilkington has been very kind to me. All I did in return was maintain the property as best as I could and drive her whenever required. And I drove her clients when she asked.'

'Did you ever drive Mr. Foxley?' Tyler asked quietly.

Farook remained with his head bent. 'I only ever drove him the one time and that would be a long time ago, many months now. It was on this occasion that he asked me if I knew where he could acquire certain drugs. From that time on I would get drugs to him when he requested, usually when he had been at Miss Pilkington's. He would approach me so that on his next visit I would have what he wanted.'

'So you are saying you only ever went to Charles Foxley's flat once?'

'Yes, sir, that is correct, just one time only. And that was because there was an incident outside Miss Pilkington's house. Mr. Foxley usually ordered a taxi to be waiting for him when his appointment was over, and this was usually lunchtimes—'

Tyler interrupted. 'Did you know who Mr. Foxley was?'

'No, sir, I did not. It was one of the rules Miss Pilkington laid down that anyone employed by her should not ask questions of any of her clients. She preferred them to all remain anonymous.'

'So, on this occasion, Mr. Farook, when you say you drove Mr. Foxley to his flat, what happened?'

Farook shrugged his shoulders. 'I just drove him to his flat in Kensington.'

Tyler continued, 'You have admitted to the murder, but we still need to know exactly what happened.'

Farook shrugged again. 'Nothing. I simply took him home.'

As Spencer made notes he wished Tyler would put some more pressure on Farook. It all seemed to be progressing very slowly and he was becoming exasperated. Then Farook pursed his lips, still remaining with his head bowed.

'It was about nine months ago, if not more. Mr. Foxley came out of the house and a woman came up to him, screaming and punching him. She was completely hysterical, saying abusive things. This is a residential area and the reason why Miss Pilkington is so particular is because she wants her neighbors to remain unaware of what is going on at her property.'

Spencer didn't find it credible that the neighbors hadn't noticed people coming and going all day. He was starting to mistrust everything Farook was saying.

Farook raised his hands. 'She was a very attractive woman, a blonde woman, but she was frightening because she was accusing him of being a pervert. She was so violent towards him, I intervened. She had actually punched him in the face and he was distressed. He asked me if I could help him get away, which I did. I drove him home and he told me the woman was his ex-wife, who was mentally disturbed. So that is how I knew where Mr. Foxley lived.'

'Did you ever see this woman again?' Tyler asked.

'I've only ever seen her one more time.'

It was as if pieces of a jigsaw were beginning to come together as Farook told them the only other time he had seen this woman was when, on the day of the murder, she was coming out of Foxley's flat and he recognized her. She had seemed agitated.

'What time was this?' Tyler asked.

Farook said it was exactly five minutes to five in the afternoon. Tyler and Spencer knew this was close to the time on the parking ticket that had been found in Justine's coat. It further supported her version of events when Farook said he saw her driving away and took her parking space. He gave a strange, guttural chuckle.

'It was lucky because in that area it was always difficult to find somewhere to park.'

Spencer couldn't believe how unemotional Farook was. If anything, he seemed to almost be enjoying the process. The only sign of nerves was the glistening sheen of sweat on his round face.

He did not raise his voice nor did he lift his head to look either of them in the eye as he began to describe the chilling events that followed.

Farook rang the bell of Foxley's flat. He heard a dog barking, but he was certain Foxley was at home, not just because he had seen his ex-wife leaving, but that afternoon Foxley had asked him to deliver drugs.

Farook began to gesture with his hands as he described how Foxley seemed dazed and was holding the side of his head. He had said that his ex-wife had just hit him with a cricket bat. He had even shown him the bat. Foxley also seemed drugged because when they walked up the hallway, he lurched against a wall.

Farook chuckled horribly again as he described watching Foxley slide down the wall in the hall. Farook had picked up the dog and put it in the kitchen because it wouldn't stop barking. Then he had gone into the bedroom and taken his clothes off, even removing his socks. When he came out of the bedroom Foxley was conscious, staring in horror as he tried to stand up and get out of the flat. That was when he had struck Foxley on the back of the head, then swung the bat again and given him an equally hard blow on the left side of his skull. Foxley had fallen to the ground and he had dragged him to the bathroom.

Tyler and Spencer sat listening as Farook seemed to take pleasure in describing every detail of the brutal act and its aftermath, even down to showering and dressing himself afterwards. The one mistake he had made was leaving the cut-throat razor.

Spencer slid his notebook over to Tyler. He had written the word: *handcuffs*. Tyler glanced at the note and looked back to Farook.

'Mr. Farook, did you bring the cut-throat razor and the knife to Mr. Foxley's?'

'Yes, sir, I did.'

'Did you also bring handcuffs?'

He grimaced and then shook his head, beads of sweat falling down his face. 'No, I did not. If I recall correctly, he was wearing one attached to his wrist, but I did not bring them. I only brought the razor and a large serrated butcher's knife.'

Spencer wondered if Justine Harris might have brought the handcuffs, but the important point was that by admitting he had brought the weapons with him, Farook had told them the murder was premeditated. What he still hadn't given any indication of was why he had planned it.

Tyler looked at him for a moment before resuming his questioning. 'Mr. Farook, you have admitted killing Mr. Foxley, but you haven't told us why. You were supplying him with drugs. Did he owe you money? Is that why you did it?'

Farook shook his head. 'No, he did not. And he was not a heavy user. He told me he was a very busy man and needed the amphetamines and the cocaine as he was sometimes putting in lengthy hours at his office.' Again, there was that unpleasant gurgle of a laugh. 'Perhaps he also needed help with his sessions at Miss Pilkington's.'

'Did you find it amusing that Mr. Foxley preferred a certain type of woman?' Tyler asked.

Farook rubbed the end of his nose. 'That was not my business. Some of them were nice and they were only doing it to earn a few quid.'

'Were you aware of any other immoral activities that Mr. Foxley had been involved with? We have discovered that he was using young girls to entertain film producers and movie stars.'

Farook showed no reaction.

Tyler shook his head. 'Personally, I find what he was doing despicable. Some of those girls were underage, you know. Innocent young girls.'

Farook still didn't react, but Spencer could feel a shift in atmosphere as Tyler continued.

'I mean, to be honest, if I had discovered that my daughter had been involved with Foxley's so-called "escorts", I would have taken serious action.'

Tyler now slowly removed the photograph they had taken from the KatWalk agency from a file in front of him. He laid the photograph flat and moved it closer to Farook.

'What about this girl? Does she have any connection to the way you killed Mr. Foxley?'

Farook refused to even look at the photograph but it seemed to trigger a blinding rage. With surprising agility, Farook exploded out of his chair with a cry of rage and swung a fist at Tyler's face. Tyler ducked the worst of the blow, simultaneously hitting the alarm button, and two uniformed officers rushed in. They each grabbed an arm and managed to pull Farook away from Tyler before he could land another blow, but he continued to struggle and it took some time before they could handcuff him and drag him down to the cells.

As Tyler went in search of a medic to tend to his face, where a bruise was already showing, Spencer came and explained to Jane what had just occurred.

'You were right, Jane. It must be his daughter. When Tyler showed him the photograph, he went berserk.'

Jane nodded. 'We showed the photograph to a number of neighbors, but none of them could positively identify her as Yasmin Farook. However, I have the name of Farook's brother-in-law's daughter, and the school she is attending, so if Farah Fareedi and Aiyla Farook refuse to tell me Yasmin's whereabouts, I'm going to see if I can question Midilah Fareedi.'

CHAPTER TWENTY-SIX

Jane was just packing up her desk when there was a call from Dabs asking if she could meet him at the labs in the ballistic section where he was doing some testing while waiting for Elliott.

When she didn't reply right away, he asked if she was all right.

'I'm fine, Dabs. I can be there in three quarters of an hour.'

Spencer looked over and asked if she would like to come for a quick drink.

'Sorry,' she called across. 'I've got a date.'

'Who's the lucky—' Spencer started saying, but Jane was out of the door before he could finish.

* * *

Dabs was waiting for her in the small reception area of the lab. He gave her a shy smile.

'I'm sorry about the subterfuge, Jane, but Elliott swore me to secrecy.'

They walked through the glass double doors, heading past the various labs.

'Elliott told me you were doing some ballistics work for him,' Jane said. 'But to be honest, I'm still trying to fathom out what the hell is going on.'

'If Elliott's hunch is right, you're going to find out a lot more, Jane. And it's pretty sickening.'

The ballistic testing area was empty and Dabs went to a secure lock-up section and brought out a twelve-by-twelve-inch green metal box with a secure lock. He carried it to a trestle table and unlocked it, removing a handgun with walnut inlay handgrips and a separate magazine with bullets in it. The gun looked familiar, but she'd seen many different firearms during her career, especially during her short time on the Flying Squad.

'This is a Smith & Wesson .39 automatic pistol made in the US in the late 1950s, capable of firing eight nine-mill rounds before you need to reload the magazine. It was originally seized by the Flying Squad in 1976 when it was left in a stolen car by the fleeing suspects after robbing a Securicor payroll van outside the *Daily Express* head office.'

'Was Murphy part of the investigation?'

Dabs nodded. 'The suspects got away, but it was Murphy who found this weapon in the stolen car. He was a DI on the squad at the time.'

Dabs put the magazine into the gun then walked over to a large grey metal water tank about three feet wide, ten feet long and three feet high. Jane followed him.

'We need to test-fire the gun. Friction from passing through the water slows the bullets down and they end up on the bottom of the tank in good condition to examine them on a comparison microscope.' He held the pistol out to her. 'Do you want to fire it?'

'No thanks, I'll leave that to you,' she said, worried something might go wrong if she fired it.

Dabs placed the muzzle of the pistol in an open tube at the end of the tank and fired three rounds, which he then removed from the water using a soft rubber grabber, so as not to make any scratch marks on the bullets. Wearing soft white cloth gloves he delicately dried the bullets with non-abrasive tissue paper, took one and placed it on one of two microscopes mounted side by side and connected by an optical bridge. He then removed three small tagged cardboard exhibit boxes from the pistol case, which Jane knew were used to store bullets fired at crime scenes. He opened a box with a tag marked *Daily Express Robbery 1976*, removed a slightly damaged-looking bullet and placed it on the other microscope and started to look for any similarities in the striation marks between the two bullets. Dabs took his time comparing the two bullets while making notes, and nearly five minutes had elapsed when Elliott walked in.

'How's it going?' he asked Dabs, who looked up from the microscope.

'Bloody hell, you were right. The bullet I just test-fired is a match to the one recovered from the *Daily Express* robbery.'

Elliott looked cautiously pleased. 'Are you sure?'

'Take a look for yourself. I've got the groove marks lined up perfectly.'

Elliott spent a minute looking at the two bullets in the microscope. 'That's brilliant work, Dabs. What about the bullets from the other two robberies?'

'I'm just about to check them. It'll take me ten or fifteen minutes. If you want a coffee while I do it, my office is down the corridor.'

Jane went with Elliott to Dabs's office. She flicked the kettle on.

'If the gun Dabs just test-fired was lawfully seized in 1976 by Murphy and matches to a bullet recovered back then, I don't see how that's evidence of corruption.'

'The gun was booked out of the lab in early 1977 by the then Detective Inspector Murphy. He said he needed it for the interview of a suspect believed to have been involved in the *Express* robbery. The suspect was never charged and the gun was never returned to the lab. I believe Murphy threatened the man he arrested and said he'd fit him up unless he got a cut of the proceeds. From information I've received, I think Murphy then provided his suspect with what he thought was a now untraceable gun, which was then used in the September 1977 Williams & Glyn's Bank payroll robbery and the *Daily Mirror* robbery in 1978.'

A stunned Jane nearly dropped the milk bottle as she removed it from the fridge. 'Oh my God, a security guard was shot dead during the *Daily Mirror* robbery.'

'That's right, and when Dabs comes back I think we'll discover the bullet that killed the guard was fired from the same gun and will match a bullet recovered from a wooden door frame at the Williams & Glyn's robbery.'

'But shouldn't the recovered bullets from different robberies have been compared and cross-checked?' Jane asked.

'Comparisons are only made if specifically requested by the investigating officer to link a particular gang to a series of crimes. The investigating officer in the three cases I just mentioned was . . . '

'Murphy. But how did the gun end up back here at the lab?'

'It was down to you, actually. Remember the stash of hidden guns you uncovered at George Ripley's garage?'

Jane nodded. 'I thought that Smith & Wesson pistol Dabs just test-fired looked familiar. It was one of a number of guns we found with the money from the Shoreditch job hidden behind a fake wall in the vehicle inspection pit. But how did the gun end up in the Ripleys' hands?'

'Dabs, as you know, worked with Murphy at Rigg Approach. He had this niggling feeling Murphy might be corrupt, but he had no evidence to prove it.'

'Was this before or after I was on the squad?' Jane asked, wondering why Dabs had never said anything to her.

'It sort of started after you found the gun at the Ripley garage. The squad DI, Stuart Kingston, told Dabs to take all the guns straight up to the lab for examination and cross-check against any recent unsolved armed robberies where bullets were fired. When Murphy saw the garage scene photos, he asked Dabs where the guns had gone and went nuts when he found Dabs had taken them up to the lab without his "personal" authority. And yet he never yelled at Kingston.'

'He obviously got panicky about the Smith & Wesson being the one he'd stolen.'

'You bet he did. He also told Dabs to cancel any cross-checking on it as no witness had said a pistol with a walnut handle was used in the armed robberies the Ripleys were suspects in. Dabs felt his whole reaction was OTT and reckoned identifying the grip as "walnut" so easily from a photograph that wasn't even close up was a bit more than mere coincidence.'

'So Dabs informed Countryman about his suspicions?'

'Yes. It took a lot of guts, but the tipping point was the way Murphy treated you. Dabs suspected he did you in because you found the pistol and therefore posed a threat to him.'

'I knew there was more to it all,' Jane said, feeling sick to her stomach.

'Anyway, with Dabs's help, I covertly researched every robbery case Murphy was involved in since his first posting to the Flying Squad in the mid-seventies. The only two instances where a nine-mill Smith & Wesson .39 automatic pistol with a walnut grip was seized were the *Daily Express* job and the one found by you at the Ripley garage. What also stood out is the fact the witness at the '77 and '78 robberies described the gun that was fired by a robber as black with a brown handle. Do you remember your last job on the Flying Squad, just before you left?'

Jane looked confused. 'You know it was the one where I was shot at and my colleague got hit trying to protect me.'

'What exactly happened?'

Jane took a deep breath. 'I was in a static observation point overlooking the bank, watching for the suspects to arrive. When they did, there was a massive shoot-out with my colleagues.

From my raised OP I saw one of the suspects sneaking along-side some parked cars and making his way towards an alleyway. I put a call-out over the radio and went after him. I confronted him in the alleyway and shouted "armed police".'

'But you weren't armed, were you?'

'No, I just thought it might make him stop or hesitate so I could arrest him. But as you know, it didn't work out that way.'

Elliott took a photograph from an envelope. It showed a dead man lying on the pavement with a pool of blood coming from his chest and head.

'Do you recognize this man?'

Jane was still calm but she couldn't help her emotions welling up. 'Yes! He was the man who shot at me. For Christ's sake, are you trying to play mind games with me? You obviously know who he is and what he did!'

'And who shot him dead, Jane?'

'Fucking Murphy did!'

'And where was Murphy before he shot him?'

Jane shook her head. 'I don't know, my eyes were closed and when I opened them, he was standing over the man and then he kicked a gun away from him. Murphy told the local uniform officers to take me back to the station because I was in a state of shock.'

Elliott replaced the photograph in the envelope. 'The man Murphy shot dead was Harry Burton – the same man arrested and interviewed by Murphy for the 1976 *Express* robbery.'

Jane's eyes opened wide. 'Are you saying Murphy set Burton up and deliberately shot him dead?'

Elliott nodded. 'I also think Murphy originally nicked Burton knowing full well he was involved in the *Express* robbery and did a deal with him, then made sure that no one was watching Burton or his gang prior to the '77 and '78 robberies. Over half a million pounds was stolen in the three robberies. I think Murphy gave Burton the gun and helped set up the robberies, for which he got a big payoff.'

Jane swallowed, finding it difficult to take it all on board. She thought about the fact that after the incident she had not returned to work at the Flying Squad after Murphy had accused her of unprofessional conduct.

'Am I in danger?' she asked.

Elliott shook his head. 'You were, but now Burton is dead he doesn't pose a threat to Murphy, and with you off the squad he thinks his worries are over.' He gently touched her cheek and leaned close. 'I'm very proud of you.'

An excited Dabs hurried into the room. 'The bullet recovered from the Williams & Glyn's robbery and the one from the body of the security guard at the *Daily Mirror* job both match to the Smith & Wesson .39. We've got the bastard!'

Elliott held up his hand. 'Not yet. I want to give him enough rope to hang himself.' He turned back to Jane. 'And I need your help.'

* * *

When she got home, Jane knew she wouldn't be able to sleep. She poured herself a large whisky and lit another cigarette from the now depleted 'emergency' pack. Elliott had said he couldn't tell her exactly what he wanted her to do until he got authority from his chief constable who was leading Countryman. She was trying desperately to make sense of what Murphy had done and the fact her life had been put in danger because of him. It was as if her brain refused to accept it could all be true. She was more determined than ever to bring Murphy down, but right now it was all too much to process. And she couldn't let herself be distracted from the Foxley murder at such a crucial point in the investigation. She started running through what they knew about Ahmed Farook.

She knew he had been in the UK for twenty years, and that he had spent time in prison for assault. He had worked for Mandy Pilkington for the past six years and they had ascertained that his brother-in-law, Ameer Fareedi, held a responsible job with a chain of butcher's. They also knew Ameer's wife, Farah Fareedi, had a university education, but they had found little information about Aiyla Farook. She had come to the UK after marrying Farook, bringing his five-year-old daughter. They had not found a birth certificate, and the name on the immigration records, Rania Yasmin Farook, could mean that the girl from the modeling agency was actually someone else, even though her aunt and her mother had agreed the girl in the photograph was Yasmin. Jane recalled Spencer telling her how Farook reacted when they had shown him the photograph and he was certain that is what had sparked his murderous rage.

Jane was topping up her whisky when the phone rang. She was in two minds about answering it. When she did, she almost wished she hadn't, as her sister Pam launched into a lengthy diatribe about a woman in her hair salon who had asked for a perm and then complained about it being too curly, so they had re-set her hair in large rollers and she then said that she should have had it cut—

Jane interrupted. 'Pam, I've had a really long day—' But before she could say any more, Pam exploded.

'You've had a long day! That wasn't the only client who made me want to throttle them!'

Jane sighed. 'You try interviewing two Muslim women who refuse to speak to you. One can't speak English and the other one is lying, and I'm concerned about the whereabouts of her fifteen-year-old daughter who I think could possibly have been sexually abused.'

Pam sighed. 'OK, sorry, Jane. That sounds awful.' After a moment she added, 'Did you see that documentary on ATV?'

'What?'

'It wasn't that long ago, all about the execution of Princess Misha'al.'

'What on earth are you talking about?' Jane asked.

'She was a Muslim. It was what they called an "honor killing", and they were never convicted because she had disgraced the family name.'

'She was executed?'

'Yes, that's what the program was about. Their faith is so strong that if you disrespect the family's honor, you pay the consequences.'

Jane started thinking.

'Hello, Jane? Are you still there?'

'Sorry, Pam, I've got to go. Listen, I'll come and have a haircut soon, OK?' Jane put the phone down.

She put on her pajamas and got into bed. She sat there for a while, going over it all in her mind. Aiyla Farook appeared to speak no English, but her sister Farah Fareedi most definitely did, and Jane was going to suggest they bring her in for questioning.

Jane put her head on the pillow and closed her eyes. She didn't understand why, but she started to cry. For so much of her time with the Flying Squad she had suppressed her feelings when she was being deliberately humiliated, and now the emotion poured out of her. Finally letting go felt good – but it also triggered something in her memory, something she had come across when checking through a report. There had been significant inconsistencies in the monies discovered in every robbery she had been involved with.

Jane sat bolt upright. It was the missing cash that she had brought to Murphy's attention. He had warned her to keep out of it and told her he would deal with it personally. Without her knowing it at the time, she'd struck a nerve.

* * *

The briefing kicked off at 8 a.m. DCI Tyler had a bruise just below his eye and seemed out of sorts, but Jane was feeling a renewed confidence, having dressed smartly and blow-dried her hair, as she joined the now diminished team around the boardroom table. There was still no feeling of a job well done, despite Farook having been formally charged with Foxley's murder at 11:30 the previous night, because they still hadn't found the motive, but they knew they were getting closer.

It was at this point that Jane asked if she could express her thoughts. DCS Walker had taken charge, and gave her a small nod as she opened her notebook.

'I think our priority should be to locate Farook's daughter, Yasmin. Her aunt said that she had returned to her family but we need to check if that's true.' Jane could feel the skepticism around the room, but she was not going to back down. 'I think there's a strong possibility Foxley's murder could be connected with family honor. We know there was an incident at a premiere involving Yasmin. We have evidence that a number of underage girls attached to the agency were being paid for sexual favors.'

Tyler rapped on the table with his knuckles. 'Detective Sergeant Tennison, I have read all your very detailed reports but there is no confirmation that the incident you just referred to involved Yasmin Farook.'

'Yes sir, but that's because I have been unable to interview her. I only have her aunt's word that she returned to their country and is living with a relative there. I do have details of a niece who is being educated in England and I would very much like to have an interview with her to get further information.'

'Sergeant Tennison, at this briefing we do not need suppositions, nor possibilities, but corroborated evidence that can be put forward as a motive for this man's butchery,' Walker said dismissively.

There was silence as everyone looked at Jane.

'Sir, Farook asked Michael Langton if Foxley was a famous film producer. Farook had said that his daughter was no longer part of his family . . . '

Walker held his hand up. 'If there is a situation regarding Farook's daughter, and we are unable to ascertain her whereabouts, I suggest your information is taken to Missing Persons.'

After the briefing, Spencer brought Jane a cup of coffee. 'Look, Jane, I know Walker was being a bit harsh, but we've got our man. He's admitted he did it. Case closed. Why don't you just go with the flow?'

'I can't let it go, Spence, because in my opinion it's a big loose end. If you'd been at that cold, empty flat, you'd feel the same way.'

'Actually, Jane, I don't think I would. I suppose you've heard the vice squad are going to be hauling in Mandy Pilkington. I think they'll make sure she's not only out of business but losing some of her blubber in Holloway for living off immoral earnings, not to mention tax fraud.'

Jane found his cheery manner irritating. 'What about Michael Langton? If Mandy's place is closed up, where do you think he will go?'

Spencer grinned and went over to his desk. He opened one of the larger drawers and took out a painting wrapped in a linen cloth.

'This was delivered yesterday. I meant to show it to you but with Odd Job spewing out his guts, I forgot.' Spencer flipped the cloth aside to show the painting of two horses jumping towards the viewer. 'Michael had it delivered before going back to live with his parents.'

Before he could say anything else, Tyler called him into his office. Jane was thinking about following him when her desk phone rang. It was Dabs.

'Sorry for calling you at the station. I know you're heavily involved in the murder inquiry.'

'Not as heavily as you might think, Dabs. I've not been given any assignments for today.'

'Can you meet me in Regent's Park?' he asked before she could continue.

'Which entrance?' Jane said quietly, not wanting to be overheard.

'The one nearest your flat.'

'I can be there in fifteen minutes.' Jane put down the phone. She wondered for a second how Dabs knew where she lived, but then dismissed it. If Tyler and company didn't feel it necessary for her to be around, she wouldn't be. Always the professional, she told the civilian clerk she had no assignments and would be at home if needed.

* * *

After parking near her flat, Jane hurried into the park, crossing the circular road and heading past Sussex Mews, before seeing Dabs standing smoking under the trees.

'You don't have one for me, do you?' Jane asked.

Dabs gave her a little grin. 'I didn't know you smoked.'

'I don't.'

Just as he was about to take the pack out of his pocket, Elliott, in his obligatory tracksuit, joined them. He was slightly out of breath, as if he had been jogging.

'Some good news: other members of my team have discovered Murphy's wife has huge sums of money in various accounts under false names and property abroad.'

'Christ, don't tell me, Murphy's got an effing villa in Spain,' Dabs interrupted. 'He gets over there and we'll never get him back.'

Elliott smiled. 'Murphy's got too big an ego to mix with all the common villains holed up in Spain. He's gone one better and bought a big place in St Lucia. I've been given the green light by my chief constable. He wants us to go ahead without using the solicitor Anthony Nichols as an informant.'

'So you're going to arrest Murphy?' Jane asked.

Elliott sighed. 'Not right away. As I see it, Murphy will be surveillance-conscious and our main problem is finding a way to approach him when he's off-guard and on his own.'

'I know where you could pick him up on his own,' Jane said.

Elliott leaned forward. 'Go on . . . where?'

'He has a routine. Every morning at around eight, he drives up to the Flying Squad office at Rigg Approach in Leyton. It's in the middle of a big industrial estate—'

Elliott frowned. 'Yes, I know that . . . and I doubt you'd be allowed in the building for a pleasant chat with him,' he added sarcastically.

'If you'd let me finish,' Jane continued, 'I was going to tell you Murphy is a creature of habit in the morning. He parks up, and as he goes into the building, he signals to the mobile burger van owner to get his usual breakfast ready. He dumps his briefcase on his desk and leaves the building to collect his bacon sandwich and coffee from the van.'

Elliott shook his head. 'With how many of his team following him like a herd of sheep?'

'No, she's right,' Dabs said. 'He's like a dog without a bone if he doesn't eat and have a coffee first thing in the morning. He's always on his own because if anyone from the team is out there at the same time, he makes out he's left his wallet on his desk and gets them to pay – and never gives the money back. They generally wait until he's got his order and returned to the office before they go out to the van.'

Elliott folded his arms. 'OK, we'll give it a try, but I'm going to need to get a surveillance van that won't stick out like a sore thumb.' He cocked his head to one side. 'When he gets his breakfast, are there a lot of punters around?'

'There might be a couple, but usually one person collects a big order for the rest of the office workers,' Dabs said.

Elliott paced back and forth for a while, then told Dabs to take a short walk. Jane saw Dabs hesitate and then do as he was asked.

Elliott put his arm around her shoulder. 'You can say no, Jane, but tomorrow morning I want to wire you up and coax that bastard Murphy into revealing himself as the rotten, corrupt copper he is.'

* * *

Jane stopped off at the local tobacconist and bought herself a pack of Marlboro Lights. Elliott had told her that he would organize the surveillance with the obo van and the tech guy, and would call her early in the evening. Jane lit up a cigarette and made herself a black coffee but knew there was no way she would be able to sit in her flat, just waiting patiently. She decided if no one else on the team was interested, she would re-interview Julia Summers just to keep herself from going mad.

She drove to Julia Summers' mews but was frustrated to discover there was no one at home.

She had just walked back to her car and was opening the driver's door when a taxi passed her, heading towards the mews.

Tanya, wearing a very short mini skirt and a fox fur jacket, got out. Jane called over to her as she paid off the taxi driver. Tanya turned around and then waved.

'Oh, it's you. I thought it was Julia. This is her fur coat and she'll go apeshit if I'm caught wearing it.'

Tanya opened the front door. 'If you want to speak to Julia she'll be back later.'

Jane followed Tanya into the house. 'Actually, it's you I want to talk to.'

'Oh, I've been at an audition. I get really pissed off as they always tell me I'm too tall. Most actors must be midgets. But then I'm not tall enough for modelling.'

Jane was going to say perhaps Tanya shouldn't have worn her platform shoes for the audition then, but decided against it. She looked around the untidy lounge, which now contained some battered suitcases along with a number of smarter Louis Vuitton ones and large cardboard boxes. She watched Tanya take off the fox fur, open one of the smart suitcases and stuff it in.

'What do you want to talk about? Because I have to sort out my stuff. Her bloody father is making her go back to live at home, so I'm kicked out at the end of the week. I dunno where I'm gonna go. It's all right for her – home's a fuckin' palace. She said it was your fault because Annalise's parents were going apeshit and calling her father.'

Jane moved a pile of clothes from an armchair and sat down, taking out her notebook. Tanya perched on the arm of the cluttered sofa and rummaged in her handbag, pulling out a pack of cigarettes.

'I need to ask you some questions and I want you to be truthful. If I think you are wasting my time, I will have you brought into the station.'

Tanya used a box of matches to light her cigarette and inhaled deeply as she crossed her legs, tossing the match onto the carpet.

'I dunno what I can tell you about anything that I haven't told you already. I've done nothing wrong.'

Tanya began to tap one foot up and down as she inhaled and flicked at the ash on her cigarette. Even with too much make-up she was a very pretty girl, with wide slanting eyes and a small turned-up nose. She had a large full-lipped mouth and a pixie quality that probably made her very photogenic. But there was no innocence to her, and she was very obviously not posh like Julia Summers.

'How old are you?'

'I'm nineteen.'

'How long have you worked for the KatWalk agency?'

She shrugged. 'When it started I was one of the first girls on their books, not that I would say they're much good. I got a few photoshoots for teen magazines but they were only just start-ing up and Simon Quinn wasn't there until months later. He's useless – he doesn't know anything about the industry.'

'So who approached you to join the agency?'

Tanya got up and went to the kitchen, tossing her cigarette butt into the stacked sink of dirty dishes.

'I was actually applying as a part-time sort of secretary to work on the reception when Rita or Angie were on holidays. I can't type or do shorthand and my main idea was maybe getting an agent for acting. I met Charles Foxley and he suggested I get represented by his new modeling agency. He also asked if I had any model friends that would be interested.'

'Is that where you met Julia Summers?'

'Yeah, but not until she came to work for Foxley. She men-tioned that she needed someone to share her house, to pay half the rent. I've been here since then but I owe her because I've never had much.'

'Did you earn extra money from the premieres and first-night events?'

'Yeah, that's how I could keep staying here. I've done quite a few.'

Jane listened as Tanya giggled about always getting a bit extra, charging for expensive evening gowns that she'd actually borrowed from friends. Julia had even allowed her to wear some of her clothes.

But she began to grow tense when Jane asked about the other activities at these events. Eventually Tanya admitted to being aware of just how much she could earn if she was 'accommodating', but it took a while before Jane got her to admit that she had actually had sex. Not always full sex, but often giving blow jobs. The following day she would report to Foxley and he would pay her in cash, on the condition she signed a confidentiality document.

'That's how I mostly paid my rent here, because he was very generous. It was always a one-off and I was not to make any contact with whoever I'd been with. I know a lot of the girls were doing the same thing but some exaggerated what had taken place to get more cash. We all sort of knew what was expected of us, and as long as we kept our mouths shut, we'd get more work. There were a lot of girls.'

'Like Annalise Montgomery?'

Tanya chewed her lip, and then said that Julia encouraged her to go but she doubted that Julia really knew the extent of what some of the girls would get up to. With Annalise it all went badly because she was so naive and she ended up in a terrible state. She came around to the mews when Julia was out, so Tanya had told her to complain to Foxley and he would see she was taken care of.

'Tell me about the girl called Yasmin.'

Tanya lit another cigarette. Jane waited as she took a deep drag. Eventually she sighed.

'I feel bad about her because in a way it was my fault. I mean, if you thought Annalise was naive, then Yasmin was like a child, with no concept of how to deal with the situation. She was very star-struck. I got her dressed in one of my evening gowns. We did her hair. My God, she had the most amazing hair down to her waist and it was so silky. She was so excited, she kept on saying that she felt like a princess because we put in earrings and a flower in her hair. She was a bit coy about the dress being low-cut and kept on telling us she had never worn anything revealing as her parents never allowed her to even uncover her hair.'

'So you brought Yasmin to the agency?'

Tanya nodded.

'How did you meet her?' Jane asked.

Tanya stood up again to toss the cigarette butt into the filthy sink.

'I met her about six months ago. It was by the Royal Albert Hall. She was sitting on a bench reading and I was just walking past her with an ice cream. This guy on roller skates careered into me and I fell over and cut my knee. He didn't even stop and I started crying. She was so sweet and came over to see if she could do anything. Because I lived close by, she helped me walk home. My knee was bleeding and she had a scarf that she wrapped around it.' Tanya shrugged her shoulders. 'When we got home it was obvious that it wasn't that bad, but I made her a cup of tea and washed her scarf. We just got talking. She told me that she had very strict parents and was studying for her O-levels from home. Her aunt was helping tutor her, but it meant she had hardly any friends and no social life.' Tanya frowned. 'I felt really sorry for her. I don't even think she knew she was beautiful. When I told her I was an actress and a model, she said she could only ever dream about doing something she really wanted. She said she would have liked to study drama and the only free time she had she spent watching movies. But if her parents knew, they would disapprove.'

Tanya then told Jane that Yasmin said she was trying to find some kind of work that would allow her to save money.

'She told me she wanted more than anything to run away from her family and have her own life. That's when I told her that I could maybe get her a job with the modeling agency. To be honest I didn't think she'd do it, and she didn't say anything straightaway, but a week or so later she appeared on the doorstep. Like I said before, I felt sorry for her because she was so sweet. I know her parents were very strict.'

'Where did her parents think she went when she was with you?'

Tanya shrugged. 'Funnily enough, I asked her that, but she kept on telling me that she couldn't do this or couldn't do that. It sounded to me like they kept her a prisoner. But she said that she had told them she was going to her local mosque for religious instruction and that she persuaded her cousin to back up her story. Anyway, a friend of mine took a couple of photographs and then a few days later – wearing some of my clothes – I took her into the agency.'

'What happened next?' Jane asked.

'Well, I didn't see her for a few weeks, maybe even more. I don't know if she did get any modelling work. Then she came around again and told me she had been chosen to go to a film premiere and I agreed to get her all dressed up. I was not around when whatever happened to her happened, but I know she created a big scene because something had gone on in one of the hotel rooms.'

'Was she sexually abused?' Jane asked.

Tanya frowned. 'Listen, I'm telling you all I know. I've just said I wasn't there when the shit hit the fan. But I did my best to calm her down later and I told her if anything bad had happened to her, she was to tell Charles Foxley and he would give her more money than she could dream of.' Tanya gave a nasty laugh. 'I think she took my advice but I never saw her again.'

'Do you know how old she was?' Jane asked.

Tanya shook her head. 'I don't know. I never asked any of the other girls. Now I hear Simon Quinn's lost his job after what happened to Mr. Foxley, so I suppose that's me fucked.' She smirked. 'Literally.'

Jane stood up. 'Thank you for being honest with me, Tanya.' As she opened the door to go, she looked back. The tough-as-nails Tanya seemed on the brink of tears.

'I hope nothing bad has happened to Yasmin after that night, because she was not only beautiful, but really sweet and kind.'

Jane closed the door behind her.

* * *

Jane drove to South Thames College in Tooting. By now it was after 3 p.m. By the time she got to the entrance a number of teenage students were leaving and she was concerned that she might be too late to speak to anyone. She stopped a young Asian boy and asked him if he knew Midilah Fareedi. He gestured behind him and Jane saw a young woman wearing a hijab. Jane approached her.

'My name is Detective Sergeant Jane Tennison. Are you Midilah Fareedi?'

The girl's beautiful dark eyes immediately became wary, glancing towards the street.

'I cannot speak. I must return home,' she said quietly.

'I just need to have a few moments of your time, Midilah, to talk about Yasmin Farook,' Jane said.

Midilah kept walking. 'I cannot speak about my cousin. Please.'

Jane kept pace with her. She kept her voice calm and polite. 'I'm sorry but I'm concerned for Yasmin's safety. I need to know where she is.'

Midilah stopped, keeping her head bowed. 'It is a private family matter.'

Jane could feel the tension as the girl clutched at her satchel.

'Please, I just need a few moments of your time, Midilah. My car is parked very near. I really don't want to ask you to accompany me to the police station, but we could drive somewhere more private.'

Jane felt slightly guilty saying that, as she would not have taken her to the station, and she actually had no authority to even be talking to her, but it seemed to have worked. After looking around quickly, Midilah nodded.

After they'd gotten into the car, Jane drove to a small side street and pulled into a parking space. Midilah kept her head bowed, holding her satchel tightly on her knees.

'Thank you for talking to me, Midilah. I really appreciate it,' Jane said, trying to make her feel at ease. 'Now, do you know where I can contact Yasmin?'

Midilah sighed. 'I have been told she has been taken to live with relatives in Pakistan. I do not know the address. My father arranged everything.' She gave Jane a furtive glance. 'Have you spoken to my father?'

'No. I am hoping it won't be necessary,' Jane replied.

Midilah looked away. 'My father is a very good man, but he would not approve of me speaking to you. My father is head of the family and he brought Yasmin and her mother to England because my uncle had got into trouble when he was working as security. He felt that reestablishing the family would be good for him when he came out of prison.'

Jane nodded encouragingly. 'OK, go on.'

'Yasmin found it very difficult as she did not speak English, and my aunt still has poor English. She eventually went to a comprehensive school but she began to disrespect my father, who had arranged for their accommodation. No matter how supportive he was, Yasmin blatantly lied to his face. I tried to persuade her to cooperate but I was forced to tell tales about her behavior.'

Jane found it strange that after being so uncommunicative, Midilah had, without any real encouragement, started revealing her family's intimate business. Her intuition was that it sounded rehearsed.

'When you say you were forced to tell tales about her behavior, what are you referring to?' she asked.

For the first time, Midilah showed a spark of defiance. 'I've just explained everything. We were not close friends. I am older and I plan to go to university. If I behaved in the same way as Yasmin, there would be severe consequences.'

Jane recalled the empty, austere flat with the two single beds. 'Did you live with Yasmin and her parents at the flat in Wandsworth?' Jane asked.

'Sometimes I stayed with my aunt and uncle, but my father has an apartment above his business.'

'And that's where you live now, is it? Above a Halal butcher shop?'

'Yes, I live with my father,' she said, her hands still holding tightly onto her satchel.

Jane reached over to the back seat of the car and picked up her briefcase. Midilah flinched, as though she felt Jane was going to assault her.

'I'm sorry,' Jane said, gently tapping her shoulder. She removed the photograph of Yasmin from the envelope in her briefcase. Midilah was pressed against the side of the passenger door as Jane held the photograph in front of her.

'Have you seen this picture of Yasmin before?'

Midilah gasped and reached for the handle of the car door.

'I have to go. You have now made me very afraid that my father will find out that I have spoken with you. I am begging you not to speak about this with him. You have no idea of what could happen to me,' she said.

Jane slid the photograph – now one hundred percent sure it was Yasmin – back into the envelope.

Midilah pulled the door handle, then turned towards Jane. Her eyes were brimming with tears.

'You do not understand. Yasmin was far more beautiful than that photograph, but she was also the sweetest, most generous child, with dreams that she would never be allowed to fulfil. Her disobedience was shameful to the family.' Midilah opened the passenger door and hurried away.

By now it was almost 4 p.m., and Jane, afraid she would miss Elliott's call, drove back to her flat. She had only been at home twenty minutes when Dabs called. He explained briefly that Elliott had managed to acquire an obo van and one of the best tech guys to wire Jane up. She would be collected at six the following morning.

Jane took a deep breath. 'Are you going to be there, Dabs?'

'No, afraid not. This has all been very hush-hush, and to be honest, I just want to get on with my life.'

There was a pause. 'Tell him I'll be ready.'

She quickly replaced the receiver, not wanting Dabs to say anything more. She had heard his concern for her in his voice. She lit a cigarette and began pacing her small kitchen. All she wanted now was to confront Murphy.

* * *

Jane left her flat at 8 p.m. and drove towards the Winstanley Estate. In the darkness, the run-down building seemed ominous. She felt nervous, not just because she was on her own, but because she was aware it was against regulations. She knew if she didn't get some answers, she could be in real trouble.

She rang the doorbell and waited. Eventually it was opened cautiously by Farah Fareedi, the obligatory lock chain still attached.

'Farah, it's Detective Tennison again. I really need to talk to you. I am by myself and have no other officers with me.'

Farah's dark eyes seem to bore into Jane as she hesitated before slowly sliding the key chain free.

'Are you alone?' Jane asked.

Farah nodded. 'My sister has gone to help my husband Ameer package the meat for the deep-freeze section.'

She stepped back from the door to allow Jane to enter and then relocked it. She was wearing a niqab and was dressed in a fine black wool dress, black stockings and black lace-up shoes. She ushered Jane into the drawing room and sat on one sofa as Jane sat opposite her on the other.

'I am sure you must be aware that your sister's husband has admitted killing Mr. Charles Foxley.'

Farah showed no emotion but simply nodded.

'He has also refused to explain why he did it and has become deeply distressed when asked to reveal his reasons.'

Again Farah showed no sign that what Jane had said meant anything to her. The woman's luminous eyes did not stray from Jane's face but remained without expression. Her beautiful hands, with long nails, were folded impassively in her lap.

'When was the last time you saw your niece?' Jane asked.

'It was some while ago. At least two months. I received a distraught call from my sister and I immediately came here.'

'Can you tell me what your sister was so upset about?' Jane asked.

Farah waved her hand in the air. 'Yasmin had been wearing make-up and I believe she had taken money. She had a confused mind and started questioning our care. To begin with, we were lenient. You have to understand that when Yasmin came to this country, she was very young and her mother, my sister, was also very childlike. My brother-in-law was so much older and yet financially dependent upon myself and my husband.'

She turned away from Jane to glance at the clock above the fake fire, and then turned back, her lips drawn in a thin line.

'Please go on,' Jane urged, gently.

'My daughter Midilah is academically bright and obedient and obeys our religious codes, whereas Yasmin had a selfish desire to paint her face and watch Hollywood movies. When she was unsupervised, what unfolded caused us terrible anguish. My husband had no option but to send her back to Pakistan.'

Jane didn't want to hurry her, but was concerned that Farah was expecting her sister or husband to return and then she would clam up.

'Do you know where she is in Pakistan?'

Farah shook her head. 'I was not privy to the arrangements. My husband oversaw all of that.'

Jane nodded. 'Do you also live with your daughter, above your husband's business?' she asked.

There was a flash of anger in Farah's eyes. 'That accommodation is used infrequently and only when necessary. My brother-in-law was often away on business at weekends and it was those times when we were concerned about Yasmin's behavior.'

'But he worked for Mandy Pilkington as her chauffeur and security guard. Why would it be necessary for him to be away on business at weekends?'

Farah clasped her hands together. 'I am not privy as to exactly what business he occupied his time with. All I know is he met people to do business for his employer.'

'Are you aware Ahmed supplied drugs to Miss Pilkington's clients?'

Farah's lips tightened and it was a moment before she replied. 'No, I was not. I really feel that it is time that you leave.'

Jane closed her notebook, as if she was preparing to go. She noticed Farah relax slightly.

'Did you know Charles Foxley?' Jane asked.

Farah hesitated a beat too long, before standing up.

'I am aware of his name, but I never met him. Due to the reports in the newspapers, I obviously know that my brother-in-law has been charged with his murder.'

'Do you know why Ahmed did what he did?' Jane asked.

Farah's composure suddenly seemed to waver. 'He had no choice. He found out that man defiled his daughter and had paid a considerable amount of money for her to remain silent about it.'

Jane looked up. 'How did they find out?'

'Obviously from Yasmin. I don't know the details, just that my sister was deeply distressed and so I came to see her, as we were both appalled. At this time my husband suggested that perhaps it was time she went back to live with relatives. Now I would really like you to go.'

'Did Ahmed ever work for your husband in his butcher shop?'

'Yes, in the beginning. Before he started working for . . . that woman in Clapham. Now that is all I am going to say. I think you should be aware, detective, that Ameer and I are leaving the country and taking my poor sister with us.'

Jane couldn't conceal her shock. 'You're leaving without seeing your brother-in-law again?'

'That man has only brought shame upon my family,' she said bitterly. 'None of us wish to ever see him again.'

'Are you going to join Yasmin?' Jane asked.

Farah reached out and touched Jane's hand with her cold fingers. She then gave her an odd smile.

'Oh yes, we will all be together again.'

CHAPTER TWENTY-SEVEN

Jane wanted to be ready in plenty of time so set her alarm for 4:30 a.m. As soon as she woke up, she showered, washed her hair and chose her clothes carefully: her usual tights, black skirt and an underwire bra, as she knew it would assist in hiding the microphone. The white linen shirt had a Peter Pan collar, V-neck and covered buttons, and instead of a fitted suit jacket she chose a heavy wool box-shaped one with pockets. She was made-up, hair perfect, and had even managed to have coffee and toast, with plenty of time to spare, knowing how obsessive Elliott was about time.

Her doorbell rang promptly at 5:45 a.m. She looked out of her bedroom window to check that it was Elliott before pressing the buzzer to open the downstairs door and waiting for him to climb the three flights of stairs to her flat.

Jane opened the flat door and he gave her an appreciative once-over before taking a small plastic case out of his pocket. Inside was a miniature microphone.

'I need you to find the best position for this to pick up.'

Jane was not surprised when he opened her jacket for her.

'I already have an underwire bra and I think it would fit between my breasts,' she said evenly.

He peered at the buttons on her shirt. 'Good thinking. OK, open your blouse.'

She took the microphone and found the perfect position for it between her breasts.

'It's important the small wire hangs loose but isn't visible.' He stepped back as Jane carefully buttoned her blouse. He glanced at his wristwatch. 'Time to go.'

Whatever Jane had expected from her previous experience with surveillance vehicles, she was impressed by the obo van. The large vehicle was disguised as a drainage company van. Inside there was an electronic console, surveillance screens, cameras and three men wearing well-worn overalls with the drainage company logo. There were no windows. The rear entry door into the van was a high step up and Jane was grateful for Elliott, who almost lifted her in. He quickly closed the door behind him.

'Did you pick up?' Elliott asked one of the men sitting by the console.

'Clear as a bell.'

Only then did Jane realize that the microphone she was wearing was live. As she was shown to a seat, she wondered if the men had also overheard Elliott instructing her to unbutton her blouse. He made no introductions, and without any signal, the van took off.

Elliott passed Jane two pages of notes. He spoke very quietly. 'Just read them through and decide for yourself how you could bring the subject matter up. The priority is that you don't give the game away. Stay relaxed and be ready for the fact that he will be surprised to see you there. I've given you a few notes as to what you could say, or maybe you can come up with something better.'

Jane nodded and concentrated on the notes.

No one spoke throughout the drive to their destination. Then Elliott picked up a set of headphones and started looking at one of the surveillance screens. She could hear the driver saying they were on Rigg Approach. Elliott leaned towards Jane as they listened to the driver tell them the mobile hamburger van was just opening up. He would do a U-turn and park in their prearranged position.

Elliott then showed Jane a small drawing. He pointed to the mobile hamburger van, then to the Rigg Approach offices of the Flying Squad, and then showed where his team would be working on the drainage manhole. Jane remained seated as the back doors were opened and, from beneath the van, a massive pump was hauled out as two men went into the roadway, removing a large manhole cover. It was now almost 7 a.m.

Elliott listened into his headphones. 'No sign of our suspect yet.'

The waiting was beginning to get to Jane and it didn't help that she couldn't see what was happening outside the van, but had to have everything relayed to her via Elliott. She took a deep breath and felt herself relax.

Elliott turned to her and asked her to say a few words. 'Just to make one hundred percent sure the microphone's working perfectly.'

'What is the distance from the burger van to you?'

'It's quite a distance, Jane. We couldn't get any closer as the industrial estate is so empty. But what I'm going to give you is a code word. If you feel any kind of threat, use the word "mustard".'

'Mustard?' Jane repeated. 'Not "help"?'

He gave a soft chuckle, believing if she could make a joke now, she had the nerve to pull it off. 'Dabs said you were a good 'un.' He quickly turned his attention back to his headphones. 'We have eyeballs on target.'

Pulling into the courtyard of Rigg Approach was a dark blue Vauxhall with Murphy at the wheel. He got out and held the car keys in his mouth as he reached over to pick up a duffle bag from the passenger seat and what looked like a file of papers. He then kicked the car door shut, took the keys from his mouth and locked it. On his way to the building he whistled to the burger van owner to get his attention and gave him a thumbs up. The man in the van waved back.

'Looks like he's placed his order and is now going into the building. Let's wait and see how long before he comes out.'

Murphy was out more quickly than they had anticipated.

'He must be hungry,' Elliott chuckled. At the same time, an unexpected vehicle drove in. Elliott looked at Jane. 'We have a male driver in a Ford Cortina.'

Jane nodded. 'It's one of the officers, nicknamed the Colonel.'

'Shit,' Elliott muttered.

He heard Murphy call across to the Colonel, asking if he wanted breakfast. He was relieved when he saw him shake his head, but then the tension went up a notch as Elliott saw Murphy pointing towards the obo van. The two men were looking directly at them and the open manhole. Then Murphy turned away and headed alone towards the burger van.

'Stand by, Jane,' Elliott told her. 'We just need Murphy to turn his back so you can get out unobserved.'

Murphy greeted the van guy loudly and then they could hear him saying, 'It's about time they cleaned the fucking drains. You can't even flush a toilet around here.'

Elliott nodded. 'Go.'

Jane was out, heading towards Murphy, as he was handed his large Styrofoam cup of coffee with double cream and two sugars. She waited until she was a few steps away to say anything, but it was the van driver who noticed her first, and said, 'Blimey, I haven't seen you for a while. Black coffee, well-done bacon sandwich?'

Murphy turned and looked at her in surprise. 'Where have you come from?'

'Well, after all the nasty rumors you've spread about me, I thought I'd be lucky to be directing traffic.'

'I know – I heard you were working out of Belgravia now. What brings you back here?'

Jane waved a hand. 'We're searching that warehouse over there for boxes full of goods stolen from Harrods. I've come to get some breakfast for the lads.' Jane turned to the van man. 'Tommy, I need three hamburgers with bacon and one with an egg sunny-side up.'

Murphy laughed. 'Theft from Harrods – my, my, you are working some big cases now.'

'I'm happy in my work and the DCI's a decent bloke . . . unlike some,' she said with a frosty smile.

Murphy pretended to look hurt. 'I hope there's no hard feelings between us, Jane.'

'Of course not,' she said with another brittle smile. 'But as I'm here, there is something job-related you might be able to help me with.'

Murphy took a gulp of his coffee. 'I don't have many dealings with shoplifters these days, I'm afraid, but how do you think I can help you?'

'I recovered a firearm on a house search. It's similar to the one I found in George Ripley's garage and I wondered if you might be interested in getting it checked out by ballistics against any of your outstanding cases.'

Murphy took another sip of his coffee and licked his lips, then rested his cup on the shelf. 'We haven't got any outstanding cases.' He turned to Tommy, who was cooking the burgers. 'I don't want my egg runny. Make sure you flip it over.'

'That's strange,' Jane said. 'I thought you had three outstanding cases.'

'Well, you thought wrong,' Murphy replied.

Jane gave him an inquiring look. 'What about the *Daily Express* robbery in '76? Then the Williams & Glyn's Bank in '77? Oh, and the *Daily Mirror* robbery in '78?'

She noticed his right eye twitch as he licked his lips again.

'They were investigated by the Flying Squad at Tower Bridge, not Rigg Approach.'

'Yes, and you were the DI at Tower Bridge and involved in the investigation of all three robberies. You recovered a Smith & Wesson .39 automatic pistol with a walnut inlay on the grip.'

Murphy shook his head. 'I've been involved in hundreds of investigations in my time on the Flying Squad, and seized hundreds of guns, so don't expect me to be able to remember every one of them.'

'You submitted a model .39 to the lab, then booked it out for an interview and never returned it to the lab.'

Murphy laughed, then, moving quickly, reached out and placed his pudgy right hand on Jane's chest between her breasts and moved it down towards her crotch.

Jane stood her ground, glad that she'd secreted the microphone so well inside her bra. She kept her voice low. 'The only wire on me, sir, is the stuff in my bra holding up my tits.'

In the obo van, Elliott was on his feet, checking his gun in his holster. He inched open the door and could see Jane and Murphy at the hamburger van being handed their orders. He gave a radio signal to the two men working on the drains to be on alert.

'If you're not wearing a wire, then why are you really here, Tennison?' Murphy asked with a glare.

She smiled. 'Payback.'

He leaned forward so his face was nearly touching hers and whispered in her ear, 'Listen, you stupid little girl, you've got nothing on me and you never will have. I didn't return the gun to the lab because I gave it to the armorer at Tower Bridge to destroy. I've still got the paperwork to prove it.' He bit into his burger, leaving a residue of tomato ketchup at the corner of his mouth. He wiped it with a napkin.

'Paperwork can be forged,' she said. 'It's the same gun I found at the Ripley garage.'

'Then the fucking armorer must be bent and he gave it to a bank robber. Now fuck off back to the hole you crawled out of.'

Jane decided to go for broke. 'I know you arrested Harry Burton in '76 on suspicion of the *Express* robbery and released him without charge so he'd work for you. You helped plan his robberies and gave him the Smith & Wesson.'

Murphy turned sharply to face Jane again. 'In case it slipped your mind, I shot Harry Burton dead after he tried to kill you.'

'That's right. You were scared the gun from the *Express* robbery could be traced back to Burton and he'd grass on you. That's why you set him up on a robbery and used it as a way of murdering him.'

Murphy's eyes started to bulge. 'Well, he can't help you now he's dead, can he?'

Jane smiled. 'It'll help when I ask the lab to do ballistics testing with the Ripley revolver and they prove it's the same gun you seized years ago and was then used in two more robberies – one where a security guard was killed. You'll be spending the rest of your life in prison where you belong.'

There was a chilling expression on his face as he spoke softly. 'Your studious homework should have made you realize what I'm capable of . . . and that I'm always one step ahead of the game.'

'Your arrogance will be your downfall, Murphy.'

'You better keep your mouth shut, sweetheart, or I will shut it permanently and you won't be able to tell the lab to do anything.'

Jane could see the two undercover officers in drainage uniforms approaching Murphy from behind, one carrying handcuffs. She knew Murphy had said enough to incriminate himself and Elliott had made the order for him to be arrested.

She leaned forward and whispered in Murphy's ear, 'You're too late, Bill. Operation Countryman have already spoken to the lab and you're fucked.'

Murphy turned and saw the undercover officers. He started swinging wildly, but then Elliott appeared and, with an almighty right-hander to the jaw, knocked him unconscious. He fell to the ground in a crumpled heap.

* * *

Jane was impressed by how fast it all went down. It seemed only a matter of a minute or so before an unmarked car pulled in and Murphy was pushed roughly into the back seat with his hands cuffed. The two officers had removed their equipment from the manhole and stashed it in the obo van as Elliott took the box of burgers from her and told the men they could have their breakfast.

He touched Jane's elbow. 'Get in the van and let's get that wire off you.'

Elliott helped her inside while Tommy looked on in total amazement, unable to fathom what had just gone down. Shaking his head, he went back to scraping his hot plate.

Inside the obo van, Elliott had turned his back while Jane removed the microphone. She was just buttoning her shirt when he turned with his hand out to retrieve it.

'What happens now?' she said, licking her lips. Her mouth felt so dry.

'Depends on whether Murphy puts his hands up and pleads guilty, which is unlikely. Whatever happens, I'll make sure you get the credit you deserve. Without your input, we wouldn't have got an arrest.'

'You'll probably need me to give evidence in court, then,' Jane said.

'Yes, but we won't go broadcasting what you did around the Met. There are some officers who would regard you as a turncoat.'

'Then they're no better than Murphy.'

He nodded. 'That's the attitude.'

There was a tap on the door. Elliott opened it, then turned to Jane. 'I've got a car here to take you home.'

'But I should be at work at the station.'

'Up to you, but don't make it too celebratory. The fireworks may be over, but this is still a covert operation.'

Jane gave him a small nod. 'Will I see you again?'

'Sometime, maybe.'

She could feel he was eager for her to leave. There seemed nothing else to say. He passed her her bag as the driver started up the engine.

'Got to get this truck back. It's needed,' he said as he helped her down.

There was so much more she wanted to ask him, but the door shut behind him.

As she got in beside the driver, Tommy called over from his mobile burger van: 'See you again soon!'

* * *

As Jane arrived back at the station, she was in time to see Tyler and Detective Chief Superintendent Walker returning from the magistrates' court, where Farook had pleaded guilty to the murder charge. Bail had been refused, and he had been taken to Wandsworth prison to await trial.

'Could I have a word, please?' Jane asked them both.

'What about?' Tyler replied with a note of impatience.

'Er, could we speak in your office?'

Tyler sighed. 'The boardroom. Two minutes.'

She was waiting for them nervously when Spencer walked in, looking pleased with himself. He pulled out a chair and sat with his legs either side of it.

'Walker's just congratulated me on all my good work. He's going to encourage my application to the regional crime squad. I've never mentioned this to you, Jane, but deep down that's where I've always wanted to go.'

She cocked her head to one side. 'Really?'

He nodded. 'You see, Jane, I have this obsession with fire-arms and the training is absolutely shit hot. If I'm accepted, I know it will change my life.'

Jane wanted to congratulate him but found it hard to believe his demotion wouldn't go against him.

Before she could say anything, Walker and Tyler walked in carrying mugs of coffee. They sat down side by side opposite Jane.

'You've got the floor,' Tyler began, 'but make it brief. We've had a long day and an even longer night. I, for one, would like to spend the weekend with my kids.' He touched the bruise on his cheek, as if to underline his point.

Walker seemed more intent on the cleanliness of his nails.

Jane cleared her throat. 'I may not have had your approval but I was nevertheless determined to uncover what I now believe to be the motive for the murder of Charles Foxley.'

Tyler sighed, while Walker just folded his arms. Spencer was the only one who looked interested, leaning over the back of his chair with an expectant look on his face.

Jane knew she had to keep it concise and get through it without disclosing that Farah had revealed the new information. She got out her notebook and, trying to keep her voice under control, began by explaining how Farook's brother-in-law, Ameer Fareedi, had brought Farook's wife and daughter to England after Farook had been released from prison, and how the family had been financially dependent on him.

'I think, Tennison, we already have all that in Farook's statements, so can you get to the point?' Walker said, making his irritation obvious.

'Yes, sir.' Jane gritted her teeth, determined to make them listen. 'Yasmin Farook was exceptionally beautiful. She was only fifteen years old and had begun to distress her family because of her refusal to obey them and follow their strict religious code.'

Detective Chief Superintendent Walker sighed and glanced at his wristwatch.

'I do think this is very important, sir. I found out that Farook himself was often away for lengthy periods and I believe this could be down to him securing drugs for Mandy Pilkington. Whatever the reasons, he was often absent at weekends.'

'We already know this,' snapped Tyler.

'Yes, sir, of course. But one of these weekends, Yasmin met Tanya Lyons. Tanya managed to persuade Yasmin, who was eager to get out of her home, to agree to accompany her to a film premiere.'

It was now Spencer's turn to look skeptical. 'I don't know about this.'

Jane ploughed on. 'At this event, Yasmin was sexually molested.'

Tyler held up his hand. 'This hasn't come up before. Do we have a witness?'

Jane felt like shouting, but instead took a deep breath. 'Sir, it's not in any report because I have only just found it out. Yasmin managed to hide what had happened from her family until she told Tanya.'

Spencer was frowning as he started to piece it all together.

'Tanya encouraged her to talk to Charles Foxley, who gave her a large sum of money to keep quiet. I think it's possible that later he gave her more money, because according to Tanya, Yasmin wanted to run away.'

Jane, at last, had their full attention. She continued to explain that Farook had uncovered the money his daughter had hidden, and found out she had been assaulted.

'For a man like Farook, if a woman loses her honor, it is gone forever. Farook believed that Charles Foxley was responsible and I believe this was the motive behind Foxley's murder.'

'And will this girl Tanya confirm everything you have just told us?' Detective Chief Superintendent Walker asked.

'Yes, sir, I am sure she will.'

'Have you spoken to Yasmin Farook?' Tyler asked.

'No, sir. I've been unable to trace her. She has no belongings left at the family flat. I was told that she has returned to live with relatives in Pakistan.'

'Do you believe that?' Tyler asked.

'No, sir. Her aunt and her cousin both said that she had gone to live with relatives but they didn't give any details.'

There was an uneasy atmosphere in the room. Tyler glanced at Walker and Spencer, avoiding eye contact with Jane.

'Have we had any alarms raised by the family regarding this young girl's whereabouts?'

'No, sir. This is why I really feel it is necessary for us to make finding her a priority.'

Jane watched as Walker slowly got to his feet, pointedly looking at his wristwatch again. 'I recommend, Detective Tennison, that you should immediately contact Missing Persons and—'

'But I do have grave concerns, sir,' Jane interrupted. 'Yasmin hadn't been seen for a considerable time before the murder.'

Now Tyler stood up. 'But you have only this Tanya's word that she was paid off for something that happened at a film premiere. Have we ever had any complaint regarding this incident?'

Jane could hardly contain her frustration. 'No, sir, because they were paid off by Foxley to keep quiet. You have to understand how very young and naive these girls were.'

'Yet again, Detective Tennison, your intentions are good, but in reality we will require much more solid evidence. Hopefully we will gain that when Missing Persons are brought on board. Until that time, we have a man pleading guilty.'

Jane watched in astonishment as Walker and Tyler left the room.

Spencer got off his chair and swung it around to place it back under the table.

'You're not OK with all that, are you?' he said quietly.

'No, I'm not,' Jane said, shaking her head in frustration. 'I have a strong feeling that something bad happened to that girl. She was an innocent fifteen-year-old. If you could have seen that hideous room her parents kept her in . . . But I don't have any evidence.'

Spencer walked to the door. 'You know, I think Foxley was a scumbag. I'm not saying he got what he deserved, but maybe we have to leave it to the family.'

Jane banged her chair down, shouting, 'Leave it to the family? Spencer, her father has pleaded guilty to disemboweling the man we suspect of paying Yasmin hush money.'

Spencer shouted back, pointing at her. 'This is all hearsay. You don't have any evidence. I'm not saying you shouldn't feel for this girl, but you have to leave it to her mother, aunt and uncle to report her missing if that's what she is.' He turned on his heel, slamming the door behind him.

Jane sat for a few minutes, trying to get her emotions under control. Then she completed a report and filed it. There was a buoyancy in the incident room as it was going to be the first weekend off a lot of the officers had had for a while, and they were hell-bent on enjoying it.

Jane slipped out as quietly as she could and went home.

By the time she had had a shower and washed her hair, it was almost 8 p.m. Yet again she was on her own; she thought about ringing her parents but knew she wasn't in the right frame of mind to go and see them. She hadn't had time to think about what had happened earlier that morning, and she didn't know if she would ever see Elliott again. She doubted if Dabs would call again. She wasn't even sure she would continue going to the rifle club. But the one positive was that she would finally have her name cleared and get the credit she was due.

The doorbell rang. Jane checked the time, wondering who it was. She went to her bedroom window to look down into the street. She knew she shouldn't, but she couldn't resist. She went to the intercom and picked it up.

'Hello, Dexter.'

'Hello, Jane. Long time, no see. I've got a chilled bottle of Chablis. Can I come up?'

'Sure.'

She replaced the phone and opened the front door. She could hear his footfalls on the first, second and lastly the third floor. He smiled, holding up the bottle of wine.

'Have you had a good day?'

'No,' she said. 'But I think it's getting better.'

AUTHOR'S NOTE

Operation Countryman

Operation Countryman was an investigation into police corruption in London. The operation was conducted from 1978 to the late 1980s. Eight high-ranking police officers were prosecuted, along with many uniforms, due to evidence provided by a 'Supergrass', an informer occupying an important position in the criminal underworld. The 'Supergrass' claimed that many officers, including members of the elite Flying Squad, which dealt with commercial armed robberies, were receiving bribes from criminals in return for warnings of imminent police raids or arrests. They were also charged with fabrication of evidence against innocent men and having charges against guilty criminals dropped.

ACKNOWLEDGEMENTS

I would like to thank, as always, Nigel Stoneman, Tory Macdonald and Veronica Goldstein, the team I work with at La Plante Global.

All the forensic scientists and members of the Met Police who help with my research. I could not write without their valuable input.

Cass Sutherland for his valuable advice on police procedures and forensics. He is always there when I need him.

The entire team at my publisher, Bonnier Books UK, who work together to have my books edited, marketed, publicised and sold. A special thank you to Kate Parkin and Bill Massey for their great editorial advice and guidance.

Francesca Russell and Blake Brooks, who have introduced me to the world of social media – my Facebook Live sessions have been so much fun.

The audio team, Jon Watt and Laura Makela, for bringing my entire backlist to a new audience in audiobooks. Thanks also for giving me my first podcast series, *Listening to the Dead*, which can be downloaded globally.

Allen and Unwin in Australia and Jonathan Ball in South Africa – thank you for doing such fantastic work with my books.

All the reviewers, journalists, bloggers and broadcasters who interview me, write reviews and promote my books. Thank you for your time and work.

Finally, a huge than you to my readers. Your feedback, messages, and enthusiasm for my characters and books is what keeps me writing.

Dear Reader,

Thank you very much for picking up *Blunt Force*, the sixth book in the Jane Tennison thriller series. I have loved exploring the beginnings of Jane's police career and how she became the strong woman we know from the *Prime Suspect* series. I have also been delighted by the response I have had from readers who were curious to find out more about the early days of her career. I hope you enjoyed reading the book as much as I enjoyed writing it.

In *Blunt Force*, Jane has been unceremoniously kicked off the adrenaline-fuelled Flying Squad after the events of *The Dirty Dozen*. Now working at a quiet police station in Knightsbridge, she finds herself relegated to solving petty crimes and desperate for a case she can get her teeth into. That is, until she discovers that big-time theatrical agent Charlie Foxley has been found viciously beaten to death with a cricket bat, dismembered and disembowelled. Suddenly Jane is thrust into the salacious world of show business, with a brutal murder to solve – and a chance to prove herself as the smart, skilled officer she is. I enjoyed exploring how Jane deals with a hit to her policing career and manages to prove herself once again in a society where women often struggled to climb the career ladder.

If you enjoyed *Blunt Force*, then please do read the first five novels in the series: *Tennison*, *Hidden Killers*, *Good Friday*, *Murder Mile and The Dirty Dozen* are all available in paperback, ebook and audio now. I have also reworked my first ever novel, *Widows*, which was turned into a major feature film directed by Steve McQueen. This is followed by *Widows' Revenge* and *She's Out*, which are also out now. I also recently published *Buried*, the first book in a whole new series which introduces DC Jack Warr, a brand new character who has really taken hold of my imagination. In *Buried*, Jack is drawn into an investigation into the aftermath of a fire at an isolated cottage, where a badly charred body is discovered, along with the burnt remains of millions of stolen, untraceable bank notes. Jack's search leads him deep into a murky criminal underworld, but as the line of the law becomes blurred, how far will he go to find the answers? The book is available now, and do keep an eye out for the next in the series, which will be published in 2021.

If you would like more information on what I'm working on, about the Jane Tennison thriller series, or about my new series featuring Jack Warr, you can visit www.bit.ly/LyndaLaPlanteClub where you can join my Readers' Club. It only takes a few moments to sign up, there are no catches or costs and new members will automatically receive an exclusive message from me. Zaffre will keep your data private and confidential, and it will never be passed on to a third party. We won't spam you with loads of emails, just get in touch now and again with news about my books, and you can unsubscribe any time you want. And if you would like to get involved in a wider conversation about my books, please do review *Blunt Force* on Amazon, on GoodReads, on any other e-store, on your own blog and social media accounts, or talk about it with friends, family or reader groups! Sharing your thoughts helps other readers, and I always enjoy hearing about what people experience from my writing.

With many thanks again for reading *Blunt Force*, and I hope you'll return for the next Jane Tennison adventure.

With my very best wishes,

Lynda

JANE TENNISON
from the very beginning

TENNISON
HIDDEN KILLERS
GOOD FRIDAY
MURDER MILE
THE DIRTY DOZEN

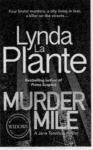
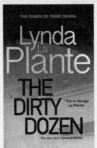

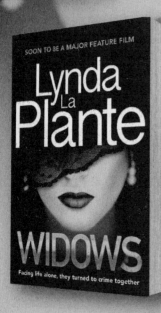
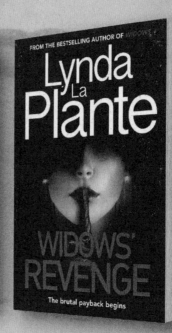